STOLEN LIGHT

STOLEN LIGHT

An Art History Mystery

by Claudia Riess

PRAISE FOR
STOLEN LIGHT...

"A fascinating combination of suspense, art history and love story, taking the reader from Havana, Cuba to Manhattan, to Florence, Italy, and back."

~ Elizabeth Cooke, Award Winning Author of
the Hotel Marcel Series

"Stolen Light is a beautifully written and compelling story filled with intrigue, twists and turns and leaves the reader wanting more from this author. Wonderful!

~ M. Glenda Rosen, Author of
the Senior Sleuths Mysteries

Stolen Light
An Art History Mystery

Second Edition | March 2019
Level Best Books
www.levelbestbooks.com

This is a work of fiction. Any references to historical events, real people, or real locales are used fictitiously. Other names, characters, places, and incidents are the product of the author's imagination, and any resemblance to actual events or locales or persons, living or dead, is entirely coincidental.

Trade Paperback ISBN: 978-1-947915-10-7
Also Available in e-book

Printed in the United States of America

In memory of Jonathan

PROLOGUE

Guantanamo Province, Cuba
April 3, 1958

William Delaney held his rifle tightly splinted against his side, as much for support as protection. He was still lightheaded from the shock of having seen military trucks lumbering up his stately drive, spotting them quite by chance from the main house living room window as he chatted with the manager of his sugar plantation, Jeff Davis, about the latest market prices. They had each grabbed a rifle from the display cabinet and fled, along with the cook's assistant, down to the basement storeroom where they were now positioned behind its bolted door.

Delaney's manager stood alongside him, clutching one of the fancy rifles, and just behind them stood the cook's young aide, Rosa. The cook himself had chosen to find refuge of his own. There had been no sound of gunshots from overhead, an indication, though not a certainty, that he was safe.

Delaney thought of his wife, in town getting her hair done, as blissfully ignorant of the turn of events as the child in her womb, and he prayed to God for her continued protection, even as Rosa's nearness trifled with his lofty prayers. He adored his wife and was dutifully faithful to her, but the girl stirred his manhood more deeply. Sitting at the desk in his study, he would sometimes imagine being transported with her to Gauguin's island paradise, the artist's seductive vision of Tahiti facing him on the wall opposite.

As the girl's pungent odor of fear mixed with his own, Delaney's unwavering fidelity to his wife felt sanctimonious to him. Even as his friendship with Castro had tricked him into believing he was out of harm's way, so his marital rectitude had beguiled him into believing he was morally superior. He was, in fact, neither.

At least five minutes had passed since the overhead tramping had stopped. "We would not have heard the trucks pull out," he said, turning to his companions, the steadiness of his voice belying his emotions. "They took what they came for and left. Let's go."

"Maybe give it another couple of minutes," Davis said, glancing at the girl, then placing his free hand on her shoulder. "You're shaking. Steady, now."

"I'm okay, sir," the girl said quietly. She listed toward him, hung there an instant, then righted herself.

Rosa's small action filled Delaney with an overwhelming sense of abandonment. Suddenly he envisioned the walls of his home stripped of his precious art collection, nurtured over time like his fantasy of tropical romance. He imagined stark white rectangles against a gray-white ground, like gravestones in the moonlight; then the undoctored reality: bare walls but for a stubble of useless picture hooks. "I don't want to wait any longer," he said, galled by his helplessness. Cradling his rifle in the crook of his arm, he unfastened the bolt and pushed open the door. "Follow me."

The cavernous basement was only dimly lit by the narrow rays of sunlight filtering in through its two high-set windows. With a beckoning motion to the others, Delaney cautiously led the way toward the foot of the staircase. When he was within ten feet from it, he thought he heard a shuffling noise overhead. He halted, indicating with a raised hand that his companions do the same.

The sound of the shot was so unexpected that his astonishment, more than the bullet's impact, brought him to his knees. The second round ignited pain and sent him sprawling across his rifle, the side of his face smacking the concrete floor. In his last tic of consciousness, his vision exploded into a brilliant firework of Van Gogh yellows and oranges, transforming all of existence into a dazzling sunflower and drawing him helplessly into its blinding core of madness and divinity.

New York City

2015

CHAPTER 1

After shimmying out of her coat, Erika Shawn checked the condition of her décolletage created by her form-fitting black strapless cocktail dress. All was in order, her breasts securely moored. As the coat-check attendant draped her serviceable wool coat over his arm along with a resplendent mountain of mink, Erika amiably cautioned, "Don't mix us up." She plucked her receipt from the polished oak counter and dropped it into the jacket pocket of her friend Rodney Smitts' tux. More herself in jeans and T-shirt than gala attire, she had to admit it felt benignly frivolous to play dress-up every now and then. From Rodney's irritable clawing at his collar, she guessed he was not similarly inclined. She slipped her arm through his and pressed him gently but firmly forward, down The Pierre's elegant hallway.

The entrance to the hotel's reception area was essentially a broad stage overlooking the main room, affording them a panoramic view. Below them the auctioned artworks were exhibited in a conscientious sprawl, permitting none the advantage of centerpiece status. The remaining space was devoted to the art of drinking and circulating. Cocktail tables draped in white linen were strategically situated along the periphery of the room, and a brigade of neatly clad servers passed among the throng with trays of colorful hors d'oeuvres. At the far end of the room, a bank of palatial glass doors revealed the dining and ballroom area beyond.

Erika glanced at her watch: 6:40. Just ten minutes into the reception hour, and already the place was hopping. She was hardly a charity ball maven, but she knew "fashionably late" no longer applied. The hour of independence before being relegated to assigned dinner tables had become prime time for networking. With champagne flowing, silks and satins caressing, and all aglow beneath fairytale chandeliers, the scene was set for players in the art world to glide into new alliances and collaborations. Her own *raison d'être* for the occasion had already been assigned her by Sara Masden, her boss at *Art News Magazine*, and she was at once eager and anxious about it.

"Let's see how your painting's making out," she prompted Rodney with a gentle tug at his elbow.

"I hate this shit."

"I know."

"Hawking myself, kissing ass. The name of the charity's a joke. PAPNEA. Who can remember what it stands for?"

"'Partnership to Aid and Promote New and Emerging Artists.' Be kind. Its mission is to help subsidize guys like you."

"I help myself by posing for life drawing classes," he shot back. "Sorry, I'm just feeling edgy," he added, hardly contrite.

She nudged him toward the stairs descending to the main room. "Over here," he directed as they wended their way through the spaces between displays and roving guests.

Erika stood before the easel displaying Rodney's oil-on-canvas. Amid snow-covered dunes beneath an ominous gray sky, a nude man and woman were passionately entwined on a lifeguard's chair, the chair itself half-buried in the snow. The cold and somber colors of the scene in stark contrast to the couple's soft, salmony skin tones intensified the heat of their embrace. Despite the unsettled quality of Rodney's creative muse, every new work, however experimental, was executed with a sureness of hand that never failed to surprise her. An art critic had once called his work "facile," the adjective wreaking havoc with his gallery bookability. He was still feeling its effects.

"Well?" he prodded. "What's the verdict?"

"The bodies, they're like the heat of the sun—incredible, the effect you get with a minimum of detail." She turned toward him. "Since when do you need my approval?"

"Mind if I barge in?" came a polite but resolute request from behind. "I'd like to get a better look." The speaker came into full view as she adroitly stepped between them.

The woman was statuesque. Erika, of average height, felt petite next to her. Willowy and sleek, the woman reminded her of a portrait by John Singer Sargent. The brilliance of the bezel-set diamond sparkling at the nape of her neck was diminished by the play of light on the ivory satin gown clinging to her elegant form. "This is a very effective piece," the woman remarked, directing her gaze at Rodney's painting, her rose-tinted lips gently curving into a pensive smile. "These lovers are clearly oblivious to the snow, a dramatic metaphor, I think, for the irrelevance of the external world on the inner life."

"That's a mouthful," Rodney observed, drawing himself up to be at eye level with her.

The woman turned toward him.

"Meet the artist, and don't mind him," Erika entreated, flashing him a warning look. "This is Rodney Smitts."

"I see," the woman replied, smiling, her focus remaining fixed on Rodney. "Accepting a compliment doesn't seem to be your strong point. Luckily, this doesn't affect the virtue of your work." She stepped up to the table alongside his painting. "I'm making a bid on it."

"Am I expected to fall on my knees?"

"Not at all." She scribbled her entry into the notebook provided. "However, I recommend an intensive course in behavior modification." With that, she sidled past him into the collective arms of the gathering.

"What was that all about?" Erika asked, arching her brow.

"Foreplay, I hope."

Smiling, Erika leaned in to study the data logged in the notebook. The woman's bid, the first one registered, leaped off the page. "Seven thousand dollars—way over the required minimum!" She suddenly blanched. "The bidder—it's Helen Gilmore."

"You mean the one who wants—"

"There you are—Erika!"

She heard Sara's cry before spotting her coming her way. Just as she arrived, a server carrying a tray of crab cakes brushed by Erika's elbow, and she nervously plucked one from the arrangement. "I think I just blew my first meeting with Gilmore," she said.

"How so?" her boss asked, inclining for the token cheek-to-cheek kiss.

"No doubt she thinks the woman will take her for a wimp for not giving me hell for my rudeness," Rodney supplied.

Erika elaborated.

"That's terrific!" Sara chirped, responding only to the news of the generous bid.

Erika bit into the crab cake, not really wanting the thing.

"Where do you put it?" Sara asked, giving Erika's figure the once-over. "You look positively svelte."

"In black, who doesn't?"

"Like me, apparently, accepting compliments is not her forte," Rodney commented, with a proprietary glance at his companion.

"So I won't tell her I love her new shoulder-length bob," Sara returned.

"I'll hold you to it," Erika said, grinning. "Hey, you look pretty fantastic yourself." In truth, Sara looked smashing in her navy silk suit, ultra-tailored, with the punch line of a daringly low closure.

"Thanks. My husband likes the conservative hooker look, and I like to keep him happy. What do you think of the art? Quite a diverse sampling, yes?"

"I haven't done the tour," Erika said. "I was going to get a drink, then check it out."

"I'll come with you. I'm due for another." Sara gave Rodney a patronizing smile. "Try and behave yourself, darling."

"Not if I can help it."

Together the two women forged their way to the nearest bar where Sara procured a martini for herself and a wine spritzer for Erika. Drinks in hand, they edged their way into a pocket of undisturbed space.

Sara took a sip of her martini. "So, did you study the fax I sent you—the 1954 inventory of William Delaney's art collection?"

"Very impressive." Erika hesitated. She was only one of a stable of contributing editors and at twenty-seven, the second most junior. "I'm flattered you thought of me, but—"

"I didn't. Helen Gilmore thought of you."

"I don't understand. Of course I want the assignment, I just didn't know you considered me an investigative reporter, much less a sleuth."

Sara uttered the staccato laugh that never varied: two piping eighth notes followed by two lower-pitched quarter notes. "No sleuthing required. Helen told me that her father, William Delaney, a U.S. citizen who owned a sugar plantation in Cuba, was allegedly killed by a group of revolutionary wannabes in 1958. With Castro it was a matter of bring-your-own weaponry, and Delaney's art collection would have fetched these hopefuls a mega-load of rifles."

"Are you saying Helen wants us to track down the missing art works, period?"

"Wants you to track them down, yes—or at least try to. The magazine will have exclusive rights to the story, whatever the outcome."

"Why did it take the family so long to start the search?"

"Delaney's widow, who recently passed away, was traumatized. Let's leave it at that for now."

"I'd also like to know why Helen didn't contact agencies like Interpol or IFFAR before she called *Art News*."

"I don't know, maybe she did. Suffice it to say, she wants you to make the inquiries, be her ombudsman."

"Why me?"

"She's come to admire your style—correction, 'spunk.' As an example, she mentioned your recent piece on the artist Mother-Fucker's graffiti. She thought it took tenacity and courage to interview the artist on his own turf."

"He's eleven years old, weighs fifty-six pounds."

"You'll have a chance to tell her yourself. She was delighted to come tonight, but on such short notice she could only make it to the reception."

"So you agree I'm qualified to—"

"She pledged twenty-five thousand dollars to PAPNEA. That makes you qualified."

"And you, excuse me, my pimp."

Sara uttered her patented laugh. "I didn't ask for a dime. The fact is, she's quite smitten by the organization's mission." She took another sip of her drink. "Before I properly introduce you to her, I think I should tell you that I used my pull to seat you and Harrison Wheatley at the same table. You know him?"

"No," Erika replied cautiously. "You're not trying to fix me up, are you?"

"In a sense, I am. Wheatley teaches art history at New York University's Institute of Fine Arts. I met him through PAPNEA in my capacity as a board member. He was in on the initial planning phase and contributed quite a generous sum to help jump-start the organization, with the stipulation that he remain anonymous. Rumor has it the man has serious issues about being wealthy by fiat—old money, or something of the sort. I don't really know. Getting to my point, he has the reputation of being a meticulous researcher, so I took the liberty of sending him a copy of Delaney's inventory."

"Why?" Erika asked, surprised by her tone's petulant twang. "Because I thought an academician might be useful in authenticating any of the recovered paintings, as well as establishing historical context. He expressed interest, particularly in the oldest of the missing works, the Vittorio da Lucca. Predictably, he refused a consultation fee."

"I guess you lack confidence in my ability to handle the assignment," Erika said. She took a hearty swig of her wine spritzer, the aromatic spray of bubbles causing her nostrils to flair, matching her emotion.

"Watch it, darling, your ambition is showing." Sara smiled. "Seriously, you're the undisputed person in charge." Gesturing with the hand holding the drink, she directed Erika's attention to a small circle of guests standing no more than ten yards away. It was hard to miss Helen Gilmore's shimmering white gown and Rodney's grand gesticulations.

Sara looked questioningly at Erika. "Smitts have the opportunity to study that inventory?"

"Not intentionally. He dropped by to grab some of his art supplies, parked with me while he looks for a place of his own. Right now he's in a group rental, apparently unacceptable. He peered at your fax over my shoulder as you were sending it." Erika glanced his way. "I guess he's trying to impress."

"To the rescue," Sara commanded.

Rodney was sounding off about the Delaney inventory. "Looks like a Who's Who in collectible art—Degas, Van Gogh, even a couple of sixteenth-century compadres. There's one dated 1504 by a Vittorio da Lucca, of soldiers bathing, riding off, skirmishing, whatever—inventory includes copies of the works, poor quality photos, but remarkable." Members of his audience were either listening intently or captivated by his good looks.

Helen was the first to notice the newcomers. "Sara," she said quietly, "I was looking for you. I thought you were going to introduce me to Erika Shawn."

"Here she is," Sara replied. "Erika, Helen—I believe you've met, in a manner of speaking." She smiled wickedly.

"I was more or less the mute bystander," Erika explained, grasping Helen's extended hand. "I'm flattered—excited—you chose me to help recover the artwork. I'll try to live up to your expectations."

"Oh, I'm confident you will," Helen assured her. She bestowed a heartwarming glance at Rodney, who smiled solemnly, appearing to acquire gravitas from her acknowledgment. "Is there someplace we can find a bit of privacy?" she asked as she and Erika, along with Sara and Rodney, broke ranks with the group.

Erika wondered if Rodney was to be part of the entourage, but her question was answered when Helen took his arm as they started for the room's exit.

They found a private niche, furnished with a billowy couch and side chairs upholstered in deep-colored floral silks. Helen and Rodney gravitated to the couch, Sara and Erika to the flanking chairs.

"Beats me why we need to be all this secretive," Rodney gibed. "Helen's been telling everyone within earshot about her newly discovered treasure trove."

Helen smiled. "I'm usually quite close-mouthed, although you'd never know it. It's just that I'm still on a high." She shifted her weight, causing her thigh to come into contact with Rodney's. Whether by accident or intent, no correction was made. "I want to give you some idea of where I'm coming from," she began, suddenly serious. "All my life I've been wanting to learn about my father, to fill the void"—her hand rose to press against her chest—"here. He was killed in 1958, three months before I was born. My mother was in town when the incident occurred, and I think she always bore a certain survivor's guilt, however unreasonable. She fled Cuba within days. She broke all ties with her friends, and all business interests were left behind. It was as if she was afraid the violence would track her down—track us down. I knew my father had owned a sugar plantation and collected art and that his art collection was stolen the day he was killed. This is all I could coax out of her. She refused to understand how important it was for me to know who he was, not what."

"Did you ever try to convince her to try to track down the stolen pieces?" Erika ventured.

"To no avail. If she'd needed the money, maybe it would have been a different story, but she was a wealthy woman in her own right." Helen placed her palm over the dazzling gem at her throat, as if she meant to negate it. "I want to recover what belonged to my father and to memorialize him in every sense of the word. I'm adding a codicil to my will designating all items recovered as donations to The Metropolitan Museum of Art."

"Is this a terrific lady, or what?" Rodney asked proudly, as if he had something to do with it.

"Never mind that," Helen said, brushing the air. To Erika, "You know the document Sara faxed to you? Well, imagine how I felt when I came across it in a pile of old bills at the back of my mother's bedroom closet two weeks ago when I was getting ready to put her house in Southampton on the market. For the first time I was looking at something uniquely his, an inventory of art my father had actually chosen to hang on his walls.

"And here's the most crucial part. Yesterday, the executor handed me a testamentary letter allowing me access to a safe deposit box in a bank in Southampton. My father had rented it in the spring of 1957 on one of his trips to the U.S., and it's never been visited since. I assumed my mother must have been paying rent on it all these years, but I was wrong. His will provided for its perpetual maintenance.

"What I found in that box! Photographs, letters, diplomas, newspaper clippings, address books, and more! He probably planned to spend his golden years on the family estate writing his life's story. Instead, Mother fled and spent the rest of her life keeping it buried.

"When she died, I felt ambivalent about launching an all-out search for the art. It felt disrespectful to her. I needed to put a loving face on the project. That's why I called you, Erika, rather than one of the international agencies. Then yesterday, when I saw the contents of the safe deposit box"— she paused, her expression defying interpretation—"the importance of conducting a private investigation became even greater. I found, for instance, a dedication pamphlet for the 1956 opening of the Museo Nacional Palacio de Bellas in Havana, listing my father as one of its principal founding donors. I also found letters from Fidel Castro, who was, I discovered, a classmate of my father's at the University of Havana law school. I have no idea what, if any, relationship they had at the time of my father's death. I only know if there's so much as a particle of good will for him in the present regime, I don't want to kill it with a heavy hand."

Like a racing boat whose engine is cut, Helen went suddenly silent.

"Gee," Erika commented, the single syllable bobbing in the narrative's wake.

Rodney touched Helen's hand. "What about the updated inventory—the one you mentioned when we were talking with the others—dated April 1957, you said?"

"Of course!" She turned to Erika. "The faxed inventory you saw was dated 1954, but there was an updated version in the safe deposit box. It will be in the parcel I hand over to you." Helen scanned her audience, her focus coming to rest on Rodney, their eyes meeting in an undisguised look of mutual approval.

Erika found their uncensored enthusiasm disarming. Along with Rodney's newfound patronage, maybe Helen's discovery of her roots was so close to her discovery of her handsome young artist, the two events were unified in spirit.

It was time for Helen to rush off to her other engagement.

At the coat check area, Helen gave Erika a peck on her cheek. "I hope to see you about our project before the week is up." She turned to Rodney. "Later, dear," she said as he helped her into her coat.

"'Later, dear'?" Erika quoted, teasing, after Helen had gone. "She's ordered me to top any competitive bid on my painting, and I'm delivering it to her apartment," Rodney replied, affecting innocence. "Oh, and also, I'm moving in," he added smarmily.

"Fast work," Sara marveled.

"I told her I'm in transition, and she invited me to move in until I find permanent quarters. She has an empty wing. I'll have a place to work without getting in anyone's face."

"Sounds ideal," Erika said.

"She's commissioning me to do another painting. It'll be a gift, in lieu of rent."

"What about a husband—is there one?" Sara asked.

"Separated."

"Children?"

"We spent ten minutes one-on-one, you think I know everything about her?"

Sara shrugged. "Close to." She pinched his cheek. "Just joking, lighten up."

"I haven't spotted our guy, Wheatley," Sara later remarked as she and Erika paused before a large still life of fruit. "I wanted to introduce you before dinner."

"If he's at my table, I think I can find him."

When Sara's table was located, one degree of separation from dais-worthy, she informed Erika she'd look in on her in a while.

Erika's table was in Siberia, but on the right side of the tracks. Rodney pulled out a chair and waited for her to sit down, then claimed the place beside her. Two couples had already settled in and were engaged in tight conversation. Perfunctory introductions were exchanged. As the apparently exclusive conversation resumed, Rodney alerted Erika to an impending visitor. "One o'clock, mother hen approaching."

"I hope Wheatley's not standing us up," Sara fretted on her arrival.

"We can always schedule an office visit," Erika reminded her.

"I don't know. I'm beginning to get bad vibes."

"Take an aspirin and call me in the morning," Rodney directed. "Enjoy your dinner."

As if to confirm Rodney's point, a waiter stepped up to the table and began distributing appetizers, morsels of lobster à la something in a translucent white sauce.

"Yes, they'll be coming," Erika advised, as the waiter hesitated behind the two vacant chairs alongside hers.

Sara headed back to her table.

Twenty-five minutes later the first glasses of wine had been decanted, the PAPNEA mission speech had been delivered, and the main course was being served. Erika was about to slice into her roast beef, when the laggards finally arrived. She put down her utensils.

"Sorry, I had a faculty meeting—computer science," the woman announced. "Jennifer Tuttle and"—she tapped her escort's arm—"my friend, Harrison Wheatley. And you are?" Roll call was accomplished as she efficiently shook hands with each of her tablemates. When it was Erika's turn, "Lovely hazel eyes," Jennifer said authoritatively, as if without her approval they wouldn't be. Harrison acknowledged each with a friendly nod.

They were a tall, attractive couple in their late thirties, Erika thought, although they didn't quite mesh. Jennifer looked like a purebred WASP whose smartphone was programmed for life. Her ash blond hair was pulled back in a hardball knot, and her streamlined olive green suit could have used an army officer's insignia. Harrison, on the other hand, seemed to be someone who didn't put much store in perfection. His hair—darker than her own chestnut brown—looked to have been tousled by nature rather than by design, and his elegant tux was topped off with an askew tie, which Jennifer would surely correct any second. Erika found him unconventionally good-looking, his strong, slightly irregular features distinguished by his penetrating brown eyes.

Harrison helped Jennifer take her seat before sliding in next to Erika. "I was looking forward to meeting you," he said reservedly. "Your assignment sounds intriguing." He turned toward Jennifer, who was examining her lobster appetizer. "You can have mine, too, Jen. I'm not all that hungry." He turned back to Erika.

"Same here," Erika said in response to his opening thought. "Sara told me about your scholarly prowess. It made me wonder if I was up to the task." She picked up her knife and fork. "Well, not really. Actually, when she told me she'd called you without consulting me, what I felt was mad. I got over it."

"I should hope so," he said. "I'm not all that forbidding"—he turned to Jennifer—"am I?"

A critical frown suddenly marred Jennifer's brow. "Look here." She wiped her hands on her napkin and reached up to set his tie right.

He ducked before Jennifer had completed her ministrations. "By the way, Smitts," he said, skewering a couple of green beans onto his fork, "I saw your work when it was in the selection phase. I liked it a lot. How did it go tonight—any luck?"

"Helen Gilmore bought the piece."

"Great. Don't get entrepreneurial, now. Stay true." To Rodney's grin, "No, I'm serious. I've seen any number of artists lose spontaneity by trying to reproduce what their buyers like about them." He studied the green beans then laid down his fork.

"Don't worry," Erika said, "Rodney's the least likely artist to imitate himself."

"Especially since he's not allowed to speak for himself," Rodney declared, giving Erika a playful jab with his elbow.

Jumping subjects, Erika began filling Harrison in on her

brief conference with Helen earlier in the evening, finishing up with Helen's discovery of the 1957 inventory found in her father's safe deposit box.

Looped out of the conversation, Rodney asked Jennifer to dance. When the couple had moved off, Harrison looked down at his plate, then began picking at his food as if he were collecting scientific data.

Why the sudden distractedness? "Recovering stolen art is not exactly my field," Erika said, breaking the silence.

"Nor mine." He put down his knife and fork, edged away a bit. She wondered if she'd offended him. "I feel restricted by Helen's reluctance to contact the international agencies," she managed without a glitch.

"Her precautions don't preclude checking out websites, do they? You needn't register a formal inquiry. You can see if any of Delaney's pieces have been reported missing by subsequent owners or if any are offered up for auction. Plus I know someone involved in art theft investigation who's the model of discretion."

"I don't know if Helen would approve."

"From what you've told me about her, my guess is she realizes her ambivalence about this project could hang it up. You know what she wants to accomplish. Don't let her stand in her own way." He folded his arms—another distancing gesture. "You'll be trying to track down items through their provenances, too. The 1954 inventory is pretty well documented in that regard, and better still, you'll be getting the later one when you meet with Helen. You can go on from there."

"With your help."

"Oh—of course," he faltered, before returning to the intense study of his food.

That did it. "I need to stretch my legs," she said. "Let's dance." Bring it to him.

"I don't know if I'm—"

"Let's go," she said breezily, not quite believing her nerve. She stood up.

He rose from his chair. "I was going to say I'm not quite feeling up to...but since you put it so..." With a smile of apology, he gestured for her to lead the way.

A foxtrot was in progress. She was expecting their first stance to be awkward and was surprised when they fell into position and into step in one clean movement, as if they'd been doing it for years. He held her formally, almost at arm's length, yet as they moved to the music she felt his imprint on her as if their bodies were in contact. "It must be you," she said, something near a laugh warbling her words.

"Pardon?"

His stiff, slightly alarmed delivery was so contrary to the willful grace of their bodies, it made her laugh outright. "Sorry, I meant it must be you who's doing the coordinating. I'm usually not such a good follower."

He smiled tentatively. "I'm usually not such a good leader. It must be the band."

"The band, yes," she replied without conviction as they flowed into a dip then out of it, as naturally as drawing breath.

"You know, after a dry spell I'm finally getting back to my research," he said sedately, as they and the music lilted on. "I don't think I would have gotten involved in your project if it hadn't been for that drawing, the one attributed to Vittorio da Lucca. A copy of it, along with copies of the other stolen works, appeared in the 1954 inventory faxed to us. Do you recall the Vittorio?"

"Yes." What she did not recall was ever feeling such a painful tug in her groin while carrying on a cerebral conversation. "It was the oldest item in the inventory."

"Did it raise any particular questions in your mind?" he inquired professorially.

"In what way?"

He was about to reply when the foxtrot came to an end.

Erika turned away to mitigate the tension in her belly. "Rodney and Jennifer are going back to the table. We should join them." She took a step in their direction as the band broke into a no-holds-barred samba.

"Just a minute," Harrison exhorted. "I want to talk about the drawing. Let's step outside."

The reception area was relatively empty. A security guard stood by the art exhibit, and off to the side a few exiled cigarette smokers were puffing away in varying degrees of urgency.

Harrison started right in. "From the poor quality of the fax, it's hard to properly examine the drawing, but given the subject matter, the Florentine origin, I can't help but wonder about a possible reference to Michelangelo's Battle of Cascina. It's a reach, but hard to ignore."

"Not for me," Erika said. "I majored in English, with a minor in art—inadequate, it seems."

"Such a drawing would be incredibly valuable in every sense—most importantly, historical."

At that moment a woman emerged from the dining hall and made a beeline for Erika, only to ask directions to the rest room. Getting them, she prepared to take off. As she turned, one of her stiletto heels got hung up in the carpet, causing her to tip into Erika, who in turn was thrown against Harrison. The woman dashed off, no harm done, but Harrison, having prevented further mishap by grabbing hold of Erika's shoulders, released her as if he'd been singed by a hot iron.

In that telling instant, what Erika had sensed on the dance floor became clear: Harrison was offended not by her, but by his attraction to her. Their connection had been physical, plain and simple, and she wanted to say if this was his reaction to basic instinct, she'd hate to think what he'd be like the morning after giving in to it. Lucky for him, there was no danger of it happening; her motto was sex without complications, and he had complications written all over him. She might have uttered a defensive remark, were it not for the interruption of his cell phone.

"Excuse me," he said, before taking the call. "Hello... Hello? Yes, I am, don't worry about it...What? I can hardly hear you, sweetheart!" He walked left, then right, searching for better reception. "I'll come, of course I'll come. You're breaking up. I'm leaving now, do you hear me?" He waited silently then clicked off. "Damn these things!" He shoved the instrument into his pocket.

Her frustration with him quickly turned to concern. "Are you okay?" she asked. She was aware of the tiniest, most injudicious nip of jealousy.

"I'm okay, everything will be okay, but I've got to leave now. I'll be in contact with you. Will you tell Jennifer to meet me out front? Thank you!"

Jennifer thanked Erika for Harrison's message, and left.

Erika resumed her place next to Rodney. The evening, deprived of Harrison's challenging presence, suddenly seemed interminable. She politely pushed aside her dinner plate. Feeling an inexplicable loyalty to Harrison, she would be kind, but unforthcoming to Rodney's curiosity. And Sara's.

CHAPTER 2

The trees bordering the Long Island Expressway were touched by the colors of early autumn. Whizzing by them created a lovely counterfeit Monet, its beauty intensified by Erika's excitement. She and Harrison were heading east to the Delaney estate in Southampton, where Helen was to show them the contents of her father's safe deposit box. "We're making great time," she said, gazing out the window. "You think we should call and tell her we might be early?" She decided not to suggest a coffee break. She was feeling her way to a professional comfort zone, nonthreatening yet amicable, and the guidelines were still too tenuous to risk the intimacy such a face-to-face might engender.

"Sure. I'll give her a head's up."

They were sitting in the back of his hired Lexus. She could hear the sound of his chinos brushing leather as he reached for his cell phone. She turned toward him as he was removing it from his blazer pocket, causing the open neck of his white cotton-knit shirt to tug open a bit more, his vulnerability twitching her into crossing, then uncrossing her legs. She herself was covered from head to toe in a tan turtleneck sweater, black corduroy jacket, black jeans, and boots. No skirt to rise up, blouse to skew open, shoe to reveal a sassy toe. She wanted to send him the message that she had no plans of trying to compromise him in any way and that he, and for that matter his "sweetheart" had nothing to be concerned about.

"Do you have Helen's number?" he asked.

She drew a legal-sized notepad out of her black leather tote bag and found it.

Helen picked up almost at once, and Harrison got right to the point. "She's okay with us arriving early," he said afterward. "An agent is showing the house at three-thirty, but it shouldn't take long. You want anything? Soda, Snapple, candy bar? Bill's got the works."

"No thanks. I'm good." Their splayed hands were inches apart on the leather seat. It would have been so easy, so sweet, to slide her hand into contact with his. Yet under these circumstances, with her gauzy feeling threatening to overcome her good sense, no. There would be no romance: Sleeping Beauty segueing from coma to dream world, never truly waking up. She knew from experience that the real ending of the story was disappointment, energy wasted. Their fingers, fanned against the smooth gray leather, were well matched. Fight it. The untenable longing will disengage, like white noise. She folded her hands in her lap.

As if he were on the same wavelength, he drew his hands to his lap almost simultaneously, with an audible intake of breath.

"Everything turn out okay the other night?" she asked.

"I...yes, everything turned out fine."

She would inquire no further, show him she had no desire to invade his space. "That's good."

"You think we should be in Southampton about four?" He looked at her intently, then down to his hands, folded stiffly.

She looked at her watch. "Three-twenty. I guess so." She turned to regard him in profile. His mouth, in particular, was disturbingly sensual. "We just passed the exit for Patchogue," she said, tearing herself away. She looked out her window, then irresistibly back at him, only to catch him studying her. Instantly, they restored the decorum with phony tight-lipped smiles.

Actually, she thought, since the Pierre gala three days ago, they had been in direct contact for barely an hour. The arrangements for their meeting with Helen had been handled solely through his department's secretary. What was she worried about? For a potential minefield relationship still in its infancy, they were doing pretty damn well. "Helen said she was reluctant to transport the material to Manhattan," she said, almost chipper. "Afraid it might blow out the window, get hijacked."

He nodded. "I should know. I have nightmares about losing all my research and having to start over again."

"Real nightmares? Literally?"

"Literally. I'm standing at the rail of an ocean liner, sorting through old CDs containing years of time-consuming work, and suddenly a gigantic swell knocks me off balance, and my CDs start hurtling out to sea, like so many Frisbees. I want to jump overboard and save them, but something holds me back."

"You can't swim," she said, grinning.

"You'd make a compassionate shrink," he replied, grinning himself. "The truth is, I don't know what it is. It feels like my feet are bolted to the deck."

"You're serious, aren't you?"

"Perfectly. What did you think?"

"I didn't—think."

"Ah, I suppose I didn't either," he said cryptically. He shook his head, as if to clear it of needless introspection.

In Southampton, they turned onto North Sea Road, and in a bit Bill pulled off to scrutinize his GPS screen.

Harrison pressed the speaker button. "Problem, Bill?"

"Just checking the lay of the land, but we're good. The house is on an inlet off Peconic Bay—Wooley Pond. Couldn't be more than a half mile away, but the lanes wind every which way. I'm just figuring it out."

Bill turned into a rural area where modest homes were

tucked in among the native maple, white birch, and fir trees, the natural landscape hardly disturbed. The occasional import—golden bronze hydrangea, butterfly bush with silvery foliage—seemed not to stake a claim on the land, but to pay homage to it. Erika sensed this respect for nature almost as a distinctive smell, like freshly baked bread, drawing the residents together.

"Peaceful place," Harrison said, dovetailing her thought.

They were silent as the car slowly made its way along the unpaved road, winding through a maze of picturesque places. Soon the housing came to an abrupt end on the outskirts of what appeared to be a large expanse of wooded land.

"Coming up," Bill announced, as they approached a clearing that shortly proved to be the foot of a gravel drive flanked by a pair of weather-worn pillars. The name "Delaney" was etched into a simple brass plaque attached to one of them.

The beauty of the estate did not appear in one jaw-dropping view, the white oaks and pines revealing only a tantalizing glimpse of the house and waterway beyond. It was only after they'd driven past the tall trees and into the swath of heather and sedge, that an unobstructed view could be appreciated: a sprawling white colonial standing on the shore of a secluded inlet.

The name "Wooley Pond" had conjured up images of a swimming hole for Erika, but this body of water, while forming a protected and private haven, flowed into the bay. She could see herself setting off on a little adventure around the bend in the bay to explore friendly shores. Foolishly, she imagined Harrison manning the oars, the image no doubt derived from the generic movie scene of a Victorian virgin in flouncy skirts floating along a lake with her ardent suitor. Exquisitely repressed, of course, both of them.

"Isn't this a wonderful spot!" Harrison observed, coming in at the tail-end of her reverie, instantly scuttled.

"Yes," she clipped.

"I'll wait here," Bill said, stopping in front of the house.

Erika slung her tote over her shoulder and headed for the entranceway. Harrison caught up at the foot of the steps leading to the wraparound porch, furnished with white wicker tables and thick-cushioned chairs.

As Erika reached for the brass knocker on one of the twin oak doors, she noticed the door was slightly ajar. To avoid opening it further, she held onto the doorknob while knocking.

There was no response from within. She knocked again.

After the third try, Harrison called Helen's number from his cell phone. "Recorded message," he said. "Helen, you there? It's us, Erika and Harrison. We're at your front door." He paused, then punched off.

"Maybe she's outside." Erika strode quickly to one end of the arced porch. She hurried down the wooden steps and continued around the house, checking out the rear deck, and then, nearer the gentle shoreline on a carpet of crushed white shells, a domed gazebo. She jogged around to the front door, where Harrison was waiting.

"What do you think?" he asked.

"I say we should just take a look." She pushed the door open a little more and peered inside.

"Well?"

"Nothing." She opened the door and walked in, instantly feeling like a trespasser. She stood in a foyer with a view on her left of a sprawling den. On her right was a formal living room and directly ahead, a broad oak staircase. The floor throughout consisted of tiles in the palest travertine, simulating an expanse of fine sand, raked smooth. She stepped aside, hugging the wall to minimize her invasion. "Helen?" she called tentatively. Harrison slipped in beside her. "Helen?" she called more forcefully.

"She's not here," he said.

"She must be. She's expecting us."

"We shouldn't have walked in."

Heedless, she strode past him to get to a room hidden from view.

He went to overtake her.

She froze in her tracks. "Oh god!"

In the far corner of the elegant dining room, Helen lay on her back, motionless, her arms flung outward, her legs awkwardly angled, her hiked skirt pulled taut against her thighs. Her head was resting against the marble base of a bronze sculpture, a slender, wing-like form, whose energy seemed to soar upward in opposition to the figure below.

Erika sprang forward, dropping to her knees by Helen's side. There was a bloody rip in a deep welt on her forehead. The injury looked as if it had been caused by a hard object striking with extreme force. "We're here," Erika whispered hoarsely, gently grasping Helen's hand. "We're calling for help." She looked up at Harrison for assistance. He already had his cell phone to his ear.

"We're here," she repeated, choking back emotions that were alarmingly familiar. She listened to Harrison reporting the location of the house and tried in vain to allow the steadiness of his voice to comfort her. "They'll be here soon," she said, tightening her grip on the hand, unwilling to accept its stillness.

Harrison knelt on the other side of Helen. He gently tugged down the hem of her skirt to reduce her exposure. He pressed his fingers to her neck to feel for a pulse. "I think she's..."

Erika wanted to cradle Helen's head, but was afraid to. She drew still closer, hoping to hear a whisper in her ear. "Don't leave me," she heard, but only in her mind. "I won't," she mouthed, her throat constricting. She could hardly breathe, reliving her mother's pain as if it were her own—rising in her belly, her heart, her head, as it had in those last moments with her. Until then she'd understood her mother's suffering, but only distantly. Her true affection had always been for her father and their wit-matching conspiracy. Even through his periodic flings, he'd remained true to her, his daughter, and to their unconditional, impishly pure love. It was only in those last moments, when her mother was pleading for her not to leave, that she'd dizzyingly comprehended that neither of them had been irreplaceable, that by never looking in on them through all the months of her mother's sickness, he had willfully abandoned them both. *I'm sorry, I'm sorry*, she wished she could tell her mother, *for not having loved you enough.*

At last the distant whine of a siren increased in volume, then stopped with the sound of tires rolling over gravel.

"They're here," Erika whispered into Helen's ear, refusing to believe what she knew.

There was a knock at the door followed by a noisy entry. "EMT!"

"Back here—hurry!" Harrison called.

A police officer appeared, with two paramedics at either end of a collapsed gurney following close behind.

Harrison jumped to his feet, making way for the medical team—a tentative-looking young man and a woman with cropped hair, clearly in charge.

Erika would not let go of Helen's hand.

"Out of the way, miss," the officer ordered. Even as he went into a crouch, his back was ramrod straight, as if his vertebrae had been fused.

"Okay," she mumbled, without acceding.

The female medic had already taken over Harrison's yielded space and was checking for vital signs.

The officer grabbed Erika's upper arm. She pulled closer to Helen.

"She's gone," the medic said.

The officer jerked Erika to her feet. She stared down at Helen as the medics were moving her onto the gurney.

"You two, don't either of you move," the officer commanded, zeroing in on Erika and Harrison. He went into a quick huddle with the medics, who then headed for the exit with Helen's inert form.

"Lieutenant John Mitchell, Southampton police," the officer resumed. "My partner is out there talking to your driver." He took a pad from his jacket pocket and unclipped the pen attached to its cover. "Your names?"

Erika and Harrison identified themselves and explained what had brought them there.

"What was Gilmore's condition when you found her—did she tell you anything?"

Inwardly, Erika was in turmoil, yet reason and speech seemed to be functioning as if drawing energy from a source outside herself. She shook her head. "She was obviously hit by a—"

"I'll do my job, and you answer the questions," Mitchell broke in. Harrison glared at him. "You don't have to be rude, Lieutenant."

"My apologies," Mitchell offered disingenuously. "You said you came to look at papers of some kind in reference to stolen paintings?"

"Yes," Erika said, before Harrison had a chance to answer. "The theft took place years ago. We're not looking for suspects, we're doing research."

"You know where these documents you're so interested in are located?" Mitchell asked.

"Somewhere in the house. I told you we were here to pick them up. They were taken by the person who attacked her, don't you think? You will tell us if you find them, won't you? Helen would want us to have them. If we find out anything on our own, we'll let you know."

"That would be good of you," Mitchell replied sarcastically. He handed them each his card. "You won't object if we call you in for questioning, will you?" he added in the same vein.

"We'll cooperate any way we can," Harrison said dryly, pocketing the card. "Are we free to go now?"

"You are, but don't touch anything on the way out, and

don't take any side trips." Mitchell turned on his heel. "I'll walk you to the door."

As Erika prepared to follow him, she took a look around, her scan ending at her feet. There, beside her left heel, lay a brown leather object, at least the edge of it. The rest of it was hidden under the sideboard. While Mitchell's back was to her, she let her bag slip from her shoulder and drop to the floor. Harrison's eyes were on her, but he said nothing, even as she scooped what appeared to be an address book from under the sideboard and into her bag.

Bill was standing rigidly by the Lexus when the threesome exited. He looked like someone expecting to be handcuffed. A police car was parked nearby, and inside it a police officer sat behind the wheel, his right arm slung over the back of the passenger seat.

Bill visibly relaxed when Mitchell walked past him en route to the police car. "What happened? I saw the medics carry somebody out."

"There was an accident," Harrison evaded. He turned to Erika. "You look pale."

"I'm okay," she said distractedly, as she watched Mitchell conferring privately with his partner. Had he seen her swipe the book, and were they deciding what to do with her?

Mitchell gave a confirmatory nod to the officer then briskly returned to Erika and her companions. "My partner's got your name and where we can reach you," he stated flatly to Bill. "And you two can go," he advised Erika and Harrison in the same tone. "We will want to question you further, so stay available." He motioned for the officer in the police car to come join him, then started back to the house.

After seeing his passengers safely ensconced in their seats, Bill slowly cruised around the grassy island, then cautiously passed the police car and headed out. "After what you went through, maybe you need to, I don't know, walk around somewhere, get something to eat."

Erika and Harrison glanced at each other. The unspoken decision was mutual.

Harrison pressed the speaker button. "We'd like to head back, Bill—unless you need a break yourself."

"No, no, I'm fine," Bill demurred, picking up speed a notch. "Don't forget, there's drinks and snacks back there."

Harrison tapped Erika's tote bag, between them on the seat. "You'll have to explain this, but first you need some nourishment. In fact, maybe we ought to stop. You need something more than a candy bar."

"I want to go home."

"Let me at least get you a drink. You really do look... shaky, Erika."

"Soda, then."

Harrison pulled open the door to the refrigeration compartment. He removed a can of Coke. He started to pour the soda into a glass, but she soon put up her hand to stop him. He gave her the glass, then poured the same amount for himself. "Well?" he asked. She knew what he was asking. "Not now," she said quietly, glancing at her bag.

"When we get there, I'll walk you to your door—you'll tell me then?"

"Yes." She looked down at her glass. Without warning, the emotions she'd felt when she was holding Helen's hand hit her full force, like a slap across the face.

"What is it?"

"I was just thinking of Helen," she said, not quite in control of her voice. She put her glass to her lips, then changed her mind. She handed the glass to Harrison, and he delivered it to one of the empty niches. "My mother died in my arms," she revealed with sudden openness. "It brought it back," she mumbled, retreating.

"I'm so sorry, Erika." He stowed his glass in the compartment next to hers. "You want to stop for a while, get a breath of fresh air? How about it?"

She shook her head. "Home, okay?" She could hardly speak. She closed her eyes. The image of her mother sharpened. She opened her eyes and focused on the scenery out the window, willing herself to be calmed by it.

He let the silence prevail.

She looked back at him. He was gazing at her intently. She smiled wanly. "I'm not going to fall apart, you know. You don't have to stand watch."

"I understand."

"I know you do," she said, meeting his gaze. "Okay. I'm going to make one call. I think I can catch Sara before she leaves for the day."

"Please. Make as many calls as you like."

She peered into her tote, spying the smuggled address book. She felt more curious than guilty about it. As she groped for her cell phone, she decided after they'd gleaned any useful information from the book, she'd hand it over to Lieutenant Mitchell, along with an exculpatory white lie, when she appeared at the police station for her interrogation.

She called Sara's private line.

"There you are—you alright?" Sara exclaimed, without introduction. "I left you a voice message—you get it?"

"I haven't checked. There's been a terrible—"

"I know, I know. Before I called your cell, I tried reaching you at Helen's. A police officer answered. He told me what happened and questioned me at length about you and Harrison. I think he has enough for a book. I've been worried about you. Where are you?"

"In the car, heading back to Manhattan," Erika replied, nonplussed by Sara's misplaced concern.

"You sure no one's following you? Tell the driver to turn off at the next exit, then right back on at the next entrance ramp. See if anyone sticks with you."

"I don't understand—"

"Shush. Do as I say. Tell the driver."

"What's going on?" Harrison asked.

Erika repeated Sara's orders, and Harrison, without questioning her, relayed them to Bill.

"Well?" Sara demanded.

"We're on it," Erika said, as Bill eased his way over to the right lane.

Erika swiveled round to peer out the rear window. Harrison did the same.

"A truck is pulling off with us," Erika reported to Sara, "and behind him, a blue SUV."

"Ford Explorer," Bill modified.

"Ford Explorer," Erika repeated to Sara. "Yes, I heard him. Anything else?"

"Are we looking for anything specific?" Bill asked with a touch of impatience.

"No!" Sara snapped. "Erika, I'll fill you in in a minute. You can get back on the expressway now. Keep an eye on the SUV—the truck, too, it can't hurt."

Erika and Harrison remained on the lookout as Bill drove the short hop to the next entrance ramp, then onto the expressway.

"There's no one behind us," Erika informed Sara.

"Don't think you're home free. I want you to be very cautious. You shouldn't stay in your apartment tonight. You can stay over at my place if you—"

"Sara, what's going on?" Erika forcefully interrupted, turning to face the direction they were driving, Harrison remaining on watch. "Wait. First listen to this. It couldn't have been more than five minutes after Harrison picked you up at the office, when James Fitch Junior called and asked to speak to you. You know him, of course."

"Yes." James was the younger associate of Fitch & Son, a small but prestigious Madison Avenue art gallery and an occasional source for Erika's periodic reports on trends in art collecting.

"Well, I told him you weren't in and asked him why he was calling. Oddly, he was reluctant to tell me at first but finally agreed. Listen to this. He was at the Pierre gala— who noticed him in the crowd?—and it seems he overheard

Rodney holding forth about the Delaney inventory, complete with photocopies and data. He said when the Vittorio da Lucca drawing came up, it threw him for a loop because it sounded like a drawing hanging in his parents' living room. There's no signature on the drawing, but he remembered the date because it impressed him as a kid—1504! He didn't want to discuss it before checking its provenance. Apparently, the documents for the family's privately owned art works are kept in the Fitch Gallery's safe, along with those agented by the gallery.

"Anyway, he checked it out, and the drawing is indeed credited to Vittorio, bought from none other than William Delaney himself, in 1957—my guess, it coincided with Delaney's trip to New York. Unfortunately, Fitch doesn't trust the security of email. He wants to see you in person. At least we were able to review the subject matter of the drawing over the phone, and it does sound like a match for the item on Delaney's 1954 inventory."

"That means it was legitimately bought," Erika said, "but more importantly, it's been found!" She felt a surge of excitement—more on behalf of Helen than the art world. She turned to Harrison, who was becoming eager to the point of agitation. "Wait, Sara." She quickly relayed the information to him.

Harrison found his voice as Erika was returning her attention to the phone. "This is important!" he exclaimed, in tandem with her equally impassioned "What?" into the phone.

"You heard me right, Erika," Sara replied. "That's why I had you do the expressway maneuver. We received an anonymous email directed to you, warning you not to pursue Helen's project and threatening you with bodily harm if you did."

Erika felt a frisson of fear, its passage leaving her with a heightened sense of her mission. "Can't you identify the source of the email? Can't we send a reply at least?"

"Get Fitch's business or cell phone number," Harrison interjected, unaware of the dramatic change of subject.

"No on both counts," Sara answered Erika, her voice nearing shrill. "It was sent from an internet access point from who knows where!"

Erika took a couple of seconds to fill Harrison in. "Erika?" Sara impatiently prodded.

"The emailer is obviously connected to the assault," Erika directed to the cell. "We have to put Lieutenant Mitchell on it."

"He already is."

"Good. Maybe he can trace the e-mail. I'm not going to be afraid."

Sara and Harrison berated her fiercely, insisting she back off the project at once, let the appropriate government agencies take over.

Erika was adamant. "That's not what Helen would want. When we talk to the authorities we'll give them whatever information and help they need, and if we're lucky, they'll give us feedback. The two objectives, tracking down Delaney's paintings and nabbing Helen's killer, are not mutually exclusive."

"No painting is worth risking your life!" Harrison vehemently objected.

"I appreciate your concern," Erika answered almost tartly, masking the warm rush of gratitude. To Sara: "Can you give us Fitch's business and cell phone numbers? And please hurry? My cell's blinking, the battery's running out."

Resignedly, Sara obliged.

Erika scribbled the numbers in her notebook. "Think what a coup for you if we succeed," she placated.

"We're not in the business of solving crimes, at least not violent ones," Sara replied, the tiniest bit of archness revealing her ambivalence. "You'll at least promise you won't go back to your apartment tonight? If you refuse, I won't be asking, I'll be ordering you off this assignment. Do I make myself clear?"

"Yes. I promise."

"You can stay at my place, but we've got an engagement tonight, and I don't like the idea of your being alone, even for a couple of hours. How about a hotel? The magazine will pick up the tab."

"I'll stay at a hotel," Erika agreed.

"You'll do no such thing," Harrison objected. "You'll stay at my place. There's more than enough room, and we'll have the opportunity to discuss the safest way to proceed with your assignment, since there appears no chance of talking you out of it."

"No, I'll be fine, but thanks." To Sara: "I'll call you later. After I'm checked in. Don't worry about me."

The call ended with Sara's recitation of precautions. The instant she signed off, Erika punched in James Fitch's cell phone number. To the generic canned message, she left a noncommittal message of her own, asking him to call her as soon as possible, either on her cell phone, or on Harrison's— dictated on the spot. She tried his gallery next, reaching his phone service, to whom she gave the same message.

"Where is he—were you told?" Harrison asked, as she punched off.

She shook her head. "Only that he's gone for the day," she said, somehow feeling sorry to be disappointing him. She tapped in the numbers to access Manhattan information. "Warwick Hotel, Fifty-fourth and—"

"Excuse me," Harrison gently intruded, extracting the cell phone from her grasp. He terminated the call. "I thought we discussed this."

"We did not discuss this. You decided I would stay at your place, but I'm not taking advantage of you. We can plan our agenda at the hotel, and then you can go home and take a break." She snatched back her phone.

"Look, Erika, I don't think the safest place for you right now is a hotel room. At least take a look at where you'd be staying at my place. If you disapprove, you'll be conveyed to the hotel of your choice. Humor me."

"I'm not afraid of being alone tonight," she insisted, channeling her fear into her determination.

"That's what I'm worried about, your unreasonableness."

"Well, if you're going to lose sleep over it, it'll defeat the purpose." She shoved her phone back into her bag. "I hope the battery holds up, in case James calls."

He gave a sidewise glance at her still open bag. "And then," he

said meaningfully, clearly alluding to the purloined item.

She nodded her understanding.

"Good. Then we'll decide—you having the final word—where we go from there."

"I hope we'll have spoken to James by then."

"Hell, yes."

CHAPTER 3

It was nearing sunset when the limo drew up in front of an elegant residential building on the corner of East Seventy-eighth Street and Madison Avenue. The street lamps had not yet come on, and the natural evening glow flattered the red brick and limestone façade like a lover bathed in candlelight. Only three stories high, yet with massive frontage and a perfectly proportioned entrance flanked by Doric columns, the building's character was at once welcoming and prestigious. Erika guessed that no more than five or six families were ensconced under its roof.

After escorting his passengers to the entrance, Bill took off quickly, leaving Erika with the panicky feeling that she had not been given time to change her mind. "Maybe I'll catch a cab," she said half to herself.

"Disapprove already?" Harrison asked, with raised brow. He unlocked the wrought-iron gate guarding an impressive oak wood door, tapped the shiny digits of the alarm pad on the door frame, staccatoing like a child playing a piano tune by heart.

"I didn't mean to be rude," she said apologetically, noticing his stance was slightly awkward, wondering if he was consciously obstructing her view so she couldn't memorize his code. This small act reminded her, as if she needed to be reminded, that she did not know Harrison at all, that even after fifty years of living with him, sharing toothpaste and edited secrets, she still wouldn't know exactly what he'd been thinking at this critical moment.

"Come in," he said, motioning her inside.

She sidled past him, careful not to make contact.

The lobby was a compact version of the Metropolitan Opera House, in white marble and red carpet. The carpet was badly worn in spots, and she wondered why it hadn't been replaced. On the far left, an imposing yet whimsical statue of what had to be a Botero stood beside the gilded door of the lobby's elevator. Centered between the elevator and the staircase was a plush arrangement of couch and chair with a marble-ledged floor lamp nested between them.

Harrison tossed his satchel onto the couch as Erika registered the open hallway with its wrought-iron balustrade at the top of the staircase. This was not a multi-family dwelling; this was a private home.

She was usually unimpressed by wealth. What she valued were the accomplishments of an individual, his or her mark left on the world, in particular on the arts and sciences. This leaning, a form of snobbery all its own, was nevertheless as natural to her as her love of Snickers bars, having been acquired too early in life to be considered an affectation—on her father's knee, the familiar smell of him as bound to his reading of Will Durant as the moon to the tides. She was not immune, however, to the amazement of having been, without preparation, dropped into a royal abode.

Her amazement was unspoken, but it must have been plastered across her face, because she saw its response flash across Harrison's: a frown of disapproval that cut her to the quick. "What a lovely place," she remarked, transforming her clearly inflammatory awe into a crisp appraisal, as if her own digs were the equivalent of his. "Thanks," he said, with a twinge of remorse, in all likelihood realizing that his judgment of her, coming from who knew where, had been misplaced, or at least premature. "It was my grandmother's."

"Oh," she said flatly, just as a figure emerged on the landing above.

A small woman who had to be at least in her eighties, her spare frame garbed in a starched little black dress with scalloped white apron, stepped up to the balustrade and looked down on Erika and the master of the house. "Good evening," she greeted pleasantly, in a thin, but mellifluous voice.

"Hi," Harrison replied, peeling off his blazer. "Grace, meet my colleague, Erika Shawn." He flung his blazer alongside his satchel. "Erika—Grace Jones."

"Hello," Erika said, with a little wave.

"Erika may be staying overnight with us. Will the Blue Room be okay?"

"Yes, of course. Will you be dining in, Mr. Harry?"

Erika smiled at the affectionately formal address that somehow ascribed a youthful buoyancy to both Grace and Harrison.

"Don't trouble yourself. If we do, we'll order something in." He turned to Erika. "Okay?"

"Of course."

"The guest rooms are on the third floor. Grace, would you show Erika the room? I'll be in my study—you'll bring her there afterwards?"

"Yes, Mr. Harry." To Erika: "I'll meet you on the third floor." She nimbly moved off, down the hall and out of sight.

The rooming decision felt unilateral, reviving Erika's misgivings. "This is very kind of you, Harrison, but if you think it's unsafe for me to be alone tonight, what makes you so sure it'll be safer tomorrow, or, for that matter, the day after? It doesn't make sense. I might as well hire a twenty-four-hour bodyguard."

"Not a bad idea."

"You're serious," she said, disbelieving.

"I am, but let's take it one day at a time. Go take a look at the room," he urged, gesturing toward the elevator.

"No," she said, without budging. "We had an agreement."

"I mean no, you won't be treating me like a doll in a china shop.

Tomorrow I'm going back to my place. Un-chaperoned."

"If that's your decision."

"It is." In a conspicuous show of self-reliance, she strode briskly to the elevator. "What do I press?" she asked smartly. She spotted the lone button. "Oh." She went to press it at the same time as he did, their hands colliding midflight. "Sorry," she said, giving way. The door slid open at once, revealing a small, oak-paneled compartment with carpet matching the lobby's. Harrison pressed the 3 button on the brass wall panel and ushered her in. With his hand on the door to prevent it from sliding shut, he said, "See you in a couple of minutes." He released the door, and it soundlessly closed.

She emerged from the capsule with a polite smile plastered on her face and her heart beating a mile a minute.

Grace was waiting for her. "You're afraid of elevators," she observed pleasantly.

"How'd you guess?"

"You're not blinking." She turned on her heel. "Come, follow me."

Erika was guided down the wide hallway, her footsteps silenced by the thick beige carpet etched in a pattern of twisting vines, faded from years of being tread on. She was led past four closed doors she assumed opened onto bedrooms—maybe one or two were "drawing" rooms, she posed inwardly, toying with the word's ramifications, feeling at once unsettled and morally above it when confronted by the disparities of social class.

Grace stopped in front of the fifth door, leading to the corner room. She cupped her hand around the ornately hammered brass doorknob and opened the door, performing the act with a decorous flourish. "This is the Blue Room," she proudly announced, as if she'd designed it herself. "It's my favorite." She stepped out of the way for Erika.

As she crossed the threshold, Erika's breath caught. For a few seconds she stood at the entrance, staring at the large oil painting on the wall facing her, above the headboard of the four-poster bed. The tender, yet meticulous style of the impressionist was unmistakable. She walked up to it, as close to it as she could get. "It's beautiful," she said, leaning in, as if she'd be able to experience it more intimately.

From behind, "It's a Mary Cassatt," Grace reverently informed her.

"I know," Erika replied, admiring the delicate brushstrokes up close, then backing up, skirting around Grace in order to view the captivating oil from the foot of the bed. The subject of the painting was a young woman in the palest blue dress. She was knitting—concentrating, head slightly bent, hair parted and pulled back, the line of the scalp, with its brilliantly conceived stroke of white, creating a heartrending vulnerability. She was seated on the grass, her long dress gathered about her feet. A straight path with a footbridge was in the background.

"It's not a portrait of her, but she looks just like Harrison's grandmother," Grace said wistfully. "That's why his grandfather bought it for her." When she turned to Erika, her eyes were glistening. "It reminds me of both of them, you see. They were such generous people, and of such fine, upstanding character." She paused. "Just like Harrison," she pronounced, the gentlest warning in her gaze, clearly stipulating don't mess with him. Claws retracted, she concluded, "You'll be very comfortable in this room."

"I'm sure I will be," Erika agreed, touched by Grace's protectiveness for Harrison. She surveyed the room, trying not to think of him. She focused on the simple furnishings, the polished wood floor, the light filtering in through the filmy white curtains, the embroidered coverlet folded at the foot of the bed.

She gave Grace a knowing look.

"Yes," Grace said, "it's named after the dress in the painting. It's the only blue in the room." She lovingly smoothed her apron, as if it were the painting itself, or the woman it reminded her of. "Here, let me show you the bathroom." She crossed the room and opened the door to the adjoining chamber.

Erika peered over her shoulder and spied what she would have described as a mini-spa, complete with sauna and Jacuzzi. "It has all the amenities," she said, sounding absurdly like a potential buyer. "Did you bring a suitcase with you?" Grace asked coolly. "I didn't see one."

"No," Erika said, realizing it hadn't occurred to her.

"No problem. There's a new toothbrush in the drawer under the sink. There are clothes in the closet. I believe about your size, or close enough."

Erika kept her question to herself.

"They're Harrison's sister's," Grace said, answering it. "She comes for visits every now and then."

"Would she mind? I'd only borrow a robe?"

"Of course not. Just leave it out on the bed for me in the morning."

The agreement struck, Grace waited while Erika used the bathroom facilities then accompanied her to Harrison's study on the first floor, via a hidden staircase at the opposite end of the hallway. Grace lightly tapped on the closed door then glided off, indicating Erika let herself in.

As she turned the knob, she heard a woman's strident voice demanding: "Why don't you just—!"

The utterance was cut off as Erika stepped into the room.

Harrison's hand was shooting away from the answering machine on his desk.

"I was getting a couple of things done," he explained, jumping up from his maroon leather chair.

"I can wait outside," Erika suggested, wondering how

the woman's statement ended.

"No, no, have a seat." He glanced down at his phone center, his focus on the answering machine.

"Where?" she prompted. This was obviously a one-man study, with packed bookshelves occupying all the available wall space and an assortment of library tables taking up the slack. Alongside his L-shaped mahogany desk stood an armchair piled high with papers and bulging folders. The only other possibility was a massive brown leather recliner at the other end of the room, but that, too, was occupied, though exclusively with folders.

"Sorry," he said, looking up. He promptly began hauling the piles on the armchair to the area under his desktop. "So, did you find the accommodations acceptable?" he asked with transparent casualness, temporarily out of sight behind his desk.

"It's a beautiful room—yes," she answered, with equally feigned nonchalance.

"Good," he said, rising to fetch the last of the folders. He crouched again, out of her line of vision.

A tiny whimpering sound came from beneath the desk. "Harrison?"

"It's only Jake." Harrison rose from behind the desk. "He doesn't like being disturbed when he's sleeping, which is pretty much all day long—right, boy?"

In response, a large, somewhat overweight chocolate Lab shuffled out from behind the desk. He peered up at Erika with a slightly bewildered look, then at Harrison.

"This is Erika. Erika, this is Jake," Harrison said, the loving gentleness in his voice caressing her name as well as the dog's, though she knew it wasn't his intention. "He's an old guy, and a great companion."

Jake plopped down to a sitting position then rolled onto his back.

"Hi, Jake," Erika said, slipping her bag from her shoulder and placing it on the floor beside the cleared armchair, then crouching beside the dog to rub his belly, obviously his goal.

"Not very subtle, is he?" Harrison said, in that same loving tone. He crouched beside her to stroke Jake's head, his chinos pulling taut against his knees.

The dog sighed in ecstasy.

Harrison stood up. "I'll have to take him out soon." Erika gave Jake a final pat and rose to her feet.

Harrison returned to his desk chair, and Erika sat down in the armchair, the dog righting himself, only to thump down at her feet.

"He seems to have taken to you."

Jake nuzzled his snout against her ankle, as if to prove the point. "You have a dog? You seem like a dog person."

"I think I am, but I can't be sure. I never had one. My father was allergic, and my landlord doesn't allow them." She bent over to caress Jake. "Good boy," she said, and was rewarded with a look of undying love. She straightened up, leaving Jake clearly disappointed. "I'm sorry, boy."

Harrison was smiling. "He'll make you feel guilty if you let him," he warned.

"I can see that." She tucked a lock of hair behind her ear. "Unreal, isn't it, sitting here as if what happened today never happened, as if we were as uninformed as Jake."

"A defense mechanism to keep us on an even keel. Relatively."

The murder scene flashed before her, impossible, but too vivid to disbelieve. "I have to focus on what Helen set out to do. It's the only thing that will compensate, I mean begin to....You understand, don't you?"

"Of course, but I'm worried. Doesn't that threatening anonymous email to you concern you at all?"

"I won't let it. I want to start. Tell me your theory about the drawing, how it relates to Michelangelo's Battle of Cascina. Let's start with that."

"Okay," he yielded. "Before I left the Pierre, we had just

gotten to the subject. Where were we?"

"At the beginning. Don't hold back. Lecture me."

"Well, then. Vittorio's drawing is of men bathing, others riding off on horseback, and others engaged in battle. Given the drawing's date—1504—and Florentine origin, one can't but wonder."

"I remember Michelangelo's studies for Cascina," she interrupted, "but not with all that going on."

"Right. No studies tell the whole story Let me put it into context. The Florentines were obsessed with re-conquering Pisa, a coastal city that had come under French domination in 1494. So, to rev up its citizenry to battle-ready mode, and, while they were at it, to glorify the state, the powers that be commissioned Leonardo and Michelangelo to decorate its enormous new Council Hall with victory scene murals."

"The frescoes, never completed."

"Exactly. The subject of Michelangelo's section of the wall was, appropriately enough, to be the Florentines' victory over Pisa at Cascina that had taken place back in 1364. Now, besides Michelangelo's grand mural never having been executed, the only cartoon he executed was that of the planned mural's central section, "Bathers," as it's generally called. The cartoon was in all likelihood destroyed by overzealous artists trying to copy it. A 'cartoon,' let me explain, is—"

"A full-scale drawing used to transfer the design directly onto the surface to be painted," Erika recited. "My education's inadequate, not nonexistent."

"Of course," Harrison replied, with a genuinely remorseful smile, but the barest break in narration. "The most notable work giving us some idea of the scope of Michelangelo's final design is a copy of the central section cartoon, made prior to its loss or destruction, by Aristotile da Sangallo, a pupil of Michelangelo's."

"Isn't there a study by Michelangelo at the Uffizi?"

"There is, but it's kind of a work-in-progress, and not his final concept. Anyway, da Sangallo's painting depicts a composite of two episodes immediately preceding the battle scene itself. The Florentine army is encamped by the Arno River, bathing in the heat of the day as their leader lies ill." Harrison raised his hand, demarcating the break in action. "A soldier—the hero—raises a false cry of alarm, proving the army's lack of readiness, prompting the men to get their act together." He paused. "In the end, they defeat the Pisans. Although there's a hazy reference to a battle scene in the background of the Uffizi study, no clear and complete renditions of the soldiers riding off to battle and the battle scene itself exist —more accurately, have as yet been discovered."

"Good," Erika said. "Now, here's where I get confused. Granted, there's a hazy reference to a battle scene in the background of the Uffizi study, and I think I remember seeing a couple of Michelangelo sketches of horses supposedly made with the mural in mind, but where's the certainty that the da Sangallo copy portrays only a portion of the final concept?"

"Well, as a civic commission, a mural portraying soldiers caught with their pants down would not have been a grand enough message for the public's edification. In my opinion, the proposal would have been rejected. Without an actual battle scene or riding off to victory, the depiction would have been more or less a typical genre piece."

"That explains it. So, when exactly was Michelangelo commissioned to do the mural?" Erika asked, studying Harrison's hand, imagining it as a Michelangelo study, the strength of it evoking the beautiful un-rendered body.

"It's presumed the summer of 1504, because in September of that year he was assigned workspace for the project. In October a payment was made for the paper to be used for the cartoon, and in December another payment was made for putting together the pieces of the huge drawing." He paused. "You see where I'm going with this, don't you?"

She nodded. "You think Vittorio may have been an artist friend or even an apprentice of Michelangelo's, and on hand when the master was planning the mural."

"Yes, but listen. From what I can make out from the photocopy on William Delaney's faxed 1954 inventory, I can't help thinking, or wishing, that Vittorio's drawing is a more complete—well, if not representation, interpretation of Michelangelo's conception of the mural in its entirety than any we've ever seen. What a thrill to uncover such a work," he speculated, fire in his eyes. "I'm really looking forward to Fitch showing us that drawing."

"I can see why—now," Erika said. Anticipating what would come next, she reached over the arm of the chair to retrieve her bag. "Here it is," she said, pulling out the leather address book she had removed from the Southampton residence, then handing it over to him for first perusal.

He thumbed through the pages, careful not to damage the already fragile binding. "I don't feel comfortable doing this. I think we should turn it over to the police."

"We will, of course, but not yet. When Helen was enumerating the items found in her father, William Delaney's safe deposit box, she mentioned address books—plural. I remember it clearly. This book must have been the only thing overlooked by whoever swiped the rest of the material Helen had ready for us. Maybe it was kicked under the sideboard in the struggle. I'm convinced the cops are not going to find any of the safe deposit contents on the premises. We'll relinquish the book, but Helen would want us to examine it first. It's our obligation. May I?" She extended her hand, and he obligingly gave her the address book. With care equaling his, she began turning pages, not knowing what she was looking for, hoping it would come to her.

Harrison rummaged for something on his desk. "Here it is, Mitchell's card. I'll call him—or do you want to?"

"I will," she said, without looking up. "Here's a name with the letters 'a g t' tacked on in parentheses. Probably an agent, even an art agent. The entry dates back fifty or more years."

"Oh?"

"I kept my mother's address book, which dates from the Stone Age. For instance, my grandparents' exchange is listed as 'Dewey 9,' even though the 'DE' was officially changed to '33' years ago." She turned the book so he could look at it, keeping her finger on the entry she'd referred to. "See where it says 'Cloverdale 8'?" She lay the book down in front of him. "That means it's now '258.' We could dial that number today."

"What about the area code?" he challenged.

"That would be '718,'" she said without pause. "'Dewey' and 'Cloverdale' were both Brooklyn exchanges."

He smiled. "A thief and a detective."

She tried not to let the appealing creases around his mouth affect her. She felt herself growing warm from the ambient temperature or from her own body heat, she wasn't sure which. She wished she could take off her corduroy jacket, then asked herself why couldn't she? She peeled it off and then draped it over the back of her chair. When she turned back, her turtleneck sweater felt tighter than ever. Slumping would advertise her awareness of this. She sat up straight, despite the fact that she could feel his eyes on her.

Jake, apparently awakened by her jostling, looked up at her. She bent over and caressed the dog. When she righted herself,

Harrison was sliding Mitchell's card toward her.

"Here," he said, rising from his chair. "You make the call, and I'll start photocopying the book. That way we can study the entries at our leisure. How does that sound?"

"Like a good idea."

"Partners in crime, then?" He extended his hand.

She shook it, not wanting to let go, but quickly pulling away.

The copying machine was sitting on one of the book-laden tables. She watched him move across the room, their eyes meeting for a final corroboration.

She punched in Mitchell's number, realizing, with the first ring, that she hadn't sufficiently prepared herself.

"Mitchell here" cut off the second ring.

"It's Erika Shawn," she panted, sounding as if she'd just run a marathon. She took a breath.

"Yeah. You think of something?"

"No, I only wanted to ask you where I should turn in an address book I accidentally picked up. You were rushing us to the door, and—"

"You walk out with anything else?"

"No."

"Where are you?" She told him.

"I'm on duty in Suffolk County. You know where the nearest police station is in your area?"

She asked Harrison. It was three blocks away. Mitchell ordered her to deliver the book to that station within the hour or he'd have her run in.

She started to explain just how completely she understood. He cut her off. "I'll be at that location tomorrow morning, nine a.m. sharp. Be there for questioning, with or without your lawyer. Your choice."

"I thought we answered all your questions at—the scene," she said, with attempted equanimity. "Now we've got a couple more, haven't we? Have Wheatley there, too. I'm making a special trip."

She was about to thank him, inexplicably. He hung up.

"The con job is definitely not your go-to career," Harrison commented. "Are we being hauled in for questioning?"

"Tomorrow morning, nine o'clock. We can bring our lawyers if we like. I don't have one."

"It's not necessary," he said cavalierly. "We'll be okay. I'm up to the 'M's." He lay the book over to the next two-page spread. "It's going quickly. When I'm done, we'll order food, and you can wait here for it while I take Jake out and bring the book to the police station."

Jake rose to his feet.

"In a few minutes," Erika gently promised, stroking the dog's head. "I'm taking the responsibility of delivering the book," she told Harrison, with renewed assurance, perhaps feeding off of his. "We can both walk Jake over to the station, but I'm handing in the book on my own."

"It might not be safe for you to be out on the street."

"Jake will protect me, won't you, boy?"

Confirmed, with a sloppy lick on the palm of her ministering hand.

Harrison smiled. "I don't seem to win any of these arguments."

"I'm staying over. You won that one."

"The only one." Another sheet in the steady stream rolled out of the printer. "Almost done."

"Good, because I can't believe it, but I'm starving." The surprising ease of her remark gently resonated at the base of her pelvis.

"We'll call in our order before we leave and pick it up on the way back. It'll save time." Another sheet slid out of the machine. "I'm glad," he remarked, as an afterthought.

"About what?"

"That you're starving."

"I guess you're right." The realization that he had calmed her perversely caused her pulse to quicken. Comfort, surrender, tragedy were the stages of romantic delusion, and she was clearly experiencing the first. She jumped out of her chair. "Here, let me make myself useful." She hastened over to where he was working, Jake following at her heels. She gathered up the pages from the printer tray, aligned them and waited to snap up the remaining pages.

Five minutes later the job was done. Erika placed her stack on Harrison's desk while he dug out a manila envelope. She labeled the envelope appropriately, slid the leather address book into it and carefully wedged the parcel into her tote.

Harrison came up with his take-out menus. They quickly agreed on an assortment of standard Chinese dishes, and he called the restaurant. "Ready in twenty minutes," he reported.

Jake performed a belabored puppy trot to the door to the room, cocked his head toward his master, then over his haunch at the closet door.

"You've been very patient," Harrison said, striding toward him. He produced a colorful braided leash and a small plastic bag, then snapped on the leash.

Erika slung her bag over her shoulder. "May I?" She extended her hand in an offer to take the leash.

"Sure," Harrison said, taken aback, but not unpleasantly.

She grasped the end of the leash. Jake turned toward her, flicked his tail and pressed toward the lobby. She tightened her grip into a white-knuckled fist. She could feel her face tighten up, too.

"Relax," Harrison advised good-naturedly. "Don't worry about him, he'll never run off. The leash is strictly for putting pedestrians at their ease. Halt, Jake," he prompted. Directed overhead: "Grace, we'll be back in about half an hour!"

"See you later!" bounced back from the unseen housekeeper. "Let's go," he said, releasing Jake from his command. "Relax," he reminded Erika, flashing her a smile bordering on patronizing.

She responded with a prideful sniff, instantly feeling like an aristocratic poodle. A look of unbounded and unquestioning love was suddenly beamed up at her from Jake, humbling her with its pure goodness. "I'll get the hang of it," she said, chastened.

Once outside the building in the crisp night air, Jake headed straight for the circle of sod at the base of the nearest of the maples lining East Seventy-eighth Street. Erika slackened her grip on the leash and tried un-tensing her arm to allow more play on the leash. Harrison shrugged. "It's his favorite tree. Amazing it survives."

"Maybe it would die if he didn't pee on it."

He laughed. "You may be right." More soberly, as he gestured east: "The police station is on Third and a couple of streets down."

By the time they arrived in front of the stationhouse, Erika was a confident dog-walker, realizing her transformation was due to Jake's impeccable behavior rather than her own talent. Reluctantly, she handed the leash to Harrison. "Temporary custody," she stipulated, before marching into the building.

The officers on duty had been given a heads-up about Erika's visit, so the transfer of the address book went without a hitch, and she was quickly back on the street. "Mission accomplished."

"Us, too." Harrison raised the knotted plastic bag. "Trash basket's on the corner. We have to go that way. The restaurant's on Sixty-ninth."

Erika caught up to him, taking hold of the leash just behind his hand.

"I forgot he belongs to you," he said, grinning.

Since relieving himself, Jake's gait seemed a bit livelier, but Erika was unfazed. In fact, she was perfectly comfortable strolling along with Jake in tow and Harrison alongside her, his steps synchronized with her own, his figure intermittently highlighted by the streetlamps. She wondered if to an outsider the three of them were illuminated as a tableau, a simulacrum of a family. She studied this image as if it were projected onto the wall of a museum, enjoying it from the perspective of an art critic, and no closer.

The genial expression on Harrison's face as he emerged from the restaurant discouraged dispute about who was to pay.

As they came to within ten yards of Harrison's entrance, a white stretch limo rounded the corner of Seventy-seventh Street and pulled up in front of his building. Harrison jerked to a halt, then pressed on, muttering something indiscernible under his breath.

As they arrived, a female passenger stepped out of the limo, aided by her chauffeur. "Good timing, darling," she crooned to Harrison, her tone laced with malice. "Grace told me you'd be returning just about now." She thrust a peremptory wave at her chauffeur, who instantly returned to his position behind the wheel and pulled shut his door.

Erika, standing alongside Harrison, struggled to keep the increasingly rambunctious Jake from jumping what appeared to be the reincarnation of Helen of Troy.

"What do you want, Charlotte?" Harrison snapped.

The goddess mercilessly eyed Erika up and down. "This one's cuter than your computer nerd," she commented. To the dog, seated now, but still straining toward her: "Don't even think about it, Jake. I love you, too, but not as much as Armani." She smoothed the fine fabric of her herringboned skirt.

"What do you want?" Harrison repeated. "To speak to you in private."

"This is not the way it's done."

"Maybe that's been our problem."

"Bullshit. Let me have the leash, Erika," he said, taking it.

"So it's 'Erika,' is it," Charlotte noted, flipping her corn silk locks. "I know a model with that name."

"No relation," Erika said.

"She's a clever one," Charlotte praised. "Good for you."

"Come on," Harrison directed at Erika, as he started for the door.

"You're making a big mistake," Charlotte warned. "Alex will be much tougher on you than I could ever be!"

Harrison turned to her briefly. "You either think I'm really stupid, or you just cracked your first joke."

Erika wondered, with forced indifference, if this was the person Harrison, perhaps in a more accepting frame of mind, had called "sweetheart" on that incoming call at the gala, or, by the same token, if it had been Charlotte's message she'd barged in on earlier this evening—not that she was about to try to determine a voice match.

Harrison closed the door behind them just as Charlotte was being whisked away in her limo. "Sorry about that," he said, unleashing Jake.

"She is beautiful," Erika non-sequitured.

"So what? So are you. What's that got to do with it? Obviously you don't get it."

"That was too good a compliment. Don't ruin it with an explanation."

"I have absolutely no intention of doing so," he said, without so much as cracking a smile.

Moments later, Jake had gone off to the fourth floor to sleep for the night under Harrison's bed as part of his ironclad routine, and Grace was laying out dinnerware fit for a king on the formal dining room table, second floor.

"Please don't fuss," Harrison urged. "We'll be fine."

"If you say so," Grace said. "In that case, I'll polish the brassware in the living room. I've been meaning to get to it for heaven knows how long."

"Your work day is over."

"I have to keep busy, or I'll become clinically depressed."

"You got that from a *Prevention* magazine. You can't hold me hostage with that article forever."

Essentially ordered to, Grace had no choice but to retire for the night.

"I use chopsticks," Harrison said, removing the packaged pairs from their hefty take-out bag, along with a handful of soy and duck sauce parcels. "You?"

Erika nodded. "Why don't we put away this china and eat right from the containers? I feel like we're overachieving with"—she gave a grand sweep of her hand to cover the entire royal venue—"all this—"

"'All this' is not who I am," he said caustically. "'All this' is where I live." He proceeded to put away the dinnerware, coming close to banging shut the cupboard doors.

"I'm sorry I struck a nerve," Erika said defensively.

"You caught me off guard," he said, without explaining how. He returned to the table and stood beside one of the finely upholstered mahogany chairs, indicating she take the seat cattycorner to his, at the table's end. "We need drinks. Wine? Soda?" He jumped behind the throne-like end chair and pulled it out for her. "What would you like?"

"Just water, thanks," she replied, hoping her modest request would not be taken as another offense. She began removing the food containers from the shopping bag and setting them on the floral placemats Grace had lined up in the center of the table, on either side of the Wedgwood centerpiece.

Excusing himself, Harrison strode to the French doors, parting them to fully reveal the stately kitchen, then returned shortly with two crystal glasses filled with water.

"This is the best I could do, we're out of paper cups," he said wryly, setting the glasses on the placemats from which the accoutrements of dining had been removed. He sat down, took a cloth napkin and tossed it onto his lap. "Out of paper napkins too, it appears. My apologies."

"It better not happen again."

They exchanged grins that mocked their private tensions.

Mid-meal, as they were swapping cartons, he said, "You're wondering who she is."

"Of course I'm curious," she acknowledged. "I wasn't going to pry, though."

"I know you weren't going to," he said slowly, as if just now realizing this. "She's my ex-wife, one signature shy."

"Hers?" she asked, already prying.

"Yes," he said, the barest trace of a smile expressing forgiveness. "Sorry."

"Don't be. I brought up the subject."

She could tell he was already retreating from it. "It must be a difficult time," she said, helping him close it.

"Only because there's an unresolved issue. Otherwise, I

couldn't be happier."

From the gravity of his tone, she doubted it. "Try the Hunan pork," she directed. There was no way she was going to ask him any more questions, although her restraint was causing them to multiply.

"Thanks," he said, his gratitude clearly covering more than the pork dish. He placed his carton of chicken with cashews on her mat. "For you." And then, as if freed by her discretion, he offered: "The issue is our Charitable Remainder Trust. You know the animal?"

"Not really—no, actually."

"You—and possibly the spouse, in this case the spouse —commit x amount of your estate to a charity, and during your lifetime you receive income from it without paying capital gains. After you both die, the charity receives the principal." He tasted the pork, diminishing the importance of the subject. "This is excellent."

She poked at her food; glanced up at him, hoping to convey expectation without imperative.

"Charlotte wants to invest a good portion of the principal in her boyfriend's business, some phase of strip mall development."

Erika was touched by his lack of rancor. It took some effort, she thought, judging from his stoic look. "Would that be considered venture capital?"

"Yes, and it would put the principal at considerable risk. Although we're fifty-fifty beneficiaries of the trust's earned income, I'm its sole manager, and since the charitable donation is in my grandmother's memory, there's no way I'm going to put it in jeopardy. That's the final issue."

"I hope it works out," she said, trying not to sound invasively earnest.

"It has to," he said, with a spike of ardor, as his cell phone rang. "It's for you," he said, after a brief exchange. "James Fitch." He handed her the phone. "Very mad," he mouthed.

"Why the hell didn't you pick up your cell phone?" Fitch yelled. "And what is it with your home phone—you leave it off the hook?"

"Sorry, the cell battery must have died, it was on its way out, but

I have no idea why you had trouble getting through to my landline phone."

"This is no time to be unreachable. The Vittorio is fucking gone!"

"What?"

"You heard me. Can you get your ass over here and—"

"Where?"

"The gallery. It's closed. Ring the bell, I'll let you in."

Harrison touched her shoulder. "What's wrong, what's happening?"

His hand electrified her. She tilted hers upward, indicating he hold on. "We'll be there as quickly as possible," she directed at Fitch. "We're only about twenty blocks away."

"You're bringing Wheatley?" James balked. "Your boss told me about him before the shit hit the fan."

"I'm bringing him."

"Oh, all right, only don't waste time. Come now."

"What's the emergency, I mean for me and Harrison? Didn't someone call the police? Were your parents home when the—"

"I'll explain when you get here." Silence cut into his last word as he ended the call.

Erika gave Harrison the news. Surprisingly, he seemed equally as concerned with the problem of her home phone as with the disappearance of the drawing.

"I think your apartment may have been broken into," he said, as they crammed the food containers into the refrigerator. "Let's run over there first," he suggested, kicking shut the refrigerator door with the back of his heel.

"You're jumping to conclusions," she objected, flattered despite herself.

"What if it's been ransacked? The sooner the police are called in, the more likely the vandals will be caught." They were hurrying down the steps leading to the main floor. He was ahead of her, not looking back. "Aren't you worried?"

"Aren't you worried about the drawing? It's a lot more valuable

than my television set."

"You're being ridiculous—of course I'm worried about the drawing, but I'm sure Fitch already called in the National Guard."

"Who knows, maybe I left the phone off the hook." She sprinted past him, taking the last two steps in a single bound, then headed straightaway for the study to retrieve her bag.

Back with him. "You think your battery charger would work on my cell phone?" she asked, slinging her bag onto her shoulder.

He shook his head. "I saw it. Our makes are incompatible."

Like us, she inwardly punch-lined, counter-punching somewhere deeper. "Too bad, I'll have to do without it."

"We'll share," he said, removing his keys from his pocket with more jangle than necessary, as if he meant to block out any inadmissible overtones.

CHAPTER 4

Her face nearly up against the cab driver's window, she directed, "Fitch Gallery, Fifty-seventh and Madison." Her tone left no room for debate.

The driver nodded as he turned down the volume of the lively Middle Eastern music blasting from his radio.

"You win," Harrison conceded, coming up behind her. "We'll go to your apartment afterwards." He swung open the back door. "I'm not happy with this."

She shrugged and slid into the back seat, stalling at a depression in its padding, regaining momentum only after he bumped in alongside her. She checked his face for a reaction. His features were impenetrable, and she remembered how the barely visible creases in his cheeks deepened when he smiled. "There won't be much traffic at this hour," she said, dragging her mind from the subject.

He pulled the door shut. "We should at least call someone in your building to check your place." He drew his cell phone from his blazer pocket. "Go ahead." He handed the phone to her.

She called her neighbors, the Barlows. They weren't at home, or chose not to answer.

"Why didn't you leave a message?"

"I didn't want to scare them. We'll check out my place soon enough."

The rest of the short trip was uninterrupted by conversation. "I want to tell you something," he said, as they were stepping up to the door of the gallery. "Hold up."

"What is it?" There was a pre-wintry nip in the air, and she drew closed her jacket.

"I think you should take the advice of the anonymous caller," he said.

"And quit? Never."

"Distance yourself, then."

"To where? Thirty-third and Lex sound about right? Look, there's no reason why you have to come along with me, but I'm committed to this project, wherever it takes me. You don't have to come in with me now. I won't hold it against you."

"So you assume I'd leave you in the lurch. Thanks."

"No, I'm saying your gallantry is not the determining factor."

He shook his head. "Are you this fervent about everything you commit yourself to?"

"Yes. Which is why I don't get involved with anything I'm not absolutely sure about."

"In this world there's nothing you can be absolutely sure about."

"You're right. Correction. I'm going to enter this building unless I get hit by a bus." She stepped up to the glass door and rang the bell on its polished brass frame.

He stood beside her.

"What do you think of them?" she asked, gesturing toward the window, where works of the gallery's featured contemporary artist of the month were on display: huge oils of meticulously rendered household appliances in unexpected settings—a dishwasher up a tree, a toaster in a field of daisies.

"The technique is impeccable, but they leave me cold. You?"

She nodded. "Same here—a cross between Magritte and Kmart." Through the glass, she saw Fitch emerging on the trot.

"Come in, come in," he directed impatiently, as he opened the door. "You took your damn time." He waved them in as if they were wayward pets.

"We came as quickly as possible," Erika said, slipping by him, hoping to pacify him with a look of understanding.

He was unmoved. "I blame this incident on you," he said. "If your boyfriend hadn't shot his mouth off, this wouldn't have happened." He ushered them toward the rear.

"If you're talking about Rodney, he's not my boyfriend," Erika said, following him through the dimly lit display area. "I don't see how he could have led the thief to your doorstep."

"My parents' doorstep," he corrected, guiding them into the smaller of the two back rooms. "Thank god no one was home. You of all people should know in my business there's only one degree of separation between the geniuses and the know-nothings, the good guys and the bad. Any number of guests have seen the Vittorio hanging in my parents' living room. Thanks to Rodney Smitts and his motor mouth, they and who knows how many others have been invited to ponder its virtues."

"You must realize how far-fetched that sounds," Erika said. "I would think your parents' guests over the years would have been aware of the value of a drawing dated 1504. Why would any of them choose this particular time to invade your parents' home and steal it?"

"I agree," Harrison said, as he and Erika took their places opposite Fitch, the three of them drawing their black leather and aluminum chairs up to the sleek ebony desk.

"How about you yourself?" Erika ventured, focusing past Fitch's shoulder to avoid pinning him with a stare. "Are you sure you didn't happen to mention the significance of the Vittorio to anyone at the gala—or afterward? Maybe even a stranger or two? Someone in the legal profession, just in case your parents' drawing turned out to be stolen goods?" Her focus glided back to him.

The color rose to Fitch's naturally pale cheeks.

"You're upset, so it may have slipped your mind. Is the drawing insured?" she asked, moving on to minimize his embarrassment.

"For the original purchase price of a hundred seventy-five thousand, rolled over without reappraisal. It's worth a lot more in today's market."

"James, there's obviously a connection between the theft of the drawing and Helen Gilmore's murder," she said, the word hitting her like a bullet. She watched Fitch tug at his tie. A slight man, with boyishly small features, he could pass for a twenty-five year old. She knew better only because she'd interviewed his twenty-year-old son when she was researching her article on multigenerational art dealerships.

"Of course," he said, "considering the timing."

"Speaking of related events," Harrison said, addressing her, "what do you think prompted some bastard to break into your apartment?"

Fitch's brow shot up. "That true, Erika?"

"Harrison's being an alarmist. I'm sure I left the phone off the hook."

Fitch threw her a look of impatience. "Let's get back to the subject. Call me selfish, but all I care about is the drawing." He shifted uncomfortably in his seat. "It was stupid of me to mention its disappearance to you over the phone. Have you contacted Smitts, your boss, the cops, I mean anyone about this?" He looked from one to the other. "Either of you?"

"No," they answered in unison.

"Good. Keep it that way. I want to call the shots in this investigation. For starters, I'm going to get in touch with a private company that's got the largest database of stolen art in the world."

"That would be the Art Loss Register," Harrison said matter-of-factly.

Fitch's jaw tensed. "Yes. Sotheby's and Christie's are among its shareholders. You can see why its discretion is said to be unparalleled."

"Of course," Harrison agreed. He turned to Erika. "The friend I spoke to you about, the one who can help us? He's on its board of directors."

"No!" Fitch pierced the air, restoring attention to him. "Helen Gilmore's investigation is bound to cause notoriety. I don't want mine to be associated with it in any way!"

"They're bound to connect through common provenance, it can't be helped," Erika said, trying not to sound didactic, irk him more.

"I want my inquiry to fly under the radar. If I'm asked to put up a ransom, I don't want the Keystone Kops fucking up the deal."

"Why do you think Helen asked me, of all people, to act on her behalf? Because she wanted to keep her project as low-profile as possible. She had the same goals as you have."

"Well, she had a funny way of showing it at the cocktail hour," Fitch replied skeptically. "I don't remember her telling Smitts to zip it when he was giving his rundown on the items in Mr. Delaney's inventory. In fact, she offered up a couple of intriguing bits herself, as I recall."

"She was on a high that night. She said so herself. She was all for containment, take my word for it."

"Looks like I don't have a choice. Listen carefully. I want you to be on the alert for the Vittorio, but I don't want you to go public. I know there's a fine line here, but I want you to respect it. Do I have your word?"

"Of course."

Fitch shot Harrison a questioning look.

"Yes, of course," Harrison said curtly. "Shall we sign an oath in blood?" He brushed the air. "Sorry."

"No problem. We're a little touchy is all." Fitch rose from his chair. "I'll show you the original bill of sale on the Vittorio."

"And its certificate of authenticity," Harrison said, half questioning.

Fitch nodded. "I took them out of the safe before you

came." He stepped around Harrison to get to a black metal file cabinet and reached for the single item sitting on top of it: a manila envelope a little larger than standard copy paper.

Erika's heart was racing as Fitch uncoiled the red string from the envelope's closure. He solemnly withdrew the contents of the envelope and lined them up on the desk so that they faced her and Harrison, then returned to his seat, sinking back into it.

Erika and Harrison gave a cursory glance at the date on the bill of sale: January 8, 1957, then focused on the photograph.

The subject of the eight-by-ten-inch photograph leaped up at Erika because she knew it would have that effect on Harrison. Clearly, the photocopy in Delaney's 1954 inventory was a cropped version of the original! She stole a glance at Harrison, his countenance proving he was in agreement. His lips were slightly parted, as if he were about to speak or utter a cry, yet he remained motionless as a still life. "The photo is very helpful for identification purposes," she said blandly to Fitch. She could feel Harrison's tension, didn't want to give him away. "Can you print a copy for us?"

Fitch nodded. "I know the lines aren't as crisp as we'd like, but it'll have to do, won't it?"

"You suppose we can have copies of the other documents as well?" Harrison asked almost too matter-of-factly.

"Of course," Fitch said, rising once again from his chair. He gathered up the items on the desk and headed for the entrance to the adjoining room. "Back in a minute," he said, closing the door behind him.

Erika and Harrison exchanged a look of irrepressible excitement; their silence an agreement to keep between themselves Harrison's hypothesis about the drawing's relationship to Michelangelo's Battle of Cascina.

"Later," she said, unable to hold back an audible reaction. Fitch returned with their copies and handed them to Erika. "Hot off the press," she said, not knowing if the warmth in her fingers was coming from the documents themselves or her heightened sense of the moment.

"I've put the originals away. Here, take this." He picked up the manila envelope he'd left on the desk and handed it to her.

"Thanks," she said lightly, sliding the documents into the envelope, then meticulously closing its clasp with the thin red string, if only to keep her hands from trembling.

"I suppose that will be all?" Fitch asked, stepping away from her. "You'll advise me of any progress you make, and I, likewise?"

"We'll keep in touch, yes." She started to rise; changed her mind.

"I was meaning to ask," she began, "do you or your parents—"

"Does your father—" Harrison began simultaneously.

"—own any other items purchased from Delaney?" She looked at Harrison, whose nod indicated his concern was identical.

"Good question," Fitch replied, as he returned to his chair. "When I looked up Vittorio da Lucca, I should have thought to follow up with a cross-reference on William Delaney." He pressed a tab on his computer keypad. "Give it a second to boot up." He took his seat. He watched the screen as Erika and Harrison contemplated the back of the monitor. "Here we go." Narrating his actions, he opened a program, selected a venue within it and zeroed in on the pertinent data. He bit his lip in concentration as he scrolled down the screen. "Yes," he said, stopping abruptly. "One other Delaney purchase, a Matisse, a pen and ink study for *The Piano*—you familiar with the painting? It's at The Museum of Modern Art."

"Forever," Erika said. She thought of walking through the old gallery of Matisses and Cézannes with her erudite father, her shiny black Mary-Janes tap-tapping on the marble floor, torn between wanting to let loose a really reverberating shuffle-step and trying to impress her father with a really smart observation, choosing the latter, of course, anything to get that coveted smile of pride beamed down on her. "Was it purchased the same time as the Vittorio?"

"Yes, it was," Fitch said, double-checking. "January 8, 1957. It's hanging in my parents' drawing room."

"It's listed on the 1954 inventory," Erika said, looking to Harrison for confirmation.

"I think you're right." Harrison turned to Fitch. "Any other Delaney purchases?"

"No—rather, nothing on record. We don't keep copies of sales records forever. If my father sold anything decades ago that he'd purchased from Delaney, the records may already have been dropped from the files."

"I see. Have you or your father seen a copy of Delaney's 1954 inventory?"

Fitch looked perplexed. "No, why?"

"It's possible that any number of properties listed in 1954 were not legitimately sold before his death in 1958, but acquired illegally, after it. There's always an outside chance that either one of you, more likely your father, might remember one or more of Delaney's properties passing through your hands, I mean in later years, further up the line of provenance."

"You mean after having been acquired illegally."

"You wouldn't have known," Erika said.

"Interesting. One or more of the stolen pieces may yet be in our possession."

Harrison nodded. "As I said, it's an outside chance. Same odds, I imagine, for any gallery in business as long as Fitch and Son."

James laughed ruefully. "The 'Son' was tacked on years after the doors opened. My father drafted me into service kicking and screaming straight out of law school. Where do I get a copy of this inventory?"

Erika produced hers from her tote. "I brought it along for our meeting with Helen," she said, passing it across the desk to him.

"The aborted meeting," James needlessly qualified. "Thanks, I'll check it out. If we come up with anything of note —any provenance that seems suspect, any property we recognize as our own or as having passed through our hands—I'll let you know first thing. Keep in mind, not everything on the inventory was stolen, cases in point, the Vittorio drawing, the Matisse study."

"Naturally," Harrison said edgily as he glanced at his watch. "It's understood that Delaney may have sold other items on the list between 1954 and his death. To that point, among the documents stolen the day of Helen Gilmore's murder there's an updated inventory dated 1957."

"Don't get touchy. Some of us lesser minds need to review a situation. If we find any items in our possession of wrongful origin, we'll negotiate with the executor of Delaney's estate. In fact, there's a possibility a museum donation might be arranged, if the concerned parties are in agreement."

"That would be very generous of you," Erika said. "Not me alone. My mother, too."

"And your father...?"

James dolefully shook his head. "My father's taken himself out of the picture," he said, wincing, no doubt at his unintentional pun. "He was diagnosed with Alzheimer's a year ago, and without so much as a blink of an eye, typical of him, he set about to arrange for his future. He was regressing minimally at the time, but afraid of a precipitous decline. He wanted to make sure everything was in order."

"I'm sorry," Erika said. "I didn't know..."

"We didn't put an ad in the paper. In any event, he immediately—over our protests—gave my mother and me Power of Attorney. He also checked out all the care facilities, opting to buy a condo with assisted living amenities and a rider that transfers him to a hospital-affiliated nursing home when he's no longer able to care for himself.

"That's where he is right now, in his condo in upstate New York. He's deteriorated quite a bit, and Mother's about to check him into the total care unit. She would have preferred caring for him at home, but that's not the way he wanted it. He wanted the staff at a hospital to be on hand twenty-four seven, and my mother never to see him crap his pants. That's the way he put it." He shook his head, shrugged resignedly. "So you see, Mother and I will have the final say about the disposition of property. I wouldn't worry about her, though. She knows more about this business than I do, was tight with him from the start. She still has a hand in it, in fact. She does all the bookkeeping, and at times she deals directly with clients."

Harrison glanced at his watch again. He rose. "I really think we should be checking out Erika's apartment—Erika?"

"Sure," she said, "although I'm not worried—James, would you make a copy of my inventory so I can have it back?"

James obliged, and shortly she and Harrison were out the door, all documents consigned to the manila envelope with the red string, safely stowed in the bag clutched against her hip.

They stood outside the door. Harrison did not have to say anything; his expression lit up the night. "I know," Erika said, and then, "let's walk a little way before we hail a cab. I'll feel freer, talking out in the open, and I'll burst if I can't talk freely."

"Okay, which way?"

"Which...?"

"Way do we walk. Where do you live?"

"Oh!" She laughed, giddy with the absurdity of their exchange in light of the importance of what was on their minds. "Thirty-eighth, I live on Thirty-eighth Street, between Sixth and Seventh Avenues."

He smiled. "You sure?"

"Not really, but let's give it a shot." She turned south; started walking at a fast clip.

He fell into step alongside her. The words spilled out of them: "I mean, there they were, so many more on horseback— and in battle!" she started.

"It never dawned on me that the photo in Delaney's inventory might have been a cropped image of the drawing," he said, his words overlapping hers. He spotted a cab. "Let's catch it." He started for the curb, hand in the air.

"No, no, not yet," she said, delicately tugging him back by the hem of his blazer. "I want to walk, I feel less constrained." She let go of his blazer as he lowered his hand. "We can walk faster if you like."

"That's okay, I just worry—"

"We'll get to my place in good time—so, I'm glad we tacitly agreed not to let on about your hypothesis. James would have leaked it one way or another, and the stakes would be raised, the ante would be upped, whatever those betting terms are." She jumped off the curb and started running across the street, just as the stopped cars were starting to move toward her after the light had changed in their favor. "Hurry, we can make it."

He ran up to her, hopping onto the curb alongside her. "Talk about risks. You were saying…?"

"Basically that whoever is out there interested in art, fame, ransom money, will be willing to take greater risks with his own safety as well as others, if he finds out the drawing might be far more valuable than he figured it to be."

"Yes, that's exactly why I want to keep our observations to ourselves. I think James would have screwed things up if he got overexcited about the value of the drawing. To discover that the faxed edition was actually a cropped version of the original, to see the periphery of the drawing, the combat—wow!"

"I know, I know, I saw it! Mainly because of the crash course you gave me—thank you!"

They'd come to another curb.

"No thanks needed—wait for the light to change, dammit Erika!"

They waited.

The light changed, and she took off as if at the starting

gun at a racetrack. He gallantly following suit.

"What's hard to believe," she went on, without a break in her train of thought as they stepped onto the sidewalk, "is that you can be the only one who's noticed a reference to Michelangelo's cartoon in Vittorio's drawing. The inventory doesn't mention it. James hasn't said a word about it. You think he's just being cagey like us? You think the person who stole the drawing at least gets it?"

"You write for an art magazine—did you?" Harrison gently posed.

"*Touché*," Erika gamely conceded.

"No, no, it wasn't meant as a dig," Harrison quickly rejoined, with a reinforcing tap to her forearm. "I only meant to point out that this is a very particular niche we're talking about. It can escape notice even by people in the know."

"Relative 'know,'" Erika qualified, smiling.

He returned her smile with added ardor. "Listen, we're both aware that art is big business, that to many dealers and buyers, works of art are not much more than commodities. Here, let's just suppose a homeowner stumbles upon Vittorio's drawing in his attic. He runs it over to his local dealer, who negotiates a quick turnover to William Delaney. Fitch senior buys it because it gives him a socially acceptable way to study naked men. Fitch Junior's heart is still in law school, what does he know?"

"And the thief?" Erika inquired, playing along. "And the expert he brings it to for authentication? And the connoisseur in Naples who has a penchant for cinquecento art? They just more chopped liver?"

Harrison laughed. "You're right, they may all be as clever as we think we are, but we can't do anything about that, can we? However, we sure as hell don't have to guarantee it by leaking what we know. Don't you agree?"

"Of course. It was never my intention to leak it in the first place."

"There's another reason why the correlation between

the Battle of Cascina and the drawing attributed to Vittorio may have passed notice," Harrison remarked. "Several figures appearing in both Michelangelo's only extant study for the grand design of his mural and in da Sangallo's copy of the central cartoon, do not appear in Vittorio's drawing. What I'm hoping is that the drawing turns out to be either a spin-off on Michelangelo's Uffizi study, or, better yet, a faithful copy of what we might reasonably conjecture is a later plan for the mural conceived by the master. You follow?"

"Yes," she said, trotting across another street, keeping pace. "Go on."

"Michelangelo's Uffizi study is a work in progress," he said. "It's not the final concept, but neither is it the first, apparently. On the left-hand side of the study, there are sketchy suggestions in stylus beneath the chalk. On the right-hand side, there are no such doodlings, indicating that he had already figured out what he wanted to do in that segment. We can suppose that there could have been any number of studies that preceded or followed this one."

"And if his cartoon of the central section was mauled to death," Erika interjected, "why can't we assume a couple of studies suffered similar fates? Not to mention the fact that Michelangelo was a perfectionist, known to have destroyed studies that didn't meet his expectations."

"Absolutely right. Now, listen to the time line. In the summer of 1504 Michelangelo was commissioned to fresco a companion battle scene to Leonardo's. In September he was assigned studio space to create the cartoon. In October he received the paper for the cartoon, and by the end of the year he'd finished gluing the sheets. Michelangelo supposedly never went further than the 'Bathers' cartoon for the central section of the mural, and in fact claimed he completed this before the Pope summoned him to Rome in February 1505. This claim is supported by a payment receipt dated February 28, 1505."

"Isn't it reasonable," Erika said, "to at least consider the notion that he executed a couple of studies from early summer 1504 through February 1505, and that someone, say a fan named Vittorio da Lucca, worshipfully copied one of them?"

"And that this supposed copy," Harrison dovetailed, "although different from all the known studies for and renditions of the mural, bears enough of a resemblance to them to nurture our hopes?"

"Or have us committed—yes!" She paused. "We'd have to gather hard facts to support our theory. Even with a certificate of authenticity, we'd have to prove the drawing by Vittorio isn't a modern-day hoax. An expert would have to analyze the paper, the ink."

"Difficult, seeing it's been stolen." He grinned. "No, you're right, of course. In the meantime, we can double-back on its provenance, see if we can track down another of Vittorio's works, compare it to the photocopy of Fitch's stolen drawing."

"Maybe find some evidence placing Vittorio in the right place at the right time for him to have even executed this postulated copy." She shrugged. "A lot of conjecture going on here."

"Art history is at least twenty percent conjecture."

She arched a brow. "Where did that figure come from?"

"I just made it up."

Erika laughed. She looked up at the street sign they were about to pass under. "Let's walk to Forty-ninth."

He grabbed her elbow as they crossed the street; dropped it as they neared the opposite curb. "We should be getting a move on, but—" He cut himself short as he spotted an oncoming taxi. "Cancel that," he said, making a beeline for it.

The driver swerved up alongside him curbside. Harrison latched onto the rear door handle and threw open the door. "Thirty-eighth, between Sixth and Seventh," he bid the driver. "Humor me, let's go," he beckoned Erika.

She climbed in. A block shy of Forty-ninth, it was hardly a concession.

He waited for her to unlock the door to the building.

She turned the knob and pushed it open. "The lock's been jamming so it's been disengaged."

He caught the door from her and followed her in. "There's no security system here." He pressed the door shut hard, as if brute force would fix it. "It's not safe."

"We're supposed to get a new lock installed by next Wednesday."

"Until then you're supposed to cross your fingers?"

"I'm fine with it."

A card shop occupied most of the ground floor, leaving just enough sectioned-off space for a resident entryway and an elevator the size of an airplane lavatory. She traversed the entryway to the elevator and stoically pressed the button.

"You usually climb the stairs, don't you?" he asked. "No, I always climb the stairs."

He started for the fire door. "This way?"

"Yes, but I'm six flights up. We'll take the elevator."

"You don't think I can make it?" He pushed open the fire door; waited for her.

She dipped under his arm and entered the stairwell. "I wasn't implying you couldn't make it."

He was already jogging up the staircase. "It's poorly lit —and you do this alone every night?"

"Yes." She launched onto a step, then took two at a time to catch up to him.

He picked up the pace. "Do you carry pepper spray?"

"Only a bullet-proof vest," she replied, managing to stay three steps behind him—the position she held all the way to the sixth floor.

"That was under three minutes, good time," he taunted, as she pitched herself onto the summit.

"My personal best," she acknowledged, gasping for breath.

He held open the fire door for her, then let it swing shut on its own. He stepped up to one of the two apartment doors.

"You?"

"My neighbors, the Barlows," she said, scrounging for her keys. "Ah, the neighbors you called."

She nodded. "Amy and Matt. Stockbrokers turned caterers. I'm their official taster. Our apartments were once a single loft—before my time." She was about to insert a key into the lock of the other door.

He darted to her. "Here, let me, just in case," he said, the urgency in his voice stopping the action.

"In case what?" she said, key poised. "In case someone's in there."

She handed him her key ring, letting him play hero, no harm done—comforting, in truth. She told him where to place each of the two keys.

He turned the keys one after the other. The door wouldn't open. He rotated the keys back to their original position, and the mechanism easily gave way. "This door wasn't locked," he concluded. He opened it a slit.

"I thought I'd double-locked it," she said tentatively. "You think we should call the super? I hate to bother him at this hour."

"Who's got a set of keys besides you?"

"Only Rodney—he's storing stuff here—and he's very good about locking up."

Harrison put his ear to the opening. He held the knob and slowly opened the door wider, waving her away.

She stubbornly held her ground.

They stood at the threshold and listened for sounds from within. Hearing none, they cautiously entered, Harrison leading the way.

She clicked on the lights.

He bolted the door, then turned to survey the room before him. To Erika, her half-loft was as ample as a grand ballroom. She'd furnished it sparsely in order to retain the sense of freedom she'd felt the first time she laid eyes on it.

He looked at her questioningly. "Everything okay?"

"Yes—oh!"

"What?" he fired, throwing himself in front of her. "Rodney's paintings, they're gone."

"From the walls?"

She shook her head. "No, they were lined up against the walls, three or four deep. The blank canvases are gone, too. He must have taken them to Helen's."

"Let's hope." Harrison proceeded to walk across the room. "Where's the phone? I'll check if it's off the hook." A photograph on the wall shelf caught his attention: a smiling woman with soulful eyes. "Your mother?"

"Yes."

He nodded. "You look like her."

"I'm not as nice as she was."

"What a sad thing to say. Of course you are."

"How would you know?" she clipped, annoyed with herself for almost buying his line. "The phone's right there, farther along the shelf."

He removed the cordless phone from its base and held it to his ear. "No dial tone."

"I'll check the one in the bedroom."

He returned the phone to its base, then followed her to her room.

At the threshold she flipped the wall switch, turning on the overhead light. She paused in the doorway, taking stock. "The bed's a mess," she said evenly, trying to undo the memory of having made it, the possibility of an intruder nevertheless elbowing its way to the forefront of thought.

Suddenly, heart racing, she bounded for the dresser, yanked open the bottom drawer. There was only one item she cared about. She saw it nested in its usual spot, a utensils tray she used to hold jewelry. She placed her treasure in the palm of her hand and gulped back her tears. She felt him looking over her shoulder at the gold locket cradled in her hand, its delicate chain draped over the edge of her palm. Her hand was trembling.

"You need a tissue?" he asked, not venturing a hand on her shoulder, a stroke of her arm.

"No, that's okay," she said, not taking her eyes off her palm, feeling his breath on her.

"Was it your mother's?"

She nodded. "From her childhood. It has my grandparents' photographs inside. I'll put it on, take it with me." She reached around and clasped it into place, hoping he wouldn't —and would—help her with it. She pulled the sweater away from her neck and let the locket drop. It fell against her skin just below her clavicle. He stepped aside, clearing his throat, and she turned toward him.

"The receiver's off the hook," he said, pointing to the corded phone on the desk table.

The locket, safely resting against her chest, stilled her fear, like the touch of her mother. "I must have left it off the hook, after all." She slipped past him to get to the phone, tested it, then put the receiver back.

"What about the unlocked door, the missing canvases? I'm calling 911 if you won't."

"Wait, first let me check my email." She sat down on the bridge chair and turned on her computer all in one motion, preempting his objection. He stood over her as it booted up.

The desktop icons appeared on the screen. She reached for the mouse and clicked on the site. The inbox items instantly appeared. She scrolled down the list, stopping on a message that had been received earlier in the day, at 5:32 PM, its point of origin, Rodney's email address; subject box, blank. She clicked on it and the message appeared on the screen. They read it together; Harrison over her shoulder:

From Starbucks: At your place 2PM collecting my remains. Backtrack: Nicely settled at Helen's, when hubby drops by, catches me applying oil to canvas. I explain this is called painting but he is unmoved, wants me out. I ask if he's as small-dicked-as-minded which terminates friendship. Couldn't reach Helen in Southampton. Point is, been trying to call you, but your line's non-stop busy, probably my fault. I was taking shower in your boudoir—so sue me—when I hear phone ringing. Rush to pick up. It's Amy Barlow, wants you to taste her fried emu or whatever. I ask her to hold on. I get a towel and raid frig, continuing call from living room. I'm guessing I left primary phone off hook. Left my set of keys in the cutlery drawer. Hope this proves I'm at least well-intentioned. Mea culpa and fuck you if you don't forgive me, Rodney.

Erika clicked off the site. "That explains it."

"Including the reason why the door was left unlocked. Not very responsible of him."

"Be kind. He probably thought it would lock automatically."

"I suppose we should just be grateful the place wasn't vandalized."

"Exactly." She shut down the computer and rose from her chair. "You want a cup of coffee?"

"No, thanks," he said, as they exited the bedroom, she clicking off the light on the way. "Maybe at my place. It's late. I think we should be heading back."

They'd come to the center of the main room. "And I'm thinking I should stay," she said.

"We're not going to go over that again, are we?"

"We are. We had a false alarm, and I don't see why—" She stopped short, her eyes drawn to an object laying on the floor near the door to the apartment.

He saw it too. "Mail?" he whispered without conviction.

"The mailman must have delivered a letter of mine to the wrong box," she replied in hushed tones, "and a tenant just now—"

"So why are we whispering?" he asked, with a halfhearted laugh. He started for the envelope.

She got to it first, her heart pounding as she bent to pick it up. It was legal-sized, white, its flap tucked in. She turned it over. "Blank," she said, sinking to the floor.

He sat down beside her as she pulled out a folded sheet.

It revealed a color-print of a painting she immediately recognized. "Oh god," she expelled, almost inaudibly, as Harrison jumped to his feet, charging for the door.

He released the lock in a flash. "Move!" he uttered. She had risen, lurched for the door, jammed her shoulder against it.

"It's too late!" she cried. "Don't be a hero!"

"That makes sense. How can I be a hero if it's too late? Out of the way. Please!" With deliberate force, he half-shoved, half-lifted her to the side, then opened the door wide enough to get out.

"Harrison!" she called, as the door shut behind him.

She threw it open. "Come back!" she called after him, as the fire door began its closing arc.

Her instinct was to pursue, but she knew it would be futile.

She ran to the window, hoping to spot someone darting away or jumping into a car, register some scrap of ID—jacket color, car type. She thrust aside the vertical blinds. Nothing unusual. An SUV rolled by, heading east toward Sixth at moderate speed. Across the street, an elderly couple, arm-in-arm, sauntered west.

Forget logic. She'd go after him.

They nearly collided in the stairwell between the first and second floor, as he was heading back up.

"What are you doing?" he asked, his tone almost pleading. "Someone might be lurking out here waiting for you!"

Without a pause, she turned to sprint up to her floor. "Whoever delivered the message is gone. It was only meant to scare me."

"Didn't it?"

"Of course it did! But—"

"Let me guess—come hell or high water you will not be deterred."

She slowed down, let him catch up to her. "Why didn't you take the elevator?"

"On the way down I thought I might catch the son-of-a-bitch in the stairwell. Up, I saw the elevator was in transit, on its way—Erika! Did you lock your door?"

She knew what he was thinking. "The guy's gone," she assured him, nevertheless picking up speed.

When they reached the door to her apartment, he again insisted on playing point man. After crossing the threshold and doing a quick survey, he nodded, signifying an all-clear.

Behind him, she bolted the door. "With all the commotion, it's amazing the Barlows haven't come by." She glanced at the anonymous document lying face down on the floor and felt a shudder run through her. She bent to pick it up, examine it properly, when she realized she ought to be taking care to maintain the integrity of the sender's fingerprints. Not that she expected there'd be any. If he'd had the sense to tuck in the envelope flap rather than give away his DNA by licking it, he'd probably taken the precaution of wearing gloves.

"Don't touch it," she warned him.

"We should have thought earlier about preserving fingerprints." She strode to the kitchen area and pulled out a cabinet drawer. "Tongs should work," she said, foraging for them in the pile of cooking tools. "And we'll need a Ziploc bag."

Having found those, she returned to the envelope. He was sitting beside it on the floor. She sat down opposite him and handed him the plastic bag. She took a deep breath and grasped an edge of the paper with the tongs. Her heart was racing as she flipped over the paper.

The painting was both eerie and menacing in its simplicity. Centrally, it depicted a splotch of blood on a plain wood floor. The combination of the floor's receding perspective and the absence of junctures between the side and back walls gave the dark splatter prominence. A single overhead bulb with a pull-cord, along with a wall switch of unknown purpose, made the precipitating event all the more enigmatic. "It's a

Francis Bacon," she said, staring at it. "It's called *Blood on the Floor*."

"Yes, it's not one of his more famous paintings. I think the sick bastard who concocted this isn't a stranger to the art world."

There was a note neatly printed in black ink across the bottom of the sheet, just below the margin of the picture:

Drop Delaney or retitle this self-portrait

Erika shook her head. "We talked so much about the Vittorio da Lucca, I almost forgot the main point. Helen was counting on us to recover her father's collection, not a single work." She bent her wrist so that the paper was turned toward Harrison. "This reminds me."

"I know," he said quietly, his voice laden with remorse, as if his interest in the Vittorio drawing had provoked this threat. "I'm sorry."

"Don't be, I was making a comment. There's no cause-effect connection whatsoever." To emphasize her point, she flapped the paper with a baton-like wave of the tongs. "Besides," she added, catching his eye, "our hunt for the drawing is perfectly consistent with the assignment. It might even add light to it."

He held her gaze. "You know just what to say."

"And you know just how to respond." She gestured toward the plastic bag. "Let's put it away."

He opened the bag and she maneuvered the sheet into it, having to use more dexterity than she'd anticipated. "Now the envelope," she said. She grasped the tip of its flap with her tongs and carefully slipped the item into the bag.

He zipped it shut. "We can give it to Mitchell tomorrow morning rather than drop it off at the police station on the way back to my place.

She did not object.

Fifteen minutes later they were poised just outside the door to her apartment. The keys were in her hand. A carry-on suitcase and a small duffle bag stood on the floor between them. The suitcase contained a couple of articles of clothing, a pair of sneakers, a pair of flats, cell charger, toiletries. The duffle bag held her passport, insurance papers, credit cards, and any other items she might need should it become necessary to steer clear of the place for any length of time. She did not anticipate this, but Harrison insisted on her being prepared.

CHAPTER 5

A t 5:30 A.M., energized by a cumulative hour's sleep and a pummeling shower, Erika was ready for action. The anonymous letter had been transformed overnight from a physical threat to a challenge to her intellect, a dare. Although she prided herself on her independence, she realized, not without some resistance, that her diminished fear was partly due to the fact that she was sharing it with Harrison.

She towel-dried her hair and tossed on a pair of jeans, white shirt and sneakers. Dropping her cell phone, now fully charged, into her shirt pocket, she set out for the kitchen.

The aroma of freshly brewed coffee greeted her midflight down to the second floor. When she arrived she realized that the coffee-maker had been set on automatic and that she would be the first to pour herself a cup from the full pot.

Three table settings and a covered basket of assorted rolls had been neatly arranged on the countertop alongside the coffee-maker. She reached for the handle of the coffeepot. The delicate sound of paw nails striking travertine stopped her midway and she turned to greet Jake, trotting toward her.

"Hi, boy," she crooned, as the dog unceremoniously flopped at her feet and rolled onto his back.

Erika sank to a sitting position on the floor and started stroking his belly. "Not even so much as a hello?"

Jake offered a token yap.

Erika laughed and kissed his ear. "What a guy."

"He grows on you, doesn't he?"

Startled, she turned toward the doorway. Harrison was standing there in chinos, white T-shirt and sneakers.

"Yeah, we're pals," she answered, returning her focus to Jake. "You need to take him out?"

"Not yet. About six-thirty's his usual time. Back in plenty of time for us to plan things and get to our nine o'clock...talk with Mitchell." He sat down on the floor on the other side of Jake and caressed the dog's head.

"What?" she asked, looking up, the sound of his voice worrying her.

"It was reported on the news late last night."

"Helen."

"Yes. Her death was reported as a probable homicide. The direct cause, cerebral hemorrhage. I hesitated telling you, but I don't want to keep anything from you." He withdrew his hand from Jake's head; touched her forearm. "I know you felt a connection with—" Her tears stopped him. They came in a sudden, noiseless torrent, surprising her as much as him. She covered her face with her hands, didn't want him to see.

He respected her privacy, said nothing, did nothing.

Without reflection or intention, the images of her mother and Helen separated, the deepest feelings adhering to the memory of her mother. She wiped her cheeks with her hands; uncovered her face.

Jake nudged her knee with his nose, urging her to resume her ministrations. She cooperated. It did not seem possible that she could be sitting on the floor and caressing a dog after her outburst.

"I know, it's hard to process," he said, answering her silence.

"Yes." She withdrew her hand from Jake's belly and began exploring the surface of the travertine tiles, her fingers dipping into the natural knots and nitches.

Jake sighed and rolled back onto his stomach.

Her finger stalled in an unusually large fault alongside her knee. "When I was a kid I used to write wishes on tiny scraps of paper

and stuff them in there," Harrison said.

"Like the Wailing Wall in Jerusalem," she mused.

"That's what I used to think—I mean, later on, when I knew about such a place."

"Do you still do it?"

"Stuff my wishes in there?"

She nodded, her finger loitering on the site. "No, but I think about it sometimes."

"Is that why you never changed things—the wallpaper, the carpeting—to keep things the way they were when your grandparents were alive? I'm sorry, that didn't sound right. I'm not suggesting you change things, I actually like the way it feels—I mean looks."

"I know exactly what you mean. It holds memories intact. Charlotte never accepted that. She wanted to renovate the place, top to bottom. I think part of my resistance was perversity, I didn't want to give her the satisfaction. Which is just as childish as stuffing wishes into a hole in the floor." He stood up. "Come on, let's have some coffee." He extended his hand to help her up.

She rose on her own. "You're not childish," she pronounced.

They sat at the kitchen table and solemnly sipped their coffee and ate their breakfast rolls.

Grace, in uniform, wandered into the kitchen, bringing the pair into closer communion. "Good morning," she stated with a touch of formality. "Would either of you care for eggs, hot cereal?" She poured herself a cup of coffee and took a seat apart from them at the table.

Harrison looked questioningly at Erika. She shook her head.

"We're good, but thanks—and thanks for the spread."

He rose, Erika joining him. "If you want me for any reason, Grace, after we take Jake out we'll be in my study for a bit, then off to an appointment. In an emergency, you can always reach me on my cell."

Erika sat across from Harrison at his desk. They had walked the dog in virtual silence, and he was already hunkered down in his usual spot under the desk.

"What do we do?" Harrison asked.

"What Helen would want us to do—begin," she said with sudden force.

He slid their copy of the presumptive William Delaney address book between them. "We'll go through it quickly, see what hits us."

"Right." She turned it so it half faced him and began slowly leafing through it, waiting for his nod before going on to the next spread.

The review took a half hour. She jotted down five entries that might be of some use to them, the most promising being the probable art agent. Of the four others, two were relatives with the Delaney surname, and two were appended with asterisks for no discernible reason. They were debating advantageous times to contact these people, when Erika's cell phone sounded from the pocket of her shirt.

Tensing up, expecting nothing but bad news: "Hello?"

This is Natalie Gilmore, Helen's daughter—Erika?" The voice was clipped without being brusque, to maintain self-control, it sounded.

"Yes. Natalie, I'm so sorry—"

"I got your number from Rodney. After he failed to reach my mother in Southampton, he looked me up and we connected. He's here with me if you want to speak to him."

"It's okay. How can I help you? Ask me anything."

"That's kind of you. Mother spoke very highly of you. I wish we could have gotten together under better circumstances. We can talk over the phone, but I prefer face to face, and besides, I'd like to meet you. I'm driving out to Southampton this morning to make the funeral arrangements. I'll be back tonight, but too late to meet. Is tomorrow morning okay?"

"Of course. What time and where?"

"How early do you get up Sundays?"

"Very."

"I'm on Eightieth and Third, but I'd rather not meet here. I don't know who'll be dropping by, and there are people I'd like to avoid. Any ideas?"

"I'd like to come with a colleague, Harrison Wheatley. He's—"

"Yes, yes, Rodney mentioned him—what's convenient for you?" Erika took a moment to confer with Harrison, whose suggestion, the dog run in Carl Schurz Park, at East Eighty-sixth Street and East End Avenue, was mutually agreed upon. At the benches, 8:00A.M. Natalie owned a dog too, and not-withstanding tragedy, dogs needed to be tended to.

By the looks of it, so did grieving protégés. "Is it cynical of me to suspect Rodney's latched onto Helen's daughter?" Erika asked, after the call.

"I take it you mean for motives of self-interest? Maybe. Why?

Are you jealous? Never mind, that was out of line."

"Way out. Yes, I did mean for self-promotion. He's been hungry for patronage, although I think acting purely out of self-interest would be out of character."

"Don't be so sure about what's in or out of character. It can get you into big trouble. I should know." He waved off the issue. "Let's give the Corelli Gallery a call. It's midday in Florence, a good time to make contact."

According to Delaney's 1954 inventory, dittoed on Fitch's 1957 bill of sale, the previous owner on record of the drawing attributed to Vittorio da Lucca was the Corelli Gallery on the Via della Scala in Florence, Italy. "The gallery may no longer exist," Erika said, "but yes, let's try. Since there's no signature on the drawing, it would be nice if Corelli can direct us to other works attributed to Vittorio—you know, the strength in numbers theory?"

"Exactly what I had in mind."

"Even better if one of those works bears his signature."

"Right. I wish we could go farther back in time with the drawing's provenance. Maybe Corelli, or the present proprietor, has access to these records, can direct us to an earlier owner we can pursue independently."

"Let's start by Googling 'Corelli Gallery Florence,' see what we get."

Within a moment, the words appeared on the screen. "I'm amazed," Harrison commented, "although I shouldn't be. Longevity of Italian art dealerships is the rule rather than the exception." He clicked onto the referenced website, the You-Go Travel Agency, and swiveled the monitor so Erika could share his view.

The Corelli Gallery was listed among the business establishments in the environs of the Montebello Hotel, stopover on one of the agency's packaged tours.

"Not much here," he remarked, "but it does verify the address and gives us alternative ways to make contact. You want to email?" She shook her head. "I'm worried about launching our interests into cyberspace at this point. I'd rather communicate one-on-one."

"I hear you—how's your Italian?" He scrolled down the File column, clicked on Print. "Nonexistent—yours?"

"I can get by if we keep it simple and slow." The printed sheet slid into the receiving tray. He retrieved the paper, checked the phone number. "Are we ready? You want to rehearse?"

"I trust you to wing it."

"Appreciate the confidence." He grabbed the cordless phone from its cradle. He started to call out, then clicked off. "You should be in on it. Wait, I'll get you a phone."

Resettled, he punched in the required fourteen digits as Erika held the spare phone to her ear. She pressed the "talk" button after the connection had been made.

"*Buon pomeriggio,* Corelli Galleria, *posso aiutarti?*"

Harrison clamped his hand over the mouthpiece and quickly translated for her: "'Afternoon, can I help you?'" Taking his hand away: "*Ciao, sono* Harrison Wheatley, *professore storia d'arte* a New York University—*ho bisogno di parlare con signore Corelli.*"

"*Signore Corelli?*" came the puzzled reply.

"*O lo proprietario,*" Harrison amended. He glanced at Erika, who waved off the need for translation, the key words coming close enough to English.

"*Vuoi suo nipote—eccolo!*"

A rapid-fire off-line exchange in Italian ensued.

"He's talking to Corelli's nephew," Harrison explained in the break. "The owner."

Erika nodded as the signore in question came on the line:

"*Ciao, Signore* Wheatley, *sono Mario Depoli, posso aiutarti?*" the question posed in a pleasant, deep baritone.

"*Grazie,*" Harrison replied. "*Io chiedere informazioni di...* pen and ink drawing, *pennae e inchiostro...*brown, *maronne.*"

"*Buono italiano!*"

"*Parlo un po' di italiano. Ma me la cavo meglio a leggere.*"

"You say you read Italian better than you speak it? So, for email I write Italian, on phone we talk English, yes?" Mario laughed, joined by Erika and Harrison.

Harrison introduced Erika as his partner in an art recovery assignment—"actually she heads it. Erika Shawn. She writes for the magazine *Art News.*"

"*Ciao,*" Erika said over Mario's "Excellent! I am *impressionato*—impressed!"

Their comments dovetailing, Erika and Harrison explained their mission, particularly in regard to the drawing dated 1504 and credited to Vittorio da Lucca. They related what little they knew of its provenance, namely that William Delaney, according to his inventory, had purchased it from

Corelli in 1951, and that their objective was twofold: to trace it farther back, and more generally to flesh out their understanding of the artist—his life, his work. They expressed their concern that the gallery's records might not go back as far as the 1950s.

Mario laughed. "The Corelli Gallery was established in 1873, and from that date all records are kept *per sempre*— forever!" He hastened to qualify that the records in question might not have been stored in perfectly neat order, but neat enough to be found in reasonable time. "We have the email, yes, but we do not keep important records on the computer, we store in basement, no viruses in basement, *capisce*?"

"Absolutely," Erika said, a Luddite herself at heart. "When do you think—?"

"Give me two days and I will tell you everything I know about this Vittorio da Lucca you speak of—*tutto*."

"I'd say that went pretty well," Harrison remarked after the call had ended.

"To be on a roll, we have to make at least one more contact," Erika said. "Any suggestions?"

"We could try reaching Cuba's Ministry of Culture."

"Maybe we should wait to check with Natalie. She may have her reasons, political or otherwise, for us not to go there."

"My guess is she'll give us free rein."

"Mine, too. We can prepare for it. Let's look online for the name of the curator of the National Museum in Havana, the museum Helen said her father helped finance in 1956. Also check any sites that might help us with protocol, determine how or where we should send Delaney's 1954 inventory."

"Or if we should send it," Harrison countered. "Right."

"Speaking of which, I hope Lieutenant Mitchell tracks down the stolen material from Delaney's safe deposit box, particularly that alleged 1957 inventory, to give us a more accurate idea of what was hanging on the walls of Delaney's plantation estate house at the time of his murder. I have to say,

I'm pessimistic about it. For that matter, I'd like to track down the sales records on any of the artworks so we can dig deeper into their provenances."

"We know the updated inventory was in the safe deposit box because Helen said it was, but do you think the sales records might have been there too?"

"I have no idea."

Erika shrugged. "I don't know why, but my gut feeling is that whoever killed Helen was after this information, and not for anything of political or historical consequence."

"You mean nothing that might call into question Castro's legitimacy, or that you could sell on eBay, like a letter from Hemingway?"

She nodded.

"Then trust your instincts, they're valid more often than not." A bitter smile flashed across his countenance. "Although I've had my share of the 'not.'"

She guessed what he was referring to. "So," she quickly tossed out, "how about we find the site for the National Museum in Havana, then try reaching our supposed art agent?"

Within seconds Harrison was scrolling down a badly translated history of the National Museum and Palace of Beautiful Arts, Erika scanning along with him.

"Wait," she declared, halfway down the second page, "back up." When he started to do so, she added, "More, almost at the beginning, to the date of—there, stop."

"Why—? Oh."

"Yes. It was the dictator Batista who inaugurated the museum.

Maybe William Delaney's patronage of the museum is a sign he wasn't on good terms with Castro by 1956. I mean, Delaney must have appeared on the same dais as Batista, the man Castro overthrew!"

"You're saying the present curator of the museum may not be so eager to cooperate with us."

"Worse. He may decide—or be ordered—to make

trouble for us." She shook her head. "I don't get it. Delaney couldn't have become disenchanted with Castro as early as 1956. Even to most Americans, never mind law school mates, he was still a hero at that point."

"Agreed. In any event, I think whatever persuasions the museum's movers and shakers hold dear, their desire to ever-improve relations with the Unites States will take precedence. They'll cooperate with us." He scrolled down a bit, stopping where the text indicated that in 1959, after the revolution, the museum's collection had been beefed up by confiscated art. "This could include the Delaney loot. One way or another, we've got to look into it. Through a reliable agent, if you're still worried about making direct contact."

"I'd like to avoid middle men as much as possible."

"Can't have it both ways."

"I know, I know....I was thinking..."

He smiled. "You do a lot of that," he said affectionately.

"I was thinking maybe Delaney's patronage had nothing to do with Batista, that it had only to do with his dedication to art and to providing public space for it, regardless of who got the photo op."

"Good point. Your conclusion being...?"

"We proceed, but cautiously."

"Okay." He printed the article, then exited the site, returning to the computer's desktop. "Now we try calling the guy we think may have been Delaney's art agent."

"It's a little early. We should probably wait until we're back from the police station—but agreed. We've got momentum, I don't want to lose it." Referring to their notes, she tapped in the 258 number in Brooklyn while he waited, his phone to his ear.

"Hello?" a female voice sounded just as they were about to give up.

"Hi, this is Erika Shawn. I'm with *Art News Magazine.* May I speak with Mr. Bertram Morrison?"

"Mr. Morrison is deceased. This is Mrs. Morrison."

"I'm sorry to hear that—"

"What's the nature of your business?"

"I'm doing a piece on the late art collector, William Delaney, and Mr. Morrison is the agent of record," Erika boldly stated, taking a leap of faith. "Maybe you can provide me with some information?"

"I doubt it."

"You may be surprised. I'm sure any personal stories would add depth to—"

"I don't think I'll be able to help you, but perhaps talking to you would provide some closure—ridiculous word, 'closure.'"

"I'm so grateful," Erika said. "When's the best time for us to visit?"

"'Us?'"

Erika gave Mrs. Morrison a brief précis on Harrison while he discreetly held his tongue.

Mrs. Morrison, her good spirits ostensibly holding, informed Erika that it was okay, provided she and her friend brought credible photo IDs plus some evidence linking them to the art world. "Times being what they are, I'm sure you understand. How does two-thirty sound to you?"

"Two-thirty today?"

"Yes, today. Saturday. You require more notice?"

Erika glanced at Harrison, as wide-eyed as she. "Oh, no, today is perfect," she said.

"Good. I prefer you come with your questions prepared. Do you need directions how to get here?"

"Thanks, I think we can find our way."

"Good going!" Harrison commended after they'd clicked off. "Lucky. You have your mandatory credentials?"

"Two in one—my photo ID from NYU's Institute of Fine Arts. You?"

"My driver's license, and if you happen to have a copy of Art

News, my name's on the list of editors."

"No problem. We'll type up a list of questions for Mrs. Morrison when we get back from our interrogation."

"Unless we're arrested on the spot," Erika quipped, countering her trepidations. "Let's go."

"No problem." He swiveled the monitor so it faced him more comfortably. "Let's get started."

Erika had elected to be questioned first, and while Harrison waited on the bench in the police station's modest reception area, she was sealed off with Lieutenant Mitchell in a small room furnished only with a folding metal table and four bridge chairs. They sat opposite each other. Mitchell was taking notes on a legal pad. A tape recorder, its green light blinking, was perched in the middle of the table. The Ziploc bag containing the anonymous threat to Erika lay beside it.

Erika had explained the circumstances under which she and Harrison had discovered the threatening note, and how Harrison had unsuccessfully tried to waylay its bearer.

"Getting back to the address book," Mitchell said presently, checking the top page of his lined pad, "why did you surreptitiously remove it from the crime scene?"

"I believe I told you that, Lieutenant," Erika answered respectfully.

"Tell me again."

"I thought Helen—Mrs. Gilmore—would want me to. When she told us—"

"Told who?"

"Me, Sara Masden, Rodney Smitts—at the Pierre gala."

"Go on."

"When she told us what she'd found in her father's safe deposit box, she mentioned address books. I'm sure the one in question was part of the group of items she had ready for me and Harrison to pick up. She wanted us to examine everything."

"For what purpose?"

To help recover art works stolen from her father's estate in Cuba in 1958."

"As I recall, you said at the crime scene your purpose was research, not tracking down suspects."

She felt herself redden. "The primary goal—Helen Gilmore's primary goal—was to recover art, not prosecute criminals. Helen was planning to donate all of the recovered works to The Metropolitan Museum of Art. Now that she's gone, that's what her daughter, Natalie will probably want. Natalie is counting on me to follow through on this."

"Be honest, you were trying to deceive me, weren't you?"

"I was trying to tell you as little as possible," Erika said, annoyed at the petulance in her voice. "Helen wanted the matter handled as discreetly as possible."

Mitchell leaned toward her. "Now that she's been murdered," he said intently, "you'll have to be more forthcoming with me, understand?"

"Yes."

"No room for your little delicacies."

Note of condescension received. "I won't feel free to share information if I think you'll go public with it."

"Don't tell me how to do my job," Mitchell chafed. Softening, he said, "I'm not as heavy-handed as you think. I do get it."

"There was a 1957 inventory of William Delaney's artworks in the safe deposit box," Erika said, as a peace offering. "It would have helped us determine more accurately the art that went missing. The inventory was stolen from the Delaney residence in Southampton, along with the other items meant for us."

"So you say."

"There would be no reason for me and Harrison to steal the items, since Helen was going to hand them over to us."

"To borrow."

"Yes." Erika's tension was rising. "There must be corroborating calls. Helen's call to Sara describing my assignment. Another verifying Harrison's and my appointment in

Southampton. If you check Helen's Manhattan phone records, the landline in Southampton, the cell phone records of Harrison's driver, Bill, as well as—"

"You're telling me how to do my job again."

"I'm sorry." She swallowed hard. "You're not suggesting I'm a person of interest, are you?"

"For sure, you're an interesting person," he returned, offering the barest of smiles. He clicked off the tape machine. "You're free to go, but we'll keep in touch. I'll see your friend, Harrison Wheatley now."

On the walk back to Harrison's, they compared interrogations and concluded that their performances were, if not stellar, at least respectable, and that they were in no immediate danger of arrest.

On arrival, they headed for Harrison's study to prepare their questions for Bertram Morrison's widow. They sat at his desk; he, in front of the computer.

Harrison opened a new document and began rapidly typing. "We want to know if Mrs. Morrison has any of William Delaney's records, sales slips, inventories," he said, his fingers skimming over the keyboard.

"Separate questions. We don't want to assault her," Erika said.

He swiveled the monitor to show her. The issues were framed as separate questions.

They exchanged smiles.

She gestured for him to rotate the monitor back to face him. "Let's ask her if Delaney bought any major items not long before his murder. She probably won't know, but it doesn't hurt to ask such an important question."

"Yes." He typed Erika's suggestion.

His hands hovered over the keyboard. "What else? Does she remember if there were any other agents who did business with Delaney?"

"Or any art dealers or collectors Delaney may have had contact with?"

The rapid-fire typing continued, each question spawning another. By noon they had enough for a full-length documentary.

Time to call Harrison's driver, Bill, and arrange for a 1:15 pick-up, leaving room for traffic hold-ups.

Bill's wife answered the phone, immediately handing it over to him.

After a pause, Harrison's upper body shot forward. "Oh, no, who's responsible you think—kids?" He listened, shaking his head, then apologized, insisting Bill let him pay for the damages.

After the call had ended, Harrison was silent. "What?"

"He says he can't work for me anymore. He's got a wife and four kids, and he's unwilling to put them in jeopardy. I don't blame him. His car lights were smashed, all of them."

"Does he know who did this?"

Harrison shook his head. "His service told him an anonymous caller said he had to drop me as a client or they'd take out their disappointment on his family. That was the word they used—'disappointment.' He asked me not to call the police, and I won't."

"You think that's wise?"

"Screw wise, I'm not going to call."

There was a lull in conversation. Was Harrison about to cut and run? "What do you think?" she asked, a useless question to fill the silence.

A bitter smile touched his features. "I'd say someone's trying to discourage us."

"We've known that for a while."

"It's starting to hit home."

"I wasn't implying you didn't get it. I'm only worried this incident will—"

"I'm not mutinying, if that's what you think—is that a word, 'mutinying'?"

"I don't think so—wait, maybe it's obsolete."

They smiled, no bitterness in evidence. She felt a well-spring of relief, followed by a stab of guilt. "Maybe you should consider backing out."

"You really must think I'm a wimp, Erika."

"No, no, I—"

"Okay, then let's not go there again. Agreed?"

"Okay."

"We'll grab a cab to Brooklyn." She nodded. "Right."

"Did you take something from your apartment you can work on until then?"

"I did. A piece on pointillism and the Benday dot technique."

"Seurat and Lichtenstein?"

"Yes. On the subject of style—does it come from the perception of the real world, or political conviction? The material's in my suitcase."

"Interesting. It'll keep you busy while I polish up a chapter?" She said it would; asked him about his book.

"On the early nineteenth century French painter, Gericault. I'm finally back on track with it, now that I've got my life in order."

They arranged to meet in the kitchen at one o'clock for a quick bite before heading out for their interview.

Erika retired to the Blue Room. Harrison buckled down in the study.

She knew her way around Flatbush because it was where her grandparents had lived, the rest of Brooklyn a labyrinth to her, its indecipherable geography frozen in her earliest memories and never redrawn.

When they entered the familiar zone, she directed the cab driver to Avenue M, whose basic character, as far as her inner child was concerned, had remained unchanged since the beginning of time, still bustling with many of the same small businesses—bakery, deli, lingerie, stationery—she'd been trotted out to in her early days. She could almost feel the clutch of her grandmother's hand just below her wrist, her own tiny fingers wiggling like trapped minnows as she tried to pull free, her grandmother securing her from child snatchers and madmen before paranoia would become the norm.

At Seventeenth Street she had the driver turn south to Avenue N, then head east. "The address is twenty-seven nineteen," she said with budding confidence, "which means the house is between Twenty-seventh and Twenty-eighth."

One block from the busy commercial thoroughfare, Avenue N was solely residential. As the street numbers rose, elegant three-story private homes were crammed together like stars at a cocktail party, each with a meticulously groomed patch of lawn nourished to a green that defied nature. The paved sidewalks were lined with grand elms circumscribed by neat patches of dark soil.

Most of the houses were garageless, resulting in heavy curbside parking. Midway between Twenty-seventh and Twenty-eighth, the driver double-parked, turned off his meter, and announced what they owed him, including the toll for the Brooklyn Battery Tunnel. He added sullenly that the trip had been an inconvenience and that it was unlikely he'd find a fare for his drive back to Manhattan, his mood lifting when Harrison offered to pay him high-end chauffeur's rates if he agreed to wait for them. He did, and a deposit amount was quickly negotiated.

They were a half hour early for their appointment. "You want to take a walk around the block?" Harrison asked as they slid out of the back seat, dragging briefcase and tote.

"Sure, but let's check out the house."

The Morrison house, they discovered, was directly across the street—white-shingled, with broad stucco pillars and a wooden porch furnished with an old-fashioned upholstered glider and chair set.

As they stood before it, its massive front door was abruptly flung open, and an elderly woman, tall and ropey, clad in slacks and cardigan, stepped onto the porch. "I saw you from the window," she said in a buttery soft voice that contradicted her form. "Are you the people who wanted to see me?"

"Mrs. Morrison?" Erika ventured. "Yes. Are you Erika Shawn?"

"Yes, and this is my colleague, Harrison Wheatley."

"Come here, then," Mrs. Morrison beckoned.

"Would you like to check our IDs?" Erika asked, arriving.

"You look honest enough." She nodded toward the glider. "Sit."

They obeyed. Two robots.

Mrs. Morrison turned one of the adjacent chairs to improve her prospective line of sight, then sank into it. "I forgot to ask if you'd care for coffee or tea. Would you?"

They declined.

After a hesitation, Mrs. Morrison spoke. "I'm afraid I might have allowed you to come all this way for nothing. I don't want my husband or myself represented in your magazine...or highlighted in any way."

"Nothing regarding you or your husband will ever be printed without your approval," Erika said. "You have my word."

"Mr. Wheatley?"

"Mine, too."

Mrs. Morrison folded her hands prayerfully in her lap. "It was so long ago, from another life, it seems, but I know the past can crop up as fresh as ever, devastate old folks like me, now that we're less resilient. Truth be told, I was terribly jealous of the Delaneys. I met them just after Bertie and I were engaged, and they'd known him for years and seemed to have that special relationship that comes only from familiarity. Sometimes I imagined William and Bertie spoke in code just so I wouldn't understand them, but of course they were only talking over my head about art. There was a special bond between them, they could talk for hours about what was really good art and what was smart to buy. When William came to New York for business transactions, they'd do so many things together. They had the same taste in food and clothes, even sports." She uttered a short, not altogether bitter laugh. "Sports. Poor Bertie. To think of him after he suffered those strokes—but what a racquetball player he was."

Erika nodded, encouraging.

The trace of nostalgia disappeared from Mrs. Morrison's features. "When William was slaughtered—the only word for it—Bertie was devastated. Worse. It wasn't only the shock of losing his friend, but he couldn't—wouldn't—accept the circumstances."

"My understanding is William Delaney was killed by rebels planning in essence to convert his paintings to guns, and that he himself was—"

"Collateral damage," Harrison finished.

Mrs. Morrison parted her hands, turning them palms up with a shrug. "Of course, and there was no evidence contradicting that, except my husband was relentless. He was certain Castro would have brought his wrath down on those bandits if that had been the case. I'll say on Bertie's behalf, that although there may have been a political falling out between those two, Castro and Delaney had a friendship that went deeper than politics. Still, all evidence pointed to the rebels. Bertie alone fought tooth and nail against it. Delaney's wife stayed out of it. In fact, she was not on the premises when the event occurred, and she fled the country almost immediately afterward, would have none of it. Such a disaster. The main house was torched, would have burned to the ground if the rains hadn't come. Of those on the premises, the Delaney's cook was the only known survivor. Jumped out a second floor window, we were told. Such a diligent young man, with the bluest eyes—oh, you never know what small things will stick in your mind. The manager of the plantation and the cook's assistant—pretty little thing—were never found, perished in the flames, it was said."

"Who did your husband think committed the crime?" Erika asked, resisting the urge to lean forward and possibly come across as threatening.

"Someone on the staff, an acquaintance, a field hand. He wasn't sure."

"There must have been witnesses, at least signs there'd been looters on the property," Harrison stated, the question implied.

"Yes, yes, Bertie didn't doubt that, but the authorities, such as they were, didn't conduct much of an investigation—for political reasons, Bertie said." She paused, musing. "Things haven't changed much in that regard, I suppose."

"Did your husband try to get to the bottom of what he believed to be the truth?" Erika spurred.

"Oh, yes," Mrs. Morrison said, more animated. "He thought that the rebels provided the real murderer—or murderers—with a perfect cover. He spent thousands on detectives trying to prove he was right. Thousands!"

"Did he come up with anything?"

"Gastritis is what he came up with—had it to his dying day."

Erika's reactive smile gave her a twinge of guilt. "How frustrating it must have been for both of you."

"Yes. We felt helpless, though for different reasons." She slid forward to the edge of her seat, her glance flitting from one to the other, her hands suddenly restless, fidgeting in her lap like impatient children. "He gave up his pursuit—I made him give it up after only a few weeks—a month—when I saw what it was doing to him. I sometimes wonder how things might have turned out if I hadn't been such a harridan."

Erika was about to protest the self-recrimination, but Mrs. Morrison, anticipating her, raised her hand to stop her. "Bertie was never the same," she said, as if there had been no break in thought. "He cut himself off from the art world completely, went into business with his brother. Became a furniture dealer, if you can believe it. Not his thing, as they say nowadays; not his thing in the least."

"You've been very kind to speak with us," Harrison said.

"Yes," Erika agreed. The list of topics for discussion lay folded in her tote. "Is there anything about William Delaney, about his art collection, I mean, that you can tell us? Do you know, for instance, if your husband helped him acquire paintings shortly before the—tragedy?"

Mrs. Morrison rose from her chair. "I can't talk anymore about this. I should have known. I'm terribly sorry."

"No, I'm sorry we bothered you," Erika said, as she rose from the glider. "Please rest easy," she added warmly, over the squeak of the glider as Harrison pushed off from it. "Not one sentence about your husband will be published without your consent." She paused. "Would it be an imposition to ask that you get in touch with us if you come across any relevant files, or if any names come to mind you think might be of interest to us? Or if you think of one now, off the top of your head—say, one of the detectives on the case? We'd of course be discreet, wouldn't give away our source."

"Thank you," Harrison added.

"I don't think I can help you." Mrs. Morrison gave each of them a brief, but firm handshake. Then, as if drawn by a magnet, she took a step backward, toward the door. "But if you give me your card..."

Erika dove for one from the inside pocket of her bag, pressed it into Mrs. Morrison's hand. "Thanks, and I hope your memories of Mr.—"

"Bertie. And I'm Tina."

"Bertie—I hope your thoughts about him become more —peaceful."

As they walked down the stoop, Harrison whispered, "That's okay," having picked up on Erika's fluster. "There's no good way to sign off in this kind of situation; everything sounds glib. You did great."

"You're such a comfort," she said, more seriously than her cocked smile would indicate.

Their cab driver was listening to hard rock, thumping his palm against the steering wheel. He turned down the volume barely a decibel as they slid into the back seat.

"What do you think of Bertram Morrison's take on the cause of death?" Harrison asked Erika below the buffer of the music, as the driver pulled away from the curb. "You buy it?"

"I don't know enough to say one way or the other, except the possibility puts a new slant on things." She wriggled farther away from him so she could turn her body to face him without their knees bumping. "I mean, we know someone wants to squelch our investigation. The question is, why?"

"You think Fitch's drawing was stolen not because of its inherent value, but because it might lead us to William Delaney's murderer?"

"Who after more than fifty-five years might be dead himself? But yes, I do. It might be a source of evidence in Helen's case as well. Anyway, who said the motivation couldn't be twofold—profit and cover-up?"

"Good point." He leaned toward her. "I keep coming back to the updated inventory from 1957, that it could be a factor in establishing true provenance, that someone has a damn good reason for preventing it from coming to light."

"Yes, but who, except a thief—and I don't mean any of those rifle-toting rebels—would have any interest in suppressing it?"

"A thief, yes, who might also be a murderer."

She frowned. "But the artworks were stolen by the rebels."

"Aha—maybe not all the artworks!"

"How smart of you! Maybe some other party, or parties, took advantage of the general pandemonium to run off with booty of their own, knowing the rebels would take the blame for grabbing the entire lot! And if William Delaney were to lose his life that day, who would believe it was in any way but at the hands of those rebels?"

Harrison sat back. "My point exactly."

"Try not to look smug."

"Am I looking smug?" he asked, taking her seriously.

She laughed. "No, it was only a warning."

He smiled. "I feel better."

"We'll have to investigate the idea thoroughly. We can't depend on Tina Morrison to offer up any names or events of that time, so we'll have to—"

"Bad sign," he interrupted, "your eyes are lighting up. We'll pass on our theories to the authorities, let them do the delving."

"What a spoilsport you are."

"If that means I'd prefer not to die prematurely, yes I am."

"I see your point."

"I hope so." They were just exiting the Brooklyn Battery Tunnel into the daylight of Lower Manhattan. "Jennifer and I, we have a standing get-together Saturday nights. Very casual, pasta and a movie sort of thing, and I'd like—"

"Excellent timing, actually, because I'm going to be leaving—"

He angled himself to confront her more directly. "Leaving?

What do you mean, leaving?"

"Not leaving town, just home—your home."

"Absolutely not. Certainly not before we hear from the police about that threatening note."

"And if the issue's never resolved?"

"We've discussed this. We had an agreement."

"You had an agreement."

"Are you afraid you're going to hamper my style, is that it?"

"Bluntly put," she said. "You surprise me."

"That's not an answer."

"Yes."

"Yes, what?"

"Yes, I'm afraid I'm going to hamper your style."

"You're being ridiculous. I have no style."

She looked out her window to escape his penetrating

look.

"I can't believe we're having this discussion. All I was going to do was invite you to join us."

"For pity pasta? Thanks, no." She turned toward him. "Sorry, that was uncalled for." He was shaking his head, looking down at his knees. She felt emboldened. "This is how it is. I go back to my apartment, you get on with your life. Tomorrow we meet Natalie as planned. Monday we call Corelli Gallery, also as planned. I'll be in my office Monday, so we can arrange a conference call to Florence."

"Forget it. I'm canceling tonight. Your safety's not going to be jeopardized by a bowl of linguini."

"You're impossible. All right, a compromise. I'll stay until Monday, but only if you keep your date with Jennifer. I'll have dinner with Grace. We'll make our own pasta. Unless she has a hot date herself."

Harrison smiled. "Her boyfriend's sky-diving this weekend—no, I think she'd love that."

"Shall we stop at the grocer's, or are we set?"

"Set."

"Good. Until then, I work on my article, and you, on your book."

The drive uptown was remarkably smooth, the traffic lights turning green for them as if custom-sequenced.

The driver pulled up in front of Harrison's building. As Harrison leaned in for an accounting huddle, Erika got out to wait for him on the sidewalk.

Without a pedestrian in sight to pinpoint the historical era, the building itself elicited images of Old New York and the grand, yet restrained romance of Edith Wharton's Age of Innocence. Prison or safe-house, it was curiously enchanting.

She would have to remain alert to that.

CHAPTER 6

"Lovely view of the river, isn't it?" Harrison said. He, Natalie and Erika were sitting on one of the Schurz Park benches outside the dog run overlooking the East River this brisk October day, the sun doing its best to keep the summer in recent memory. He was sitting between the two women, and he looked politely from one to the other. "Jake and I try to come here every Sunday. He's made friends with a number of the regulars."

Jake, not yet released, looked up at Harrison from a prone position at his feet, then back out at the dog run and the river beyond, lifting his face to take in the smells, or maybe only to feel the wind brush against his nose. A contented grunt issued from him, drawing a laugh from the humans, relaxing them with the naturalness of his being.

Natalie reached into the side pocket of her structured tote and lifted out her restless Yorkshire terrier, placing the silky-haired imp at her feet, careful not to let go of the leash. "Now try to be still for a minute, King," she tentatively ordered. To her benchmates she said, "He doesn't need the workout, but he craves meeting new friends."

"Pretty courageous for a guy his size," Erika remarked, as King, with a tiny barbaric yelp, tried to jump Jake, but was prevented from doing so by Natalie's reflexive tug on his tether.

Natalie smiled. "Six pounds of pure energy."

The words echoed in the silence, colliding with Erika's memory of Helen Delaney, her animation. "You look like your mother," she said, confronting the memory head-on. "More exotic, with your brown hair and eyes, but beautiful in the same way."

"Thank you, I'm more than flattered." Natalie brushed her thighs, clad in tightly creased jeans. "I miss her, and yet it's almost intellectual, as if it hasn't really sunk in. I'm going through the motions, making arrangements..."

Jake adjusted his position and sighed. King took this as a cue for another try at conquest but was thwarted by the tension on his leash.

"One minute, boys," Harrison appealed, focusing on Natalie, pressing her to broach the point of their meeting.

Natalie looked out at the river. "I want you to go on with it, as if she—my mother—were still here." She paused. "Unless you feel it's too...dangerous for you."

"Of course we'll go on," Erika said, looking straight out before her as well, as if at some point in the distance their gazes would converge.

"That's understood," Harrison submitted.

"I mean, I want to be clear about where I stand," Natalie said. "I'm every bit as committed to this project as she was."

Erika turned toward her, reaching across Harrison's lap to grasp her hand. She heard his intake of air and was unnerved by the thrill of it. "Natalie, you can be sure of us." She withdrew her hand, clearing Harrison's lap so high it looked as if she were waving at someone on the opposite shore, in Brooklyn. She couldn't help thinking of last night, how she'd caught herself listening for the sound of his return from his date with Jennifer, frustrated she couldn't hear anything beyond the closed door of the Blue Room, her alertness embarrassing her in her own company.

"I knew I could count on you," Natalie said, refocusing on each of them in turn, "but I had to be reassured in person.

I also needed to make it clear that although my mother never had the chance to draw up her codicil, I know her intentions, and I'm going to honor them. Any artworks you manage to recover will be donated to The Metropolitan Museum."

"Your family agrees to this?" Harrison asked, skeptical.

"All the known works in my mother's estate, and any that may be added 'until the end of time,' I believe is the phrase, belong to me." Her voice bit the air like a cold snap. "My brother's fine with it. My father can go cry on his girlfriend's shoulder."

"Oh," Erika said, the barely audible syllable laden with recognition.

Natalie brushed her forehead, as if she meant to sweep back an unruly thought. "He isn't as bad as I make him sound," she said almost contentiously, as if she'd been bullied into a forgiving frame of mind. "It's just that he's been behaving badly. Toward Rodney, for one. Rodney's been wonderful, a great help to me. I feel ashamed telling you this, even though it isn't my doing, not the slightest, but my father has taken it into his head that you're responsible for my mother's death, and he doesn't want you at the memorial. I'm telling you this to avoid a scene."

"I was going to ask you about the services," Erika said breathlessly.

"I know you were, that's why I—"

"That's why I'm outraged!" Harrison fired.

"Don't make it more difficult for me," Natalie said. "He doesn't believe you literally took her life."

"Oh, well, that's good of him!"

"Harrison, please," Erika urged, though her sentiments mirrored his.

Natalie pressed her fingertips to her forehead. "He only feels you stirred up unfinished business from the remote past, who knows what. He's angry you took the project on, listened to her, that's all." Her fingers sprang away from her forehead, leaving two pale depressions.

Harrison abruptly rose from the bench. "I'm sorry, I didn't mean to take it out on you."

Jake lumbered to his full height, King responding with an excited twirl, his long silky hair catching the sunlight.

"That's okay, I don't blame you," Natalie said, rising herself. She directed a questioning look at Erika as King hurtled to the end of his tether and strained forward with a choking gasp.

Erika shook her head. "I've read the sign. Only one human per dog allowed. You go ahead. Your dogs have been very patient." She waved them off.

Resting an arm on the back of the bench, she watched the foursome cross the narrow pavement to the chain link fence bordering the dog run. As Jake sat and King fretted, Harrison lifted the latch to the gate. He gestured for Natalie and King to precede him, then followed Jake into the grass-carpeted corral, briefly pausing to re-latch the gate.

The dogs relieved themselves immediately, lifting their legs in perfect unison, reminding Erika of synchronized swimmers. She smiled at the absurd thought as Harrison detached Jake's leash, her smile lingering as Jake loped in his dear fashion toward the center of fun, Harrison holding back, watchful but unobtrusive. Whether to protect King from the other dogs, or the other dogs from King, Natalie chose not to set him free, allowing him to pull her maniacally from one canine attraction to another.

Dividing her attention between the exuberant Lab and the fitful Yorkie, Erika sat back to enjoy the show. The morning sun played on the river's surface, adding to the scene's inspiriting effect.

She sensed the presence behind her, the breath on her neck, the tug at the base of her scalp in too rapid a sequence to react outwardly, except to sound an alien bleat. Frozen in a kind of marveling—the hand must have swept under her hair and captured it in one smooth motion—she failed to defend herself.

One hand wrenched the hair upward, the other pushed against her forehead, immobilizing her, insuring the tension on her scalp. The rip of pain activated her defense mechanism, along with a fierce remorse that it had not done so instantly. With a grunt, she reached up and tried to grab at those hands, but he—she?—held fast, the back of her neck jamming up against the back of the bench. She could not see the face, and the musk odor of it, and the breath, hot against her cheek, mocked her ignorance.

Lips brushed against her ear, the whisper penetrating like a tongue: "Get it? Stay off Delaney."

And then a letting go.

She jumped up, spun around, her savage scream unrecognizable, a new sound from her, blocking the words she meant to cry out: Stop him! She meant to run after her assailant, but he had vanished, or seemed to have. To her left: a small boy running, a woman in pursuit of him; a jogger, already turning away from the outburst. To her right: passersby, one stopped in his tracks, the only one, taking the cell phone from his ear, holding it toward her, Want to call 911? the unspoken question. She waved him off—wait, was he the man who had just—? She felt her knees buckle.

Coming from behind, someone caught her around her waist.

She rallied, flailing. "Erika, stop! It's me!"

"Oh!" She turned in his grasp. "Did I hurt you?" She threw her arms around Harrison, instantly pulling away, her courage to do without his help returning with his comforting presence, the paradox barely nicking her consciousness.

"I'm fine," he said, rubbing the spot on his head where her fist had connected. "What happened? I heard a scream, turned, and it was you!"

She told him what had happened as Jake, nudging and pawing at the fence, was attempting to break out, wanting to be part of it. She went over it again after Harrison had come back from fetching Jake and summoning Natalie with a wave.

Natalie could not hold out to the end of the story. "Anyone see what just happened here?" she cried out to the indifferent air, as if she were delivering a line from the stage of an amphitheater. "Anyone?"

There was an instant of frozen attendance by those within earshot, but no verbal response, only a shying away.

"Forget it," Erika said, her scalp still stinging. "No one saw, it was too quick."

"Did you at least call 911?" Natalie asked Harrison, her freneticism turning officious.

"No," Erika answered for him, "there's no point." She was trembling now, internally, invisibly. "We'll tell Mitchell —the officer we've been in contact with from the beginning. It's okay, we'll manage."

"What do you want to do, Erika?" Harrison asked, his look a balm.

The trembling abated. "You mean about the project?"

"Yes. You must know I want you to quit, but it's up to you. Entirely."

"I want to continue with it."

"Of course. I knew you would."

Natalie squeezed Erika's shoulder. "Thank you, thank you, I'm truly grateful." She scooped up King and carefully tamped him into his assigned compartment of her bag. "You must promise me, though, that you'll contact the police about this."

Erika nodded vigorously. "We will, we will."

"I can't believe you can be so with it," Natalie marveled. "I would be a basket case—as it is, I am a basket case!"

Harrison bent down to stroke the top of Jake's head. "Good boy," he said, from no apparent cause other than a sudden spike of affection.

After parting with Natalie, Erika and Harrison set out for his place. Whether from the sudden reliving of her attack or from the withering realization of it as an event to be remembered, Erika found herself feeling a bit unsteady, having to make a conscious effort not to let it show in her gait.

"We should call Lieutenant Mitchell," he said. "Immediately."

"From your place."

"Okay. By the way, I think you're very brave."

"I don't know about that, but thanks."

They walked for a time, then at Jake's cue stopped alongside a hydrant; waited for him while he lifted his leg.

"May I hold the leash?" she asked.

He handed it to her. Jake looked up at her, then walked on.

There was a security in the tug of him, and a comfort in his trust in her—no demands, no expectations, merely the assumption of her being there.

CHAPTER 7

E rika pocketed the receipt for her carry-on suitcase and apologized to the clerk for its having taken up most of the cloakroom's floor space.

"You look tentative," Harrison said, his voice close to a whisper, as she slid alongside him. "Were you followed?" He glanced toward the entrance of the café, aptly named The-Hole-In-The-Wall.

"I don't think so." She tried not to notice the colliding of their thighs, unavoidable given the snug quarters of the corner banquette. Their faces were almost touching.

"I sometimes come here to grade papers or read; they pretty much leave you alone."

"It's good we don't feel rushed." She looked about her. The place was small enough to take in at a glance. None of the ten or so patrons engendered suspicion, at least not immediate. "What are you drinking?"

"The house white, a Pinot Grigio, not bad." He beckoned the waiter, already on the way.

She ordered the same, and the waiter handed them a small hand-printed menu to share.

They reviewed the menu, deciding on a couple of simple chicken and vegetable appetizers to share as dinner.

As they unhurriedly made their way through the dishes and nursed their wine, they went over what they'd been up to.

Harrison had, as they'd agreed, called the Corelli Gallery. Turned out the only papers its proprietor, Mario Depoli could come up with were the sales transactions of the stolen Vittorio drawing: the gallery's acquisition in 1933, and William Delaney's purchase in 1951. "A complicated story," Harrison said, "but, bottom line, the balance of the Vittorio folder belongs to a family—the Fabbris—living in the town of Montevarchi, about thirty miles outside Florence. Thanks to Depoli, we have an open invitation to their villa."

For her part, Erika had focused on getting her hands on Michelangelo's Battle of Cascina-related reprints—good reprints, especially of his drawings assumed to be studies for the background scenes. Sizeable areas of those works had been drawn with light, thin strokes, and it was difficult to make out individual figures or ones that had been superimposed on. If they could take a look at prints crisper than those in book format, maybe they could distinguish a minor character or two with counterparts in the Vittorio drawing. This would strengthen their argument linking the drawing to the master's own conceptualizations. Probably a wild goose chase, but intellectually irresistible.

To this end she'd contacted the British Museum in London. She was told that a complete set of reprints associated with Cascina did not exist, and was expecting to hear back from the curator by the end of the week to see if reprints could be made. She'd emailed a similar request to the Ashmolean Museum in Oxford and was waiting to receive a reply.

After obtaining Natalie's go-ahead to explore the Cuban connection, she'd also composed two letters—"feelers"—one to the Cuban Minister of Arts, the other to the curator of the National Museum in Havana. She'd brought the rough drafts for Harrison's input—or censorship. He read them, praising her tact. "Good move, asking the museum to send you a catalogue and sending them, in turn, a copy of Delaney's 1954 inventory. Shows an openness on our part, a gesture of good will."

"That's what I'm hoping."

"You were going to talk again with Lieutenant Mitchell today," he gently prodded, as she returned the drafts to the tote bag at her feet.

Yesterday morning their conversation with Mitchell had been confined to the incident at Schurz Park. Mitchell had approached it from every perspective except the dogs', and purportedly would contact Natalie Gilmore for her first-hand account. Later that evening Erika and Harrison had finally decided it would be best to give Mitchell a full disclosure of their research activities. Although Erika had offered a few crumbs at her interrogation, she'd done so begrudgingly. Their tactical turnabout was based on two factors. First, a free exchange of information between them and the detective would benefit both sides of the investigation, criminal and academic. Second, Harrison said he'd abandon ship if she didn't agree to it.

"I did talk to Mitchell today," Erika said. "I told him everything."

"You don't sound very enthusiastic," he said. "More than anything this is about safety, yours especially."

She shook her head. "I gave him all the names—Morrison, Fitch, Depoli—even Bill, your driver. I feel disloyal."

"Come on, you didn't go before The House Un-American Activities Committee. If anyone can provide so much as a scrap of information that leads to the person who killed Helen, or the person who attacked you, it's worth the qualms." He smiled, almost to himself. "And I'm sure you stressed the importance of confidentiality."

"I made him swear to it."

"I thought so."

"You'll be happy to know he's alerting the patrolmen in my neighborhood to check up on me at regular intervals. Starting tonight."

He paused. "That probably won't be necessary."

"What do you mean? I am going back to my apartment

tonight."

"Well, I made arrangements."

She held his gaze. "What did you do, Harrison?"

"I booked us a flight to London, then on to Florence. We depart JFK at 3:30 A.M. Our return gets us back to JFK Friday night." He returned her gaze with equal intensity, undaunted.

"You're kidding."

"There were only two seats available. I didn't want to take the chance of losing them. They're first class, so we have the option of exchanging them for a future date without penalty, if that makes you feel any better."

"Oh, so much. And did you decide what I should wear to the airport?"

"I thought your pink pants suit—you know, the one with the butterflies on the—"

"Harrison!"

"Seriously, I thought it would be a good idea to remove you from harm's way, give the authorities some time to do their probing, also spark a little fear and trembling out there."

"So you think news of this... probing will somehow reach the perpetrators and discourage them from taking more chances, being more aggressive?"

"That's my hope. Besides, sooner or later we should make this trip, see the art first hand. Why not sooner than later?"

"I'm not saying it's a bad idea. I'm objecting to the way you took charge."

"I acted impetuously. Not typical of me. I'm sorry."

"You're forgiven. I guess." She lifted her wineglass, realized it was empty.

"You want another?" He looked for the waiter.

"I better not. I should stay alert for what you're going to pull next."

"Nothing—well, except that I should tell you I ordered a rental car for us to pick up at the airport in London. I hope you don't mind."

She laughed. "And lodgings?"

He nodded.

"Nonsmoking?"

"It didn't occur to me."

"Thank god."

"Why? I didn't think you smoked."

"I don't. I'm only happy you didn't think of everything." She ran her finger around the rim of her water glass. "You know, this may not work out at such short notice. For one thing, I'll have to get permission to take time off."

"Why don't you call Sara on her cell phone right now?"

She nodded. "For another, I'll have to apply for travel expenses, and I don't think authorization can be made on the spot."

"No problem. I'm paying."

"Oh, no you're not."

"Please don't give me a hard time." His look came close to a glare. "I've got the money. I'm uncomfortable enough about it. Don't make it worse."

She was taken aback. "Why don't you give it all away, if it makes you so touchy?"

"Because my cagey grandmother knew that's what I'd do, so she put a big cap on charitable donations in her will, if you can believe it. She knew it might not hold up in court, so she added an emotional plea, designed to make me feel guilty if I defied her."

Erika smiled, a bit guilty herself. "She wanted you to live it up, enjoy life." She added a taunt: "You were such a serious child. Self-denying."

He looked surprised.

"No, I didn't research your past. I guessed."

It took a beat for him to process this. "Okay, the matter of expenses is settled. Don't bug me about it again. I'm still hungry, are you?"

"A little, yes."

They ordered seconds on the chicken dish. While they

were waiting for it to be brought out, she called Sara.

"What was all that nervous laughter about?" he asked after the call had been terminated.

She looked down, fiddled with her utensils. "Sara was quite agreeable with the arrangements. She thought our leaving town for a while was a good idea. In fact, she says if anyone asks, she's going to say we're on a retreat in the Himalayas."

"And that's funny?"

"Well, she made a comment about our running off on a romantic holiday. It was her wording that was amusing," she added, fighting off a surge of adolescent jitters. Now that I think about it, the rumor might actually serve a purpose. It would explain our inaccessibility, put people off our scent, as it were." What a gaggle of syllables!

He nodded, either in agreement or in acknowledgment of the waiter, just arrived with their chicken dish.

As Harrison slid the communal dish in her direction they accidentally bumped elbows, and she was startled by her acute awareness of his nearness, feeling it as a kind of vibration, as if she'd been struck like a tuning fork.

They shared a silence, poking at their food, she wondering if he had glimpsed her senseless longing for him, if there had been a glitch in her demeanor. She stole a glance at him, catching him in mirrored theft, their gazes locking for an infinite second before retreating to safer ground.

"We'll have to make some last minute calls tonight," he said at last.

She nodded. "We've got to call Mitchell, get his permission to leave the country."

"Already did."

"Guess he either trusts us or has no legitimate reason to detain us. I should call Natalie...alert the Barlows..."

"I've already gotten in touch with my teaching assistant. Reliable guy, I can always count on him to fill in for me... and Jennifer, I should call her..."

Erika stiffened. "You think she'll approve?"

"Of what? My teaching assistant?"

"Of your gallivanting off."

"I guess she could consult with Rodney, see if he approves."

"Rodney is irrelevant in this context."

"As is Jennifer—say, are we having our first lovers' quarrel?" He smiled broadly.

The lapse in his guard was thoroughly disarming. "Sara would be tickled pink if it were," she said. There was a grain of pepper on his lower lip, and she saw herself licking it off and hurling them into a delicious tangling of souls. How indelibly the suspension of judgment was built into her! She took a deep, restorative breath. "About tomorrow morning, do we meet at the airport, or should I call a car service, swing by your place?"

"Neither. The only sensible plan is for you to stay over another night."

"No, Harrison. I'll be perfectly safe. We had a deal. I've got my suitcase in the cloakroom."

"This isn't about safety, it's about efficiency. We've got to be at the airport at two in the morning. If we're lucky we can catch a couple of hours of sleep."

She had to admit he was right. If she held out it would appear to be out of presumptuous coyness. She yielded.

Later, over coffee, she suddenly came out with a staccatoed "Oh."

Holding his cup motionless midway between the table and his lips, "What?" he asked, his frown blooming.

"Grace probably stripped the linen in the Blue Room. My staying an extra night will be such an inconvenience for her!"

Harrison set down his cup and smiled, his emotion hard to decipher. "Oh, Erika," he said softly, "you are so refreshingly not to the manor born."

The grain of pepper had disappeared from his lip, yet it took all her effort not to be swept away by the image it had conjured.

CHAPTER 8

Erika rested her head on the back of the tub and breathed in the delicate floral scent of the beaded bathwater. She opened and closed her legs, the gentle rhythm agitating the water just enough to stir desire without inflaming it. Although she had reservations about setting herself on a surface enjoyed by strangers, the self-confidence exuded by the Russell Hotel, grand Victorian overseer to the splendid urban garden of Bloomsbury's Russell Square, dared her to imagine that no other nude body had ever made contact with the glistening porcelain.

Amazing to think it had only been...let's see, deducting the five hours time difference...fifteen hours since they'd taken off from JFK. Her sense of time, disrupted by jet lag, was as swirly as the bathwater. She'd been too jumpy to sleep before their departure, and the two Mimosas she'd had once they were tucked on board had dipped her in and out of dozing like a bobbing apple. Harrison, too, had napped intermittently, only under the influence of Bloody Marys. During periods of mutual waking, their talk had ambled into art, politics and family history, and their compatibility had blossomed into a kind of fretful ease.

Harrison had phoned the British Museum as soon as the plane touched down in Heathrow. Within minutes he was chatting with its assistant curator, Brian Latham, who knew what they were after from Erika's email. His suggestion, as Harrison relayed it: "Sorry, chaps, but it's too late in the afternoon for a proper visit to the Michelangelos, but come by at ten tomorrow morning and I'm all yours. Meanwhile, for amusement, why don't you pop over to Norfolk and have a look at da Sangallo's grisaille panel at Holkham Hall?" It would be after closing, but Brian said he knew the principal caretaker who lived on the grounds. Top-notch fellow, he'd give them a private tour of the place, Brian would see to it. No need to check into the hotel prior to their jaunt; reservations had been guaranteed by American Express. Plans were finalized before the plane had taxied to a full stop.

Erika rolled over and languidly rippled about. Then slowly, her belly pressed against the floor of the tub, she arched her back, pushing up on her hands, her breasts breaking the surface of the water. She held the position in the stretch, feeling herself to be a sea creature. Then she relaxed, submerging, turning to rise, to sit, human after all. She smiled, twirling a hand in the water. It had gone so smoothly—at least so it seemed from her sybaritic vantage point—picking up their rented car, installing the Global Positioning System with the desired coordinates, and cruising off on the wrong side of the road to the picturesque north coast of Norfolk. Splitting up the driving and sharing the adventure of seeing a landscape for the first time, they'd eluded exhaustion, chatting up a storm the entire trip, celebrating their second wind.

And wasn't it worth it, to see rising out of the friendly countryside and cloaked in the mystery of dusk, the grand, no-nonsense Palladian style mansion, Holkham Hall. Built in the mid-eighteenth century and once home to the Earls of Leicester, this broad and stolid edifice seemed to capture the arrogance of that family's dream of substantiation, and of a civilization's, to endure. What gave the effect its impact was the structure's natural setting: twenty-five thousand acres of nature reserve, they were told later by the caretaker, Jason, over tea and scones in his one-man cottage, at his insistence and long past the call of duty. Pinewoods and creeks, marshes, nature trails, and windswept dunes along the bay, lovely to stroll along. "You two should visit when you have more time," he'd said. Wistfully, as if he were wishing he were younger, or remembering when he was. "We have a few lovely little cottages on the grounds...very private, rates quite reasonable...."

She might sit here forever. The aroma was intoxicating. Must let the water out, she prompted herself. Reluctantly she obeyed, finishing up with a quick shower and shampoo. Her final indulgence of the long day: massaging into her skin, top to bottom, the body cream, same scent as the bath beads. She used up the entire contents of the amenity tube, the last dollop applied between her legs, her palm briefly lingering, nurturing.

Soft and slippery smooth, she slid between the welcoming sheets and drew the thin coverlet up around her shoulders. Drifting into sleep, she replayed their walk through the mansion, experiencing again the wonder of being its only visitors...through the high Marble Hall, "in truth Derbyshire alabaster," Jason had said...more translucent than marble, and softer...admiring its grand, classic colonnade...entering the staterooms, surprisingly opulent in contrast...surprise after surprise with Harrison...coming upon the da Sangallo, its style more stilted than its reproductions would have predicted...examining its details, the force and direction of brush strokes, a game almost, matching limbs to torsos, especially in its crowded left half...awed not by the greatness of the work but by its historic significance...standing close to it and to each other, Jason standing apart from them, not a member of their circle...further on, pausing before the portrait of the Duke of Arenbury about to gallop off to battle, Jason near them here, looking from one to the other, explaining how the massed army in the background had appeared only after Van Dyck's painting had been cleaned, the discovery reminiscent of Michelangelo's horsemen missing from da Sangallo's rendering, she and Harrison exchanging knowing glances about this, Jason, with his sly smile, reading something more into this...Without looking back, she knows they are alone, wandering through the park earlier seen, but as a painting, a sweep of the eye, a scanning. Now they are lost in it, without orientation, Holkham Hall behind a curtain of trees or disappeared altogether. She doesn't care where they are, only how the grass prickles her bare feet, staining them moonlit green, how her white dress flutters, his transparent shirt ripples as he moves...the sky an impossible blue...Enchantment draws them into the night, quickens their pace...She speaks with her eyes—this way, yes—and he moves with her from lawn to winding path, thicket-lined, and canopied by lavish trees. They walk quickly, deeper into the thickening wood, the path narrowing, overgrown, past the boundaries of the estate, past the caretaker's caring, inviting still, but with a wisp of foreboding. They are pressed into single-file, he in front. She is starting to fall behind. The gap is widening. She wants to call out to him, but she can't catch her breath. Her heart is racing, and she hears the rising pressure of her blood, the susurration itself intensifying fear. She runs faster than she thought she ever could, never minding the brambles underfoot, the pain nothing to her, a curiosity. Fear gathers like a storm, shaping itself. Clarifying into something behind her and closing in. She can't turn because seeing it will stop her cold. Ahead, the billowy shirt droops as he stops, turns toward her, casually, as if to remark about the fine day. Even from this distance she can see her terror mirrored in his features, or does he see what is behind her, what is suddenly upon her, nailing onto her shoulders, wrenching her backward. He is running toward her, but it is too late. She claws the air trying to grab at the thing, but it's ripping her away like a hawk, she the prey. Thoughts flailing, clawing wildly at hope, she sees him running toward her, losing ground...

She woke with a sharp intake of air, and lay there in the dark, the map of the room lagging into consciousness.

She turned on her side and peered at the night table's

digital clock. A fluorescent 3:11 winked to 3:12. Time was meaningless. She was wide awake and lonely in the silence. The dying scent of flowers emanating from her skin made it worse, like a taunting love song.

She half-adapted to the room's faint ambient light and fumbled her way to the bathroom. When she flicked on the light, the space blazed into high-noon intensity. She squinted at her image in the mirror, startled by her nakedness, as if she'd awakened to find herself on a public beach.

She clicked off the light, unsure of what to do next. She didn't want to be alone though she'd never minded it, mostly enjoyed it, in fact. Except that in this moment, whatever the real time was, if such a thing existed, being alone wasn't equivalent to self-amusement, it was uneasy solitude, and vaguely threatening. She wanted to snuggle into conversation, hear her voice mingle with another's. Merely imagining this was a comfort.

Minutes later she was poised in front of Harrison's door, securely wrapped in the terrycloth hotel robe, its belt tightly knotted. Beneath it she had on her only pair of cotton underpants, to prove to herself her innocent intentions.

She knocked lightly on the door, intending the sound to be heard only if he were awake. She waited. She would not try again.

She started back to her room. His door opened. "Erika."

"I'm sorry," she said, returning. "I didn't want to wake you up."

"It would have been okay, but you didn't. Anything wrong? Come in."

The hotel robe was shorter on him, falling just below his knees. Its belt was securely tied, but not tightly knotted like hers. He was barefoot. She wore the hotel scuffs that fit her like clown flippers.

He closed the door behind them.

"Nothing's wrong," she said. "I had a disturbing dream, and I couldn't go back to sleep, and now I feel like an idiot."

"Don't be ridiculous. Come sit down." He moved toward the arrangement of upholstered armchairs and small decorative table. Stood there, waiting. "Tell me about the dream if you want to. Or not."

She noticed his open laptop on the desk. "You were working." He was silent.

"I'll go," she said, without moving a muscle.

"No. Please don't."

"You said for a long time you couldn't work. I don't want to interfere with that."

"Charlotte's mission was to replace my interests with hers. You're not that person."

She started walking toward the desk. "How many pages did you write tonight?"

He met her at the desk. "Ten. Ten pages." She studied the screen. "You mind?"

"Of course not."

She read silently: Gericault's classical rendering of the human form and structure of composition, in contrast to the dramatic nature of his subject matter, form a link between neo-classicism and romanticism. In particular, The Raft of the Medusa, painted in 1819...

"I found myself wanting to share them with you," he said abruptly.

She looked up at him. "What? Share what?"

"The pages."

"Oh. That's...nice."

"You want to talk about your dream?"

"No, I just wanted to talk." She paused. "We were in the woods. In Norfolk. Some creature was coming at me from behind. Obviously a remake of the Schurz Park experience."

"I didn't save you."

"How do you know?"

"Because you would have slept through it."

"But you were on your way. I just happened to wake up."

"So technically I might have saved you."

"Eventually."

They chorused a nervous laugh. "Erika," he said, softly.

"What?—Don't say it." Not knowing what he was going to say, yet wanting him to, despite her denial.

"I have to touch you. I mean, I want to."

"It's not a good idea," she said, holding his look.

He—they—reached out—they summoned each other, and embraced. They gazed. Kissed. Gently at first, then deepening, consuming, impossible to have known how good it would be, but knowing.

"Burning," she said, in a parting of their lips, an unbearable parting.

"Mine too. My skin." Marveling almost.

They opened each other's robes, laughing a little at the difficulty of her knot.

He was bare underneath, she, in her prissy underpants. She slipped them off, kicked them away, along with the scuffs.

They closed in on each other, robes parted, burning one to the other, the melting sharpening the awareness of distinctness: my flesh touching yours.

Her legs buckled with the wonder of it, and he pressed her to him, and her right leg found him under his robe and drew up around him, and his hand, and then his hands, were under her, under her robe, and he was lifting her, carrying her to the still-made bed, lying her down on it.

"Take it off," she said, peeling the robe from his shoulders—"mine, too"—as he helped her with hers, together awkwardly, avidly, freeing themselves of the final impediment to complete presence.

He stroked and kissed her everywhere, she, limp from his hunger. She started to cry, keeping the sound of it inside, her chest heaving.

"Why are you crying?"

"I don't know."

He kissed her cheek, licked away the tears. "You don't know?"

"I feel like I'm crying into you."

"Is that a good thing?"

"I don't know."

"I think it is. It is." His hand swept over her. "You are so new to me, but…"

"You know me."

"Yes."

She could hardly move from the yielding, her energy siphoned to an aching pinpoint below, her eyes roving where she longed to explore with her lips and tongue, her eyes closing with the image of it, opening to see his face, the tears coming again, still, her hands weakly sliding down his back, her tongue tasting without touching over the curve of him.

He pressed his hands against her inner thighs, and she spread further to the urging, her anticipation intensifying as he entered her, her hips rising to bear him deeper, pleasure swelling from the glazed friction of him.

He stopped, held her still. "I don't have—I didn't think we were—"

"I'm on the pill," she said, her words contrasting with the fire within. "I mean it's not like I—"

He kissed her. "I understand. This is different."

"Yes."

He moved in her, thrusting deep, and then again and again. Anticipation, heightened by its brief thwarting, spilled into waves of unexpected force, rip-tiding through her, undamming her whole being.

In the ebb of it, "Harry," she whispered hoarsely, not knowing the word until it was spoken. "You were with me."

He burrowed his face in her neck. "Yes." He nudged her with his pelvis, inadvertently setting off a delicate flutter.

She shimmied up against him, teasing up another. "So good." He laughed softly. "You content?"

"For now."

* * *

She was the first to wake up, entangled with him under the bedclothes to where they'd slipped some time ago. Lifting his hand from her breast, she wondered how long it had been, knowing that the question itself was the harbinger of reality, the tearing herself away from the myth.

She rolled to her side. The digital clock read 6:24. She turned back, propped herself on an elbow, stared down at him. His lips were parted, and every cell in her body hungered for him. She drew down the sheet to reveal more of him, this man she hardly knew but to whom she'd been conjoined, or had felt so, when reason, in one of its rare comas, had left her.

Still, his body, the slope of it—the slope of him—drew her downward, and she rested her head on him and listened to the sounds of his belly and mocked herself for thinking they were beautiful.

He stroked her head. "What a nice way to wake up. Hi."

She propped herself back up on her elbow. "Good morning."

"You look pensive. Should I be worried?"

"Worried about what?"

"That you're having second thoughts."

"I never had first thoughts, that's the problem."

He cupped his hand to her face; explored it as if he were sightless. "Erika."

The sound of her name never sounded so sweet. His hand smelled of him, of her, of their love-making. "It's all downhill from here," she said, joking, to lighten the truth. "This is as good as it gets."

He rolled onto his side and swept his hand down her face, her breasts, under the bedclothes to her belly, pressing its way to her center. "How about this? This better?"

She said nothing.

He gently kneaded. "This?"

"I don't know. Yes."

"Why?"

"Why what?"

126

"Why is it better?"

"I don't know." She pushed his hand away. "That's why I know this is as good as it gets. I'm not thinking. You're not thinking. Just wait. You'll start thinking, and reality will kick in, and poof goes the magic. Guaranteed."

"You call this not thinking? Sounds like you're thinking to me."

"Don't try to trick me. I mean not thinking properly."

"You mean not thinking cynically."

"No. I mean not thinking realistically."

"Careful. If you predict bad things will happen you'll make them happen. Don't do so much expecting." He kissed her, tipping her off the fulcrum of her elbow. "Were you expecting that?"

Fallen, she lay on her back looking up at him. "No."

"It made it nicer, didn't it?"

"For now. Yes."

"For now is what our lives are. Our time on earth. Breathing.

For now."

"Okay. The early part of for now, then. As opposed to the later part of for now."

"Later, as in next week?" he asked.

"As in next year."

"Next year, or week, for that matter, we might be—"

"Dead? So let's live in the moment? You don't really think that way. If you did you wouldn't be so keen on getting your book done, achieving something that transcends death."

"Now you're trying to trick me."

"How?"

"By pitting love against ambition. Different authority, sweetie, like faith and science." He tweaked her where his fingers had momentarily played. "Do I have to make law review before you let me in again?"

"Don't distract me," she said, dislodging his hand. She pushed him onto his back and rose to her knees. Hovered over

127

him.

He flung out his arms in abject defeat. Smiling.

Splayed beneath her, he was irresistible. She resisted. "So how about Jennifer? She faith or science?"

Suddenly serious: "Jennifer has been a companion."

"While you heal."

"Yes. We do not sleep together."

The words hit her full force, accusatory. She looked away. "What, is that impossible for you to believe?"

She turned back to him. "No. It isn't. We're opposites, that's all."

"Opposites? Oh. You mean I deal with my trust issues by being celibate. You deal with yours by being—I'm guessing —promiscuous."

"I'm not promiscuous."

"Indiscriminate then. How's that?"

"Better."

"Please. Can we call a truce? Can we pretend this moment exists outside of time? Outside our hang-ups?"

"I don't know."

"Erika."

"What?"

"Be quiet and kiss me."

She studied him. Couldn't help foretasting his mouth, his tongue. She negotiated with her better judgment: no harm done, just this once more; self-deceit, being known, is rendered harmless.

"Outside of time," she murmured, descending into the kiss.

CHAPTER 9

The words had completely slipped her mind, and now she couldn't get them out; I can hardly hear you, sweetheart. It was the phrase Harrison had spoken into his cell phone at the Pierre gala. Ritualized into a nagging chant. I can hardly hear you, sweet—

"Here we are, chaps," Brian Latham beckoned, upstaging the chant. He waved her and Harrison into the British Museum's Study Room. "We're all ready for you."

Erika paused just inside the entrance. It was impossible not to be awed by the staggering number of precious works she knew were housed within these walls, yet the significance of this was understated by the inviting look of the place —ruddy brown wood in the cabinetry and moldings, study tables surfaced in warm green leather, burnished gold table lamps, sky-blue carpet. She moved along, falling into step with Harrison, who was adjusting his gait to make it unavoidable. Inwardly, she kept her distance.

Brian headed them to the far end of the room. "Morning, Katherine," he greeted in passing.

A tidy matron looked up, smiling. "Morning, Brian," she intoned with a reverence either for him or the work at hand. Clad in white knit archival gloves, she was about to open a large leather-bound portfolio. A collegiate-looking young man sat beside her at the table, waiting with refreshingly unabashed eagerness.

"Who?" Brian asked, looking back as he continued en route. "Tintoretto," Katherine answered.

"Ah. Marvelous—carry on!"

Brian led them to a cul-de-sac behind a bank of rosewood filing cabinets. On a desk table illuminated by the table lamp craned just above were two drawings displayed side by side on a long wood easel.

Erika's breath caught. Harrison snapped to attention. Brian laughed. "Good lads. I see you're properly riveted."

"When they take you by surprise..." Erika began.

"Precisely." Brian waved them toward the two straight-back chairs pulled out from the table; he stood behind them once they were settled. "You recognize them, of course."

"From art books," Erika said, sitting forward.

Harrison touched her arm, marking the moment as shared.

The drawing on their left was of a seated male nude twisting to focus on a point behind him. This was the central figure in the "Bathers" portion of Michelangelo's planned Cascina mural. Having so recently viewed a rendition of this figure in Holkam House, Erika was sensitive to their differences.

"Da Sangallo hardly approaches the master, eh?" Brian posed, reading her mind.

She nodded. "This is more animated somehow, you can feel the torsion. Da Sangallo's isn't a bad copy, but his figure is a little more barrel-chested and, well, the energy isn't coming from"—she patted her stomach—"within."

"That's good," Harrison praised. "The force in Michelangelo starts in the midsection and flows outward. In his studies there often isn't all that much attention given to the extremities and the head. In this case the typical cap worn by the model is drawn with a thin light line, indicating the outline of the skull, but not the sculpted form achieved elsewhere with the use of light and dark shading, chiaroscuro modeling."

Erika looked from one drawing to the other. The study

on the right was of a standing male nude, also in a twist position, in black chalk with lead white, recognizably one of the pole-wielding figures in the "Bathers" scene. "The drawing on the right seems to achieve the effect of form—of mass—with less effort," she said. "The chalk lines, the cross-hatching alone"—she pointed selectively, careful not to touch—"may even create a greater sense of strength and movement. Am I off base here?"

"Absolutely not," Harrison said. "In fact, Michelangelo basically simplified his highlighting technique by eliminating the wash medium for the balance of his studies, at least those extant."

"Learned from experience," I suspect, Brian chimed in. "See here, in the pen and ink drawing, how the brown and gray wash achieves form—beautifully, of course, but a bit arduously, not swiftly, not stunningly. And look, here, in the right portion of the drawing, how the lead white, meant to highlight, rather mucks it up a bit, whereas in the chalk drawing, the white positively illuminates, wouldn't you say."

Erika smiled. "I see your point, but it's hard for me to be the least bit critical of anything Michelangelo put his hand to."

"Everyone's starry-eyed on their first date with the man," Brian said. "You'll get over it. Nobody, even the greatest among us, is perfect. And that's the beauty of it, don't you see, what draws us to him, his quintessential, his perfect, if you will—humanness."

"Well put," Harrison said, addressing Brian, but touching Erika again.

"Yes," she said, her simple affirmative, regardless of what it was directed to, switching on the chant: I can hardly hear you, sweetheart—beat one, two, three—I can hardly hear you, sweetheart....

Harrison had said he was celibate, but that did not rule out affection. Jealousy rose like bile from the dark corners of her mind. How she despised her weakness. There was no way she would accede to it by asking who sweetheart was and sink deeper into that loathsome ache. No danger of this kind of thing with Rodney. She'd never felt the desire to fuse with him, to count on him never to leave her. Where there's no faith, faithlessness is not an issue; possessiveness, the underbelly of dependence, not an issue. She must stay intact. I can hardly hear you, sweetheart....Go ahead, sing on. Eventually all earworms play themselves out.

"The chalk study," Harrison began. "It's from the Teylers Museum in the Netherlands, if I'm not mistaken. Did you recently purchase it?"

Brian laughed. "No such luck. Actually, we're mounting another Michelangelo exhibition, more comprehensive than the one held here years ago, and this is one of the Teylers on loan. They're lending us several more than last time, trust us more this time around, I imagine. Conservation precludes lengthy hang times, for us no more than six weeks. We keep our drawings in acid-free boxes, removed from light, temperature, humidity fluctuations and, well, you could say the Teylers are cautious to the point of paranoia.

"Also, the Ashmolean has added to their commitment a couple of drawings they've acquired from private collections. These are being held offsite until they've completed their most recent round of renovations. They've entrusted the balance of their Michelangelos to us, so I dare say they mean to bring out the new ones with a fanfare."

"I didn't realize the museum was undergoing renovations," Erika said. "It's probably why we haven't had a response to my email."

"The museum's remaining open during the renovations," Brian declared, but their administration's preoccupied." He strode to the adjacent desk table. "On the bright side, you're spared a trip to Oxford." There was a metal box sitting on the desktop, and he reached for the pair of archival gloves beside it. He slipped on the gloves, removed a set of leather-bound portfolios from the box, then, in a scrupulously choreographed ritual, exchanged the two drawings on display with two others, from the Ashmolean collection. Both were putative studies for the battle scene portion of the mural, with details far more discernible than in reproduction.

Erika tried to contain her excitement. She wanted urgently to take out their copy of the Vittorio drawing, hunt for similarities.

"Getting closer to the core of your mission, I take it," Brian ventured. "It's my understanding that you're studying —piecing together, as it were—the evolution of the Cascina mural. Am I correct?"

"How it evolved, yes," she said. "What aesthetic principles motivated the changes in form. How Michelangelo's mind worked as he approached the final design." She hesitated, wondering if they should let Brian in on their investigation. In fact, tell him that their interest in Cascina was an offshoot of their primary mission, to help recover a cache of artworks stolen over a half century ago. An important figure in the art world, Brian could be of help as a networker. Surely Helen would have approved. It didn't look like he was going to leave them alone with the drawings, so if they didn't fill him in, they'd have to talk in code and take mental snapshots of them—photographing them was prohibited—and copy selected figures to jog their memories later, when they could freely examine the Vittorio and make comparisons. She caught Harrison's glance. Should we? she radioed.

He answered with a tic of a shrug, spiked with eagerness.

She directed herself to Brian. "There's a bigger picture here," she began. "I mean beyond our interest in Michelangelo."

"Which is...?" Brian prompted.

She explained, starting with the ransacking of William Delaney's art collection and ending with the theft of a work that had once been part of it: the pen and ink drawing attributed to Vittorio da Lucca.

Brian brought a gloved finger to his chin. "So, your interest in the alleged Vittorio da Lucca drawing is a spin-off of your primary assignment."

"Exactly," Harrison answered. "In truth, I initiated—instigated!—particular interest in the drawing credited to Vittorio when I noticed its possible connection to Michelangelo's Cascina. We think there's a chance his drawing is a copy of one of Michelangelo's conceptualizations of the mural, the grand scheme of it. What we'd like to do is search for correlations between the drawing and the fragments, so to speak, of the master's work in progress. We'd prefer to do this openly, in your presence, but worry we may not be able to secure your absolute confidentiality."

Brian raised a brow. "This is terribly sinister. Come clean, you're not C.I.A., are you?" He smiled, his geniality touched with hauteur. "There have been threats, assaults—a murder," Harrison said quietly. He related the violent side of their story, left out of Erika's account. "Any breach in confidentiality could touch off further violence."

"I see," Brian replied solemnly. "But of course you can trust me." Erika reached in her bag for the copy of Fitch's stolen drawing.

She passed it to him.

Again, the raised brow. "Interesting," he said, non-committal. "The quality of this—well, one can hardly call it a print—is very poor, but of course you know that." He pulled over a chair from the adjacent table and sat beside them. "Fill me in, if you would. I've never heard of this Vittorio fellow, but then my knowledge is not encyclopedic."

"We know basically nothing," Erika admitted, "except that an unsigned drawing dated 1504 is credited to him on its bill of sale. We do hope to obtain more information in Florence."

"Have you tried Googling the man?"

"Unsuccessfully."

"Unlike my younger colleagues, I'm not of the opinion

that if it can't be Googled it doesn't exist. That said, I remain skeptical." He held the drawing at arm's length and cocked his head. "Although it does arouse curiosity, I'll give you that."

"The fact remains," Erika said, keying in to his interest, "even if this is a wild goose chase, the chase itself makes for a good story."

Brian lit up. "Publishable."

She smiled, shameless. "As a piece in *Art News*." She paused. "Quite possibly a more ambitious project, aimed at a broader audience."

"A book."

"Yes, I could see it. Of course we'd give you ample credit," she added, prostituting herself further.

"You're too kind."

"If you blow our cover, you'll see how kind we are," she replied, her smile subtle enough for varied interpretation.

He laughed, but not heartily. "I understand."

Harrison was staring at her as if she'd just executed a triple toe loop.

Brian handed her back the drawing. She placed it on the table between Harrison and herself. Instantly they were immersed in the task, hunched over the table, eyes flashing from the Vittorio to the drawings on display.

The first of the drawings on loan from the Ashmolean was a pen and ink depicting, by consensus, members of the Florentine cavalry pitted against Pisan infantrymen. The second was a black chalk sketch of a nude man helping another mount a horse.

Erika was the first to speak. Pointing at the first drawing: "What do you think? Look at Michelangelo's horse, this one here, it's not very well defined, but the positioning of the forelegs—see how they're crossed?—and the general attitude of the body"—she pointed at one of the horses in Vittorio's background—"isn't this the same horse, only in reverse? Do you see what I mean? Am I seeing it because I want to so badly?"

Brian leaned forward from behind, grasping Harrison's shoulder for support. "Not so farfetched," he commented, scrutinizing the drawings. He stood back up. "In fact, we have another Michelangelo drawing from the Ashmolean, 1503, 04, I'll show it to you in a bit, that portrays a horse at least one art historian has claimed is the same animal portrayed upside down in the Fall of Phaethon, circa 1533, by Raffaello da Montelupo. Indeed, this historian, Parker, proposes that Montelupo is the draughtsman of both works. I am not, shall we say, of this persuasion, but what this should suggest to you, Erika, is that you should feel comfortable about exploring your observations."

Erika nodded excitedly, not in response to Brian, but to her possible discovery. "Harrison?"

He laid his hand on hers, which was splayed against her notepad. "I see it, yes. I agree."

"Look at the posture of the heads."

"Uncanny. Yes."

She slipped her hand from under his so she could record the observation in her pad.

Excitement mounted as they pored over the series of drawings Brian subsequently displayed for them on the long easel, but it was not until a particular pair of them—one from the British Museum, one from the Ashmolean—were perched side by side, that they simultaneously made another significant observation, she the more breathless: "Look here, the figure on the horse, you can just about make him out!" She was pointing at the upper middle portion of the drawing owned by the British Museum, a crowded battle scene of overlapping shapes, the pen strokes so light, the shading so minimal it was hard to distinguish one form from another. "You see it?"

"The horseman—here," Harrison declared, overlapping her words, and pointing at a figure in the right foreground of the Vittorio. "The same—well, almost identical. We might not have spotted it on a reproduction."

"I don't think so, no." She scrutinized the melee a

moment more, then switched her attention to the other exhibited drawing, of three nude men, with another two emerging from the smudgy black chalk background. There were no discoveries there, but searching for them, the physicality of it, their brow-furrowing, adrenaline-soaring excitement was intense and consuming. At the peak of it, she felt a sudden regret for her mother, that her mother had never seized the opportunity to experience this kind of high for herself, her intelligence forever dedicated to maximizing her husband's ease in attaining his. This rush of regret broke the surface of her joy, but just as quickly was absorbed by it, the greater, more powerful force. In the end, with two strong correlations made between Michelangelo's studies and the Vittorio, she and Harrison felt more strongly about their theory.

Brian did not share their optimism. "My gut tells me Vittorio da Lucca never existed, and that your discoveries today are just subtle enough to suggest authenticity, as I believe they were meant to."

"In other words, it's too good to be true," Erika prompted. "Exactly."

"My gut tells me otherwise," she said amiably, her excitement not to be diminished.

Brian grinned. "Good for you, I admire your optimism. But you should work from the premise of doubt, of having to prove Vittorio da Lucca is not the invention of a very clever draughtsman—early twentieth century, I suspect." To Harrison, with a glint in his eye: "Perhaps an art historian like yourself."

"Everyone knows art historians are notoriously bad artists," Harrison said flatly.

Brian laughed. "As are museum curators. Seriously, though, I think if you recover the filched drawing, or come across any of this alleged sixteenth-century artist's other works, you should have them analyzed, and I don't mean cursorily."

"We're not babes in the wood," Harrison replied, bridling.

"Erika and I have seen our share of fake antiquities, and we're aware of a broad range of counterfeiting techniques. You can be sure we'll avail ourselves of every means of authentication. We know, for instance, that the ink in Michelangelo's day was made by boiling oak galls, or the excrescence of insects of the genus Cynips, with ferrosulfat. This was then mixed with gum Arabic, a combination of saccharine and glycoproteins, to control the ink's viscosity. The process took two to three weeks. The ink will be one of the first items we'll have analyzed."

"The age and composition of the drawing paper should also be determined," Brian submitted.

"We know that, too," Erika said, adding her ego to the mix. Finally chastened, Brian began, "I didn't mean to suggest..."

"That's okay, neither did we," Harrison jumped in, his boyish smile redemptive all around. "You've been a great help. We'll be asking for your guidance again, I'm sure. You must know the most experienced technicians in the field of documentation."

"I do, yes."

"And we'll be calling on you for your critique—I should say contribution—on material intended for publication," Erika reminded him.

"Absolutely. You must be sure to keep me updated on your...adventure."

After preparing the drawings for storage, Brian peeled off his archival gloves and extended his hand to Erika and Harrison in turn. He then excused himself, encouraging them to stay and chat as long as they liked.

They watched him walk off, the metal storage box held before him like a royal presentation.

"'Excrescence of insects'?" Erika softly pronounced. "I'm impressed. Truly."

"There's more where that came from, if you're interested."

"I'm sure there is."

They began putting away their notes, reviewing them as they did so. She felt a kind of mystical conspiracy between them, their faith in Vittorio's authenticity illuminated by Brian's skepticism. With it, a mischievous titillation, piquant as sexual tension, but with none of the pitfalls. In their sharing, he was largely responsible for the excitement this project brought her. As a lover, though, as this man's lover, she knew she would fall prey to her own impossible expectations and tip the balance between sharing and dependency: the endless nag to retain his affection.

She watched him as he tucked away the last of his notes into his briefcase. Studied his profile. Remembered the smell of his neck. Taunted herself with their passion, at the same time muting it, channeling her fever for him into a nobler sharing. She listened for the pestering earworm. Silence. She tried to chafe it into existence, testing herself. I can hardly hear you, sweetheart. Her brain would not catch the meter.

He snapped shut his briefcase and turned to her. He must have seen something in her eyes. "Regrets already?"

"I wasn't prepared."

"Neither was I."

"I want to...slow down."

"You want to stop."

"I want to—"

He touched his fingers to her lips. "Don't say it. I'm sorry." He took his hand away. "I want you to be comfortable with me."

"I am—very—and I want it to stay that way."

"I understand. I'll take your lead."

She smiled. "Thanks."

"Slow, slow," he said—crooned, almost.

Such tenderness in his features, she could hardly correct him.

* * *

They had originally planned to visit the Ashmolean that afternoon, but since Brian had eliminated the need to, they decided to take in the British Museum more fully and then drop by the Wallace Collection, where Harrison could view a little known painting by Gericault on exhibit.

They ended up spending more time than anticipated at the Wallace Collection, a national museum converted from an historic London townhouse, reminding them of the Frick Museum in New York City, another art venue once a home on the same order of magnificence, and, as they discovered, a favorite roaming place for both of them. They wondered if their paths had ever crossed; wanted, somehow, to believe they had.

They were starving by the time they were kicked out of the Wallace at 5:10, ten minutes past closing. Understandably, since they'd taken only one quick and early dining break: tea and scones at the British Museum café.

"Shall we pick out a restaurant? What are you in the mood for?" he asked.

"I don't know. I'm kind of beat. I'd just as soon order in."

"Room service."

"Yes—no. It's a rip-off."

"Good. It's decided then." Smiling, he set off for the hotel.

* * *

They chose her room only because it was her door they came to first.

He ordered poached salmon; she, fish and chips. A split of champagne to share. No desserts.

While they were waiting, they checked their emails. Nothing essential for her; one for him, a short but tantalizing message from his friend on the board of trustees at Art Loss Registry. He'd made a couple of "interesting discoveries" that he suggested they discuss over lunch the following week. He was hoping to meet "your Ms. Shawn."

"A turn of phrase," Harrison quickly explained. "All I did was mention we were working together."

It was the only uncomfortable moment of the evening. They sat across from each other at the table wheeled in with their dinners and talked about what they'd done that day, their findings, their impressions, trailing off with their plans for the next day, in Florence. When they at last bid each other good night, there was a graciousness about it, a gallantry. Not so much a shaking of hands, but a respectful brush, a leaning in, a nod, faces almost touching. As if last night had been a glitch in time, a break in the continuum. A lovely aberration.

* * *

Alone again, she performed her nightly rituals, sat for a while in the easy chair by the window and read the local newspaper, then crept into bed.

She felt good, purposeful about the next day's itinerary, the trip to Florence. She clicked off the light, the sharp little sound marking order in her life.

She lay on her back in the center of the bed, closed her eyes, stroked the space on either side of her, measuring her space, her right palm cruising over the barest lump in the surface, a fold in the mattress cover. She returned to it, caressing it more particularly, something fleshy about it, nodal, stimulating. She remembered the feel of him, the heightened insignificance of everything other than the feel of him...Harrison...Harry....

And then it flared up, vengefully, perhaps to silence her heart, hold her to her course—the notice of her father's death, chanced on one lazy Sunday morning as she was leafing through *the New York Times*. The summary was absolute and cold as death itself, except that nowhere was she named in the reckoning, as if she'd been airbrushed out of existence like an unwanted face in a photograph, and no invented excuse or pardon could ease her absence. She felt it now, rawly, as she did then.

She breathed deeply, forced herself to, the deep breathing easing her back to the pulse of being. As an exercise in concentration, she focused on one of Michelangelo's drawings, narrowing her scope to the barest outline of a horse, coaxing him into prominence with strokes of black chalk, adding dimensionality with inked cross-hatching and highlights of white, working on the figure as if it were her own shape she was creating. She stroked its smooth and solid flesh, felt it as she felt herself, down her arms, her sides, feeling her own dimensions, the presence of herself, drifting off to sleep in her own embrace.

CHAPTER 10

October at its gentlest, and in Florence!

It was a day to make one regret ever having to die, the sun illuminating the colors of the world to almost unbearable beauty. Flamboyant pinks and corals of flowers in the window boxes of shops along the Ponte Vecchio, muted in the Arno's translucent gray-blue. Pastel yellow of buildings, sienna of clay-tiled roofs, deep green of surrounding hills crisply delineated against clear azure, here and there tips of cypress trees breaking the line.

Blue-tinged black of her contoured skirt and unbuttoned jacket, pristine white of her tank top flashing as a playful breeze tossed at her lapels. In the worn cobblestones she detected subtle flecks of ocher, molten purple, pink, and remembered discovering the flecks of hazel in Harrison's dark brown eyes, feeling a kind of proprietary glee, as if she'd been the only one ever to have come close enough to notice. She studied the tops of her espadrilles and smiled at her naiveté.

"What?" he said, ever observant.

She looked up. "Nothing. Only what a lovely day."

"Despite the disappointment?—I mean at the Uffizi, no hidden images emerging from the Michelangelo."

"That's okay. We were spoiled by the British Museum. We expected too much."

"I suppose," he said.

"But I loved walking around the galleries, seeing the Botticellis again, the Caravaggios, this time with your astute commentary!"

"You're sufficiently enlightened, then," he gibed. "Well, here we are."

They'd arrived at the Accademia Gallery, Via Ricasoli, home of Michelangelo's *David*, the original, the real thing. On her only visit to Florence, the blink of an eye on a post-college whirlwind tour of Europe, she'd missed seeing the sculpture because the gallery was closed on Mondays, the one tour day allotted to the City. This time she was determined to see it, and it looked as though Harrison was determined to see it with her. Together they had hustled the languorous Grand Hotel Villa Medici attendant through check-in and its more celeritous manager to drum up museum ticket vouchers. Without further ado—never mind ringing for the bellhop, they'd find their way—they tossed their bags into their adjoining rooms, she gasping at its elegance, he immune, then dashed off to the Uffizi with barely three sips of the hotel's complimentary latte—heavenly, sinful not to sit and savor over—under their belts. All this to give them time to fit David and at least an exquisite pretense of a leisurely tour of Florence into their already challenged itinerary.

"Shall we?" he asked, ushering her toward the gallery's entry checkpoint.

She knew the layout from guidebook descriptions, knew that *David* was situated in a "beautifully lit Tribune," a vaulted recess at the far end of the Galleria dei Prigioni, and that on either side of this long corridor striking unfinished sculptures by Michelangelo were displayed, including the controversial *Pieta da Palestrina*, ascription to the master disputed. She'd seen reproductions of *David* in public squares and on sale in museum shops. His form was as ubiquitous as the Statue of Liberty's.

She thought, therefore, as she approached the threshold of the hall, that she was prepared for the sight of him. She was not. His sheer size, colossal, impossible to have imagined, at the same time wrenchingly human, the stance casual, tensed, vulnerability captured in the slightly odd proportions: largish head and torso—evoking newness, innocence? Irrelevant, the debate over whether this was sculptor's error or intention! She felt the tears well. Impatient, she wiped them away, clearing her vision. She did not believe in a personal god, nature was all, and wondrous in itself, but this statue, pinnacled at the nexus of life and art, was an absolute in itself, stirring an old yearning to worship. She walked toward him, Harrison by her side, his closeness seeming to breathe life into the marble.

She reached up, stroked the carved right foot with her fingertips, then brought them to her lips.

"This is what the devout do at St. Peter's Basilica in Rome," Harrison said.

"I know that. You think I'm hokey, don't you?"

"I think you're lovely."

She knew her memory of *David* would forever be stroked by those words. "That's sweet of you," she said in a sisterly fashion, covering up. "And thanks for helping make this happen. If it weren't for you—"

"Please. No keynote address. Segnor Depoli's waiting for us." She glanced at her watch: 1:35. Already five minutes late.

Wasting no time, they paid brief homage to the Michelangelos en route to the exit, then hurried off to the Via della Scala, and the Corelli Gallery, where they were scheduled to meet its proprietor.

Mario Depoli was every bit as compact and lively as his stick-shift Renault. "I never tire of seeing our countryside," he declared ebulliently, punctuating this with a wave of both hands, leaving the steering wheel momentarily untended, the vehicle zipping along the SR408 like a puppy off its leash. "*Per favore,* would you pass me another slice of the pecorino?" he asked Harrison in the rear seat, increasing the excitement by turning to address him directly. "*Grazie*," he sang, as Harrison pressed the cheese into his hand with the efficiency of a relay racer, at the same time delicately cautioning: "The road, Mario, the road."

"It's so good of you to drive us!" Erika burst out, sitting beside Mario and hoping to engage his focus if not on the road in front of him, at least on something nearer to it. With a flourish she tore another wedge from the orange she'd been working on.

Mario polished off the cheese and wiped his fingers on the cloth napkin in his lap. "This is my pleasure, *signorina*. I have not been to the Fabbri estate in many weeks, and it is always a treat. I only wish my wife could have accompanied us, but she is having to watch over the shop today. The orange, it is to your liking?"

"Delicious, the juiciest navel orange I've ever had."

"You are just on time, arriving in October. This orange is only available from now through May. You must return in December to enjoy the moro orange, with the juice of deep red. Perhaps my wife will be available then, too." He smiled merrily, his eyes on the road, and within. "'Delicious,' yes. A lovely word." He breathed deeply, as if smelling it. "My wife, I have not told you, is the owner of a superior wine and cheese shop."

"Then we have her to thank for the cornucopia of goodies back there," Erika said.

"Which are going fast," Harrison joined in. "You shouldn't have left me in charge—what is this cheese, semi-firm, wrapped in prosciutto?"

"Provolone," Mario replied. "Smoky sweet, the best on the market. My wife carries only the best. In wines, too. Her most select are from the Fabbri vineyards. Signore Gian Fabbri is the proprietor of an award-winning wine estate. In fact, his son Aldo is his—how do you guys say—ah, sales rep. He comes around the shop from time to time. A nice young man, maybe a little irresponsible. Look at me, I sound like an old man—

mamma mia, I am an old man!" He gave a shrug of cheerful resignation. "So you see, our association with the Fabbri family extends beyond the world of art. But of course I would say pleasing the palate is an art in itself. Yes?"

"Yes, except your wife didn't have to go to the trouble of pleasing our palates," Erika suggested.

"She thought we would not care to stop for lunch. Also, she packs me a basket of food if I am going around the corner to buy a newspaper."

"Well, thank her for us, anyway," Harrison said, with a laugh. "This is great."

"She will be happy for your enjoyment."

Mario maneuvered a bend in the road, and their breaths caught in unison. "I always expect this view," Mario said, "but it is always a surprise."

Like a Fragonard painting, the scene was complete in itself, yet seemed to call for a narrative. A stone villa arose in the distance, magnificent, but so in keeping with the landscape as to appear at ease in it, unimposing. Farther off lay the rolling hills of Tuscany, holding the building in visual embrace.

The broad drive to the villa was paved in cobblestones and lined with cypress trees spiraling to the clouds. On stone plinths, busts of Roman senators and ancient deities were stationed at intervals along the tree line, like sentinels. Sculpted in such divergent styles and temperaments and purposely angled to face every which way, a tongue-in-cheek humor appeared to be aimed at human posturing. Erika smiled to herself.

Mario, creeping at a snail's pace for a change, spotted the smile. "You get it, I see. Signora Fabbri was at first against it, but in the end she saw that even her anger was part of the joke and gave in to her husband. We take ourselves too seriously, yes?" He uttered a confirmatory grunt in answer.

The cobblestone drive continued past the end of the tree line, forking at the head of a courtyard studded with intriguing statuary and sweeping past it on either side. Mario tooled up the left path, Erika craning her neck to keep the courtyard in sight for as long as possible.

"Time enough to see all," Mario assured her as he pulled up alongside a dark green Maserati coupe. He turned off the engine.

As they stepped from the car, a figure emerged from behind the foliage at the rear of the estate house. "I thought I heard you sputtering up the drive—hello there!"

Erika raised a hand in greeting. Their welcoming party was a tall, lean man she guessed was in his mid-thirties, a composite of Mediterranean and Madison Avenue: hair, dark and thick, tastefully salon-touched with deep golden highlights; attire, Ivy League except for highly polished black leather shoes. His stride was long but markedly slow, as if he wanted either to slay them with his strikingly good looks or gently ease them into his aura.

"Aldo Fabbri," he said, offering his hand to Erika as if it were a gift, as he looked her up and down. "Charming," he concluded.

Mario completed the introductions, and Aldo led his guests up a gentle incline and around back, to a veranda poised on the crest of the estate, where a party of three awaited them, all eyes trained in their direction. They were seated around a glass and wrought-iron table. Four full bottles of wine stood in the center of the table, about a dozen glistening wineglasses alongside them.

"My family," Aldo declared, on approach, as the only man at the table jumped to his feet. "My father, Gian, mother, Maria, and my *bella nonna*—grandma." He bent to plant a kiss on her cheek. The woman, a wizened archetype of Aldo, gave Erika much the same once-over as he had. "*E il tuo fidanzata quello?*" she eagerly directed at him.

"*Sfortunatamente, no, nonna,*" Aldo replied through a baritone laugh. "She asked if you were my fiancée," he said, responding to Erika's puzzled look. "Don't be alarmed, she asks that of every pretty young woman loitering anywhere near."

"Never mind that," Gian advised Erika, extending his hand to her. "My son's a confirmed bachelor, and my mother-in-law means to badger him into conversion. We're delighted to meet you, Miss Shawn—may I call you Erika?" His hand-shake was every bit as warm and lively as his demeanor.

"Please—and thanks for having us over, especially on such short notice."

Her gratitude was waved off, and they shook hands all around.

As they pulled up chairs around the table, Erika angled hers so she could take in the full panorama stretching before them, the rows upon rows of grapevines laid out as flawlessly as computer-generated art—infinite, but for the Tuscany hills.

"We like to preview our wines before releasing them to the public," Gian declared. "You'll of course join us?" He proceeded to uncork one of the wine bottles as Aldo reached for another. "This one's our signature—Chianti Classico riserva, made from the sangiovese grape. We let our chief steward make the selections on accompanying hors d'oeuvres; he has an incredibly sensitive palate. He should be along any minute."

Harrison, along with Mario, who appeared to know the drill, graciously accepted. Erika excused herself. "I want to be perfectly clear-headed when I study the Vittorios," she said.

"Exactly why you must indulge, my dear!" Aldo's mother protested. "Wine opens your mind for the immediacy of experience!" Erika smiled.

"I'm perfectly serious. Wine makes the senses more acute. Admittedly, too much wine and they become fuzzy. There's a fine line."

"Well then, I will have a taste," Erika cheerfully yielded. "Brava on foisting your theories on the woman," Aldo commented to his mother. He was sitting next to Erika,. He gave her knee a friendly stroke, then went back to uncorking the third bottle.

Harrison, on her other side, made a point of resting his arm on the back of her chair.

The steward emerged from the interior of the house wheeling a cartful of meat and cheese delicacies, along with a supply of bottled water.

During the course of the wine-tasting—what with all the "buono!s" and "magnifico!"s, Erika had a sip or two from each of Harrison's glasses—the history of the Vittorio da Lucca folder was recounted. "It has been in the Fabbri family's possession since 1505," Gian informed them. "You see, my forebears owned a boarding house in Florence on what has since been named Via Raffaele, and from the chits enclosed in the folder, it appears that Vittorio da Lucca rented a room from them in 1504 but was quite negligent in his weekly payments. When he died in1505, there was a sizable sum outstanding on his account, and the folder, which included a number of his drawings, was assigned to the Fabbris to cover the debt."

Erika and Harrison exchanged grateful looks.

"What?" Aldo prodded.

"Vittorio da Lucca's existence was questioned by our contact in London," Harrison supplied. "What we've just heard surely counters that."

A mildly explosive statement in Italian issued from Grandma. "*Va bene, nonna,*" Aldo soothed. To Harrison: "She thinks I dissed my heritage by studying in Oxford, therefore she hates everything English. In fact, she understands every word we're saying, but you won't catch her admitting it"—turning to her—"*eh, nonna?*"

His grandmother raised her wineglass in answer, drawing an adoring laugh from her relatives.

Gian suggested his son give Erika and Harrison a tour of the family's art collection rather than taking them directly to the folder of drawings. "Keep in mind," he added with a touch of pride, "the Vittorio portfolio has been preserved virtually intact since it has been in the family's possession. Except for one drawing, sold in 1933 to the Corelli Gallery, when my parents were feeling the impact of the Great Depression. *Sfortunatamente*, it was the most detailed drawing of all," he added with a touch of remorse. "I would have liked to have returned it to our collection, but I never pursued the matter."

"Did you know the Vittorio portfolio was a gift to me?" Aldo animatedly put forth, overlapping his father's words. "My reward when I got straight A's in third grade. When it comes to gift-giving, my parents' currency is art. The highest function of cash, they believe, is acquiring items that by their very nature devalue it. A somewhat convoluted, but charming way of thinking, yes?" He brought his wineglass to his lips; drained it. "Ah, squisito, our best Chardonnay yet. Good, then we'll excuse ourselves and"—he rose quickly to his feet —"Shall we?" He offered Erika his hand in assistance, and she accepted it rather than make a political point. As she stood, Harrison, not to be outdone, cupped her elbow and pressed it upward, further casting her as the helpless female.

Aldo began their tour by leading them round to the courtyard, a setting that seemed to spring out of the romantic imagination. At one end, a long pergola with leafy vines sheltered a carved stone bench forming a perfect harbor for whispering endearments or reading leatherbound books. At its center, a marble fountain, with tendrils of groundcover ambling up its base, showered on a playful commune of dolphins, water nymphs, and river gods. "An example of Valerio Cioli's neo-paganism, mid-sixteenth century," Aldo informed his visitors, as they stood near, reaching into the spray to be nearer still. "Valerio was in Raffaello da Montelupa's workshop, as you may know, and he, in turn, was a pupil of Michelangelo. This is the only reproduction—I should say replication—on the premises," he quickly added, as if they needed to be reassured. "All else is as originally conceived."

They entered the building by way of the wrought-iron and glass double front door, Aldo ushering Erika through with a hand on her shoulder, keeping it there until she sidled out of reach.

The main room was furnished with oversized tapestry sofas and wing-backed chairs, heavy oak tables with ornately carved legs, Tiffany lamps and medieval sconces. Grand, but homey. A more modest décor would have been lost in this virtual museum of fine art, with its vaulted ceilings and vast floor space.

The art on display spanned the ages, representing a great olio of genres and styles. Even so, there seemed to be a vital force uniting the collection, like a wildly diverse group of individuals coming together to celebrate a family reunion. Breughel, Titian, Hopper, and Monet shared one wall, while Duchamps, Caravaggio, and Klimt shared another. On one side table, a series of Matisse busts were aligned with a heraldic lion by Donatello and a small statue of Dante by Pietro Lombardo. Above them hung two exquisite damasks, one of Botticelli's graceful nudes, the other of Redon's pristine flower arrangements.

A sweeping view of the Fabbri vineyards was the subject of a vivid mosaic of inlaid stones above the room's marble fireplace. The large open window along the same plane framed the view of that same landscape in the real world, their juxtaposition creating the effect of a Magritte painting.

"The mosaic was installed in 1901 by the Ugolini firm," Aldo said, brushing an open hand across its surface as if he were caressing a woman. "Indisputably the best Intarsia craftsmen in the world." His focus skidded off Harrison and settled on Erika.

"Yes, beautiful," Harrison declared somewhat acidly.

"Isn't it," Erika mused, deflecting from Harrison's air of contention by pretending not to have noticed it. She needed to break up their tableau.

She was suddenly impatient to get to the Vittorio drawings, to feel the kind of joyful immersion she'd experienced at the British Museum. With an agreeable smile forcing the men into a détente, she hurried off to the arched entryway to the next room, thereby turning the remainder of their leisurely tour into a jaunty walk-through.

The rooms shared by the family were eclectic, linked only by the Fabbris' refined yet expansive taste. In sharp contrast, Aldo's suite was a distillation of personal taste from the collective. The furnishings were sleek and contemporary; the art, varied but thematic photography.

The suite was a surprise at the top of an ornate winding staircase. The walls of the anteroom were painted eggshell white, perfect ground for the black and white framed photographs on exhibit.

"What a wonderful collection," Erika commented, her focus darting from one image to another.

"Hard to take it all in at a glance," Harrison added, enthusiastic, if a bit begrudgingly.

In one photograph a small boy on tip-toes was reaching for the string of a balloon floating just out of reach, the expression on his face a combination of surprise and despair. In another, a bloody sneaker lay next to a fallen bicycle, its front wheel twisted out of alignment, the bright sunlight glinting off its fender. In another, a man and a woman were passing each other on a lonely thoroughfare, their looks locked in mutual curiosity, their long strides about to part them forever.

"All so different," Erika said, "but in all, a sense of the unexpected, of change." She turned to Harrison. "You agree?"

He nodded. "The sense of the transitory nature of things—of endings. Sudden."

"Capricious," Aldo added. "I was inspired by the sand paintings of the Tibetan Buddhists, the way they sweep away in an instant their intricately designed mandalas, imaginary palaces to contemplate during meditation. Of course my inspiration stops at their idea of transience. When it comes to designs, theirs are prescribed. The subjects of my photographs are not. Then, too, the sand art demonstrates that all things are ephemeral except the eternal Buddha nature. My photographs have no such religious overtones. Whatever is is, and

153

then is gone." He snapped his fingers. "Poof."

"Amazing," Erika remarked, "that you set about to collect works with a particular philosophy in mind. I would think this would be restricting, but it doesn't seem to have been for you. How many photographers are represented?"

Aldo laughed, grasping her hand. "Only one. I'm it."

"Really!"

"Excellent," Harrison allowed, with a fixed smile.

They moved to the bedroom, Aldo keeping hold of Erika's hand as if they were old chums.

The room was the most casual one on the tour—books piled on the floor in front of a stuffed bookcase, platform bed with rumpled spread, towering chest of drawers, massive desk graced by computer and printer, white leather desk chair draped with gray throw. Over the desk, unframed black and white photographs lined two wall shelves. All the photos contained red-ink markings indicating areas to be deleted or enlarged, contrast heightened or softened.

"My darkroom," Aldo announced, gesturing toward a door on the far side of the room with the hand holding Erika's. "Have a look." He drew her toward it, dropping her hand in order to open the door halfway.

She could tell by the expression on his face, a sudden drawing inward, that this was his sanctuary, that she and Harrison would not be invited in. As he held the door open for them, she peered in over his extended arm, Harrison looking over her shoulder.

The floor, the walls, the ceiling, the cabinets were pristine white. Processing sink, wash stations, vent hood: steel gray. The labyrinth of shiny copper pipes below the equipment looked like it had come straight out of the pages of Dr. Seuss.

"My workplace," Aldo said, closing the door gently, but firmly. Erika realized up to now she'd envisioned Aldo only in the company of others, strutting his stuff. Suddenly she saw him as a solitary soul, a maverick in an age of digital photography, carefully lifting his prepared paper from its primordial bath, studying one of his images as it emerged, remembering it at its conception, maybe sadly. It made him more likeable, somehow. "It must feel magical, seeing your work come to life," she said.

Aldo grinned. "You sound like a little girl. But yes, I suppose it does."

"I feel a song coming on," Harrison said dryly.

Aldo laughed, restrained. "Then I say let's get down to business." He sidled past Harrison to get to his chest of drawers. He pulled open the bottom drawer, removed a layer of T-shirts, and heaped them alongside the chest. "Here we are," he said, carefully extracting a large, ancient-looking folder from its bed of white linens. "Our *pieces de resistance*. In their original housing." He placed the folder on his desk. "For your pleasure."

Erika flashed a knowing smile at Harrison. Aldo balked. "What is it?"

Her smile broadened. "I was thinking of the methods of conservation at The British Museum—the sealed containers, the climate control, the white gloves. Your storage facilities would cause minor heart attacks."

"You think if I kept my windows shut and vacuum-packed these drawings they would last forever?" he asked, half-teasing. "Those Brits—and for that matter you Americans —believe our glorious doodles can last for all eternity. Am I right? Funny, we Italians have more of a sense of history than you people, but we seem to know that at a certain point there'll be no trace of us, that the earth will no longer exist, that eternity exists in the now—damn, I'm preaching aren't I?"

"To the choir," Harrison said. "We're not as anal retentive as you think. Besides, what about the Uffizi? I'd say it's been pretty well—anglicized?"

"Ah, but you see, conservation methods were implemented there as a result of the damage caused by the great

Arno flood of 1961. The goal was to prevent a repeat of that tragedy—to extend the lives of our art treasures, not mummify them. The difference can be summed up in a word: hubris."

"Admit it, Aldo," Harrison said. "You've set up a straw man so your philosophy can stand out in relief."

Aldo smiled. "Well, maybe I've exaggerated our differences, but only to make a point. There are degrees, maybe not measurable, but real enough, in the way we think about art—about life in general. In the grand scheme of things we Italians take ourselves less seriously."

"You mean less puritanically," Erika clarified, as if Aldo needed her help. "I see what you're saying."

"With less of a religious zealotry, yes," Aldo said. "Thank you."

"Doesn't Italy embrace Catholicism?" Harrison challenged.

"A country's religion on record is different from its Zeitgeist," Aldo genially shot back, with a collegial glance at Erika.

"What about your grandmother, wouldn't she object to this characterization of yours?" Erika asked a bit sharply, to show Harrison she was not colluding with his opponent.

"My grandmother?" Aldo asked, throwing her a puzzled look.

"Your grandmother wants to see you married," Harrison supplied. "Isn't there a religious component to this wish?"

Aldo raised a brow, seeing the light. "Nothing to do with religion. She wants great-grandchildren. She doesn't give a fig for the eternal vows. She's afraid if I had children out of wedlock they'd be less accessible to her. Either of you married?"—he glanced at Erika's naked ring finger—"or ever been?"

"No," Erika said, with a declarative punch. Aldo turned to Harrison. "You?"

"Final stage of divorce." Equally incisive.

"So, I take it, Harrison, my friend, commitment isn't exactly your bag either."

"I wouldn't jump to conclusions."

Aldo favored Erika with a glance of approval. "The fact is, how can we commit to one woman with so many attractive ones out there?"

"An honest man," Erika mumbled. Harrison spun to face her. "What?"

"Honest—admitting you're hunters by nature."

Aldo grinned. "It's built into our hard drive, what can we do?"

"Upgrade our software," Harrison shot back, still focused on Erika.

"You know," she said coolly, belying her body flush, "we came a long way to see these drawings." She gestured toward the folder. "I don't know what we're waiting for."

Aldo gave her a genteel version of the smarmy look. "Have you ever kept a treat from yourself in order to increase the ultimate pleasure?"

"I wouldn't equate a Snickers bar with a sixteenth-century drawing," she said, disdaining the innuendo.

Aldo lay open the folder on his desk and picked up the scraps of paper covering the first drawing. A sudden breeze from the vineyards, fruit-scented and laden with indigenous micro-matter, fluttered the drawings, altering them forever, at least so it seemed to Erika, their talk of conservation so fresh in her mind. The thought of exposure to the elements was at once liberating and alarming. Her breath quickened with excitement, and she sidled closer to Harrison to share this moment with him: her colleague.

"We'll need another chair," Aldo said. "I'll get one—"

"No, please," Harrison protested. "Standing gives us a good perspective." He turned to Erika, his demeanor softened by her initiative. "Okay with you?"

"Yes." Their arms were in contact. For an instant they

were alone in the room.

"These are the chits my father was talking about," Aldo said, riffling through the papers he was holding. He set them aside. "Later." He pulled the top two drawings from the pile and laid them to the right and left of the one below. All three were done with pen and brown ink. "Don't be afraid to handle them. Gloves not required. You mind if I retreat to my darkroom for a couple of minutes?"

Erika could hardly pull her attention from the drawings. "Go ahead, we're fine."

Aldo opened the door to his private domain. "Any questions, you know where to find me."

The door clicked shut.

"Are you thinking what I'm thinking?" she asked.

Harrison kissed the top of her head. "Yes."

"No, I mean—"

"I know what you mean."

"The one in the middle is different."

"Yes. How?"

She smiled. "The teacher again."

"So tell me, how?"

The possibility made her tremble. She leaned against him. "It can't be."

"It might be."

They were silent. Studying the drawings. Holding hands, not knowing who was the first to have reached out for the other.

The drawing on the left was of a male nude standing alongside a Greek column. Although the model's stance was clearly relaxed, weight bearing on left foot, hip thrust out, hand resting on hip, its depiction was not quite credible. "His back seems too stiff to have caused the pronounced jut of the hip," Erika said. "It's a competent figure drawing, very good, really, just not remarkable."

"Good, yes, but as inert as the column. How about the one on the right?"

The drawing was of the rear view of a male figure, arms raised, face in profile, nude except for a cloth draped about the waist. "This one has more fluidity, I think, and, well, more weight, maybe because of the shading."

"He look familiar?" Deviltry in his voice. "Yes, actually —oh!"

"Exactly."

"In the background of the 'Bathers' scene—the one holding the pole!"

"Yup."

"Only here, no pole." She giggled out of sheer excitement.

Together their attention rested on the middle drawing, another male nude, this one twisted sideways, as if someone behind him had just called out to him. "It's in a class by itself, isn't it," she said, with a sense of relief, as if by mutual consent they'd remained silent about this one until they'd talked about the others, as a kind of initiation rite. "The energy stems more from the core here, the outline of the figure determined by the inner mass. The energy is diffuse in the other sketches." She looked from one drawing to another. "The shading—the cross-hatching we talked about—doesn't it seem, well, more self-assured in the...middle one?"

He laughed. "Go ahead say the word, it won't bite you."

"Michelangelo. There. So you really think it might be? Seriously?"

He gripped her hand more tightly. "Seriously."

"What would be the explanation, then? That the drawing was put in the wrong folder in Michelangelo's studio? An honest, or intentional, mistake?"

"Or a gift from Michelangelo to Vittorio." He shrugged. "Another conjecture."

"Based on the primary conjecture."

"Yes, that the drawing is Michelangelo's."

She smiled. "A pretty off-the-wall conjecture." Grinning: "That's what they told Copernicus."

"Good thing he didn't listen to them." She could feel the giddiness rise between them, like a spray of nitrous oxide. "We haven't looked at the other drawings," she half-admonished, overcompensating. "Let's do it."

She felt another surge of adrenaline as they set aside the drawings already seen in order to reveal the others, peeling off each from the rest with the meticulousness required in an operating room, as if they were delicate layers of a living organ.

They agreed that although there was a range of artistry and confidence in the drawings, eleven in all, including two that were on reverse sides of the paper, there was only one that bore the imprint of mastery. They studied it again, coming to the same conclusion.

She took a deep breath. "I'm about to go out on a limb," she warned.

"Go on. I'm with you."

"Well, if one Michelangelo was placed, or misplaced, among the Vittorios, isn't it possible that two...?" She watched him complete the thought, the boyish smile breaking out: disbelieving, yet wanting to believe. "I mean, why not? When you get down to it, isn't even the very best available photocopy of the stolen drawing of poor quality? The Michelangelo trademark wouldn't exactly have popped out at us, would it? Plus the very thought that it was one of Michelangelo's would have been preposterous to us until now"—she pointed to the drawing under discussion— "now that we've seen this!"

"It's tempting to go along with you," he said, stroking his chin, as if a professorial gesture would tamp down his excitement. "But given the varying degrees of skill demonstrated by these drawings, I'd say that in all probability when Vittorio was directly copying a Michelangelo drawing or cartoon, he was at his best."

"You're saying even the drawing in front of us—the middle one—is a Vittorio, just a really, really good one?"

"Probably."

"You're reneging."

"I'm not. I'm only suggesting we don't get carried away."

"That's better." She smiled, he reacting in kind. "Okay, let's get Aldo. He should know what he's got here. Correction. Might have here." She tapped on the darkroom door. "Aldo, can you come out?"

Aldo instantly responded, his consternation apparent as the door opened. "Anything wrong?"

"No, no, everything's fine—more than fine."

Harrison raised a hand. "Please, finish what you were doing."

"Never finished, always a work in progress." Without taking his eyes off Erika, he reached back and shut the door.

"We need to show you something," she said quickly, scooting back to the desk, where she directed his attention to the drawing singled out. Without fanfare: "It may be a Michelangelo."

"Really?" Surprised, but not jackpot-worthy.

"Before we go on," Erika said, "you should know, first, the drawing your parents sold from this folder in 1933 has recently been stolen from its present owner, and second, our interest in Vittorio da Lucca is part of a larger investigation, involving the recovery of an entire art collection. Without going into details, I must tell you, anything we discuss here is to be regarded as highly confidential. A leak could hurt our chances of recovering the drawing and the collection at large, as well as increase our personal risk."

"I understand absolutely," Aldo breezily assured her. "On another tack, I confess I haven't studied the drawings very closely, probably out of residual embarrassment. When I was given them at the age of ten, I'm sure I lacked the balls to deal with a bunch of pictures of naked men." He smiled, pleased with himself. "However, they're looking better and better. Did you turn over the sheets of paper, check for additional drawings?"

"Very cautiously," Erika said. "We sort of bent over and peered underneath as we set each aside. We tried to leave as few fingerprints on them as possible. We were afraid of accidentally marring the paper. We saw two more drawings, neither very notable."

"Anything on the back of my potential Michelangelo?" He brushed the edge of it with his thumb.

"We were especially respectful of this one," she said, trying to project her caution onto him. "But no—only a single curved line, very fine, like a slip of the pen."

"Come on," Aldo said carelessly, "life is short, give it a whirl." Baiting her, almost, he whisked the paper over. "Let's take a closer look."

She could hear herself and Harrison suck in air as the drawing came into contact with the one below it. On a visceral level, she saw the drawings abrading each other like strips of sandpaper.

"They're done in ink, not chalk," Aldo teased, reading her mind.

He cocked his head. "Look at this."

There was a faint line of script in the upper left corner. "I see it," she said, amazed. "We missed it." She glanced at Harrison to confirm their shared oversight, he nodding in return.

"The price of caution," Aldo gently chided.

"The curved line we did see seems to stem from the last letter," she said, her interest in the discovery overriding any inclination to self-recriminate. "It sort of falls from it, a little sadly, I think. Can you make out the text?"

"P-r-o-s," Aldo spelled.

"*Prostrato*," Harrison said quietly. "*Prostrato ai tuoi piedi* —"

"—*mi lamento e piango*," Aldo finished.

They were quiet, watchful, as if more words, long dormant, might stir from the page.

"Your pronunciation is very good," Aldo said at last.

"Not really," Harrison said, "but thanks. Frankly, I'm

dumbfounded." He turned to Erika. "Did you know Michelangelo wrote poetry?"

"Yes, but I never studied it."

"This line, right here, is very close to one of his published lines." Aldo's brow shot up. "You have a photographic memory?"

"Hardly. I have a book of his poetry—English translation below the Italian. I actually spent a few hours studying it before this trip, to bone up on my Italian."

"How apropos," Aldo remarked.

"That was the idea. There's a line—I remember the English—'Prostrate upon the ground, I lament and weep.' This version reads 'At your feet, I lament and weep.' I'm thinking this may have been written before the final draft, and that Michelangelo, knowing his love was unreturned, gave Vittorio the drawing sheet containing these words of anguish."

"Or maybe he simply knew Vittorio was dying," Erika suggested. "Of course—yes!" Harrison exclaimed.

"Do you know when the poem was written?" she probed. "Does the time frame jibe?"

"Great question. The poem was written about 1504. Perfect timing, in fact. Which is probably why the poem stuck in my mind."

"Not that I wouldn't be thrilled if it were so," Aldo blandly put in, "but aren't we attributing all this passion a bit prematurely?"

"Not necessarily," Harrison replied. "Michelangelo's sexual orientation was obscured when his grand nephew published his poetry with the gender of pronouns changed. They were only switched back in the late nineteenth century, when Addington Symonds published his biography of Michelangelo."

"Thank you, but I was aware of Michelangelo's homoeroticism. I was merely suggesting you were jumping the gun with this particular example of it."

"I see your point, and of course Erika and I would never

put forward our ideas before they were fully researched. I hope you understand that."

"I do now."

"Actually," Harrison went on, "ruling Michelangelo's handwriting in or out will be pretty much conclusive, given the refinements of the science. The grapheme, the smallest part of a letter and unique to its user, is examined under the microscope, and either validates or refutes a claim to authorship. Michelangelo's will be an interesting case because he consciously changed his handwriting from Gothic to Humanistic around 1500, and signs of this transition should be in evidence. It will be a more daunting task to establish, with the same degree of certainty, the authorship of the drawing."

Aldo laughed. "You try to sound objective, but your words give you away. You're not hoping for a miracle, you're counting on it."

After a reflective pause, "You're right," Harrison said. "I should be careful of that."

"No you shouldn't," Erika firmly objected. "You haven't allowed your enthusiasm to cloud your judgment, not for a minute!"

"What an advocate you have here, my friend," Aldo declared. He patted Erika's shoulder, delaying withdrawal with a languorous sweep down her back. "You're not in any way implying that a member of the Fabbri family, living or dead, would have been party to anything...untoward?" he asked, with a mischievous smile.

"It never entered my mind," Harrison emphatically denied. "I'm only withholding judgment until we have the drawing—and handwriting—analyzed. There's always a possibility, however remote, that both the drawing and handwriting are Vittorio's, and that he intended to pass off one of his own best works as the master's, for cash or favors, his death depriving him of the opportunity."

"Which reminds me," Erika declared, "we haven't looked at these." She gestured at the small pile of chits. "If Vittorio's handwriting, maybe even his signature, is in evidence here, I bet we could—I mean an expert could—rule out Vittorio as a forger."

"Smart girl!" Aldo commended. "Or stupid of us boys not to have thought of it."

"We're not competing for a prize," Erika said impatiently. "Maybe we are," Aldo suggested with a sexually nuanced wink, although once again, his sunny flair of urbanity seemed to warrant forbearance. He reached for the chits; thumbed through them. "It looks like these are all jottings from the landlord, but I'll hand them over to the experts along with the rest of the material."

"Are you familiar with accredited antiquities experts?" Erika asked pointedly, the matter too critical to pussyfoot around. "There are so many factors to consider—age and origin of the paper, ink constituents, handwriting, not to mention the style and form of the drawing itself. We can research this for you and recommend—"

"I'm sure you can," Aldo amiably cut in, "but I think I can scare up a few experts on my own. I do have my connections—friends— at the Uffizi." He started to put his folder in order. "And I will read them the riot act regarding secrecy. I promise to let you know the results of the research as soon as they're in." He gave her shoulder a brisk rub in the manner of an athletic coach.

Harrison cleared his throat. "You think we could take a couple of photos? Just to have as points of reference, you understand."

"I don't see why not. Let's see your camera."

Harrison took his micro point-and-shoot from his pants pocket. "Questo e una merda," Aldo commented dryly. "We'll use my camera." He smiled. "You look surprised. I'm not a complete retro nerd, you know. I prefer the alchemy of liquids for black and white, but for color photography I go for the resolution of digital, and for that I've got state of the art Canon. I can print you up a set of photos you can take with you today, or I can take a little more time with dimensions and lighting and FedEx the lot to you in a day or two.

Your call."

They chose the latter. Erika gave him her card listing the *Art News* address.

Aldo tucked the card in the portfolio. "Good. Now we can have a drink, unwind before dinner." To their look of half surprise, half demurral: "And I won't take no for an answer. Later, after dinner, you should have a taste of our nightlife. I'll take you to my favorite haunt, not far from here. It will be a nice break from your academic marathon."

Erika was game, but Harrison argued this would be an imposition on Mario, who surely would want to get back to his wife by dinner time.

"Mario's a big boy," Aldo rebutted. "He can drive back whenever he likes. I'll drive you two back to Florence myself, no problem. My pleasure, in fact."

"It would be rude to ask Mario to make the trip alone," Harrison said, standing firm. "Erika?"

A challenge as much as a question.

"You go then," Aldo suggested, leaping into the pause. "I'll drive Erika back after I show her the sights."

"Fine!"

"I think I should go back with Mario, too," Erika said, miffed at being third in line to decide her fate.

"No, that's okay, you stay," Harrison countered.

What was this, his idea of a loyalty test, one he was hoping she'd flunk, allowing him to trot guiltlessly back to his uncluttered life?

"Yes, I think I will," she answered, with overdone insouciance. "Sounds like fun, Aldo." Good. She'd take this opportunity to take back her uncluttered life.

* * *

"That was truly excellent spaghetti marinara," Erika claimed, so neutral she sounded didactic. She and Aldo had just enjoyed a leisurely dinner wheeled in to his suite, and she realized, as he was reaching for her hand across the small table, that she had encouraged the gesture with her purposeful flirting. She'd meant to jumpstart her old freedom of detachment, the carefree thrills and spills of sexual play. Instead, she was trapped in her own game. "You have a great cook," she said, rising from the table. "It's a wonder you're so slim and trim." She shuddered at her choice of words—it's a wonder?

He rose along with her. Stepped to her side. "I wanted to take you to one of my favorite nightspots," he said, closing in, "but now I don't know...maybe later?" He placed his hand between her shoulders, pressed downward, sloping around her waist, down toward her belly.

She'd asked for this, hadn't she?

His hand moved upward, approaching her breasts. She slid out of his grasp. "I'd like to go, Aldo."

"Out on the town?"

"No. Altogether."

"If we don't connect here and now, our moment is lost."

"I want to go."

"There were positive vibes, I felt them, and now you're uncomfortable. You think I'm seeing this through my camera lens. That I'm an opportunistic bastard."

She nodded. "Like me. That's why I'm uncomfortable."

"Why? Seizing the moment doesn't make you heartless, you know."

"You're preaching to the choir again," she said, trying to hide her impatience.

"A remorseful choir, it appears."

"Please, Aldo, you don't need to point out the inconsistency between my thoughts and actions."

"I'll be damned. You do feel remorse."

"Yes."

"But why?"

"I don't know. Can you explain why all your life you like vanilla ice cream, and then suddenly one day you wake up and you don't?"

"I never liked vanilla ice cream."

She smiled humorlessly. "Maybe you can call me a cab. It's presumptuous of me to expect you to drive me back."

"Because you didn't earn the ride? You insult me."

"I didn't mean that at all."

"It doesn't matter what you mean. I'm a gentleman. I'm driving you."

"Of course you are, I never meant to imply otherwise."

"And now," he said, slicking his hair back, "we're becoming overly sensitive and quite unbearable. Both of us."

Erika expelled a short laugh. "And now, 'poof!'" she quoted him, "our moment is—"

"*Defunto*—gone. Let's go, *amico mio*, I'm taking you back to your hotel."

❋ ❋ ❋

Uneasy from her interlude with Aldo, prolonged by their airily stilted conversation on their ride to the Hotel de Medici, Erika headed for the bank of elevators and anticipated the relieving silence of her room.

As she anxiously waited for one of the elevators to descend to the lobby, she decided it might be a good idea to decompress with a glass of wine.

Entering the quietly elegant lounge, she spotted Harrison seated at the bar, his back toward her, his face in quarter-profile. Three stools away, a woman in a blue dress sat slightly sideways, turned away from him, her legs crossed, her bare knee caught in the brightest point of light cast by the graceful chandelier directly overhead. Otherwise, it bathed the room in a soft glow. There were two empty glasses alongside the small evening bag on which her hand rested.

The bartender was leaning against the bar, his arms folded, elbows resting on the glossy dark-wood surface.

Such a stillness here, broken by her passage to the bar. The scene reminded her of an Edward Hopper painting.

"*Nighthawks*," she said quietly, coming at Harrison from behind. She hiked herself onto the neighboring stool. "Only not so stark."

"You've got a good eye, anyway," he said blandly, staunching surprise at her sudden arrival.

"Anyway?"

"Compared to your social skills."

"What?"

"Forget it. I should have known better."

"Not that I should have to explain myself, but nothing happened."

"You don't have to report to me."

"Damn right, I don't."

"All right, let's let it go, then."

"Oh, do let's," she said, dripping Jane Austen. To the stationary bartender: "I'll have a glass of white wine, please. Pinot Grigio, or whatever. Thanks."

Harrison nodded. "And I'll have another scotch."

Like a portrait come to life, the bartender sprang into action. "Lieutenant Mitchell called," Harrison declared flatly.

"Oh? About what?" she asked, her voice, trembling. "We spoke only briefly."

Was he enjoying her agitation? "About what, Harrison?"

"About your friend, Rodney. They arrested him at your apartment."

"No!"

"It looked like he'd broken in."

"Impossible!"

"Let me finish, okay? The cops had responded to a call from your neighbors—"

"The Barlows."

"—who'd heard noises coming from your place. They knew you were out of town, so they called 911. The cops arrived on the scene and caught him rummaging around your stuff. He was arrested, held in custody a couple of hours, then released on his own recognizance pending further inquiry. I can see how it went down."

"Who do I call to straighten this out? Rodney would never—"

"He admitted to jimmying open the lock, Erika."

"Then he had good cause to!"

"The story he gave is as believable as your objectivity. He said he'd left some important stuff in your apartment—papers, paint supplies, whatnot—and that he'd gone to the super's apartment to get him to open the door. He said when the super said no, he took matters into his own hands."

"The super knew him, he should have lent him the key!"

"*Eccoci*—here we are," the bartender announced, placing their drinks before them.

"*Grazie*," Harrison answered distractedly. "Your analytical powers are usually more reliable."

"*Cosa*—pardon?"

"He means me, not you," Erika explained.

"Ah, *scusi*," the bartender beseeched, withdrawing.

Erika took a swig of her wine; turned to Harrison. "You were saying?"

"Never mind. What I meant to say is that there are a number of Rodney factors you need to consider—"

"'Rodney factors'?" She waved her hand, coming close to knocking her drink over.

The woman in the blue dress slid off her stool and sauntered away, just as a young couple clinging to each other planted themselves at the far end of the bar. The bartender went to tend to them.

"Listen to me, Erika," Harrison enunciated with studied calmness, leaning in toward her. "There are facts that could be given an incriminating slant, especially when added up. First, the threatening note. Rodney knows his art, and only someone who does would have thought to scare you with that particular Francis Bacon painting. He's also fit, as I'm sure you'll attest to"—the sarcasm could be cut with a knife—"so he could easily have escaped the scene. Like he could have escaped after the Schurz Park incident."

She could not hold her silence. "That wasn't Rodney!"

"How do you know, you didn't see your attacker, did you?"

She wanted to say she hadn't recognized the distinct musk odor, but thought better of it. "I just know!"

His lips formed a tight smile. "For sure, that'll hold up in court."

He reached for his glass; changed his mind. "Also, as you're well aware, your good friend first homed in on Helen Gilmore, then on her daughter, Natalie. Without much latitude for mourning, it may be added."

"You're loving this, aren't you?"

"No! Why in hell would I?"

She let his hyper-protest echo in answer.

"Let's think like detectives," he said, more subdued. "You know yourself, Helen felt a special closeness to Rodney, that something clicked between them. What if she let him in on some critical information found in the Delaney safe deposit box? Or if he came upon it himself? What if there were documents, memorabilia, who knows what else, in that box, that he could profit by? After all, he's virtually a starving artist, isn't he? One who could shake the world with his greatness, if only he had access to—"

"Stop! What about Natalie's father? From Rodney's description of him—from what Natalie herself says about him —not only is he a damn hothead, but until recently, I bet he thought he could lay claim to his wife's art collection! Who knows what agenda's been kicking around in his head?"

"For starters, Rodney hit on his wife and his daughter, which would explain the hotheadedness. You have a point about his expectations regarding the art collection. I'm sure he's being questioned about that."

She waved him off. "Who says we should take anyone at their word in that family, including Natalie? Maybe she or her father or her brother—we don't know anything about him, do we?—maybe it's in somebody's best interest to keep certain facts from surfacing when it comes to the disbursement of the Delaney estate!"

"This was my fault, getting you riled up," he said, pulling up short. "We've got to leave the second-guessing to the authorities. Go give Rodney a good character reference when we get back to New York, if you must, but don't go deputizing yourself, for god's sake. Promise me." Again, he reached for his glass, this time bringing it to his lips, emptying it. He set the glass down. "Promise me."

She shook her head. "Promises are made to be broken. I don't make promises."

"That's cold."

"Really? And what would I call you this evening? Churlish?"

"One-night stands will do that to me every time."

She would not take the bait. "In which case I'll try to be understanding." Unflappable.

His features registered a look of disappointment ending in defiance. "Good."

"I'm going up now." She took a last sip of her wine, leaving half a glass, and slid off the stool. She reached for her wallet; thought better of it when he drilled her a stare. "Thanks for the drink. You coming?"

"Not right now. It's my turn to stay put, yours to go." He smiled humorlessly.

Her smile mirrored his. "Good night, then."

She strutted off in a manner she hoped appeared self-assured, but not overdone, on the off chance his eyes were still on her.

She packed her belongings for the trip home extra

neatly. Because, she supposed, there was a greater need to feel ordered and in control of things, or to prove she was. Too analytical for her own good, as usual, but the habit was itself comforting in a way—anchoring, defining.

Lying in bed, she thought of the passionate interlude that had taken place two nights ago, made herself think about it. Like picking at a scab, making it bleed, not to hurt, but to feel more keenly, or as punishment for having gotten into trouble to begin with. She thought of their foolhardy embrace, the illusory perfection of it. Reality masked as dream, dream, reality, their convergence so brief, so sweet, she played it over and over to prolong the blur, letting its poetry glaze over her, so dense, so deep the wanting, she held on, or tried to, losing it bit by bit to sleep.

CHAPTER 11

The skies opened up as Erika neared the entrance of The-Hole-In-The-Wall, distracting her from her angst about her impending reunion with Harrison, whom she hadn't seen since their return from Europe two days prior, when she had moved back to her apartment. She shoved her tote under a wing of her blazer and made a mad dash for it.

"Over here!" Harrison called to her, as she was shaking herself off like a wet puppy. The angst returned.

He was sitting at the same corner table they'd shared a week ago, and wearing the same blue blazer. His hair had the same gently tousled look it always had; his smile, typically awry. The sense of recognition took her breath away. The man sitting alongside him appeared insubstantial as mist.

"Hi, Harrison," she said, hardly aware of her passage from the door to the table. The men had risen to their feet. "Seems like years."

"Or minutes."

"Time is relative."

"Like everything else."

"Did I miss something, you guys?"

"Nothing relevant," Harrison answered his friend. He took a step toward Erika. "Here, let me take your jacket. It must be soaked."

"Thanks." She let him peel it off, exposing her pink

shell sweater, suddenly reminding her of blushing flesh. She combed her fingers through her wet hair.

"You cold?" Harrison asked. "No, I'm fine."

"The jacket should be hung up. I'll take it to the cloakroom." He started forward, then stopped. "I haven't introduced you two."

"Good observation," the third party said genially.

"Erika Shawn, *Art News*," she said. "And you must be Greg Smith."

"Exec board, Art Loss Register. Hi."

Erika wiped her damp hand on her pants leg and shook his hand. "Harrison said you've got some information to share, and I've got some news of my own."

"Excellent. Sit."

She chose the wrought-iron chair facing the banquette. She dropped her tote bag at her feet, as Harrison went off to the cloakroom.

"Nice spot," Greg said, sitting back down. "I know it's a favorite of Harrison's."

She nodded. "You could spend the day sipping tea, they'd leave you alone." Now that Harrison was not filling her landscape, Greg came into focus. A square-jawed blond in Nordic white cable knit sweater, he prompted thoughts of mountain climbing as opposed to the fine arts. "So...I guess Harrison has more or less filled you in with what we've got so far."

"Yes. Problem?"

"There's the matter of security..."

"I know—and a commitment to William Delany's daughter, Helen Gilmore for privacy. I'm mindful of the issues. I wouldn't last a week on my board without a fanatic respect for our clients' regard for privacy and, in most cases, anonymity."

"Is she giving you a hard time?" Harrison asked, returning. He slid into the banquette next to Greg. "Don't worry, Erika, I know this man, and I trust him completely."

"Just what Delaney must have said about Castro," she

tenderly gibed.

Harrison smiled stiffly. "Erika has trust issues," he said, locking onto her gaze.

"Only when its absence reflects the real world," she said, staring him down.

"You're losing me again," Greg said. "Shall we start with a round of drinks?" He ushered over the waiter.

Erika opted for ginger ale; the men, light beer.

"That'll do us for a while, Josh," Harrison advised the waiter. With a wink: "For like an hour, boss. Got it."

"So, how did your weekend go?" Harrison asked Erika, with studied nonchalance. "Any jet lag?"

"I was too busy to notice, starting with my face-off with Lieutenant Mitchell." She didn't mention she had also manically spit-polished her apartment, cooked and frozen a week's worth of suppers, and joined a gym. "You?"

"I graded papers and tried working on my book. Basically sat in a corner. Did you get your point across about Rodney? Clear his name?"

She glanced at Greg.

He shrugged. "No point holding back. I know the story."

"Mostly I made a fool of myself. I got my neighbors, the Barlows, to come down to headquarters with me, add their character references. They've always thought Rodney was a great guy. I thought it would help. It didn't. Then, in his defense, I brought up the email he'd sent me at 5:32 PM the day Helen was murdered. You remember his email, Harrison?"

"Yes, but what's that got to do with—"

"In the email he says he tried reaching Helen at her mother's house in Southampton."

"Yes, but he made the call from his cell. They'll have to track down where he was when he made the call. Could have been at the scene of the crime."

"I know," she said ruefully. "His cell number was on Helen's caller ID. To make matters worse, he had told Mitchell he remembered calling from a friend's land line. I reminded

Mitchell that Rodney is an artist and can be absent-minded about this sort of thing. Mitchell got a good laugh out of that. I totally screwed up."

"Not at all," Harrison said. "You made your point, and you did your best." He stood up. "And you are cold." He took off his blazer, put it over her shoulders.

"Thanks," she said, feeling the drape of fabric as an embrace. The waiter arrived and distributed their drinks.

"Maybe you'd like a cup of tea instead of the soda," Harrison suggested, sitting back down, almost reluctantly.

She shook her head. "I'm thirsty, anyway." She politely discharged the waiter then took a sip of her ginger ale. "One good thing from my talk with Mitchell. He told me Tina Morrison has a packet of letters from the 1950s she's offering to lend us briefly. Letters from William Delaney to her husband. You remember, she told us she'd pressured Bertram to drop his efforts on his murdered friend's behalf. Well, now she wants to share these letters on her husband's. 'In Bertie's honor,' as Mitchell quoted. I said it was a good thing," she added ruefully, "but I'm thinking we awakened her guilt."

"I'm not so sure how dormant it was," Harrison said.

"If it makes you feel better. Anyway, I'll pick up the material after our meeting."

"I'll go with you."

"She wants to deal directly with me. I guess she feels a certain womanly kinship. You and I can look over the letters tomorrow. And by tomorrow I hope to have Aldo Fabbri's Fed-Exed repros of his drawing in hand." She took another sip of her soda and drew his jacket closer around her.

"Okay," Greg said decisively. "You've caught up. Now, let me show you what I've got." He drew three copies of data from the slim portfolio tucked at his side and held them up. "As you know, we've only recently begun our recovery efforts. Already, I'm well into the task of circulating the Delaney inventory internationally, to galleries, museums, collectors—individual and corporate. I'm steering clear of easily accessible websites out of regard to your desire for minimal exposure, and I did not contact any possible sources in Cuba as per your instructions. I understand William Delaney had a friendly association with Fidel Castro, and for discretionary reasons you're handling this on your own." He proffered a copy of his data to each of them. "Okay so far?"

"Perfect," Erika said. As she reached for her copy, her foot slid forward, causing her shoe to come into contact with Harrison's. Without thinking, her eyes glued to the papers, she slipped forward in her chair, aware of the equivalent movement on his part only from the subtle shift beneath the table, their legs, from ankle to knee, lightly touching. She wanted to press more firmly against his solid form but resisted, as if temptation were a test of her grit. She held still, focusing hard on the papers, as if they would vaporize without her concentration. Then, with one tiny movement, she drew back her foot.

Greg took a swig of his beer. "Moving on to my query accompanying the inventory. In a nutshell: Do you recognize any of the works itemized? Do you, or any person or corporate entity known to you, presently own, or have previously owned, one or more of these works? Ditto the above in regard to any and all works citing William Delaney anywhere along the line of provenance. I figured this would cover works not on the inventory, either slipped through the cracks, or sold by Delaney between 1954 and 1958, the year of his death. I hope at least some of these buyers will be encouraged to come forward.

"I should add that the buyer who finds he's got stolen goods on his hands, and the shady guy who realizes he's been outed, are in the same boat. They've got merchandise that can't easily be unloaded. The well-intentioned individual might come forward, content with a refund or reward. The other might put his merchandise up for ransom. In either case, there's a chance the paintings can be recovered."

"And your—agents know how to let the cat out of the bag without the story ending up in the *New York Times*?" Erika asked.

"Exactly."

"You are thorough," Harrison commented.

Greg laughed. "A pain-in-the-ass Virgo, but then, nothing gets by me. In fact, I'm delighted with our initial response. As you can see, I've listed all the particulars on every piece we've received word about, even if a detail might on surface appear to be unworthy of notice. Look it over, ask me any questions."

The report was self-explanatory. There were two headings: Presumed Legitimate and Probable Theft, with subdivisions under each.

"Interesting," Erika remarked. "There are seven works listed as legitimately owned, and they all stem from that original Delaney-to-Fitch sale in 1957."

"Yes," Greg said, "and you'll notice that two of them—"

"The Gauguins," Harrison anticipated.

"Right, the Tahiti Woman sketch, and the Island Sunset oil. Neither is listed on the 1954 inventory. Delaney obviously acquired them after he issued that inventory."

"Obviously," Erika repeated, with not quite his confident ring. With her rock-solid theory of human behavior lately churning under her like a roiling sea, how could she be dead sure about anything?

"I'm looking at the list of presumptive thefts," Harrison said. He flipped to the second page. "Nine entries in all. Curious. Although I've seen every one of these works of art listed on William Delaney's 1954 inventory, his name does not appear in the line of provenance on any of them. While the alleged owners on record vary, every one of these works passed through the hands of the Milagros, a gallery in Havana."

"Milagros," Erika echoed, reaching for her tote.

Greg raised a hand, anticipating protest. "No, I did not contact this gallery. As I said, I did not include Cuba in my inquiry. The present owners of the nine works in question range from the Pushkin Museum to the Sara Lee Corporation, and all are institutions we reached out to. Incidentally, most are willing to negotiate the transfer of property if evidence of theft is proven beyond a reasonable doubt. A holdout, a collector associated with the Kelvingrove Museum in Glasgow, is invoking the statute of limitations, and as an innocent purchaser, he has every right to. Always a sticky issue. A lawyer on our board is checking into precedent-setting cases. I believe this particular collector can be worked on. I know his agent."

Erika pulled out a bunch of papers from her bag. "This is relevant," she said, snapping off a metal clip. "Letters— copies of letters—one from Cuba's Minister of Arts, the other from the curator of The National Museum. You'll see the minister yields to the curator, giving him complete authority to relinquish any and all art to the Delaney estate he deems to have been"—she air-punched quote marks—"'inappropriately acquired, providing the Cuban government receive all due credit for its just and humanitarian role in this effort.' He underlines this by going on to say that due to the traumatic circumstances pursuant to the theft, as well as the tenuous nature of Cuba-U.S. relations subsequent to it, he understands the surviving spouse's lifelong fear of reporting the loss. For this reason, his agency is willing to forego the statute of limitations claim—again, providing it receives proper kudos for doing so. The curator's letter is more specific. It's where you'll see the Milagros mentioned." She distributed the letters. "Take your time."

The men read the letters, interjecting an occasional utterance of acknowledgement or surprise.

"Super," Greg offered in summation. "A clear effort to heal— restore—relations with the U.S., as initiated by President Obama."

Harrison held up the letters. "At the very least, these are meant to inspire trust, encourage a more open conversation."

"For starters," Erika said, "the curator says he examined the local records and concluded that the owners listed in the provenances prior to The Milagros Gallery taking possession are fictitious, and that The Milagros is, in fact, the initial purchaser of all the art allegedly stolen from William Delaney."

"The fence, to put it bluntly," Harrison said.

"Looks like it, yes. Whether or not the founders of Cuba's National Museum were wise to this or shut their eyes to it in their eagerness to build up inventory, I don't know. But the present curator seems to be pretty straight about it."

Greg nodded vigorously. "Passionately so. Looking for national redemption, I'd say."

"Same way I read it," Erika said. "And keep in mind, this is the first time an inquiry about these works of art was ever put to the Cuban authorities. Delaney's wife never permitted an inquiry of any kind, not even when many works left Cuba, sold on the international market. This is the first chance for redemption the Cubans have been given—on this issue, anyway." She bumped into Harrison's gaze, took a few sips of her ginger ale to free herself.

"Fascinating," Greg said. "The probable stolen goods on my list were all bought in the nineteen-nineties, by Sara Lee and the like, either from the National Museum or from Cuban nationals."

"Exactly," Harrison said. "This was the time of Cuba's economic depression, when they were unloading some of their precious art."

He polished off his beer. "To supplement that list, the curator cites a couple of pieces that are still in the museum's possession or still owned by individuals or agencies in Cuba."

"And both our lists are works in progress," Greg said. "I'm counting on that. Certainly your Cuban connection isn't ready to drop the ball."

"Not at all," Erika agreed.

"Looks like he's going all out," Harrison said. "He's already exposed the Milagros and probably pissed off a lot of bigwigs. It must have taken some courage to do that—you hungry? Greg, you ready for something?"

"Thought you'd never ask."

With sudden intensity, Harrison posed, "Erika, you ready?"

The question covered more than lunch and sounded more like a dare. "Sure, let's eat," she said, with feigned innocence, refusing to take it on.

CHAPTER 12

"This is truly a fresh take on pointillism and the Benday dot technique," Sara commented, patting the clipped pages on her desktop. "The questions you raise on the relationship of perception and motive are right on the mark. Looks good." She raised her eyes.

"And so do you, kid. Stretch pants, and in that washed-out color, yet. How do you do it?"

"Look who's talking, in her form-fitting pencil skirt," Erika said.

"You won't catch my ass in ecru, babe." She uttered her patented four-note laugh as segue. "You'll have Jack's piece on gallery openings vetted by tomorrow, on my desk by three?"

"Maybe earlier. I'm almost done with it."

Sara fluttered a hand. "Okay, now get out of here. See you tomorrow. Do us proud."

Erika hooked the strap of her tote bag onto her shoulder. "I'll try." She grabbed the handle of her art portfolio and headed for the door.

The air was invigorating. Crisp without bluster, perfect for walking, and she loved to walk. On Sunday, her first day at the gym, the stallion who'd assigned himself to her as orientation counselor, had been visibly impressed by her virgin workout on the treadmill. She was dressed sensibly for a long walk. Besides the stretch pants, she had on a breathable cotton shirt, relaxed-cut herringbone jacket, and cowboy boots, deceptively unconstricting.

She was looking forward to seeing Harrison, going over the material in her portfolio, for starters: the packet of letters she'd been entrusted with the day before. Tina Morrison had transferred the parcel to her with such gentle care, it was as if she were parting with a living creature. Erika was saving its unveiling until her meeting with Harrison, although she wasn't sure why. Mutual revelation a safe substitute for sex, maybe.

She headed east to Fifth Avenue, then turned north for the thirty-block jaunt to Seventy-eighth Street, and The Institute of Fine Arts. They'd arranged to meet in the library, on the second floor. A quiet space, Harrison had said, with less likelihood of their being interrupted by students and colleagues than in his cramped office elsewhere in the building.

She was imagining the upcoming conversation with him, the streets in effect gliding by, when she skidded to a halt as a boy on roller blades jumped onto the sidewalk and sashayed across her path. From behind, a man's gruff "Sorry!" punched the air as his hand made contact with her shoulder, stopping his forward movement.

She uttered a sharp cry, her overreaction alarming her as much as the stranger's touch. She sprang forward, spurred by the memory of her attack in Schurz Park. To dispel it, she turned to take a quick look.

The man was nondescript—medium build, thirtyish, in generic windbreaker, jeans. Even without knowing him, he looked familiar, though in her state of heightened suspicion, there was something sinister in his blandness, the way he looked past her with studied indifference.

She turned forward, commanding herself to get a grip, helplessly accelerating at the same time, her gathering speed heightening the need to escape. Despite herself, she could feel his presence behind her, mimicking her dream that night in London, which had reflected the incident in the park.

She forced herself to concentrate on her breathing—counted: one, two, three, four, as if she were working out, cooling down to a brisk walk, refusing to look over her shoulder and give credence to her groundless fear.

Only when the art institute was tantalizingly near, just across the avenue, did the need to be there press her into making a dash for it. She hopped the curb just as the light blinked in favor of the uptown traffic and the cars lurched at her before their drivers saw her coming.

"You're gonna get killed—stop! Erika!" That same gruff voice. Impossible! "Hold up, will you, I—"

—the rest drowned out by the honking horn of the car swerving past her just before she leaped to safety. She looked back. The man in the windbreaker was loping toward her, dodging cars.

She ran for the building, hearing the screech of brakes, the detonation of curses.

She took the steps two at a time, pulled open the heavy door and tucked into the reception area, the door falling shut behind her.

The visitors' assistant looked up from the book she was reading as Erika was about to skirt past her desk. She peeled off her glasses. "One moment, miss, may I be of assistance?"

Erika started for the broad spiral staircase, rear right. "Professor Wheatley said to meet him in the library, second floor!"

The young woman shot out of her seat. "Wait! Do you have an appointment? Security!"

Erika heard the door thud shut a second time; knew who it was. She started up the stairs, her flat portfolio slapping against the scrolled wrought-iron balusters.

That voice, from below: "Wait, dammit!"

The receptionist's voice, thinner: "Come back here, you!"

Above, Harrison emerged from down the hall, alarmed. As Erika got to the next to last step, he reached for her, grabbing at her sleeve and yanking her toward him.

An elderly man in uniform rounded the spiral. The younger one who had been following her scuffed past him and onto the landing. "Don't touch me!" Erika warned. "Guard, hold him, he may be armed!" Anticipating the stranger's hand going for his gun, she dropped her portfolio and lunged at him, as Harrison tried to take charge on his own.

"I've got him, Erika, step away!"

"Get your hands off her!" the stranger ordered, in one deft movement wrenching himself free and thrusting himself between Erika and Harrison.

"Professor Wheatley, careful!" the guard cried, cautiously advancing toward them.

"Son-of-a-bitch!" the man in the windbreaker uttered hoarsely. "You're Wheatley?" To the guard, "Stand down, man, I'm effing Allsafe!"

Harrison blanched. "Oh shit."

"You got that right!"

From the foot of the staircase: "Want me to call for backup?" the receptionist militantly barked.

"No, no," Harrison answered. To the guard, "It's okay, Norton." To the others, "Let's take this outside."

"Let's what?" Erika asked incredulously.

"Trust me, come on." He picked up her portfolio. "Who's Allsafe?"

"Come on," Harrison urged, his eyes pleading. He started down the stairs.

She considered her options, then trailed after him. "This better be good."

Outside, she half expected the men to roll up their sleeves and duke it out. Her other half knew better.

The mystery man was livid. "I told my partner this was a bad idea, but what do I know!"

"It was a good idea until you blew it!" Harrison fumed.

Erika grabbed her portfolio from Harrison. "Anybody care to explain why this man has been stalking me?"

"Bingo!" the man said. "Just my point!"

"He's been guarding you, not stalking you," Harrison said. "Allsafe is his company."

"It shouldn't have gone down like this. Name's Frank Brennan, miss." The man extended his hand, put it back down when it was refused. "You should've been informed, you wouldn't have gone nuts, almost getting yourself killed—how would that have looked on my record?" He attempted a companionable grin, another failure to placate. "But no, your friend here, he thinks you wouldn't approve, so he has you protected on the sly. Of course, when you suspect something's up, right away you think your boyfriend's checking up on you, or worse, you're being stalked."

"If you'd been doing your job—" Harrison began.

"Wait a minute," Erika cut in. "You're paying this company to have me watched?"

"Protected."

"Same thing. And you're doing this behind my back?"

"Yes. I knew you'd be unreasonable about it. Just because we've had personal issues doesn't mean I stopped caring about your safety."

She shook her head. "You feel absolutely no remorse."

"That's not entirely true."

"The minutes are ticking," Brennan said, "and I'm still officially on the job. You want to terminate?"

"Of course he wants to!" Erika answered. "Oh—I thought I recognized you! In the lobby of my apartment house, Saturday morning, when I was checking my mailbox!"

"Ah that, yes. I was pretending to be a tenant."

"I bet. Anyway, you can stop the ticking now. Time's up."

"No," Harrison said.

"I'll pay whatever he owes you," she said, addressing Brennan.

"No," Harrison repeated.

"No to what?" Brennan asked.

"No to everything. There's someone out there who can come after her at any time. Why do you think she was so frightened of you? Because she knows it's true."

Of course it was true, but she would not allow anyone—the park assailant, Harrison, Harrison's hired hand—to rob her of her independence. "Don't talk about me as if I'm not here," she said, glaring at Harrison.

"I'm sorry. But you're not being reasonable. Will you at least talk about this with me in private? Later? After we're done working?"

Working. The word itself was compelling. She was suddenly aware of the art portfolio resting against her leg. "You're putting me on the spot," she said.

"Will you agree? Can I tell Brennan we'll call in our decision later?"

"My decision."

"Your decision—after my persuasive argument."

"After my persuasive counter-argument."

"That's a given." To Brennan, "I've got the number for Allsafe's central station. I'll call it in a couple of hours."

"What do I do until then?"

"Go see a movie, take a nap."

"On your dollar?"

"Yes."

Brennan tapped his forehead in the manner of a salute and took off with a determined stride, heading downtown.

Erika opened her mouth to speak.

"Not a word about it, not now," Harrison said, putting his hand on her shoulder, immediately taking it away and shoving it into his pants pocket.

"I was only going to say I'd rather not go back in there for our meeting."

"That's okay, we can go to my place, it's only a block away, on Madison."

"I'm aware of that."

"It was going to be my first suggestion, but I thought

you might think I was trying to—"

"I would never think that."

"Now I'm insulted."

She smiled unwittingly. "We're wasting time."

❊ ❊ ❊

"Hello there, Mr. Harry!" Grace chirped from the second-floor balustrade, perking up a ruffle of her starched apron. "No calls, no deliveries. Good day, Miss Shawn," she added flatly, as if she'd run out of song.

"Hi, Grace," Erika answered warmly, finding Grace's un-inhibited bias endearingly forthright.

"Will you be wanting anything, Mr. Harry? Coffee? Tea? I've made fresh scones, really quite good."

He glanced at Erika. She shook her head. "Maybe later, Grace. We'll be in the study, working."

"Shall I prepare the Blue Room?" Neutral again.

"That won't be necessary," Erika replied, beating Harrison to the punch. "I hope I wasn't any trouble last time."

"Not a bit, dear." Relief betrayed by a sunburst of a smile. Jake's greeting was more democratic than Grace's. As they entered the study, he lumbered from beneath Harrison's desk and in slow motion went for them, attacking one then the other, unable to decide whom to kill with kisses first.

"Hi, boy," Erika cooed, bending to get a better handle on calming the old Lab, but instead getting nosed off balance and toppling to an even more vulnerable position, teasing him into greater fervency.

"Down, boy!" Harrison ordered, hauling him off her.

Erika rescued her portfolio, which in the melee had ended up beneath her. She dropped her tote bag alongside it and crossed her legs, lotus style. "Here's as good as anyplace," she said, reaching for the portfolio's zipper.

"Let me clear my desk or one of the tables." She scanned

the room.

"It would only take one dumpster, two tops," he said.

"This is fine. We can spread out." The dog was struggling to free himself, get back to her. "That is, if you can sit quietly by us—think you can do that, Jake?"

"I don't think so," Harrison answered for him. "Let's give it a try."

"All right." To Jake: "You have one chance, boy, don't blow it." Still holding Jake's collar, he led him to Erika's side. "Now, lie down and behave yourself," he demanded, bristling with conviction.

Jake, appearing to understand the non-negotiability of the order, plopped to his belly and lay his head on Erika's thigh. He looked up at her, eyes asking: Aren't I the picture of domesticity?

She melted.

"Unbelievable," Harrison commented, lowering himself to the floor opposite them. Melting himself.

Careful not to disturb Jake, Erika unzipped the portfolio and lay it open. "We'll look at the FedExed prints from Aldo first, then the Morrison letters." She started to slide out the fifteen-by-twenty-inch papers.

He picked up one as it emerged, his smile fading before it set. "I see you agree," she said.

"I was expecting state-of-the-art technology from him."

"I know. I thought we could get an informal analysis on our own, but I'd be embarrassed to hand these over to an expert, the resolution's so poor." She withdrew a sheet of powder blue stationery from the portfolio. "Aldo's accompanying letter." She handed it to him. "What do you make of it?"

"'My dear Erika and Harrison,'" he began, "'it was such a pleasure to meet the two of you—'"

"I mean past the bull."

He read on, silently. "Nothing much."

"You're being generous."

"Well, he isn't very specific. He says it'll take a couple of weeks for his expert to get to the analysis."

"Doesn't even reference his or her name or business association.

You don't find that odd?"

"Taken along with the lousy quality of the prints, yes, I do."

"This is intentional. He's making it as difficult as possible for us." Harrison leaned over to pat Jake's haunch, buying time. "What are you thinking?" she asked.

"I'm thinking Aldo's getting back at you for leading him on."

Not wanting to agitate Jake, she held her reaction to an inward flinch. "Oh, really?"

"It's a possibility." A pause, hardly a warning for what was to come: "Unless he got what he wanted."

She let his words bounce back at him.

"I mean, to prove your point about the ephemeral nature of all relationships," he explained. "If only to feel better about blowing me off."

"I told you we didn't—oh, believe what you want."

"It wouldn't have been the first time I've been lied to, although I guarantee you, never for such a screwed up reason."

"Tell me we're not having this conversation."

"We are having this conversation, but"—he raised his hands in the air—"we just stopped." A smile dawned.

She tried not to be roped in by those disarming creases forming in his cheeks. She had to watch herself like a hawk. "We're here to talk about Aldo's hang-ups, not our own. Don't waste time."

"Let's hear your theory, then. What's the reason for Aldo's obstructionist behavior?"

"I've been going over our visit to the Fabbris. There are things I didn't notice at the time—no, I did notice, just paid them no mind. Aldo's father, Gian—remember, out on the veranda, when he said he'd always meant to pursue the recovery of the only Vittorio his family had sold from the portfolio—the most detailed drawing of the lot?"

"The one the Fabbris sold in 1933 to the Corelli Gallery. Our reference to the Battle of Cascina hopeful. Yes, I remember. So?"

"Aldo cut him off, didn't want him to go there."

"He was getting antsy, wanted to take us on the tour of the place."

She shook her head. "No, he didn't want us to dwell on his family's curiosity about that drawing. Consistent with that is what happened afterward, in his suite, when we told him we thought one of his Vittorios might in fact be a Michelangelo."

"He was impressed."

"Come on, Harrison, was he blown away?"

"He was showing you how cool he was. Reeling you in."

"If he was, it was to get me to tell all, starting off with the name of the current owner of the drawing his family had sold to the Corelli Gallery."

"Gian is a friend of the proprietor of the Corelli Gallery, he obviously would have been able to find out the drawing had been sold to William Delaney in 1951."

"That's right, but if he ever tried to contact the Delaney family, he would have met a dead-end. More recently, if he put out an all-points bulletin on the drawing, the Fitches wouldn't have responded. James told us his father was quite attached to it." She stroked the Lab's head, still resting on her thigh. He uttered a gravelly dog-purr, looked up at her, eyes half-lidded, then instantly fell back to sleep. "I think Aldo wants to get in on the hunt for the stolen drawing, and we're his best bet. I'm glad we withheld Fitch's name."

"This is your only theory?" She smiled. "So far."

"I don't see how it can explain why Aldo has been so tight-lipped about the expert he's hired to check out his Vittorio-slash-Michelangelo, or why he sent us such poor reproductions."

"I don't know either, but something's not right. I want to find out who the expert is, assuming there is one."

"What? It doesn't make sense for him not to find out if his Vittorio is a misattributed Michelangelo. It's worth would skyrocket if it is!"

She shrugged. "Maybe he doesn't want it outed at this time. Let's try to track down this person, maybe we'll learn something." Harrison gathered the repros together and lay them aside. "I trust your instincts. Our goal, then, is to get this fellow to talk about his client without suspecting our subversive intentions. Want me to do the detective work? I've got my sources at NYU, and from researching Gericault, I'm in close contact with a couple of top curators abroad. Brian Latham, Greg, others may be of help. I'm confident if Aldo has gotten in touch with an expert of any stature,

I'll find him. The world's not exactly teeming with these people."

"I'd start out with Florence. He mentioned the Uffizi. Are you planning to make a list of names, then more or less cold-calling them?" She cocked her head. "You have to be really diplomatic."

He smiled. "You mean I have to lie."

"To get your entrée, I guess so. What's your M.O.?"

"I'll be aboveboard with him about our interest in the possible misattribution of Aldo's drawing."

"You just won't tell him Aldo never gave us his name."

"You kidding? I'll tell him Aldo gave us his name, number and email, and urged us to contact him!"

"Aboveboard, Harrison, not overboard."

"I'll handle it. Trust me."

Trust. A loaded word. From Jake, an audible sigh accompanied by a delicate nuzzling: trust in its purest form. She stroked his side, felt the resilience of his body, could not help but relax with the ease of their connection. Stirring, Jake looked up at her with rheumy eyes. "His love is unconditional," she said softly.

Jake turned his head to gaze adoringly at his owner. Harrison laughed. "Although not necessarily exclusive."

Perfectly serious: "It doesn't matter. He gives a universe of love to each of us. How nice if it could be this simple, this...innocent..."

"Don't go biblical on me, Erika. Adam and Eve wouldn't have known."

"What?"

"The difference between love and wishful thinking. At least not before the Fall. Without getting kicked in the ass, you can't fully appreciate joy."

"Very Hallmark. What was it, anniversary or sympathy?"

"Neither. Just your way of discrediting an observation."

She looked at him hard. "Why are we always at each other? We're so alike; same fear of commitment."

"Wrong. Mine comes from a bad experience, makes me doubt my judgment and distrust women."

"How's that different?"

"I know it belongs to me, my state of mind. You turn yours into a world view."

"Sounds as though you've been giving it a lot of thought." No answer from him, only a turning away.

"Oh," she said.

"Right."

"Then you should stop thinking about it, and move on."

"I'm trying."

"I mean to our agenda. Move on to the Morrison letters." Disconcerted, he swept a hand across the top of his head —

—as hers swept across Jake's, her mind fusing her action with Harrison's, her palm feeling his tousled hair flattening with her stroke, his unease pressing on her chest.

"Would you like a bite to eat first?" he asked, gliding onto a safe subject. "Grace's scones, at least?"

"Thanks. Later maybe."

"A drink?"

"Water would be good."

He leaped to his feet. "Be right back."

"Wait. I don't mean to be paranoid, but I'm really afraid of getting something on the letters. Even water." She glanced at Jake. "Even—"

"Dog drool?"

She gave a hapless shrug. "It's just that the letters must mean so much to Mrs. Morrison because they belonged to her husband."

"Bertram—Bertie."

She nodded. "He must have treasured them. They're all he had left of his friendship with William Delaney."

"Let's move upstairs, then. I don't want you to feel uncomfortable—Jake!"

The Lab shuffled to an upright position.

Harrison motioned with his head, and Jake trotted off to his spot under the desk.

"Catch you later, boy," he assured him, following the dog's audible settling in. He bent down to help Erika reorganize her portfolio. "Got to be oblique," he whispered. "If I say 'I'll take you for a walk,' he'll go crazy. Poor guy can't handle postponement"—their faces close enough to excite—"any better than I can."

She mustered a collegial grin. A word, any word, would have fanned the flame.

They sat cattycorner from each other in the formal dining room, as they had on her first visit. Harrison had moved the Wedgwood centerpiece to the other end of the table, and she had removed the packet of Morrison's letters from its satin pouch. Her heart was racing in anticipation.

"All right," he said, not yet daring to touch the neat stack of letters between them. "Any discoveries? Since you haven't let on, I assume nothing earthshaking."

"I didn't look at them," she said. "I was saving them. For

us. Don't ask me why."

"Ah," he uttered, sounding perfectly cool, but then taking her hand and pressing it to his chest. "I'm touched," he said, lowering her hand to the tabletop without releasing it. Smiling, "Don't ask me why."

She slipped her hand from his and offered him the envelope on top of the stack.

He retrieved it gently from her keep and very delicately extracted a thin sheet of stationery from within. He could have been performing brain surgery.

"What's the date?" she asked.

"November 12, 1953. The letterhead's the Delaney Plantation, Guantanamo Province, Cuba." He held the letter so she could see it. She moved her chair closer to improve her angle. The letter was typed, with sporadic inserts handwritten in ink, faded but legible.

"Shall we divvy them up, share the good parts?"

"Sure."

"Let's read this first one together. Read it aloud. I want to hear it."

"You like prying, do you?" he asked, catching her excitement.

"Only in tandem—Read!"

The two of them were suddenly serious as he began:

"Dear Bert,

I must apologize for my delinquency in responding to your letter, but I have not had a moment's leisure since your visit. I was, first of all, swept into the drama and aftermath of Fidel's trial. I suppose being so staid, even priggish, a person myself, I am captivated by the man's fiery nature, drawn to it as a kind of voyeur. Meanwhile, I wonder what the level of awareness is in the states. Fidel Castro or Desi Arnaz—who's the more famous Cuban?

On a more practical note, the replacement for my retired

manager is working out splendidly. I had been courting him for months—Jeff Davis, a Navy man, young, and smart as a tack. While he was overseeing Supply and Purchase at the base, our sugar transactions with them were never more efficient. Of course, to persuade him not to sign on for another tour of duty, I had to compete with the Navy perks. If sales rise more than 5% this year, he'll get 2.5% of net profit. Although there are not many years between us, I dare say his vigor puts me to shame. I marvel at it. He manages with an iron hand in a velvet glove. Everyone loves him except the shirkers.

I cannot believe November 23 is almost upon us. Happy Thanksgiving to you and your family. I hope next year we can celebrate it together. Above all remember, though my letter writing may on occasion flag, my affection for you remains constant.

> *As ever,*
> *Will*

"The signature is very neat and compact," Harrison added. He looked up from the sheet.

"I kept thinking of Helen," Erika said, after a pause. "How she would have savored every word!"

"Her father, up close and personal."

"Yes." Almost wistful.

"Shall we go on?" he asked.

"Let's jot down facts, dates, as we go along."

"Want me to make copies? It won't take long."

"Mrs. Morrison wouldn't approve. She doesn't want the letters 'out there' was the expression she used. Let's take notes."

"I see your point. Got paper, pen?"

"Pencil!"

He smiled. "Like the British Museum. No pens allowed. Protect the artifacts."

"You read my mind."

"For once."

"Stick to the subject. You have a couple of pencils and pads?"

He went to fetch them from his study. Waiting, she peeled off her jacket, hung it on the back of her chair.

She hesitated. When they'd first entered the room, she noticed that a couple of framed photographs had been placed on the credenza since her last visit. Knowing herself, she squelched her curiosity about them, as if finding out more about Harrison's personal life would deepen her stake in it.

But curiosity would not be kept at bay, especially when given an opportunistic lull. She strode around the head of the table to the credenza to take a look, realizing, on the way, that her interest in the photographs was keener than in Degas' vivid pastel of a ballet class on the wall above. Not a good sign.

"I just put them out last night," Harrison said, returning with the supplies, as she stood there, engrossed. "They're nice, aren't they?" Modest pride in his voice.

"Wonderful."

He set the materials on the table and stepped to her side. "It gave me a feeling of empowerment," he said, a touch of self-mockery tweaking the pride.

She gave him a sidelong look.

"Putting them on display, I mean. Charlotte thought it was low class, showing off amateur shots nobody's interested in but you. She stuck them away in a spare bedroom. When I heard she finally signed the divorce papers, I brought them out of hiding."

"Congratulations."

"For being formally divorced?"

"For coming out of the closet as a sentimentalist."

"How boring of me."

"Never a bore." She pointed to a photo, a beach scene she'd been particularly drawn to. "This is you, isn't it?"

"At twelve, with my little sister, Nelly, and our parents. We've had a place on the Jersey Shore as far back as I can remember. My parents were teachers, and we used to spend summers there, but now we're lucky if we get to hang out a couple of days a year, when my mother and father can bear to tear themselves away from the ranch."

She pointed to a photo in which his parents, older, but still a handsome couple, were standing beside a horse against a backdrop of rolling plains. A small boy sat astride the horse, strapped to a special saddle-seat and clutching the pommel with all his might while grinning from ear to ear. "Great one— the ranch, I take it."

"Yes, the one in South Dakota. When my grandmother died, my mother spent her inheritance on a ten-thousand-acre spread in South Dakota, and others in Wyoming and Colorado, for the purpose of developing year-round camps for special needs kids. The boy on the horse is one of the regulars. He's had a whole constellation of developmental problems caused by a brain injury suffered at birth—but look at that smile. He's sixteen now, has that same radiant smile. As for my parents, they don't stop working for a minute, but it's their heaven on earth."

"They do look happy. In both photos, on the beach and here, the same look of…"

"Reverence?"

"That's it."

"For each other and for what they do." He smiled wryly. "A great disadvantage for me, their marriage."

She was standing six inches away from him, but inside her head and beneath her ribs they were touching. "How so?" she asked.

"If you never see the antithesis of trust, you don't define it. I never developed a sense of caution."

"You were trusting."

"I got over it. I had a crash course."

She smiled. "You're smarter than I am. I got home tutored, but I had to repeat the course."

"Oh, but sweetie, it was a different course."

She shrugged. "Another time, I'll show you my diary, you show me yours."

His unrestrained laugh, hers hitching onto his, cleared the air of any lingering self-absorption, and they returned to their seats to get back to work.

Very carefully they divided the unread letters, about forty in all, between them. A general survey of the postmarks indicated the letters were in chronological order, the one read aloud being the earliest. Harrison wound up with the top half, the earlier ones; Erika, the ones written from mid 1955 to mid 1957.

After jotting down the significant facts plucked from the letter already reviewed, Erika delved into her assignment, as Harrison tapped into his. With almost every document scrutinized, there were facts or commentary that each felt compelled to share.

"Here's a reference to a meeting with Ernest Hemingway," Harrison remarked, angling a sheet so Erika could see it. "January 5, 1954."

She leaned in to have a look. The paragraph referred to an animated conversation Delaney had had with Ernest Hemingway:

...the dazzlingly brilliant but troubled writer in the Floridita bar in Habana Vieja, the two of us downing Daiquiris and regaling our manhood with off-color banter that under less besotted circumstances, I would have deemed unworthy of gentlemen.

"Colorful," she said, "but I wonder if it's relevant."

"Anything that helps establish character and setting may turn out to be useful," he said, scribbling an entry in his notebook. "You never know what will tip the scale, make you see the light." He looked up; stared at her hard.

She must not be taken in by his fervor. It would pass in a blink.

She plucked the next letter from her allotment.

Seconds later, she said, "You should read this." She positioned the letter between them.

"What's up?"

"Anything that refers directly to Delaney's paintings should be processed by two brains. Read."

They read it together silently, she taking notes this time:

> *March 17, 1956*
> *Dear Bert,*
>
> *First, congratulations to you and your lovely wife on the birth of your son, Jeremy. (When last I saw you in New York even you were glowing with anticipation!) We've sent the little chap a jolly watercolor by Randolph Caldecott, which you should receive within the week. We hope it pleases him.*
>
> *Acclaim should be paid as well to your having landed the prestigious Winstons as your clients. For all their youth the couple has impeccable talent for spotting fine art. I've seen their collection and have envied it, especially for the Monets. Perhaps you can persuade them to part with one or two.*
>
> *My narrative cannot compete with yours: Recently, my cook's assistant took ill (homesickness, my unconfirmed diagnosis) and returned to Santa Clara to live with his parents. I have since replaced him with a lovely young girl, Rosa Ramirez, rescuing her from the miserly employ of our local baker. I had observed Rosa to be a dutiful worker, a wonder, given the cantankerous temperament of the baker. She will establish residence here within the week.*
>
> *I've been looking over my outdated inventory, long overdue for revision. Please assess the lot, tell me who should be better represented, or what new artists would complement the collection without offending my taste. Where I will put the new pieces, I do not know. The storage space in the basement is already cramped, and*

though I try to rotate the paintings on view, it is frustrating to me that any of them must reside in darkness, however temporary.

Harrison looked at her to find her already regarding him. "A cache of artworks in the basement," he said, question implied.

"Do you think it was overlooked by the rebels?" she asked.

"It may have been. Sounds as if it was virtually hidden."

"It may have been destroyed when they torched the place, no?"

"Unless..." he began, inviting her to go on.

"Unless an unknown party swiped the stuff, then covered his tracks by setting the fire. Tina Morrison said her husband, Bertram, always did believe someone took advantage of the opportunity, knowing the rebels would take the blame."

"But who?"

"I don't know. Keep reading."

They went back to it, curiosity rising...

You should know that I will be parting with several paintings purchased, without your mediation, in 1955. Among them, a Wilfred Lam, Braque-like, with Gauguin's sensibility, a Mario Carreno, also cubist, with a nod to Picasso, and a Carlos Lopez, with an interesting backstory, to be discussed at our leisure. I will be donating the works, all by Cuban artists, to the National Museum in Havana, whose rejuvenation has been aided by President Fulgencio Batista. Batista's critics, myself among them, must admit that whenever the man does not feel threatened, he relaxes his guard and becomes less of a tyrant. Case in point, his 1954 amnesty, which freed Fidel Castro, among others, from prison. For whatever motivation, during times of political complacency he has striven to enrich the public's cultural life, and it would be remiss on my part not to contribute to that effort. Are your eyes widening in disbelief, my friend? Yes, I know, I've never parted with a single item of my collection. Think of this as the one exception to the rule. I am still the unyielding "pack-rat" of your dubbing.

Meanwhile, I begin to worry I may have been more enamored of Fidel's charisma than cognizant of his political ambition, and that the measured intelligence I so admired in law school will one day be overwhelmed by the appetite for power.

Someday, amigo, and it may be sooner than later (I used to think it would be in my dotage), I will be a resident of New York City, and the two of us will be idling away the hours on some park bench, arguing about the state of art, you, no doubt, citing the reasons for its decline, while our wives stew about our neglect of them. I only wish they were as closely knit as we two, and could share their complaints in merry sisterhood.

My warmest regards, and again, congratulations,
Will

Erika could hardly process the last paragraphs, so fixated was she on Delaney's bombshell. "He never sold a painting! Harrison, do you know what this means?"

"It means every item on the 1954 inventory should appear on the 1957 inventory."

"And?"

"I'm on tenterhooks. And what?" His jaw dropped.

She nodded. "I can't believe it either."

He stared at her hard, as if he were checking her thoughts for confirmation. "Erika, it means the major sales transaction with James Fitch Senior was illegitimate. The drawing ascribed to Vittorio da Lucca, the Matisse study, whatever Fitch took possession of..."

"Stolen goods. I know."

"Wait a minute." He hopped to his feet. "We need to see that list of collectors who've come forward so far. Greg Smith's list. It's in my study."

"Sit down, I've got my copy right here." She reached

for the bag at her feet, accidentally brushing her hand against his calf as he sat back down. "What do you want it for?" she instantly posed, always a beat away from abashment. She handed it to him, and he held it so they could both check it out.

"I'm looking for—yes! See here"—his finger jumping from one entry to another—"and here and here. You see?"

"I think so. On every notation where William Delaney is listed in the line of provenance, Fitch is—"

"The owner that immediately follows. Right. What else?"

"I don't know. Fitch's name doesn't seem to appear anywhere except when it's linked to Delaney's. Of course. That's it, isn't it?"

"Right. This supports your theory that the works of art stored in the basement were overlooked by the rebels and hauled off by party—or parties—unknown."

Erika pressed her fingers to her forehead in an effort to pinpoint her focus. "If we look at the list with that in mind we can divide the art into two groups. The rebels' haul went through a fence, the Milagros gallery, and as a cover-up the primary source was fictionalized. As for the group stashed in the basement storeroom, the Delaney provenance gave those sales a legitimacy that would bear up under the scrutiny of the world's most reputable art collectors." She withdrew her fingers from her forehead, broadening her focus to include his expression of pride in her, deliciously unpatronizing. "Sounds right," he said. "So, let's suppose a member of the household or staff looted the basement storehouse on that fateful day, then later sold it to a legitimate art dealer, say, Fitch Senior?"

"William Delaney was killed in 1958," she challenged. "Right."

"The Fitch sale is dated 1957. Now that we know Delaney never parted with any of his art, we can only assume the sale document was pre-dated—post mortem."

"That's true." He shrugged. "Doesn't mean Fitch Senior

was in on the scam. If, say, the bogus sale was actually transacted in 1959, and the scam artist wanted to trick Fitch, he could have easily made a deflated-looking number nine that anyone familiar with Delaney's history would have perceived as the number seven. Like us. We saw the date on the bill of sale at the gallery. I bet if we take another look, the number will appear ambiguous. Obviously, Fitch made the deal with someone posing as Delaney, a smooth con man, I'm betting."

Erika waved her hand like a student anxious to be called on. "Wait. Let's think this through. The sale took place after Delaney's death. Delaney was an art collector. Fitch Senior, as the owner of an art gallery, would have known this, right? How could he have sat there and accepted Delaney's signature on a document knowing that Delaney was dead?"

"Good question. Fitch was new at his trade and might not have known about Delaney as an art collector until he was approached by his imposter. Besides, in all likelihood Delaney's death was handled low-key. His wife, as we know, was scared out of her wits and would not have written an obituary or encouraged anyone else to do so, and the Cuban authorities would have wanted the event underplayed. I'm for giving Fitch the benefit of the doubt."

"And I'm not," Erika countered. "I think he was in cahoots with the imposter, or chose to overlook the fact that he was being duped, just to get his hands on the goods. You know it's been done. Look at that case in the news not so long ago —the dealer passing off tens of millions of fraudulent modern art works for about fifteen years, all painted by a guy in his garage in Queens. The story she gave to the high-class collectors and galleries? She said she could not divulge the provenance on the works—any of the works—because the owner was adamant about remaining anonymous. Did these dealers believe her, or did they want to believe her?"

Harrison feigned a prayerful bow. "I know the case, and I concede absolutely. We won't give Fitch the benefit of the doubt. Which leaves us where?"

"Skeptical about everyone."

"Open to anything sounds more agreeable."

"Agreed."

"One question. If Fitch was in on it, how do you explain the theft of the Vittorio from his home?"

"He could have arranged it as a red herring," she suggested. "To deflect from his collusion."

"He's non compos mentis."

"Not necessarily. His son, then. His wife."

Harrison squinted, deliberating. "More likely one of the many guests in on Helen and Rodney's tell-all at the Pierre, or anyone along the grapevine, arranged the heist. It's what James Fitch Junior thinks, anyway. Remember his rant at the gallery?"

"Of course. Okay, let's put the theft of the drawing on hold. Where does that leave us?"

Harrison leaned back in his chair. "At square one. Who stole the cache of art from the basement?"

"As we said, a member of the staff, maybe a local friend or—Bertram Morrison!"

Harrison jerked forward. "You're really pushing the envelope now. You said it yourself, Morrison contended someone other than the rebels had something to do with the death of his friend, Delaney. Why in a million years would he want to draw attention away from the rebels if he was a murderer? The rebels would have served as a perfect foil for him!"

"If you want to make your innocence ironclad, what better way than to protest the closing of a murder case?"

"Darling, that is so damn convoluted. Delaney was his close friend as well as his agent."

She shifted her weight as the word "darling" shot through her. "Did a friend never turn on a friend?" she asked, sitting straight as a broomstick. "Do these letters we're looking at go up to the time of Delaney's death in 1958? No, they stop the year prior."

"Maybe the Morrisons were busy with their new baby."

"How about maybe the friends had a falling out? Morrison could have written Delaney a letter that angered him, or had it out with him on the phone."

Harrison threw up his hands. "You think of everything, Erika. Look, if you can come up with the motives and logistics, I'll buy it."

"I guess for opportunity, we'd better stick with someone local, someone in Cuba. Packed the goods in a truck, then burned the place down."

"Smart," Harrison agreed.

"You know," she said, "this still doesn't explain Helen Gilmore's murder, the need for someone at this late date to go after the contents of the safe—the inventory, the documents, memorabilia—not to mention the threats to me and your driver....We're leaving something out, something staring us in the face."

"Don't stress out. If it's there, it'll come to us."

"We hope. In the meantime, we'll pass on whatever's relevant to Lieutenant Mitchell. Which means we should give him a copy of Fitch's Vittorio da Lucca bill of sale and a copy of a letter bearing William Delaney's 'Will' signature. Mitchell can give them to a handwriting expert, confirm that the signature on the bill of sale was forged."

"Excellent. I'll make a copy—hope he won't require the original—of a page with Delaney's marginal notes, and a copy of one of the envelopes addressed in longhand. Give the expert more to work with."

"Good idea. I don't think Tina Morrison would mind, especially if you black out whatever you can of the typewritten text, for privacy's sake." She paused. "Forget what I said earlier. Let's make copies of the pertinent letters—intact, for our eyes only. If Bertram Morrison is later implicated in the death of William Delaney, his wife might decide to destroy the originals."

Harrison shook his head. "If Morrison was involved, why didn't he destroy them right off the bat, in 1958?"

"Why didn't Richard Nixon destroy his incriminating tapes?"

"Good point. So. I'll run the items discussed over to Mitchell—unless you want to."

"You do the honors, it's fine." She shook her head. "It's still bugging me there's something we're not seeing here."

"Think good thoughts. Let's get back to it."

When mention of an inventory again appeared in a later letter dated April 10, 1957, Erika shared an excerpt of it with Harrison, as much for that tantalizing notation as for its hint of soap opera:

....I was half-joking when I asked you to talk the Winstons out of one or two of their Monets. Damned if a year later you didn't go and do it, my man! I hope your hand was steadier than mine as I made note of this in my revised inventory. I will personally hand you a copy of this long overdue document on my trip to New York, in May. Thank you, as ever, for obtaining a fair and reasonable price on the Monets, and for your streamlined management of re-authentication and insurance.

* * *

I've been reviewing our phone conversation, trying to answer the question you so diplomatically posed. I see now that I've been rationalizing R's continuing on here, convincing myself that if I let her go she would be hard put to find suitable employment elsewhere. Were I more theatrically inclined, I'd say the Devil sent her to me to test my faith, but in truth I have only myself to blame for welcoming temptation into my home. Indeed, it has been a struggle, at times a torment, but with your encouragement, no less through your example, I remain anchored to my moral core....

"I'll mention the Winston Monets to Greg," Harrison said. "He might very well recognize the name 'Winston' in the world of art collection, find out if the sale to Delaney is in the family records, along with a description of the paintings. What do you make of the reference to 'R'? Rosa, the replacement for the cook's assistant?"

"I would think. After all, Delaney did present her as a kind of Poor Little Match Girl, someone who needed rescuing."

"You mean the generic male is a pushover for the type."

"You said it, not I."

"Another 'gotcha' moment. Good for you."

"I'm curious to see if the plot thickens," she said, pretending not to have caught the sarcasm. "It may be the issue that caused tension between the two friends. There are only a couple of letters to go." Reaching for one: "We should ask Tina Morrison if she'd look through her husband's files for the 1957 inventory. You think she'd feel put out?"

"Hardly. She's letting us read her husband's personal mail.

What could be more intrusive than that?"

"I'll follow through, then. Although it doesn't seem fair."

"Why?"

"Your task is more daunting."

"You mean tracking down Aldo Fabbri's expert? We're working together, Erika, what's mine is yours."

She smiled awkwardly. "That doesn't make sense, but it sounds good." She picked up her pencil. "Let's finish up."

Of the remaining letters, Harrison's were mostly filled with details about the plantation business; Erika's, with commentary about rising political unrest, with occasional excursions into the merits of remaining true to one's moral code, Delaney's tone waxing increasingly self-righteous.

Harrison made copies of the documents to bring to Mitchell and those they were keeping for themselves, after which the original letters were restored to their satin pouch and packed away in Erika's portfolio, along with her set of copies and Harrison's and her penciled notes. They planned their next move over tea and scones. "If either of us has made headway, let's meet in two days, Thursday," she suggested, dying to lick the crumbs off her fingers. "These are so good." She wiped her fingers daintily on the embossed linen napkin. "My turf this time."

"You're inviting me to your apartment?"

"Office. How about ten or so—unless you have classes Thursday morning."

"I'm free after one o'clock. Too late?"

"No, that's good," she said.

"Stay for dinner tonight."

"Sorry, the Barlows—"

"Your neighbors."

"They're trying out a new recipe on me."

"You're their guinea pig?"

"I draw the line at internal organs. You can come if you like, I know they'd be more than happy if—"

"But would you be?" he interrupted.

"What?"

"Happy."

"Why wouldn't I be?"

"Wrong answer." He studied the plate of remaining scones. "Actually, I should work on my book. I haven't been properly concentrating. Thanks anyway."

She was filled, as if her lungs had drawn it from the air, with a sudden longing for love untortured by knowledge, for a time of grace when dream and reality were one. How simple it would be, to take his hand without foreseeing the future.

"Another time, maybe," he said, patently diplomatic.

The limbic vapors were displaced by the scent of scones and lemon, the sapped wedge floating in her tea like a dead mermaid.

"Sure," she said. She glanced at her watch, although she knew what she would say. "It's time I go."

"One other issue."

"My bodyguard. I haven't forgotten. You'll call him off,

please?"

"Listen closely, Erika. Do you know who attacked you? Do you know who threatened my driver—who's responsible for Helen's death? I want to do everything I can to prevent further harm. Feel free to politicize my motives any way you choose."

She rose to her feet. "Don't think I don't appreciate what you've done, Harrison." She started to clear the table.

He jumped up. "Leave it be." He took the cups and saucers from her and put them back on the table. "There's something more important we have to clear up. I want to apologize—I should have earlier—for hiring Allsafe without telling you."

"Without consulting me."

"Okay, okay, I'm sorry."

"I'm also very uncomfortable about your paying—"

"You're not to feel indebted to me in any way—this is so damn frustrating!" He took hold of the chair-back. Gripped it white-knuckle hard.

"Don't get excited. I should have remembered your aversion to letting somebody else pay for something. My oversight."

"You should know me by now." Composed almost; grip relaxing.

"I do know you." Her answer deepened in meaning as their eyes met, and a shared memory passed from one to the other, a reflection endlessly mirrored. She made herself look away.

"You'll agree, then? I can call the station, get Brennan back?"

She removed her jacket from the back of her chair. "Only if there's an understanding that he, or anyone who spells him, will keep his distance. I don't want anyone in my face, making conversation." She fumbled with her jacket.

"Agreed—here, let me help you."

They fumbled with her jacket together, lingering over

their awkwardness, prolonging the act of departure.

"What did you say?" The phone voice indicated a rift in the speaker's concentration.

"Sorry, Mrs. Morrison. I asked if you could check your husband's files to see if you could locate—"

"Oh yes, Delaney's 1957 inventory. Forgive me for wandering, my mind's been elsewhere."

Erika looked out her office window at the darkening sky. It was becoming less and less likely she'd miss the downpour before trying to scout up a cab to Brooklyn to return the letters. "Well, as I said, in order to make up a really accurate list of stolen works, it would be helpful to see the updated inventory."

"I should tell you, after the tragedy Bertie was a little unhinged, destroying documents indiscriminately. The letters, thank heaven, were spared, only because they happened to be tucked away in a bureau drawer."

"So I guess his copy of the inventory was—"

"Destroyed, yes, I'm sure it was. But I'm so glad the letters were spared."

"Yes. We're so grateful you allowed us to share them with you."

"You know, the pain of the past never faded with time. A look used to come over Bertie, and I'd know he was reliving that day, new and raw. I used to call them his memory attacks."

"I'm sorry, but I don't think I quite understand what—"

"Oh lord, I thought I told you when you came by with your friend. The day William Delaney's place was vandalized, the main house was torched; would have burned to the ground had it not been for the rains."

"You did tell us about the fire, Mrs. Morrison."

"Ah, but did I tell you that Bertie was there?"

"At the plantation?"

"He arrived on the scene almost immediately after the attack. The place was already engulfed in flames. It was a miracle he wasn't there from the start, and if his plane had landed on schedule he would have been. He would have been killed along with the rest. Imagine, thinking you're about to visit an old friend, filled with stories, news—jokes to share! He used to describe it to me, what it was like that day. He used to be so good with words, my Bertie, before the strokes."

Moved as she was by the story, Erika's primary interest was how did it dovetail with yesterday's brain-storming with Harrison? She was still trying to wrap her mind around the fact that the list of art works on the 1954 inventory had been carried over in its entirety to the 1957 update, ideas still bursting like nuked popcorn over that one! "It must be so difficult for you," she said, almost breathlessly, the irrepressible excitement of mystery-solving spilling into her compassion, marring it.

"It is difficult for me, but how much more difficult it was for him, I can hardly imagine," Mrs. Morrison said, her voice close to breaking. "But now I'm depressing you, and that's the last thing I want to do. I'll see you in a little while, and perhaps I can make up for it. I can be cheerful, you know, if I put my mind to it." She uttered a small, doleful laugh.

The clouds burst as the call ended. Erika slipped into the poncho she kept in her shallow office closet then checked, for the third time, the packet of letters secured in the depths of her tote.

As she shut the door to her office, Brennan, slouched in a folding chair up against the adjacent wall, looked up from his muscle magazine.

"I'm taking a cab to Brooklyn," she informed him. "Basically in and out. I've gone this route before, no problem."

Brennan rose to his feet, rolled up the magazine and jammed it into the pocket of his jeans, making sure it was tucked under the flap of his windbreaker. "Let's go."

"You're not dressed for the rain," she said, with slim hope of dissuading him.

"I'm good." He reached into the pocket of his windbreaker and came up with a mini folding umbrella.

"I'm going to be in a cab, out of it for a quick drop-off, then back in. What are you expecting, a drive-by shooting?"

"I'm paid to watch out for you, so save your breath."

She could hardly complain when, minutes later, he was waving her into a cab he'd commandeered by flashing a card—business ID or Price Club membership, who knew?—under the nose of a stranger, a newly boarded passenger, causing him to bolt.

Shoving over to leave room for Brennan, Erika reeled off her destination's address. The cabbie, perhaps given the circumstances of his vehicle's takeover, put up no objections to driving to Brooklyn.

Hardly settled in, she snapped open her cell phone; punched in Harrison's number. He answered after four rings, interminable, given her rising pulse rate.

His urgency seemed to anticipate hers: "Erika!"

"I wanted to make sure we're on for tomorrow, my office."

"I was going to call you. How about first thing in the morning?"

"I thought you weren't free until after one."

"I'm calling my T.A. to take over. I've got important feedback to share with you."

"Same here."

"Really?"

"Really."

"Want to talk now?"

"I'm in a cab with the bodyguard you foisted on me. Now's not good."

"Returning the letters to Tina Morrison?"

"Yes."

"I don't know if I can wait until tomorrow."

Deep twinge in her belly. Why couldn't he have used the word it instead of I? "I can't either," she said, punishing him for his ambiguity by matching it.

CHAPTER 13

Ten-twenty, and no sign of him. Erika thrummed her fingers on her desk, trying to turn her pubescent angst to adult-worthy impatience.

As she reached for her cell phone, it rang. "Where are you?" she asked, spotting the caller ID.

"The gate," Harrison answered, sounding out of breath.

"What?"

"Boarding in minutes. Greg Smith will explain. He's probably on his way over to your office now."

"Boarding, as in boarding a plane?"

"JFK to Miami, then on to Havana. It was managed in under twelve hours."

"As in Havana, Cuba? Why didn't you tell me?" she demanded, anger supplanting surprise. "What's going on?"

"The final documents just came through. Didn't think they would. I've been running around, getting things done. I'll try to arrange a meeting with the museum curator or the arts minister. Won't have time for both. Preference?"

"Are you kidding me?" She was fuming. "Why aren't I with you? This is our project!"

"Trust me. Hear Greg out, you'll understand. I'll see you in three days. We've got a lot to talk about."

"You bet we do!"

"Going now. See you soon."

She could hear something being announced over a loudspeaker, couldn't make out the words. She dropped her ego like a hotcake. "Be careful!" she cried out before she was cut off from him.

Had he heard?

"Be safe," she added, into the void.

* * *

She was in a state of confusion spiked with renewed outrage when, ten minutes later, Greg Smith, looking as alpine as ever, was ushered into her office by Frank Brennan, her bodyguard.

"Glad I passed muster," Greg said cheerfully, clearly unruffled. "May I sit?" he asked, taking the seat across from her. "This won't take long."

"How do you know? I have no idea what's going on."

He smiled and deftly withdrew a folded paper from the shirt beneath his cable knit sweater. "This is Harrison's itinerary." He handed it to her across the desk.

She unfolded the paper bearing Greg's Art Loss Registry letterhead. "He's on a 'People to People trip run by Carlton College Alumni Adventures,'" she recited in toneless wonderment. "His lecture is on 'Environmental Art, slash, Art As Environment.'" She looked up at Greg. In her cramped office he seemed even brawnier than he had at The-Hole-In-The-Wall. "What is this trip and why am I not on it?" she asked, indignant.

"It's a long story."

"You said this wouldn't take long."

"Funny." He stretched his legs beneath the desk, his feet bumping hers. "Sorry," he said, quickly retracting. "First off, the tour takes thirty, max. It was filled months ago. I should add that these People to People tours to Cuba are run by a limited number of licensed venders." He shrugged. "Of course, what with the fluid nature of things, travel may be totally open by next Tuesday. At any rate, these tours have been around for a couple of years, even under the U.S. embargo, though nowadays it's a bit easier to hop on one of these tours."

"So Harrison was able to hop, but I wasn't. Where did the idea for this trip come from, anyway? What is your role in this venture? What do either of you plan to gain from it?" The questions were piling on like a subway at rush hour, the most disturbing, unvoiced: Was it Harrison's idea to leave me out? Her mouth was dry. She needed water.

"I feel like I'm at a press conference," Greg said, unperturbed. "A hostile one."

"Would you like a drink of water? Something else?"

"Water would be great."

This man was agreeable to a fault. She swiveled her chair so she could fetch a couple of quart bottles from the cabinet near her desk; swiveled back around and handed him one. They took a couple of draws, then replaced their bottle tops.

Greg sat forward in his seat, as if preparing for a downhill ski run. "How's this? I talk, and then you ask as many questions as you want."

"Sounds fair."

"Excellent." He sat back. "It recently came to my attention that a friend of a friend was forced to drop out of a commitment to lecture on an art tour of Cuba. Of course I thought of Harrison and you, what an opportunity to come face-to-face with your contacts in Havana. It was unlikely there would be enough time to get the paperwork done, not to mention getting Harrison accepted as a stand-in, but I've got connections in Washington, D.C. who've got connections with folks in the Office of Cuban Affairs, plus rules and regs have become less daunting. I asked Harrison if he could pull it off, and he gave me an off-the-cuff lecture that knocked my socks off. He talked about Jose Fuster, the 'Picasso of the Caribbean,' as if he were a lifelong friend. The artist has literally transformed his community in Havana with his colorful multimedia sculpted pieces. In fact, this area is dubbed 'Fusterlandia' and is one of the main tour visits. Harrison compared this permanent collection of art installations with the works of environmental artists like Edith Meusnier and Christo and Jeanne-Claude—you remember their saffron colored panels, The Gates, in Central Park back in 2005—artists whose works are more ephemeral, seasonal.

"He went on for a good while with his presentation. I told him if he edits it down to an hour and a half, he's got it made. And, as it turned out, he did have it made, but just under the wire. I'm truly sorry you couldn't go along.

"The tour is eight days—other cities besides Havana are visited—but Harrison will leave after the Havana portion. He'll be back in three days, which includes the flight from Miami to JFK. It's all in the itinerary I gave you, including the hotel the group will be staying at: the Melia Habana in the district of Miramar. He'll be getting in touch with you, I'm sure. I've overdone it. Do you have any questions?"

She felt thoroughly and childishly left out. She harnessed the feeling and looked him straight in the eye. "Why couldn't I have traveled independently? Now it's too late."

"Inquiries would have hobbled my efforts on Harrison's behalf."

"I could have made my own inquiries. Maybe you didn't want me to hobble Harrison's efforts." Why was she so reluctant to admit the possibility that it was Harrison himself who had elected not to be hampered by her presence?

Greg shifted his position, entrenching himself. "I might have thought it was easier for him to gain access to certain individuals if he was on his own, yes."

"Did you give Harrison that choice?"

"I told him you wouldn't be able to get clearance in time. We left it there." He gave an easygoing smile that stiffened into a line of obstinacy.

Greg resents women, Erika concluded, choosing the least worrisome reason for being blocked from this trip. Furious with Harrison, but giving him a damn pass. "Did you provide him with the name of anyone less prominent than the Minister of Arts to contact?" she asked evenly. "As a means to gain access, as you put it?"

"I did. I gave him the name of a lawyer associated with the office of the Assistant Secretary of State for Western Hemisphere Affairs. He's an underling, but a bright, on-the-spot young man who knows his way around the U.S. as well as the Cuban diplomatic offices in Havana. He's stationed in Havana at the moment, and I'm sure he'll be a big help steering Harrison through the maze of bureaucracy. The name's Javier Garcia. He's a Cuban-American, born in Miami. A perfect liaison for Harrison. Made-to-order."

Erika jotted down the name on her itinerary sheet. "Thank you," she said coldly.

"If you need to reach Garcia for any reason, let me know. I'll express you through. Any other questions?"

"Not now—not yet." Her unease about her exclusion was mounting by the second, along with her ability to stifle Harrison as its cause.

Greg started to rise. "You have my card? Never mind, I'll give you another one." He grabbed a card from the back pocket of his chinos; handed it to her. "Mind if I take the water?"

"What?" she said, distracted.

"The water." He raised the bottle she had given him, gave it a shake.

"Of course, take it," she said civilly, inwardly hurling expletives.

CHAPTER 14

"Come!"

Erika flung open the door to Sara's office. "It's been over twenty-four hours and I haven't heard from him, Sara, and I'm beginning to worry, really worry!"

"Breathe girl, breathe."

"I am breathing." Sara's placidity was maddening. From the vantage point of her own agitated state, Sara was comatose. "I've tried calling and texting, but he's unreachable."

"Shut the door, hon. What was the nature of your last contact with Harrison?"

Erika pushed the door closed with the heel of her foot without turning from Sara. "He called me from Miami. Then he texted me after he had checked into the hotel in Havana, then next morning after his lecture."

"How did it go?"

"The lecture? It went just great. This is what you're interested in?"

Sara uttered her trademark musical laugh. "I'm trying to calm you, give you perspective."

"Whatever that means," Erika said, walking closer to Sara's desk. She placed her hands flat on the desk and leaned forward, as if this would wake Sara up. "I'm not sure what I should do next!"

"You're looming. Take a seat. Have you called the tour

promoters?"

"Yes."

"And?"

Erika planted herself in the straight-back leather chair opposite Sara. "They said they're not at liberty to say."

"To what question?"

"Every question. I tried contacting Greg Smith, but he's either unavailable or screening my calls. I tried on my own to reach someone in the State Department who would talk to me and was shuttled from one subdivision to another until I got someone I thought would help. I gave her all the information I had, and she said she would look into it. I don't think she'll call back."

"What makes you think that?"

"A gut feeling; she sounded indifferent." Throat tightening, Erika undid the top buttons of her blouse. Still constricted, she peeled off her blazer and flung it over her knees. "I'm being stonewalled. It's as simple as that."

"What did Harrison text you, Erika?"

Erika managed a wan smile. "You mean besides how the lecture went?"

Sara's smile was more upbeat. "Exactly."

"He said he was going to meet someone in the arts ministry. The person who got him this interview was Javier Garcia." Erika related what she knew about Garcia from her conversation with Greg Smith. "I don't know what the interview was about," she concluded, anticipating Sara's next question. "At least not specifically. I don't think Harrison knew at the time either."

Sara flashed her a quizzical look. "Unless he chose not to tell you."

The idea had entered Erika's mind. She hadn't let it stick. With Sara's gibe, it nipped at her again.

"You are a naïve one," Sara said, confoundedly maternal.

"Maybe that's why you're tough on men. To protect

yourself from your innately trusting nature."

"Is there a charge for the psychoanalysis?" Erika fairly snapped. "Shall I lie down on the couch?"

"Your defensiveness speaks volumes, dear. Come on, you know I adore you."

"Sorry, I'm just very jumpy."

"No, I apologize."

"We're wasting time. What shall we do?"

The question was answered by the startling ring of Sara's office phone.

"Natalie Gilmore," Sara reported, checking the caller ID before punching in.

From what Erika could make out, Natalie was firing off a tirade, punctuated by Sara's monosyllabic utterances. "Can I talk to her?" Erika mouthed.

Sara shook her head vehemently, then scribbled a dictated number on a desk pad; repeated it for confirmation. Finally, she issued a statement: "I'm awfully sorry, Natalie. I can understand your anger. I'm quite put out myself by all this, although I don't think you should assume Harrison's motives to be nefarious."

Erika reached to grab the phone out of Sara's hand. Sara clutched if firmly as she bid Natalie goodbye. "We'll stay in touch," she said coolly, through clenched teeth, as she warded Erika off. "My god, Erika!" she cried, after punching off.

At last, Sara was fully present. "What do you mean, 'nefarious'?" Erika hurled at her. "Why didn't you put me on?"

"Because it wouldn't have been productive," Sara replied emphatically. "Natalie is furious with Harrison, and with good cause. As am I. I assumed Harrison had cleared this trip to Cuba with Natalie. At least you should have spoken to her as soon as you knew. The matter of recovering William Delaney's art is your assignment, Erika, but it's Natalie's mission. That was her grandfather!"

"I thought Harrison must have called her at some point. I should have made sure!"

"Let's not beat you up, it gets us nowhere. It was an oversight on Harrison's part. Well, probably."

"Probably?" Erika objected, her voice rising in pitch. Her chest was pounding. She tried to take Sara's word of advice, earlier dismissed: breathe. Just breathe. She inhaled deeply; exhaled slowly.

"It works, doesn't it?" Sara asked with genuine compassion. "It helps," Erika admitted. Calmer, but by no means calm, she asked, "How did Natalie find out about Harrison's trip? Did she tell you?"

"I was getting to that. Your man in Havana, Javier Garcia, contacted her. I took down his number. Natalie said a representative of the magazine should call him. That could be you, although I didn't press her. She might have said no."

"Let's do it. Please hand me the phone."

Sara passed her the portable device, along with the notepad. "You'll see zero-one-one in the U.S. exit code," she said; "fifty-three, the country code."

Erika punched in the number. The moment it took to connect was interminable.

"Hello, this is Javier Garcia, and you're on speaker phone, a youthful male voice intoned. "I see you're calling from *Art News*."

"This is Erika Shawn. We're on speaker phone, too," she advised. She clicked it on. She heard a shuffling movement in the background. "Where is Harrison Wheatley?" she demanded.

"He's right here."

Sara was patting the air as a warning to go easy. Erika nodded her understanding, but bulldozed on. "Where is 'here'?"

"His hotel room at the Meliá Habana."

"Put him on, please—Harrison, are you there?"

"I can't put him on, but I assure you, he's fine."

"I'm fine, Erika!" Harrison cried, his voice clearly strained.

"Why can't you put him on the phone? Is he tied to the bedpost? Have they hurt you, Harrison?"

A voice in the background uttered something in Spanish. It sounded angry.

"I'm unhurt!" Harrison called out. "Cooperate with Javier, he's on my side!"

"Okay now, Erika?" Garcia urged.

"I don't have a choice. Please tell me what's going on."

Garcia audibly sighed. "Thank you, Erika. Now, without getting excited, let me explain. Harrison has gotten himself into a bit of a problem here."

Erika's breath caught, but she kept her silence.

"Thank you," Garcia repeated, as acknowledgement. "So, I can't divulge the facts surrounding the case because they remain unconfirmed, but what I can say is that they concern the matter of allegedly stolen art. What I would like for you to do is relate as fully as you can the nature of your association with Professor Wheatley. There is another person in the room with us, and he will be listening to you, too. His name is Hector Martinez and he is a lawyer employed by the Cuban government. Please be assured that privacy regarding this matter is as important to Mr. Martinez as it is to the rest of us, and that everything you say will be handled with the utmost discretion. Do you understand, Erika?"

"Yes—Harrison, are you good with this?"

"I'm good with this!" Harrison replied, with a note of desperation.

Sara nodded her agreement, reached across the desk to pat Erika's arm reassuringly.

With gnawing reservations, Erika described to her unseen audience the nature of her assignment as well as her association with Harrison. Garcia asked her to further elaborate on the research that took them to England and Italy, and, at the request of Hector Martinez, posed several questions directed at establishing Harrison's character.

"Is Harrison free to leave his hotel room?" Erika asked

when her interrogators appeared to be done with her. "Harrison," she said louder, "shall I call the State Department?"

"No!" Harrison replied after an instant's pause. Erika wondered if he was being prompted.

"All sides are covered, Erika," Garcia assured her. "Our aim is to keep a low profile. To answer your question, Professor Wheatley is being detained in his hotel room until Mr. Martinez feels comfortable about allowing him to leave."

"He's under house arrest?"

"I wouldn't say that, no. After the initial stages of the investigation are complete, your friend will be released. Further processing can be transacted in the States. There are other issues at stake. We want to make sure all security measures are in place so that he can return home without incident."

"Have you confiscated his cell phone?"

"We have, yes. We'll give it back before he leaves, but he's advised not to turn it on until he's landed at JFK."

"Will he be on his scheduled flights from Havana and Miami tomorrow? Will he be landing at JFK as planned?"

In the background, a burst of agitated commentary from Martinez that Erika, a tolerable whiz at college German, was ill-equipped to translate.

"We're cautiously hopeful," Garcia said, with the decisiveness of a final offer.

CHAPTER 15

Accordingto Harrison's itinerary, his flight from Miami was scheduled to touch down at JFK at 9:32 PM. It was 9:35, and Erika still hadn't heard from him. She panicked. No surprise; it had been more or less her steady state for the past three days. Earlier, she had called the airline to ask if his name had been listed on the flight's manifest. As expected, the information could not be released due to security regulations.

She called the airline again and was informed the flight had been delayed. Revised arrival time: 10:57.

She emptied the dishwasher. Combed her hair. Sat straight-backed and immobile while every cell fidgeted.

At 11:15 Harrison called, and the sound of his voice instantly dispelled tension, like air escaping a vent. She slumped into her chair, deflated by the sudden relief. "You're safe," she whispered.

"Erika?"

"I'm here. I'm glad you're back. I was worried you wouldn't be on the flight."

"So was I."

Now that her primary concern for his safety had been happily resolved, her chagrin at having been left out of his plans reemerged. "You calling from baggage claim?" she asked, restrained.

"No. Headed for the taxi line. I've just got a carry-on. Want to meet at Hole-In-The-Wall? They're open until at least two in the morning. I can call you from the cab, give you a more accurate time of arrival."

"Sure," she clipped.

"It's not inconvenient for you? We can wait until tomorrow. We can meet in your office as we had planned a couple of days ago, before...all this."

"We can meet then, too." Her mood, as changeable as a child's, lifted again. His innocence, despite Natalie's accusations and Sara's innuendos, was abloom in his voice, the rhythm of his speech. "We had important matters to discuss at that meeting, both of us."

"Mine can wait until tomorrow," he said. "Can yours?"

"Yes."

"Because tonight I only want to catch a glimpse of you and tell you about my run-in with the law."

Run-in. Sounded as ominous as a minor traffic regulation.

* * *

They were ensconced at the same table they had shared with Greg Smith; sipping green tea and picking at English muffins, hers spread with blackberry jam; his, orange marmalade. Harrison looked exhausted, but Erika hadn't reminded him of it.

"Where's your bodyguard?" he asked, suddenly remembering. "Pacing outside. I said we could talk privately if he sat apart from us, but he chose not to." Harrison was reaching for his cup. She touched his wrist, bare below his sweater cuff. "Tell me what happened, Harrison. You've been talking around it." Doubt and resentment, tugging at her again.

"I want to," he said. "I meant to, only I'm afraid if you're questioned again it might be construed that you're, well, part of it."

"The plot?" she asked, taken aback. "You're making it worse. You better explain. I'm not afraid of becoming embroiled, if that's what you're thinking. You told me you were going to meet someone in the arts ministry. What's his name? Start there." She broke off a piece of her muffin and gazed at it, allowing him a moment to gather his thoughts unsurveilled.

"His name is Luis Navarro," he said. "He's the assistant to the Assistant Minister of Arts."

She looked up. "Thanks."

Harrison took a sip of his tea. "That felt good."

"The tea?"

He smiled. "Telling you."

"Tell away," she said, popping the broken piece of muffin into her mouth, encouraging him with her sangfroid. "How did you come to meet Navarro? Greg, by any chance, mention his name?"

"He did, actually. He said his friend—I should say connection—Javier Garcia told him Navarro was the person to see, that he was as informed as anyone in the department and easiest to gain an audience with. In fact, Garcia told me Navarro was especially eager to see me and had taken the initiative to see me. He said Navarro had some crucial information about five—he was very specific, five—of the paintings listed on William Delaney's inventory."

"I sent the minister a copy of the inventory," Erika said. "It must have been passed around."

"Exactly." Harrison chipped off a piece of his toasted muffin, then abandoned it. "Navarro had recognized five of the paintings on the inventory. He pointed them out to me. Imagine: two Matisse oils, two Gauguin, one Van Gogh. None of them are listed on Greg's work-in-progress report, and none have turned up through the diligence of the museum curator you reached out to."

"Amazing. What was Navarro's source?"

"An Italian aristocrat, down on his luck, with an unsullied family name he'd die to preserve."

"Signor Anonymousotti, I presume."

Harrison smiled. "Of course. This is a young man who's been left a number of art works by his father, now deceased. Trouble is, his father warned him that the provenance of these pieces is somewhat sordid and that he must be especially cautious if he ever decides to sell them. The son brought photos of the paintings to the ministry but withheld information about their location. He wants to sell the works for a fair price, but only to a discreet buyer, such as the arts ministry itself or a museum."

Erika was raising the tea cup to her lips. She clacked it back into the saucer. "You must have been unable to contain yourself," she said, adding sub-vocally: I should have been there!

"I offered to help the gentleman discreetly unload his art, or I should say Luis Navarro proposed that I do so. I agreed it would be a perfect arrangement for the Italian, since the only players in the game would be a respectable art professor and an aristocrat in her own right, Natalie Gilmore. I was sure if the sale didn't proceed up to snuff, those five works of art would remain underground forever. I said I would discuss the matter with Natalie, and that only she would set the terms, if there were any to set. Navarro brought up the subject of my commission, but I immediately shut down that discussion. No fees involved. Period."

Erika was relieved to hear Harrison voice Natalie's primacy in any art recovery negotiations. Surely Natalie would forgive him for not seeking prior consent for pursuing the matter on her behalf. "So far, so good," she said. "But I'm puzzled. When did the trouble start?"

"Here's where the story turns *Rashomon*," he said, gesturing to the waiter. "The tea's getting cold, I'll order two more, okay with you? Want something else to eat?"

"Just tea."

He ordered two teas and an appetizer of chicken fingers. "Two plates, thanks. We'll share."

"You think you know me better than I know myself," she said, half jesting. "Now, tell me what happened? When did it go wrong?"

"When the authorities stepped in to interrogate Luis Navarro."

"What?"

"We think alike. That was exactly my reaction. Apparently, Navarro has been under suspicion for running a black market network in the art world for some time. The mysterious Italian is no doubt one of the more discriminating members. Navarro put us together like a couple of clients on Match dot com."

"You think it was a coincidence that you were in his office at the time of his face-off with the authorities?" Erika asked in disbelief.

"Yes. A really bad one."

"But still," she wavered, doubtful, "how could this have gotten you into trouble?"

"Navarro's story is different from mine. He said I approached him with an offer to broker deals for him using my respectable position in the States as a front, and that it was I, not he, who was running the black market network. He said I tried to convince him that with the improvement of Cuban-American relations, the business of art recovery and reparations was going to pick up and that we should be on the ground floor of operations. Those are the words he put in my mouth: 'ground floor of operations.'"

"Well, that can be proven wrong!" Erika balked. "Why hasn't it?"

"I was told it takes time," Harrison said, frustration surfacing. "People have to be questioned. People who are loath to be discovered."

They were quiet as the chicken fingers and tea were delivered to their table and the first cups and saucers removed, along with the plates of half-eaten muffins.

"Where does Javier Garcia come into play?" Erika

asked. "Hardly 'play,'" Harrison commented, edgier still. "Javier is a lawyer with an understanding of all sides and an interest in bringing the matter to a just and swift end. He is also committed to facilitating the recovering of those five works of art. Natalie will of course be at the helm in that effort. The sad thing is, Luis Navarro, the bastard, is trying to use Garcia's history against him."

Needing warmth from somewhere, Erika pressed her hand to the tea cup.

"I'm taking it out on you," Harrison said, suddenly remorseful. "The only person I want to talk to."

"It's all right. I get it. What about Garcia's history?"

Harrison sighed. "Garcia is a Cuban-American, born in Miami. His grandfather was imprisoned as a political enemy at the beginning of the Castro regime. The rest of the family fled to America. His grandfather died six months before Raul Castro freed fifty-three prisoners."

"He died in prison?"

"Yes."

"That's a tragic story. Navarro must be suggesting that Garcia, because of his family's experience, is biased against Cuban officialdom and will stir up as much trouble as he can for both Cuban authority figures and, by extension, Cuban-American relations."

"You amaze me, Erika." He stood up and leaned over the table; held her face in his hands and studied her. His kiss, because she moved, landed beside her nose. When he sat back down, his arm brushed his tea cup. It wobbled but did not tip over. "Lucky," he said.

"Yes."

"You make me feel like it will be okay."

"You, too," she said, not quite why. Maybe for symmetry. "Let's not talk about this anymore, not until, or if, we have to."

"One more thing," she said, almost coyly. "Did you try to get me to Havana, or did Greg Smith persuade you not to?"

He hesitated very briefly, perhaps because it was a compound question. "Erika, Greg said there was no time to get you certified for individual travel, but still, I checked all the airlines. The flights to Havana were booked solid. Even if you could have gotten the documents on time, there wasn't an available seat. There's a big influx of tourists traveling to Cuba these days."

"You never brought up the subject of a tour."

"I didn't bring it up because I didn't think I'd be able to go. I didn't think about it until Greg called at the last minute to tell me to pack my bag."

"He basically said I would have cramped your style, Harrison."

"Listen, Greg has been campaigning for years to become president of the board. He was just out-voted by a woman who joined the board three months ago. He's become a neo-misogynist."

"I thought as much."

He laughed. "That figures."

"Are you sure Greg didn't put you up to this?" she asked, very much in earnest. "Did he know there might be a deal in the offing to retrieve William Delaney's art, and he didn't want me gumming up the works?"

"Are you saying I hid something from you?"

"Not with bad intentions," she said quietly. His look of hurt was genuine. It had to be.

"Or maybe Greg didn't let you in on the plan because he was afraid you'd reject it out-of-hand," she reconsidered.

"You're saying I might be a liar," he said, still reacting to her first comment.

"No, only naïve," she said. Like Sara said about me, she added to herself.

"Erika, do you trust me?"

"Of course," she said instantly, the line of his neck, his tousled hair, the imprint of his kiss, overriding doubt.

CHAPTER 16

Gypped out of a sunny start, October flaunted the rare brightness of morning. Every nook, every particle of dust in Erika's modest office was illuminated. Squinting out the window in its brazen glare, she felt lit through, laid bare. She lifted her face to it, imagined in exposing her innermost longings she was yielding to them. She let the sun's warmth embrace her, knowing, on a more austere level, that the warmth was produced by her temperature-controlled environment.

A call from the receptionist alerted her of Harrison's arrival. The realization that he was back from his journey and safe, struck her almost as strongly as it had the night before. She redid the waist button of her pinstriped suit jacket and ran her fingers through her hair, puffing it up. She was nervous, letting him into her inner sanctum, yet longed for it.

They spoke at once as he came through the doorway: "Can't wait to see your reaction," he started right in. "Space is a little tight here," she apologized.

"We don't need space, we need time. This meeting is four days late!" He stood his briefcase next to the folding chair opposite the desk chair; peeled off his brown wool sports jacket and hung it on the back of it. "Here good?"

She laughed. "Where else?"

"I see your point." He sat down. "Pleasant, though.

Friendly." He watched her take her seat across from him. "Ready? Okay, do you remember us discussing the obstructionist, Aldo Fabbri? The lousy photocopies he sent us of his Vittorio drawing, adding to his failure to reveal the name of the antiquities expert he was going to have check it out?"

She was suddenly lit from within by the recollection of their sitting on the floor of his study, with Jake's head resting on her lap. "You were going to try to track down this unknown expert," she said. "I had my assignment. This was yours."

"Well, I found the name Aldo was withholding from us."

"So quickly? Before your trip?" She had promised to keep the subject of his Cuban entanglement at arm's length, but an interjection was surely permissible. "Where's the expert based, Florence?"

"Surprisingly, no. If Aldo thought he could buy time by miscuing us, he was wrong. Lucky for us, we hit pay dirt with our most unlikely contact, Brian Latham."

"You mean Aldo sent his drawing to the British Museum for analysis?"

"Close. Actually, to one of the experts Brian had listed in answer to my inquiry. He's on the faculty at Oxford University. Name's Percy Clarke."

"Don't tell me you've already heard from him."

"I told you I was good—or did I?" He reached into his briefcase for a two-page document; handed it to her across the desk.

It was the printout of an email exchange between Harrison and Percy Clarke. She scanned it eagerly, disbelief mounting. Breathless almost, she fluttered the pages at him. "How could you have kept this from me?"

"I wanted to see the expression on your face." He grinned. "It was worth it."

"This man has reattributed Aldo's Vittorio da Lucca drawing—to Michelangelo!"

"Yes, he has, hasn't he?"

"Says here he used a computational tool developed by

a group of Dartmouth researchers, and that these high resolution digital images can read the signs of an artist's, quote, 'aesthetic signature invisible to the naked eye'—Harrison, do you know what this means?"

"It means the chances of the drawing stolen from the Fitch residence being a Michelangelo have just gone up considerably."

"My hands, they're shaking."

"They are." He took them in his. "It's exciting, isn't it?" Overwhelming, now she was in his harbor. "Yes," she whispered. "And did you happen to notice the date, Erika?"

"The date of Clarke's email?"

"No, the date of his analysis."

Puzzled, she slipped her hands from his to take up the pages. "I must have skipped over it." This time it popped out at her at the close of the analysis excerpt Clarke had selected for email transmission. "I can't believe it. Aldo had this analysis done way before we met him!"

"Why are you shocked? You were the one who was suspicious about Aldo in the first place."

"Only after he sent us those worthless copies of the drawing from his folder." Frowning: "But I only thought he was trying to buy time so he could get the results from his expert and then, one way or another, try to get his hands on the drawing stolen from the Fitch home."

"You mean low-ball its possessor before the individual knows he's got a possible Michelangelo in his mitts."

"Yes."

"And now you're thinking Aldo was doing more than stalling us, he was downright lying."

"Yes. To keep us in the dark. To keep us from spilling the beans before he has a chance to carry out his plans."

"Now the only thing we have to determine is how deep is he in it? Did he have anything to do with Helen's murder and the theft of Fitch's drawing, or is he just a pernicious son-of-a-bitch?"

"I figure the latter."

"Any reason?"

She shrugged. "Just a hunch. He strikes me as being arrogantly opportunistic, but not evil."

"Shall we tell him we caught him at his game?"

"You mean if Percy Clarke doesn't blow our cover? No, I'd say let it be for now, see how it plays out."

"I say we tell him. I want to see him writhe."

She smiled at the mischievous curve of his lips, his relish for revenge far short of real malice. "Let's decide later. First let's talk about my bombshell." She took a breath, preparing to begin. "It's about Bertram Morrison. I spoke to his wife on the—"

She was silenced by a commotion erupting in the hallway.

Something or someone thudded against the door, accompanied by "Get your hands off me, you nut—hey!"

Harrison leaped from his chair to hurl himself against the door, blocking passage.

Erika shot up. "Let him in, it's Rodney!"

Harrison reluctantly stepped aside, and Rodney bolted in. "Since when did this place turn into a goddamn police state?" Glaring from one to the other. "What's with the Gestapo out there?"

"My bodyguard," Erika said, with a rueful shrug, as Brennan pushed into the already cramped area. "He's okay, Frank; a friend."

"No one stopped him," Brennan said gruffly. "The receptionist must have stepped away from her desk. He was very combative when I asked for his ID."

"I said he's okay—thank you!"

Brennan hesitated, weighing the dismissal, then withdrew.

"What's going on here—plotting?" Rodney sniped, a beat before Erika began sliding a blank notepad over the copy of Clarke's email, and too late for her to abort the act.

"Hell, it's true!" Rodney sang out with sardonic delight, catching her at it.

"Nothing of the sort!" Erika protested too adamantly, glancing at Harrison for moral support.

Rodney's eyes narrowed. "Charming. A regular little cabal, the two of you."

"Don't be a fool," Harrison warned impatiently.

"Don't get on your high horse, Wheatley. If Natalie thought I'd be bumping into you today, she would have been incensed. Your unauthorized involvement in Cuba was not a wise idea. For your information, she's asked Greg Smith to turn over his Delaney file to her. He will be stepping aside. Natalie will be working with a renowned art law specialist who's been engaged by the Met Museum on many occasions. Don't expect Mr. Smith to be returning your calls." He turned to Erika. "Natalie has more or less forgiven you. She realizes you had nothing to do with the planning, only the failure to keep her up to date. Still, she tried to dissuade me from coming. 'Erika's your friend,' she said, 'why do you want to antagonize her?' So, I asked, how come after my good 'friend' puts in a good word for me, the law is breathing more vigorously down my neck? And you know what she said? 'If you're right and Erika does have it in for you, you'll get riled up and get yourself into bigger trouble!' Bigger trouble? I shouldn't be in any trouble!"

"Why don't you state your business?" Harrison curtly suggested.

"Screw you!" To Erika: "I'm an artist, remember? An observer. I wanted to see for myself. And now I have. Caught you in flagrante with your new buddy."

"For god's sake, Rodney!" Erika forcefully objected, her glance nevertheless fluttering about Harrison like a moth drawn to a flame. "Confirmed!" Rodney pronounced, again with mordant glee.

"There is something going on between you two, no use denying it!" He waved his arms about, playing it to the rafters.

"Are you protecting him, Erika? Do you suspect him, this scholar with his grand aspirations? Do you suppose he gave one of his acolytes, some puppy-eyed coed, the assignment of getting hold of the contents of Helen Gilmore's safe? Have you been leading the law away from his doorstep and onto mine?"

"Cut the histrionics," Harrison scoffed. "This is a small room, you might hit someone."

Erika thought the suggestion seemed unkind, despite its justification. "Calm down, Rodney. Sit—here, take my chair." She put her hand on his shoulder to guide him.

He recoiled. "No thanks, I'm afraid I'd be inclined to uncover what you've hidden from me on your desk. You know I'm not governed by what passes as etiquette, especially when the subject is self-preservation!"

She let his bit of showmanship ride. "Listen, Rodney, contrary to what you may think, I'm prejudiced in your favor, and Lieutenant Mitchell and his crew know it. If I clue you in on Harrison's and my findings, your involvement will appear even stickier." She felt an inner satisfaction, even a reluctant smugness, for having grasped her argument out of thin air.

"Quick thinking," Rodney said bitingly. To her look of guilty surprise: "I saw your shoulders relax. I told you I'm an observer, nothing gets by me."

"Enough!" Harrison ordered, drawing up to Rodney as if he might take a swing at him. "There's enough circumstantial evidence linking you to Helen Gilmore's death without your having to dream up our evil plot against you! You latched onto Helen and her daughter in lightning fast succession, you misled the cops about your phone call to Southampton, you nosed around Erika's apartment and covered your ass with a lame follow-up email. You later broke into her place, I take it to collect the rest of your paraphernalia. At least that's what Erika thinks. You're doing fine on your own, making yourself into a person of interest."

Erika had never seen Harrison so enraged, though despite his threatening posture and accusatory tone of voice, his anger did not alarm her. She was confident, from his even breathing, his studied gaze, that he was in control.

Rodney's mute response did frighten her. More than provoked by immediate insult, it seemed torn from some deeper order of malcontent. His eyes burned with pure hatred, unchecked by judgment or even awareness.

Harrison, on the receiving end, appeared unscathed. Erika, more familiar with Rodney's emotional range, was afraid for Harrison. Rodney's aggression had always taken the form of flaunted urbanity, a disdain for those he deemed aesthetically challenged, his biting wit executed with the precision of a meticulously drawn sketch. Nothing like this dark and brutal silence. With no thought of the consequences, she tried covering Harrison by shoving herself between him and Rodney. Harrison stopped her with a firm push against her rib cage, his hand remaining in place to bar her from further attempt.

As if suddenly glimpsing his state of mind through the shocked countenances of others, Rodney's facial expression collapsed into one of mortification. "My life's gone to shit," he complained, his sardonic tone deteriorating to a whine. He slumped into the folding chair, accidentally kicking Harrison's briefcase.

Harrison paid it no mind. "If so, it's your doing, not ours," he admonished. "Get your act together."

"Shut up, man, okay?" Rodney beseeched, with a residual flicker of resentment. He turned to Erika. "I came to cry on your shoulder, whatever, and first I'm beaten off by some thug outside your door, and then I find the two of you holed up here concocting who knows what." He threw up his hands, staving off any rejoinders. "They've got it in for me, you know? The detective and his posse, they're grilling everyone I associate with. Natalie's on my case, her father's making life miserable for me, my friends are afraid of being seen with me, and the Milgram Gallery, finally going to give me a break, postponed my show. Postponed? Bullshit, they canceled! Worst of all, I can't paint a damn thing. I stand there staring at the blank canvas, and it stares back at me. You wonder why I exploded? I'm at the end of my rope, that's why!"

"Listen, we were grilled by the detective, too," Erika said. "This bad spell will run its course," she assured him.

"You find that in a fortune cookie?" He fluttered his hand, canceling his remark. "Forget it."

She shrugged it off. "I know you think I only made things worse for you, but maybe you'll feel differently when you get your bearings."

"I know you didn't try to mess me up," he said with a trace of acrimony.

"Would you like me to give Lieutenant Mitchell a call, ask him to get off your back?"

"Or call the Milgram Gallery?" Harrison pitched in, his voice lacking enthusiasm. "I know the owner. I could put in a good word for you. It might have some clout."

"Don't patronize me, okay?" Rodney clenched his teeth. "Sorry, I didn't mean that. I resent what looks like your immunity is all. Okay, you were interrogated, but they're not hounding you—and you're not stuck in a creative vacuum." He rose to his feet. "You're busy. I'll leave now." He started for the door. "Sorry to have bothered you," he murmured, brushing by Erika.

The effect of his touch took her by surprise; chilled her to the bone. "No bother," she responded too airily.

His lips formed a tight-lipped smile. "Yeah, sure," he muttered, not quite under his breath.

The door clicked shut behind him. "'Alas, poor Yorick,'" Harrison declared.

Erika gave a start, for at that moment she was herself wondering if any part of Rodney's plaint had been an act, and if so, for what end?

"Something wrong?"

"It's nothing," she said. "Come on."

"That look he directed at you, I've never seen it before."

Her voice trailing off: "I'm thinking I may not know him as well as I thought I did."

"And you feel guilty about feeling that way."

She nodded. "It seems so...disloyal. I do respect his talent, and I've always taken his bravado as a kind of boyish trait stemming from that talent."

"In other words, his talent excused his arrogance."

"In a sense. It was harmless, a form of exuberance. Now I'm not sure. What if his intention today was to manipulate me into feeling guilty? Is that twisted of me, or what?"

Harrison smiled affectionately. "Hardly. But what would be his motivation?"

"To influence my actions. I run to Mitchell, protest his treatment of Rodney. I get overemotional, maybe Mitchell gets a bug in his head about the root of my behavior—guilty conscience, maybe?—starts focusing on me for a while, easing up on Rodney. Here's another possibility. Who knows if Rodney gave us a straightforward account of his sessions with Mitchell? Is it possible Rodney tried to lead him in my direction, and now he's accusing me of doing that to him?"

"What the shrinks call 'projection'?"

"Yes."

"So you're saying he may be unhinged."

"Temporarily."

Harrison gave a who-knows? shrug. "Having experienced one mind-blowing creative block of my own, I do know something about what he's going through." After a reflective pause: "Unless to garner your sympathy he fabricated his painting block."

"That's what I'm considering, cynical as it may be."

Harrison ran a hand through his hair. "If any of your concerns about Rodney are valid, and especially if they're not, this is no time to voice them."

"You're suggesting they might be prejudicial to the investigation."

"At the least. Besides, if Rodney has had any role, pri-

mary or peripheral, in the Delaney case, it would be unwise to
—"

"Is that what we're saying here? Do you actually believe
that's possible?"

"Nothing would surprise me. Our research has been full
of surprises."

Erika felt herself flush.

"So," Harrison segued, awkwardly backing up into the
folding chair, "I say for now we drop Rodney's game plan and
get back to our own." He realigned the chair and planted himself in it. "You were about to release your bombshell about
Bertram Morrison."

Erika skirted around him to get back to her seat, keeping him on tenterhooks. "You're not going to believe this." She
sat down.

"Try me."

She rested her elbows on the desk and leaned toward
him. "Morrison was at the scene of the crime," she said breath-
ily.

Harrison thrust forward. "He's dead. What crime?
Where?"

"Guantanamo Province, Cuba."

"You mean Morrison was at the plantation the day the
place was looted?"

She nodded. "His wife said he'd gone to visit his friend
William Delaney, and if his plane's landing hadn't been delayed he would have perished or been killed along with the
others. She said the residence was already ablaze when he got
there."

Harrison rose from the chair and began pacing back and
forth in the limited floorspace. "Bertram Morrison is at the
scene," he pondered aloud. "Too late to help William Delaney,
but not too late to help himself. He removes the hidden cache
of artworks for transportation, then sets fire to the place to
cover his tracks. Is he riddled with guilt? Do we even care?"
He came to a halt and turned to Erika. "Your scenario doesn't

seem so far-fetched anymore, does it?"

Feeling the need to be up and at the ready with him, she joined him in the open area. "No, except suddenly I'm a lot less comfortable with the scenario than I was when I came up with it."

"I don't get it. Bertram Morrison was at the scene of the crime. The elusive factor of opportunity has been handed to us on a silver platter."

She nodded. "I know, but when I look at the picture as a whole, it makes less sense."

"Explain."

She shifted her weight. "For one thing, he can't be connected to the attack on Helen Gilmore, a crime that must in some way be related to the original crimes against Helen's father, William Delaney. As for Tina Morrison, when I returned the letters to her we talked awhile, and unless she's up for an Academy Award, it's hard to doubt her sincerity about wanting to see the crimes solved, past and present. Besides, if she had anything to do with covering up the crimes of the past by perpetrating or abetting in the crimes of the present, she wouldn't have let on about Bertram's trip to Cuba."

Harrison raised a brow. "I see your cynicism has softened."

"Although," Erika reconsidered, "if we can credit Rodney with unexpected acting skills, why not Tina Morrison?"

"She's back!" Harrison affectionately observed.

"And if we can conceive of Fitch Senior creating a diversion by staging a fake theft, why not imagine Mrs. Morrison creating a distraction of her own?" She shook her head. "No, that's too much of a reach."

Harrison smiled. "No scenario should go unexamined," he recited. "You taught me that. Seriously, the thing is, however we spin it, the fact that Bertram Morrison was in Guantanamo Province at the scene of the crime is pertinent to the current investigation, and we're obligated to tell Lieutenant Mitchell."

"I agree. He can re-interview Tina Morrison, track down her husband's old business associates, and any other sources who might help connect the dots. By the way, did you approach him yet?"

"You mean to hand over the samples we made of William Delaney's letters?"

"Yes, so he can check out Delaney's signature against those appearing on the 1957 bills of sale."

"I had all the available exhibits delivered to him by messenger early this morning. He may already have gotten his analyst's opinion. I expect a call from him late afternoon."

"Good, then you can add the latest on Bertram Morrison to the agenda."

"What about Aldo Fabbri? Think we should share the latest scoop on him? Personally, I think not. Aldo's deception regarding the analysis of his drawing is too far afield for Mitchell and his team, at least at this point."

"Right. Especially since we decided it's probably more about Aldo's acquisitiveness, getting a bargain on Fitch's purloined drawing, than anything more venal. Plus I think we should let Aldo pursue his search for the missing drawing unhampered."

"Let him do the detective work for us," Harrison interpreted. "Exactly." She hesitated. "What about Rodney?"

"No place for Rodney's mood swings on the agenda."

She uttered a sigh of relief. "Thanks." She realized she was beginning to view Rodney as a mother might regard a child given to tantrums: minimize his embarrassment and hope it's a passing phase. "Also..." She paused.

"Yes? You can mention Cuba, you know," he said, with a wry grin. "I'd like to steer clear of my own mess, but that doesn't include the communications you've initiated."

"Good. I'm expecting to hear from The National Museum any day now, with more evidence of works to be returned outright, or"—she added with a grin that matched his — "politely ransomed. Of course it's understood that Natalie will be the final arbiter in all negotiations, and as sole inheritrix of her grandfather's collection, she'll have the final say on how it's deeded over to The Metropolitan Museum of Art." She felt a peculiar heaviness in her shoulders, realizing she and Harrison had just been wrapping up.

Harrison glanced at his sports jacket draped on the back of the folding chair. "So," he pronounced with strained finality. "We should plan to get together in a few days, see where we are." He reached for his jacket; slipped it on. "With luck, you'll have gotten more feedback from your contacts in Havana." The statement was not in itself a non-sequitur, but his distracted delivery made it seem so.

"I'll call you on your cell phone," she said.

"Or I'll call you."

"Yes," she replied, neither of them moving. She looked down and by chance focused on his briefcase.

"Ah," he said, "I might have left it." He picked it up.

"So," she voiced, in a belated echo, before initiating their short excursion to the door.

"Wait."

She stopped mid-step. "Look at me."

She turned to face him directly.

He set down his briefcase then righted himself in the sparest of motions, as if to avoid causing a disturbance in the air. "What were you thinking when you came between me and Rodney?"

She smiled. "I wasn't thinking."

"You should do more of that."

Her smile broadened. "Shielding you?"

"No. Not thinking."

"I'll give it some thought." The smile downright roguish.

He smiled faintly, but without play. "I'm not implying you should put yourself in danger, either for me or for yourself."

His seriousness took her by surprise; made her shy. "Of

course not. I know that."

The stillness was like a presence, an intermingling of their unspoken thoughts.

He reached for her, his hand shaping itself to her cheek, his thumb finding the corner of her mouth, then, meeting no resistance, venturing across her lower lip and inward along its satiny underside, surfacing at the opposite corner.

"Remember?" he asked softly.

She pressed her fingertips to his lips, not to silence him as he may have thought, but to complete the circuit of their kiss.

He closed his eyes, understanding, after all.

"I remember," she said, answering his question, although there was no need to.

He started to lean toward her, she toward him, when the sound of the office phone jarred them back to reality, or at least what Erika, at her most typically analytic, took it to be.

So ingrained was her defense mechanism, it was with a measure of relief she broke away. "Excuse me," she said gently, which sounded ludicrous, although what wouldn't have?

He gave a resigned shrug and stood there, waiting. She picked up after the second ring. "Erika Shawn."

"Do you have a cell phone? I'll give you my number!" A woman's voice; desperately high-pitched.

"May I ask who's calling?" Erika asked with compensatory evenness. She glanced at Harrison, indicating with a shake of her head she didn't have a clue.

"First call me back on your cell phone. I do not trust the office line." There was a trace of a foreign accent in her voice, indefinable, like distant music.

A small rap sounded as the receptionist stuck her face in at the door. "Everything okay? I took a chance putting the call through. The lady sounded frantic."

"Tell her to go away!" the woman on the phone demanded.

"It's okay, Lonnie, I've got it," Erika said.

The receptionist rolled her eyes heavenward, then withdrew. The door clicked shut.

"Is she gone?" the woman asked.

"Yes."

"Can you remember a phone number without writing it down?"

"Yes."

"Are you alone now?"

Erika put a finger to her lips, messaging Harrison to remain silent. "Yes, I'm alone. May I at least repeat the number, make sure I've got it right?"

"No. Listen carefully." The woman recited a phone number; repeated it; hung up.

Erika grabbed a pencil from her desk and scribbled down the number on the nearest paper at hand. "No area code, it's local." She reached for the cell phone sitting in its usual spot, at the base of her mail tray.

"What the hell's going on?"

"No idea. Don't move, don't say a word." She punched in the dictated number.

The woman answered mid-first ring. "Erika?"

"Yes, will you explain—"

"This is Isabel Fitch. My son, James, is confident you are handling the matter you discussed with him with the discretion it requires."

"Mrs. Fitch?" Erika turned to Harrison, who was still as a statue, barely a foot away.

"Senior," she mouthed.

"Understand, my son knows nothing about this call, including the reason for it. He would be tempted to call the police. Will you promise to tell no one?"

"You put me in an uncomfortable position. Without knowing—"

"Do I have your word?"

"Yes," Erika reluctantly lied. Of course, she would tell Harrison, if no one else.

"In turn I will give you my word that the police will be notified in due time." Leaving no beat for reply: "I received a ransom note for my Vittorio da Lucca this morning. It was slipped through my mail slot. I cannot say exactly what time it was delivered, but my assistant discovered it fifteen minutes ago. I will not tell you its contents over the phone, but I need you to come take a look and see what you can make of it. I have been associated with the art business a long time, but I am sure you are more of an aficionado than I am. Will you come as quickly as possible? Of course I will pay whatever fee you—"

"No fee," Erika protested. "If I come, there'll be no fee. If I come," she stressed. "As you wish."

"If I do, I'd like to ask my colleague, Professor Wheatley to—"

"I am not trusting my son!" Fitch volleyed. "Please— alone!"

"All right, I'll come alone," Erika conceded, surprised by her snap decision, the sudden rush of adrenaline. "What's your address?"

"We have been on the phone too long. You can find me." The connection was severed.

Erika flicked shut her cell phone.

Only then did Harrison dare move. Taking a step closer, he said almost querulously, "I'm not sure what just happened, but I know I don't like it."

Feeling him charge back into the center of her attention, Erika suddenly wondered what words would have been exchanged, what actions committed, possibly later regretted, if they had not been interrupted by the phone call. "Isabel Fitch received a ransom note for the drawing, and I'm running over there to take a look at it," she said straight out, preparing for his objection.

"Oh, great, I guess she meant to call 911, punched in your number by mistake."

"I knew you'd understand," she said, with a conciliatory smile.

Unappeased: "From what I heard, I'm not invited along."

"She sounds pretty paranoid, not even cluing in her son. Later, she'll notify the authorities."

"Thanks, I feel so much better."

"Come on, Harrison, all she wants me to do is look at the note, get my read on it. I'll have my cell phone with me, and Brennan can keep an eye on me—I mean, from a distance."

He shook his head. "I don't get it. How can you be so guarded with me and so daring with strangers?"

"It's a matter of acceptable risk."

He gave her a quizzical look.

"With you it would be harder to get over an unhappy ending," she said, looking down. She sidled past him to get to her desk computer.

"According to you, the inevitable unhappy ending," he said, refusing to be distracted.

"Yes," she said, clicking onto the Google White Pages. "Listen, I'll call or text you the second I leave Fitch's place." She paused, a new idea germinating. "If no one's looking, I'm going to try to send you a photo of the ransom note," she said.

"No spy games!" he vetoed. "You'll tell me about it later!"

"Okay, okay," she agreed, even as she considered going back on her word.

He picked up his briefcase. "I'll talk to you later. Remember to call me." He started to leave, hesitated with his hand on the doorknob; turned back.

They did a long take, staring at each other.

"My brave scaredy cat," he said tenderly. "Be careful."

If only she could let reason go and ask him to come near. In her mind's eye, they stumbled toward each other to complete their interrupted embrace.

She nodded a fond dismissal, and he turned to go, his left foot slightly toeing in with the motion, hooking her into his departure and stinging her with regret.

Erika pocketed Isabel Fitch's address. As she rose to go, Sara barged in unannounced.

"Sorry, got a moment?"

"Of course," Erika replied cheerfully, already planning her exit lines. She grabbed her tote.

Sara charged ahead. "I just got a call from Natalie Gilmore. Until Harrison's name is cleared you're not to involve him in any of your ongoing Cuban communications. Letters, emails, to be discussed only with me or Natalie."

Erika felt like a deer in the headlights. "Rodney was just here," she managed.

"Your point?"

"He was extremely hostile. He told Harrison Natalie was furious he traveled to Cuba without her consent. At worst, that's negligence. If she still harbored so much as a shred of suspicion, Rodney would have announced it on the intercom. He held nothing back, believe me."

Sara raised a brow. "Natalie doesn't share all her thoughts with Rodney. She knows he's a talker."

"Surely she doesn't believe Harrison..."

"Is involved in art running, as it were?" Sara shook her head. "No, at this point she's concerned only with his reputation. It must be unsullied if his name is to be associated with her mission. As for the matter of shady dealings, I, on the other hand, believe the jury's still out."

"I'm speechless."

Sara shrugged. "I'm more cynical than Natalie. I suppose she's a nicer person."

"Sara, you said yourself Harrison has an aversion to money!"

"Inherited money. Perhaps not money resourcefully acquired."

"Sara!"

"Who knows, maybe he could use the extra cash to get his ex off his back." She smiled tenderly, taking the edge off her words.

Erika make a concerted effort to shake off Sara's absurd hypothesis; concentrated on the more pressing issue at hand. She tightened the grip on her tote, hugging it to her side. "Sara, I've got a—"

"You run along now," Sara said, with a hand flourish. "You deserve a break." As she started for the door, "Have a nice lunch," she added, sparing Erika the need to fabricate.

CHAPTER 17

C ruising by the receptionist, Erika remarked she was off to a "project-related interview." This also served as an explanation to Frank Brennan, following close at her heels.

She elaborated on the white lie in the cab heading downtown, adding that the interviewee was extremely protective of the information she had agreed to divulge and that a stranger hanging about the place might cause her to have second thoughts. As Brennan opened his mouth to object, she cupped her hand to his ear, and in a hushed voice revealed the woman's identity, hoping he'd take this as a major concession. It seemed to work: he knit his brow and bobbed a conspiratorial nod.

On Seventh Avenue and Fourteenth Street and nearing their destination, Erika asked the driver to pull over. She paid him, and she and Brennan slid out of the cab.

They were standing directly opposite a tiny art supply store, its window crammed with easels and palettes and colorful boxes of every media. To its left, Chung's Market was fronted by stands of neatly arranged fruits and vegetables, and to its right, Petro's Ukrainian Diner posted its menu and flyers of neighborhood events on a bulletin by its door. The trio of establishments, so close they seemed to overlap, was a comforting reminder to Erika that Greenwich Village had retained its character of lively heterogeneity. Under different circumstances, she would have loved to explore the area, a favorite haunt in her years at New York University.

She turned to Brennan as the driver took off. "Until I enter Fitch's building you can keep me in your line of sight. After that you can keep an eye on the place, but from a respectable distance."

"I don't get it," Brennan objected, in a delayed campaign for inclusion. "Tell the lady I work for *Art News*."

"No way. She could trip you up on an easy question, blow the deal."

"Gotcha, but why can't I just wait for you by her door?"

"She's got a thing about the paparazzi," Erika invented. "She might see you out the window, take you for one of them. It took me ages to cultivate her confidence. Let's not destroy it now."

"So she's that famous," Brennan conjectured, eying her.

"In certain circles," she offered elusively. Turning her back on him, she started walking west, in the direction of the Hudson River, toward Perry Street. She figured she had five short blocks to go, tops. In the near distance she could see where the shops left off and the run of residential dwellings began. "Give me a head start."

"I'm coming after you if you fail to exit the premises in forty minutes," he warned.

"Only if you hear shots," she replied flippantly, the last word nevertheless catching in her throat. "Just kidding," she added, as much for her own benefit as his. She strode on.

Intent on checking address numbers, she became aware of the rural-like quiet of the area only when she was midway down the first exclusively residential block along Perry, the sense of seclusion deepened by the sheltering maple trees bordering the pavement. The Fitch house, a traditional brownstone tucked among its peers in friendly cohesion, was located near the end of the next block.

As she approached the steps leading up to the main

entrance of the townhouse, a young man emerged from its entrance below street level—the "English basement"—and proffered a friendly nod as he deposited a plastic bag into the trash can up against the enclosure's wrought-iron fence. She smiled politely in return before mounting the steps. Out of the corner of her eye, she could see Brennan, about four houses down, starting to cross the street in a slow stroll, a portrait of nonchalance.

The door was opened a crack in response to one gentle push on the doorbell. "Yes?" came a strong, high-pitched voice from behind the door, as the door-chain snapped taut.

"It's Erika Shawn."

The door was shut to allow the chain's release, then opened wide, still concealing the person behind it, except for a delicate hand waving energetically. "Hurry, come in, come in!"

Erika stepped inside, to be confronted by a woman who carried herself so erectly, Erika found herself correcting her own posture. The woman's Rubenesque figure was stunningly well-proportioned. That she was mindful of the fact was evidenced by the white patent leather belt cinched at the waist of her navy shirt-waist dress.

Erika extended her hand. "Mrs. Fitch?"

The woman nodded and gave Erika a peremptory hand-pump. "Were you followed?" she asked, flicking her glance nervously from left to right over Erika's shoulder. "You must leave at once if you even think you were."

"No," Erika unblinkingly assured her.

Mrs. Fitch slammed shut the door and refastened the chain lock in one quick movement. "Do not stand on ceremony," she said, in her just discernible accent and without the crack of a smile. "Call me Isabel, or I shall be forced to call you Ms. Shawn." She gestured toward the living room, a gracious space decorated in understated Victorian into which the entryway spilled. With a quick turn, she led the way to an arrangement of two high-backed chairs flanking a finely carved walnut table. "Please sit. Would you like coffee or tea?" She waited for Erika to select a chair, then took the other.

Erika dropped her tote beside her. "I'm okay, thanks."

"No trouble," Isabel said impatiently. "My assistant can make you either. I'm having tea."

"Tea's good."

"Two teas, Andrew!" she sang out, in a voice as tensely pitched but more melodious than the one directed at Erika. "First bring us the gloves!" She turned to Erika. "To handle the note," she explained, nodding toward the envelope on the table. She ran her fingers through her short wavy hair, natural gray and in youthful abundance. In every aspect, Isabel's real age—had to be at least seventy judging by her son's—was contradicted by her exuded age. Even her eyes, of darkest brown, smoldered with a tenacity for life. "Look over there," she said suddenly, aiming her forefinger at the wall opposite. "There, above the couch. That is where the drawing hung. All those years!"

"Please, Mum, don't upset yourself," urged the young man hurrying toward her, a pair of yellow latex kitchen gloves dangling from his fist like a trapped bird. The same person Erika had seen taking out the trash. Clad in a lily-white T-shirt, sleeves near bursting at the abs, pressed blue jeans and sneakers.

"I will try, son," Isabel promised, visibly heartened by the sight of him. She took the gloves from him. "Andrew," she pronounced with affectionate vigor, this is Erika Shawn, from *Art News*."

The two repeated the silent acknowledgment they had earlier exchanged, and Andrew went off to brew the tea.

"I didn't realize—I mean, is Andrew your son?" Erika asked awkwardly.

"No, but he ought to be," Isabel replied, slipping on the gloves. "This should prove to you that I plan to turn in the evidence to the police," she added parenthetically, holding up her sheathed hands. She reached for the envelope. "No, he is not my son, but I am quite as attached to him, as I am to James." She held the envelope in her hands, staring at it as if it had materialized from another dimension. "We took Andrew in seven years ago. My husband and I are patrons of an organization that helps troubled teens transition from juvenile detention to the real world, give them a feeling of belonging as well as a healthy work ethic. A while back we decided to do more than send in our expected donation. The usual period of fostering is three to four months. We grew very fond of Andrew, and it seemed only natural that he stay on." She waved the envelope in the air. "I suppose my biological son is right. I do trust Andrew more than I do him. I am asking you not to reveal the contents of this to James." She opened the flap of the envelope.

Erika leaned forward at the edge of her seat.

Isabel removed a sheet of paper; held it so that Erika could examine it. "What do you make of it?"

Erika gasped, immediately regretting it. "What is wrong?"

She would not let on, at least not entirely; there were too many unknowns raging around Fitch Senior's acquisition of the Vittorio da Lucca drawing as well as other works from William Delaney's collection. She pointed to the sheet of paper now fluttering in Isabel's trembling hands. "It took me by surprise. I recognized it from an art course. It's a Francis Bacon." She did not add it was the same one she herself had received, only with a different caption.

"I knew you would be able to help me," Isabel twittered breathlessly. "Tell me what it means—all that space, with only the mark of blood—was something digitally removed? What has been left out?"

"Nothing's been left out," Erika said flatly, making herself use Isabel's agitation to neutralize her own. "Its sparseness fills it with unanswered questions. It's supposed to make you feel uneasy. The caption takes it to another level." She studied it intently, forcing it to inflict calm on her, like a jab of painkiller: something left out of this room something taken from yours we talk today contact the law you too will know silence. "It's a ransom note—or, I should say, the preview of one. There's no riddle to solve here. The painting, the wording, are for effect only." She amazed herself with the steadiness of her voice.

"May I put it away now?" Isabel asked. "Are you done with it?"

"Yes—you'll turn it over to the authorities?"

"In due time, of course."

"I'll take it for you, if you like."

"Absolutely not!" Nostrils flaring, Isabel refolded the note and tucked it into its envelope. With an imperious toss of her head, she transported the parcel to a small writing desk several feet away. Returning, she snapped off the latex gloves and slapped them onto the table. "You think I am a hare-brained old lady, don't you," she said without the slightest inflection.

"Of course not!" Erika vehemently objected. "I only meant to be of assistance." She wasn't sure if she'd heard a pejorative snort from Isabel as she reestablished herself in her chair. She was about to apologize further, when the telephone on the writing desk sounded an alarm—or appeared to, given the prevailing tension.

Isabel leaped from her chair and tore over to the desk, snatching the receiver from its cradle and simultaneously pealing "Yes, hello!" into the air. "What?" she cried, pressing the receiver to her ear. "What did you say?" Her chest was heaving. With her free hand, she clutched the edge of the desk.

Erika rose to come to her aid but was cut short by Isabel's frantic head shake.

"Did you say down payment?" As Isabel listened, her free hand moved to her chest, slender fingers fanned against her bodice like a decorative broach. "I need time—yes, where? All right, all right. No. I'm not delivering anything. My assistant will be acting for me." She winced. "Take it or leave it." Her hand slid to her waist, grabbing at her belt buckle as if it was about to snap open. She nodded, listening again, then hung up.

She walked slowly back to her chair and sank into it. "Andrew?" she called weakly.

"What can I do?" Erika asked lamely, reaching out toward her. The question went unanswered, unheard or rejected.

Andrew appeared, bearing a tray with elegant tea service accompanied by a plate of assorted cookies.

"What is it?" he asked solicitously, reacting to Isabel's look of distress. He quickly laid the tray on the small table, dexterously removing the latex gloves out from under. He tucked the gloves into a back pocket of his jeans.

"I just called you," Isabel mildly chided, though clearly heartened by his presence. "You didn't hear me."

Andrew dropped down to one knee before her. "The phone rang—was it—them?"

"Yes. They are letting you act for me." She laid her hand on his head, as if knighting him. "You have to go to the bank now. I'll write a check. Put on a suit, son. I don't know why, but I would like you to." She glanced at Erika, who had remained very still. "You will have your tea, and then you will leave us," she said decisively. "I do thank you for coming."

"I don't need to have tea," Erika assured her, with a twinge of resentment that Isabel would have presumed she'd counted on refreshments, especially at this stressful time.

"It will help me to stay calm, this little ritual," Isabel said. She went to reach for the teapot, but Andrew intercepted her as he rose to his feet.

"Here, let me," he said, grasping the handle. He filled the dainty cups, placing them on either side of the tray, within easy reach of the two women. "We have milk here," he directed to Erika with a reserved smile. "And here's lemon and sugar. We don't believe in artificial sweeteners." He removed two embroidered napkins from the tray and placed one on Isabel's lap.

As he bent beside Erika to perform the same favor, their faces nearly collided.

The napkin fluttered to the carpet as Erika jerked back in horror. *No no no please no.*

Andrew swooped up the napkin and replaced it on Erika's lap. "Oops," he said quietly, urging her silence with a hooded glare.

He returned to Isabel's side. "Don't you worry, everything will be okay. Hang tough." He smiled at her affectionately.

Isabel withdrew the cup from her lips. "How do you manage to relax me, son? Have you put something in my tea? Fetch my checkbook and pen from the desk, then get dressed."

Erika watched Andrew move toward the desk, his gait unhurried, natural. She must be wrong, she tried convincing herself, as her senses, refusing to repeal their verdict, pulsed *he's the one, he's the one.* The musky scent of cologne was fused in memory with the whispered threat, the pain tearing at her scalp. Coincidence, she pleaded with herself uselessly, as she watched him reach for the requested items in the desk drawer.

There was no plan, but Erika rose to her feet, the need for privacy her sole reason. She picked up her tote bag, slung it onto her shoulder, as thoughts stuttered into being. She should leave immediately, but then she might never again be allowed access, the chance to investigate. It was okay, Brennan was out there. Her lifeline. "May I use the ladies' room, please?" She sounded as if she were asking the teacher if she could be excused.

"Thank you," Isabel said affectionately, addressing Andrew as she took the checkbook and pen from him. "Now, look like you mean business; the black suit is best."

Erika felt invisible to them.

Isabel turned to her only after Andrew had left the room. "The bathroom is down the hall," she said, as if the intervening exchange had not occurred. "Third door on the right."

Erika started to walk in the appointed direction. "Your bag, please."

Erika stopped in her tracks. "What?"

Isabel motioned with her hand. "Take out your cell phone. I'll give it back."

"You don't trust me?"

"Not one hundred percent, I'm afraid." She motioned again.

There was no choice. Erika gave an exaggerated shake of her head, overplaying her reaction to the insult, when in fact she could understand it. "Here," she said, handing over the device.

Isabel placed the instrument on the table, very gently, as if making up for her forceful tone of voice. "Thank you."

Now what? Erika wondered, leaving the room. Her link to Brennan gone, she'd be unable to warn him of possible trouble ahead. If it came down to his having to collect her, the worst thing would be to have him caught off guard. The pre-monition of a violent confrontation shuddered through her, stopping her mid-step across from a room whose door was ajar. More potent than fear, curiosity prompted her to glance into the room. Andrew, in his jockey shorts, was slipping an arm into the sleeve of a white shirt. He looked up, startled, and she turned away, unnerved as much by his wide-eyed stare as by her own audacity.

The bathroom was a few feet away, taking on the char-acter of a safe haven.

The illusion of safety vanished as she pushed in the flimsy button-lock on the doorknob. She wasn't confident it worked, but there was no way of testing it. The room was long and white—white tiles, white towels—white everywhere; she could hardly see details as she fought for clarity. She clung to her bag as if it contained the answers to all her urgent ques-tions.

Time was of the essence. If Andrew left for the bank within five minutes, she'd have maybe ten before Brennan came to fetch her. She could ask Isabel about her husband and William Delaney: when did they meet, when did they start transacting business, who were their agents? When her bodyguard Brennan hit the scene, whatever trust existed between Isabel and herself would be gone. But would Andrew allow them to talk privately? Hadn't he warned her in Schurz Park to keep out of this business?

In a minute Isabel would start wondering what she was doing in here. She flushed the toilet and turned on the tap water. For authenticity, she crumpled a paper wash towel. She looked for a waste basket. Found it tucked near a covered laundry hamper.

A set of towels hung on the rack above the hamper, the bath towel brushing the surface of the lid. There, protruding from behind the hem of the towel, lay a slim, silver object, easy to miss.

Without an instant's hesitation, she seized the cell phone and flipped it open. Brennan's number refused to come to mind, programmed into her cell phone's memory but not her own. She'd have to call Harrison's cell. Tell him to alert Brennan. She was already forming what to say to him, pleading with him not to get involved, promising to reach him later, as her finger hit the call button. A phone rang—Isabel's phone.

She punched in the end call button, realizing that in her haste to speak to Harrison, she'd forgotten to enter his number. She knew instantly what she'd done: automatically redialed the last number called from the cell phone now cradled in her hand.

She acted before the burning question had a chance to form fully. She pressed the menu button, then recent calls. The number—Isabel's number—stared up at her from the display screen—twice, one beneath the other. The entries included the times the calls had been made. The uppermost, her own, had been made seconds ago; the one below, six minutes prior, about the time Isabel had received the ransom call. She hit the clear button and began punching in Harrison's cell phone number. Though fixed on this,her trembling caused her to strike a wrong button, and she was forced to clear the screen and begin again.

She heard movement outside the door, then a jiggling of the knob.

"I'll be right out," she responded, evenly as she could, as Harrison's recorded message began what seemed like interminable caller instructions.

No time. She snapped shut the phone, ending the call.

Still clutching the phone, she swung round to the window, her bag slapping at her hip. She scanned the outdoors, hoping to spot Brennan, to signal him, convey some message, any message.

She heard the lock give way with a click. She turned toward the sound, knowing that in the next instant Andrew would appear in the doorway.

The door swung open.

"You called her!" she blurted reflexively, unprepared for the actual visual assault.

The slender screwdriver that he must have used to disengage the lock was in his right hand. He brought it up to his lips, held it there like a finger, and made a shushing sound.

He closed the door from behind without taking his eyes off her. "You do not want to scare Mrs. F," he said, slipping the tool into the back pocket of his suit pants.

"I won't give you away and risk having you take it out on her, if that's what you mean," she said, self-directed anger fueling the boldness in her voice. How could she have voiced her accusation, given him a heads-up!

"Shut the water off, it's driving me nuts."

Before she could change gears, he brushed past her, turned it off himself.

He spun around, snatching the phone from her.

As she watched helplessly, he flipped it open, nimbly swept from options to erase, then, in a staccatoed blink, deleted the record of the two calls to Isabel's number.

"This is not what it seems," he said.

"What is it, then?"

"Not a thing. You got an active imagination is all." He popped the phone into the pocket of his suit jacket.

Her frustration deepened when she remembered how quickly Isabel had answered her phone, too quick for his cell number to have registered on her caller ID.

Erika had nothing incriminating on him but the scent of his cologne.

"Andrew!" Isabel called shrilly. "What's keeping her?"

He opened the door a crack. "I'm waiting to get into the bathroom! She says she doesn't feel so good. A case of nerves is what I think!"

"It doesn't surprise me," Isabel answered. "Are you dressed?"

"Ready in a minute!" He shut the door. "Appreciate your cooperation," he said, picking up the ends of the striped tie draped on his chest, then whipping them into a passable knot, centering it with a delicate tug against the starched white collar. "How do I look? Just kidding." He took a fleeting glance in the mirror over the sink. "Okay, let's go."

Erika froze.

"What did you think, I was going to leave you alone to play mind games with her? You're coming with me."

"No!"

He held her by the shoulders, like a friend seeking her full attention. "Look, you can choose to be brave, but I don't think you want to make that choice for anyone else—Harrison, Sara, Rodney."

"Is that a threat?" she asked meaninglessly, buying time. Any minute Brennan would show up, get her out of here.

He grasped her more tightly. "I've got friends who owe me. Take it any way you like."

With a burst of resolve, she tore at his hands in an attempt to pry herself free.

In one quick movement, he drew back his right hand,

formed it into a fist and punched her, just above her left breast.

She staggered from the force of the blow but stifled her cry, determined, even at the apex of pain, not to lose control.

"Sorry," he said, gripping her forearms to steady her, "I had to make you understand."

"Get your hands off," she rasped, pulling away from him, her chest throbbing. She rubbed the point of impact, a small indulgence for the child within, still howling.

She would do as he asked until they stepped outdoors. Isabel was more vulnerable than she, an unknowing captive under her own roof. To awaken suspicion would put Isabel in mortal danger. He made her walk in front of him down the hall to the living room, where Isabel was fingering Erika's cell phone as if to divine its secrets.

"Don't give it back to her," Andrew said, drawing near. Isabel looked up, questioning.

"She was trying to call out on my cell."

"I was trying to check for messages on my land line," Erika declared over-emphatically.

"She is probably lying, but we have no time for that," Isabel said. "Did she succeed in calling out?" she asked Andrew. "Will the police interfere?"

"Don't worry, there were no calls." He stroked the back of Isabel's head. "And she's ageed to come with me. I'll keep an eye on her."

Isabel jumped to her feet. "Are you out of your mind? We cannot have anyone nosing about. We were warned!"

"It'll be okay."

"What if they've got a lookout who sees you leaving with her?"

"I've got it covered. Trust me."

"Do I have a choice?"

"Unless you want to babysit her, no." He smiled. "You have that check ready for me?" His watchfulness never wavered, surrounding Erika like a radar zone.

"There, on the desk chair," Isabel said. "In Dad's briefcase. You'll need that to hold the money."

Erika shuffled her feet. "I'd like my phone back," she said, too meekly. "Now."

"When I am satisfied all has gone well," Isabel said. "Although for the life of me I can't imagine why Andrew wants you along."

"To keep her from making trouble," he said.

"We still have to deliver the balance on demand. We cannot keep her under lock and key until then."

"Of course not," he said, side-stepping to retrieve the briefcase without letting up his surveillance. "She'll have good reason not to interfere until the mission's complete. Leave it to me."

Where is Brennan? Why hasn't he shown up?

"Get going, then," Isabel said. "It might take some time at the bank." She turned to Erika: "I am sorry to have to inconvenience you."

Erika was guided to the door by the repellant hand pressed between her shoulder blades.

Suddenly they were out in the open. In an instant of eased pressure, the hand on her back shifted to find a more secure hold on her. A chance to make a break for it. Why was she hesitating? She feared reprisals for her friends, but there was more to it. Was Andrew acting alone, or did he have an accomplice, someone who'd executed the threatening notes, Isabel's as well as her own? She wanted to know. To know she had to be there.

The instant was gone. He had her by the wrist, pulling her down the brownstone stairs. "This way," he ordered, yanking her toward the near corner. "Don't fight it."

In her peripheral line of sight, she saw Brennan half a block away on the other side of the street and about to cross it, surely headed for the Fitch residence. Again, she was faced with a choice, but she was beaten to it.

"Erika!" Brennan called out. "Hey!"

She turned toward him as he was drawing a gun from

his belt.

He raised it over his head and set out at full tilt.

"What the hell!" Andrew said gruffly, digging his nails into her wrist and launching into a sprint, ripping her along with him. "I knew you couldn't be trusted!"

She pulled back, resisting the tug, yet she moved with him, a surge of adrenaline investing fear with excitement. She would be in on the action, first-hand discovery. She skidded round the corner with him, his nails biting at her wrist, challenging her to ride through the pain, more severe with her lagging.

Brennan had not yet caught up with them, but there was no way he'd missed them turning the corner.

"This way!" Andrew ordered, veering toward the townhouse on the right. The gate leading to the basement level was unlocked. He pushed it open, then, with the full length of his body molded to her back, forced her down the few steps into the tiny courtyard. With the touch of his foot, he swung shut the gate.

"There!" he hissed into her ear. "Now!"

Within seconds, they were crouched behind the bank of trash cans set along the basement façade.

"Erika!" Brennan bellowed.

So close—directly above, she sensed. In her state of hypervigilance, she could almost hear the sound of his breathing, see the anguished frustration on his face. She held herself very still, crouching low beside Andrew, her tension mounting. Just like playing hide-and-seek—she, jam-tucked in a corner of her parents' closet, her mother's dress half-covering her face, the tension escalating as the other kid approached—crouch becoming cringe; her friend, a foe, out to get her.

From down the block, the sound of a car engine starting up pierced the breathy silence.

"Stop!" Brennan yelled, simultaneous with the screech of tires. "Shit!"

After a pause, "Wheatley? Brennan here. I think your

friend just drove off with a guy from the house—yeah, the Fitch's. Huh? I don't know. She wasn't kicking and screaming but she didn't look happy. I saw them and then they were gone. Then this car takes off like a bat out of hell. No, I didn't get the plate number."

His voice was becoming fainter. "I tried her cell. She's not answering. I'm going to the house to question the lady..."

Brennan was out of earshot.

"The lady won't talk," Andrew whispered hoarsely. He rose, jerking Erika to her feet. "We're going to walk the same direction we were headed. Don't look back." He led her out of the enclosure.

Just as the gate was clicking shut behind them, a young woman in snug boot jeans and a slouchy knit sweater emerged from the main door above, house key in hand. "Hello?" she questioned in unison with Andrew's "Hi," as Erika, taut with bridled energy, remained silent.

"Your gate was open; we shut it," Andrew explained, looking up. He flashed an even smile. "You're too trusting. You should keep it locked. He let go of Erika's wrist and slipped his arm around her waist. "We always do."

"Thanks," the woman said, turning toward her front door to insert the key into its lock. "I'll keep that in mind," she said, her voice edging on sarcasm.

Applying firm pressure to her back, Andrew urged Erika forward. "We got lucky," he whispered, finding a belt loop of her skirt to slip his thumb into.

Keeping pace with him, she said nothing; waited for him to reveal himself.

"Looks like you decided to get with the program," he said. "Smart."

A man with a dog on a leash came from around the corner, walking toward them. With all her nervous energy channeled in observation, she recorded the man's spare build, gaunt face, slightly crooked nose; the dog, a mixed breed, mostly collie.

"You'll vouch for me," Andrew said, tilting his head toward her.

The man with the dog quickly walked around them on the curb side, avoiding eye contact.

"You'll be fine if you remember what I tell you to remember,"

Andrew said.

She detected agitation in his voice. What was he after? There was more to it than just wanting to keep an eye on her, prevent her from blowing the whistle before he'd completed his mission. Was he planning on having her ID his accomplice, frame the guy so he could keep the loot for himself, maybe even offer her a small cut? Was he shoehorning her into his plan—or had he convinced Isabel to make the call to her, seeking her help?

"You'll know when the time comes," he said, infringing on her thoughts. He slackened his pace. "Coming up on Twelfth Street. Get ready to cross."

He drew her tightly against his side as they stepped off the curb and crossed onto Seventh Avenue. A bank was right in front of them. He relaxed his embrace. "Act natural."

He released her to hold open the heavy glass door for her, allowing her to slip past him into the plush lobby. The perfect gentleman. She waited for him to draw up beside her, and together they marched through the roped-in corridor leading to the tellers' windows.

They were next in line. "Be cool," he reminded her, nudging her side.

The available teller waved them over.

"Hi, Florence, how you doing today?" Andrew asked, greeting the attractive middle-aged woman.

The teller smiled crisply. "Good, yourself?" She didn't wait for his answer. "And what can I do for you, Andrew?" She gave Erika a quick once-over.

Andrew set down the briefcase and drew an envelope from his jacket's inner pocket; passed it to her under the bars.

"This here's my friend, Erika."

Erika stood expressionlessly by, refusing to acknowledge either of them; her token act of defiance.

Florence tore open the envelope and pulled out a check. Her pinky, with its plum-coated tapered nail, shot up, as did her brow. She turned the check over, nodded at the sight of its endorsement. "This is a large amount, Andrew."

"I've cashed Mrs. F's checks before."

"Yes, but this transaction will have to be cleared by the manager. I see he's over at his desk. Mr. Johnson, Ken Johnson." She passed him back the check. "I'm sure you understand."

"Security." He smiled, took the check. "Thanks, Florence." He picked up his briefcase. "C'mon, Erika." He led the way to the desk prescribed, in an enclave bracketed by low wood railings.

"How can I help you?" Johnson inquired, gesturing toward the two leather chairs opposite his own.

Andrew handed him the check as they took their assigned seats. Erika stared straight ahead, registering her lack of compliance. Johnson examined the check, searched for something on his computer, then gave his ruling. "There are sufficient funds in cash reserves, but I won't feel comfortable unless I confirm with the client herself." He looked up from the screen. "Do you know if Isabel Fitch can be reached at the telephone number on file?"

"Yes," Andrew said impatiently, "but she's had me cash her checks before. Don't you recognize me?"

"I do, indeed, and that's why I'm willing to forego the more stringent procedures. Excuse me." He picked up his phone, rechecked his computer screen, then punched in a number. In a moment he conveyed his success with a nod in their direction. "Good day, this is Ken Johnson, bank manager. May I speak with Isabel Fitch, please?—Ah, good."

After asking a series of questions requiring knowledge of previously encoded personal data, Johnson was satisfied he was speaking to the person claiming to be Isabel Fitch. He then suggested, with a self-conscious laugh, that she might consider transferring the funds in a more secure manner: electronically—"that is, if your purpose is to place them with another institution." A pause. "Thank you. I appreciate your continued confidence in us." He glanced at Erika; smiled officiously. "There's a young woman with Andrew—not that that would affect—oh, fine." With a nod, he indicated to Erika her presence had been okayed.

She remained rigid, unresponsive, silently directing him to remember her in this demeanor. There was always a chance Andrew would claim she had been involved in his scheme or even that she had instigated it. She was reminded of Harrison's Havana predicament, of guilt by association. She wanted her non-participation noted.

"Mrs. Fitch would like to have a word with you," Johnson said, handing the cordless phone to Andrew. Rising from his chair, he said, "I'll prepare the funds. A security guard will come collect you shortly." He headed for the rear of the lobby, where a massive door secured by prison bars clearly demarcated the bank's vault.

Andrew cupped his free hand over the phone. "I knew he would, Mum, I saw him," he said, slouching into himself, as if to form a private booth. "He was following us. Did he hurt you?" There was tension in his voice. "Good. Quit worrying, she's fine, a real sport. Okay, we'll make it brief." He punched the off button, then half rose to place the phone onto its stand. "Such a worry wart," he muttered, sarcasm lined with tenderness. "Your bodyguard dropped by," he informed Erika, his voice stripped of humanity. "Anybody else bothers her..." He dangled the warning between them like a rat by its tail.

She would not let the rush of foreboding betray her. Her features remained impassive, even as she imagined Harrison in a life-and-death struggle with Andrew.

The security guard arrived. He tried to discourage more than one individual from accompanying him to the vault. Andrew insisted Erika, "the brains of the family," come with him, and prevailed.

Johnson was waiting for them. He was gently cradling a bulging canvas bag, its drawstrings pulled tightly closed.

Andrew glanced at his watch. "Tight schedule," he informed Johnson. After a cursory check of the bag's contents, he transferred the cash to his briefcase, pressed the sides shut with some effort, then fiddled with the built-in combination lock. "Appreciate it, Ken. Let's go, Erika."

Johnson laid his hand on Andrew's shoulder. Andrew flinched. "You just have to sign a receipt form," he said apologetically. "Bank policy, when an amount over—"

"Understood," Andrew fairly snapped.

The requisite form signed, Andrew and Erika exited the building.

He prodded her to the curb with his briefcase. "We take a cab from here," he ordered, his voice cracking with rage. "Shit, you acted like you had a broomstick up your ass."

"You're lucky I didn't shoot my mouth off," she said, immediately regretting the snappy retort—regretting anything between them resembling conversation. In silence she was set apart: imperturbable, a force to be reckoned with.

Her stalwartness was tested on the stop-and-go cab ride to the Fitch Gallery. Trapped in close quarters with him, the heavy air oppressing her still further, she fought to maintain her separateness, her zealous self-determination. But the weight of confinement pressed in on her, making it hard to breathe. The pain in her chest from his punch flared up, prompting her to glance down at his offending hand, splayed beside her on the worn leather seat. It was an ordinary hand, imparting nothing of its violent past, the secret binding her to Andrew in an unsavory pact. Looking at the hand, she remembered Harrison's, in almost the same attitude, beside her on a smooth leather surface. Instantly, willfully, she was transported to the interior of the Lexus, Bill behind the wheel, she and Harrison trapped in the rear in bittersweet conflict, he, distrusting his judgment; she, threatened by her most tender instincts. She folded into the memory.

"We're here," Andrew announced.

His voice, like a clap of thunder, ruptured the silence of her thoughts.

We're here! she repeated inwardly, like a call to arms.

Andrew tossed a couple of bills onto the front seat, then reached over Erika and shoved open the door. He jammed his hip against her to urge her out of the cab, although she was already inching over on her own.

He waited for the driver to pull away, then pushed her toward the door of the gallery. "We're coming down to the wire," he said. "Don't screw up."

No chance of that happening, she assured herself, bolstering herself for whatever was ahead. At stake was the recovery of a drawing: Vittorio's or Michelangelo's, either way of significance to the art world—to the world at large. There was a danger it would be lost forever in the murky business of the black market. She would do whatever she could to prevent that. Whatever Andrew's primary motivation for having her on the scene, she knew what her own was.

Andrew raised his hand to the brass doorknob, turned it.

As they entered the gallery, Erika readjusted the shoulder strap of her bag, reminding herself of its contents—pads, pens—the tools of her trade. She was on assignment, she prompted herself.

Her knees were telling her otherwise.

James Fitch was standing at the far wall, pointing to the upper right corner of a colorful oil abstract. "...where the focus begins and ends," he was advising a middle-aged couple about five feet from the painting.

"...the cycle of life," the woman was interposing.

All three turned toward Andrew and Erika, James's features registering surprise, downgrading to annoyance.

"One of my favorites," Andrew said casually. "Mark my words, this painter's career is about to take off." He approached the group, his hand on Erika's back, pressuring her along.

"This is my...assistant, Andrew," James announced coolly, scarcely concealing his true feelings. "And this is Erika Shawn. She's with *Art News*." He gave her an undisguised questioning look. "Meet Mr. and Mrs. Rogers."

"Nathan," the man corrected, shaking each of their hands.

"Beth," the woman said, taking her turn.

Erika mimicked a smile. She wasn't sure it worked.

Andrew took on a serious mien. "I wonder if you'll excuse us a moment—Nathan, Beth. We've got some urgent family business."

"Of course," Beth agreed genteelly. "I hope it's not bad news. We can come back tomorrow if it's more convenient for you."

"That won't be necessary," James assured her. "Please stay."

"Actually, that would be a good idea," Andrew counterpunched.

"We'll hold the painting for you. No need for a deposit, you haven't made a commitment."

"Thanks, that's awfully good of you," Nathan said, already heading for the exit, his wife in tow.

James hastened to escort them to the door.

"What the hell's going on?" he asked, closing the door behind them. "Is Mom okay—Dad?"

"They're fine."

"Why are you holding his briefcase? What's in there?"

"Everything's okay, only you've got to leave now."

"You haven't opened your mouth, Erika."

"Listen to Andrew, he'll explain later," she said hoarsely. "Later," she repeated, no more convincingly.

"Call Mom, I want to hear her tell me."

"Fine." Andrew took out his cell phone, punched in a number, handed the phone to him. "Be quick."

After the ensuing exchange, James appeared to accept the legitimacy of Andrew's demand, but was enraged about not having been taken into his mother's confidence regarding the reason for it. "I'm expecting an explanation," he fumed, letting it out on Andrew.

"You'll get one, bro."

Nostrils flaring, James turned to Erika. "I hope you and your friend Wheatley haven't fouled up my recovery of the Vittorio. Is that what this is all about?"

"I'll talk to you tonight," Andrew answered. "Now beat it."

James took a step toward Andrew, then stopped himself, chest heaving from the effort of containing his aggression. "See that you lock up," he grunted.

"I always do."

Without comment, James directed himself toward the door with an unnatural swagger. "Set the alarm!" he added, without turning back, punctuating his departure with a deliberate slam of the door.

Andrew promptly turned the window sign to read *Closed*. He gestured toward the rear of the gallery.

Erika regarded him warily.

"We're on display out here. Our boys won't go for that. Anyway, I have to unlock the back door for them." He cocked his head at the briefcase. "And I want to get this out of sight." He started to walk to the rear, then turned back. "Come on!"

She weighed her options. Followed him.

After unlatching the door at the end of the narrow rear hallway, he ushered her into the small room where she and Harrison had met with James. In Andrew's company it felt more like a prison cell than an office.

"Give me your bag," he said, hauling it off her shoulder. "They'll think you've got a machine gun in that thing." He tossed it onto the top of the file cabinet; the briefcase after it, more gently. He glanced at his watch. "They should be here any minute."

"Who, your collaborators?" she asked, unable to hold back. He laughed derisively, loosened his tie. "Relax."

"There's no one coming, is there?" she baited.

There was no reply. His eyes revealed nothing.

"You want to make a deal with me, is that it? Split the ransom, is that what this is all about?"

Bad joke. Wrong timing.

He stepped toward her.

She backed away, jamming into the desk. She felt behind her for some solid object. She pictured a letter opener, smooth and tapered, imagined the weapon's arced trajectory, its deadly plunge. "Stop!" she ordered—or meant to, the sound more like a bird's cry.

He sprang at her, reaching around, grabbing her. Bearing down on her, he raised her arms over her head and pinned her across the desktop, his face hovering inches from hers.

"Get off me!" she shouted. She tried to free herself, but her wrists were cuffed in his iron grip, her legs jammed, her torso trapped under his weight. Still, she struggled.

He lifted her hands, then banged them back against the desk. Their faces were almost touching. The hem of her skirt, risen in the skirmish, pulled taut against her thighs, heightening her vulnerability and unreasoned shame. He paused, holding her still, and she could see in his eyes that he savored this frieze of absolute domination.

Into the cruel pause: a flashback so gentle, of Harrison tugging at the hem of Helen's risen skirt, trying to cover her, knowing Helen would have wished him to.

The colliding of events exploded into revelation.

With a surge of unrestrained force, she punched out her hands from his vise and ripped his other hand from her neck, pushing him back and off balance. She lunged at him, kneeing him in the groin before he had sufficiently recovered. When he instinctively grabbed at himself, she went for the screwdriver she remembered he'd shoved into his back pocket. She almost got to it. He pried her away, pressing her arms against her sides, finally outstripping her strength.

A sudden bang at the front door prompted him to pull her in close, riveting her against him in an iron embrace. Securing her with one arm, he clamped his free hand over her mouth.

A double rap, then the door opening. Then slamming shut. She realized what was about to happen. She felt the head-snapping punch, then nothing more.

CHAPTER 18

The police officer planted himself in the sculpted plastic chair beside the hospital bed. He was a big man, dwarfing everything in the room. He made the chair look like it was meant for a toddler. "Hello, Erika, I'm Captain Tom Brody. Are you feeling up to a couple of questions?" he posed, at once concerned and impatient.

"I'm okay," she said, her left temple throbbing with pain. "I have to get out of here."

"They want to observe you overnight. You were not out very long, but a concussion's a concussion." He squeaked the baby-chair closer. "To be on the safe side. No internal bleeding, though. That's good."

She felt at a distinct disadvantage, half-reclined and in a flimsy cotton hospital gown. She tried hoisting herself to an upright sitting position, but the slippery plastic mattress casing made it difficult. "What do you want to know?" she asked defensively. After this interview she would demand to be discharged. They couldn't keep her against her will, could they?

"Don't strain yourself. You want me to raise the bed for you?"

"No, it's all right. Go ahead."

"Okay. Can you tell me why you were at the Fitch Gallery today?"

"Didn't Andrew tell you?"

"Yes, but I want to hear it from you."

Erika hesitated, but only a beat. "Isabel Fitch got a threatening note from the person who stole her drawing. A very old and valuable drawing. I was in her home taking a look at the note, when she got a call from this person, giving her instructions."

"And?"

"She was afraid I'd let the cops in on it and mess up the deal. And I thought—well, maybe I didn't think it through—I should be there when the money—the down-payment—was transferred."

"Why's that?"

"I write for *Art News*. It's a good story."

"I see. And did the individual show up at the gallery?"

She gave a helpless shrug. "I remember getting there. There was a couple looking at a painting with James—James Fitch. Then the three of them left. I don't remember anything after that. Maybe when my head clears I'll remember more. I'm sorry."

"You don't have to apologize."

"Could you tell me what happened—what they say happened?

Maybe it'll help jog my memory."

"Well, I'm not sure I should..." He frowned, weighing protocol, then leaned forward. "James Fitch says he was annoyed he was left out of the loop, so he returned to see what was what. He says Andrew was calling for help from the back room so he ran back there, where he found Andrew trying to revive you. They called for emergency assistance, and you were brought here. Andrew says what went down, the pick-up guy was trying to take you hostage, make sure Isabel Fitch would come through with the rest of the ransom. When he heard James coming in the front door, he must have thought it was the police. Whatever, the pick-up guy high-tailed it out the back door."

"With the cash?"

"Without the cash. Is this bringing it back—your memory, I mean?"

She shook her head. "No, but maybe it will after it, you know, sinks in."

"I hope so—look, there's a bodyguard, name of Brennan, sitting outside your room, very vigilant. He made me show him my badge. I thought he was going to bite it, make sure it was real."

"I'm sure he feels responsible for what happened to me. It wasn't his fault."

"Is it true he was hired by a Mr. Harrison Wheatley?"

Her heart leaped at the name, even now, when she felt beat to hell. "Yes."

"Are you able to tell me why?"

"I remember everything up to walking into the gallery with Andrew, but it's complicated. Do I have to tell you the story? You could talk to Lieutenant John Mitchell—Southampton, Long Island—he could fill you in."

Captain Brody took a pad from his pocket; dug around for something to write with.

"There's a pen here," Erika said, reaching for it on the bedside table. "You think this could be enough for today?" she asked, handing him the pen. "I'm really tired, and my face hurts when I talk." The officer scribbled some notes in his pad. "Of course," he said. "Let me verify your address, phone number, et cetera." He flipped through the pad; found what he was looking for. He began reciting her address.

She stopped him midway. "You have it. That's me."

He hauled up from the chair; shoved the pad and pen into his jacket pocket. "Okay, you feel better now." He patted her leg with his meaty hand; gave it a squeeze for good measure. He started to leave.

"Officer?" He turned. "My pen?"

"Oh, sorry." He handed it to her, then left, holding the door open as a nurse, as petite as he was king-size, rolled in her cart bearing the tools of her trade.

Erika put the pen back on the table as she tried to raise herself up.

The nurse hastened to the bed to work the controls until Erika was more comfortable, then inserted a small device into her ear. "Temperature slightly elevated, normal range." She took her blood pressure, recorded it. "Good. There's a gentleman waiting to see you—very impatient."

"Where is he?" Erika asked anxiously.

"In the waiting room. Says his name is Harrison Wheatley. Shall I let him in?"

"Yes."

"Back in a jiff," the nurse said, rolling the cart toward the door. Moments later she returned, Harrison at her heels. She stopped.

"You want me to..."

"You don't have to stay," Erika answered. "We'll be fine." To Harrison, once they were alone: "Are you okay?"

He looked like he had been caught in a wind tunnel: shirttails half out of his khakis, collar of his blazer askew, hair more undisciplined than ever.

"Am I okay? Oh, Erika, look at you!" In a sudden burst, he rushed to her, swooping down to press his face against her uninjured cheek.

"So, I look that bad," she said wryly, hiding the flood of emotion. "I never should have let you go," he said, his voice breaking. "Why did you go? Thank god you're all right!" He crouched beside her, seized her hand to hold it to his chest.

"Sit down, Harrison, and let me talk to you." She kissed his hand, moved it along her aching jaw and cheek, the touch of him, a balm. "Come, sit."

He nodded, then complied, pulling the chair as close to the bed as he could. "When I found out they'd brought you to Lenox Hill, I tried to get a cab, but I couldn't, so I ran up here, only to find they wouldn't let me see you until you'd been questioned by the police."

"I'm so sorry you had to go through—"

He flung up his hand. "Don't go there, don't you dare."

"Okay, listen, we have to talk. I have to get out of here." He shook his head. "No way. Not until tomorrow."

"They're being overcautious. We'll tell them I won't drive, I won't work any heavy machinery. You'll vouch for me."

"I don't like the sound of this. You're scheming again."

"How did you find out what happened?"

He raised his brow, clearly suspicious of her evasiveness, then yielded. "First, Brennan called to say you'd gone off with some guy from the Fitch house. Not all that willingly, he thought. He said he lost you when the two of you drove off."

"That wasn't us."

"What?"

"We were hiding behind trash cans. I heard Brennan phone you."

"You mean you went off willingly?"

"Not exactly. It's complicated."

"Everything's complicated with you."

"What happened after that?"

"I called Isabel Fitch."

"Nobody was supposed to have known I was going to see her. You heard me give her my word."

"You think I cared at that point? I was frantic. Besides, Brennan was on his way over to her place to shatter those vows."

"That's true. What did she tell you?"

"Not a damn thing. Nothing that would help me find you, anyway. Although I will say she seemed genuinely concerned about your well-being. She said she'd call me about you as soon as Andrew—the guy you went off with—gave her the go-ahead."

"Did she tell you why?"

"Only later, when she called to tell me you'd been taken to Lenox Hill. She said she hadn't given me any information earlier because she was afraid I'd interfere with the delivery of

281

the ransom money."

"As you would have."

"Damn right. You think I would have sat by knowing you might be in danger?"

"Even if it meant losing a drawing possibly worth millions?"

"Untold millions."

"I'm touched." If only he knew how deeply. "Andrew was the person who attacked me in the park, you know. Schurz Park."

He grabbed her hand, as if to pull her to safety. "What? How can you be sure?"

"His cologne."

"His cologne," he repeated.

"Right, not exactly what you'd call ironclad proof."

He sighed, dropping their clasped hands to his knee. "Proof enough for me. For the most part"—he smiled—"I trust your instincts. You told the police, of course."

She shook her head. "Come on! Why not?"

"I have my reasons, Harrison. Good reasons. I'm not being coy." She must be careful not to reveal everything, not yet.

"Erika, Erika," he said plaintively, "what am I going to do with you?"

"Help spring me from this place, for starters. Look, nobody was trying to take me hostage. It was much worse than that. Andrew was about to kill me, when he was interrupted, I assume by James, who apparently bought Andrew's cock-and-bull story, as did the cops, at least for now. Without my story, I'm sure all the available accounts corroborate Andrew's. I have no doubt he's planning to finish the job. I wanted to stall him, buy myself some time, a couple of hours, anyway, to do some planning myself."

"Why didn't you tell this to the cop who interviewed you?" Harrison asked, stunned.

"Couldn't take the chance. Maybe he'd think I was disoriented after the concussion. Even if he took my word for it, there's no way he could throw Andrew in jail and keep him there. Sooner or later, he'd get me, I'm the only loose end. After I'm out of the way, the ransom plot could go into rewind. I need to pay Andrew a surprise visit tonight at the Fitch's, and I'd like Lieutenant Mitchell to be there, if possible with on-call back-up. He's been in on the case since the beginning, and I want someone present who represents the law. Think you can arrange it?"

"Maybe—but only if I can come with you. Are you going to tell me what this is all about?"

"No."

"That's blunt. How long am I to be kept in the dark?"

"Not long. You know I trust you more than anyone in the world, don't you?" She realized this startling truth only as it was uttered. "That's news to me," he said, shy almost. "Good news—if I can believe it."

"You can," she said, inwardly scuffling her feet in embarrassment. "All I ask is that you play along with me. Don't contradict anything I say."

He smiled wryly. "I'm to be your puppet, then. It's come to that, has it?"

"Not exactly," she said, ricocheting his smile.

"What makes you think Andrew hasn't skipped town?"

"Because I'm the only snag, and for the moment I've got amnesia. After I'm out of the way he's home free, and with a rich and doting surrogate mom, he's got too sweet a deal going for him. So. While I get dressed you'll call Lieutenant Mitchell? Strike the question mark. You will call him. Use your persuasive powers. Tell him about the threatening note Isabel received. Have him set up a routine visit with Isabel, Andrew and James. Nothing alarming, have him say he wants to pick up the note, ask them a couple of questions about the stolen drawing, was it insured, that sort of thing. I promised Isabel I wouldn't let the police in on this, but sorry, the assault changed the rules for me. Ask Mitchell to tell her that. It might appease her. Also, see if Mitchell will give my assigned doctor, Tim Jason, a call, pressure him to wait twenty-four hours before registering my discharge. I think he'll do it, with Mitchell's authority. If Andrew calls the hospital I want him to think I'm here overnight."

"That all?" Harrison asked, marveling. "Maybe we should get the message through to Andrew that you're going in and out of consciousness," he suggested, not totally serious. "He might just believe it, coming from Mitchell or the hospital."

"Perfect! This might just put him at ease for a bit." She threw off the covers and rose from the bed. Head spinning, she fell back to a sitting position. "Too quick, is all," she said, anticipating his remonstrances. "I'm okay."

He shook his head. "I don't approve of this. You're not supposed to strain yourself or get upset."

"Harrison, with or without your help I'm going to do this. Without your help, it'll be much more of a strain, in all ways. What'll it be?"

"What do you think?" Resigned, he shoved his chair away from the bed and dug in his pocket for his cell phone.

Erika rose from the bed again. Harrison reached out to help, but she demurred with a definitive wave of her hand. In as dignified a manner as possible, she shuffled barefoot to fetch her belongings from the closet.

When she emerged from the bathroom ten minutes later, dressed and combed, Harrison was ending his call to Lieutenant Mitchell.

"We're all set," he informed Erika, pocketing his cell.

"I got scared when I looked in the mirror. I put on lip gloss." She smiled wanly. "It doesn't help much." She had combed her hair to one side in an attempt to hide the swelling and discoloration. That hadn't helped much either.

"You look like Mata Hari," he said.

"Thanks for the try." She sat on the edge of the bed, across from him. "When's Mitchell planning on getting to the house?"

"Eight o'clock. He'll call my cell to confirm it's a go." He sighed. "Although I'm not happy about this. I don't like second-guessing doctors."

As if on cue, a stocky man in a white jacket, stethoscope draped around his neck, chart in hand, stepped into the room. "What, up and about, are we!" he declared, clearly nonplussed.

"Doctor Jason, this is my friend, Harrison Wheatley; we are leaving now," Erika said emphatically. She picked up her bag from the bed and swung it over her shoulder to underline her point.

Harrison gave an innocent shrug. "Don't look at me, Doctor. I got my marching orders."

"This is a matter of life and death—you can say I went AWOL," Erika said, preparing for an argument. "'The patient flew the coop against my advice.' I'll sign a form saying I'm releasing myself without permission. Only please wait twenty-four hours before you enter it on the records. Anyone asks for me, I'm here overnight, slipping in and out of consciousness. You'll be getting a call from a Lieutenant John Mitchell to back me up on this." She threw back her shoulders, tried to look the peak of alertness.

Dr. Jason uttered a nervous laugh. "I see our patient is showing no immediate symptoms of trauma," he said, slipping his hands into the pockets of his jacket. He thought for a bit. "Very well," he sighed, I'm willing to go along with your request, but only because it looks like I might be placing you in greater peril if I don't. Of course I'd prefer keeping you overnight for observation. However, if you're determined to leave, I won't stand in your way. You must remember, though, a hospital is a relatively controlled environment. You can't do anything, well, foolish here. You understand what I'm saying?"

"I do, Doctor. I promise to cancel my kick-boxing match. Harrison will watch over me like a hawk. If I keel over for any reason, he will call you. Right, Harrison?"

"Absolutely."

"I'm holding you to it—both of you," Dr. Jason said. "Wait here, I'll be right back with the form. If you leave without signing it the deal's off. You are outrageous, you know."

True to his word, he was back moments later with a notated release form. Erika signed it. Before he could have second thoughts, she started for the door. "Thanks, Doctor," she said, as Harrison looped his arm through hers. "Thanks for everything."

Brennan jumped up from his folding chair when he saw the pair of them. "Where are we going?" he asked Erika. "I thought we were here for the night—gee, you look like you hit a wall."

"Thanks for your honesty," Erika said kindly. Harrison shot him an angry glare.

"About what happened to you," Brennan said, "I could've done more, and I'm real sorry. When Wheatley called to tell me you were here, you could have knocked me over with a feather."

"Please, it was not your fault in any way," Erika consoled. "And you are not to misunderstand me when I tell you that you don't need to come with us."

"In fact," Harrison put in, "it's a good idea if you stay right where you are until morning. We want it to look like Erika hasn't left the room. Please don't tell anyone—boss, relatives, friends, anyone—that she is leaving."

"You notice I didn't object to your crazy decision," Harrison said when he and Erika were waiting for the elevator doors to part. "I think I deserve a commendation. So, where to? I think you'll be most comfortable at my place. You can put up your feet, let Grace fix us something before we head downtown."

"Something simple," she said, as they stepped into the empty elevator. "That'll be nice."

Her knees buckled as she reached for the ground floor button.

He pulled her close to keep her from losing her balance.

"You're not up to this, you're still too weak!" He pressed the button.

"I'm not weak," she protested, as the elevator began its descent. In truth, she had been literally swept off her feet by a sudden wave of anticipation about what would take place at the Fitch residence later that night. "I'm fine, really fine," she assured Harrison, wishing she could share with him all that was on her mind.

CHAPTER 19

Andrew's expression skidded from horror to confusion. "Looking pretty good, Erika. Considering." Without removing his foot from the doorway, he addressed Harrison. "And you are...?"

"Professor Wheatley," Erika replied, poker-faced. "I'd like to talk to you and Isabel. Is she in?"

Andrew glanced over his shoulder, as if to check. "This isn't a good time, actually, but give me a message. I'll pass it on."

"Who's there, Andrew?" Isabel Fitch sang out from within.

"Erika Shawn and a Professor Wheatley."

Isabel responded after a pause. "Lieutenant Mitchell says to let them in, it's okay."

Andrew grudgingly moved his foot, providing a narrow passageway.

Erika and Harrison were holding hands; stuck to it, even though it made for an inelegant entrance. She could have made this visit on her own, but how much easier it was with him at her side! She squeezed his hand; he squeezed back.

Above his frozen smile, Andrew's eyes lasered Erika with a look of warning.

"Oh, my dear!" Isabel cried, jumping from her chair as Erika came into her line of vision. She clapped her hand to her chest. "I'm so sorry! It was entirely my fault!" She glanced at Andrew, squinting as if to shield herself from the sun's glare. To Erika: "Does it hurt terribly?"

"Not as bad as it looks," Erika said, taking in the room. Despite the commodious couches at the far end of the room, and possibly to avoid the unease of thigh-to-thigh contact, the evening's seating arrangement included the two high-backed chairs that were part of the permanent décor and two others that had been added.

Two chairs in the makeshift circle were occupied by Lieutenant Mitchell, in off-duty garb of jeans and sweatshirt, and James Fitch.

Lieutenant Mitchell rose from his chair. "Erika—Harrison. Join us. Isabel Fitch, James and Andrew here have just been bringing me up to date with their accounts of today's events." He held up a large spiral pad opened to a page of cramped script. "Speaking of which, Mrs. Fitch gave me your cell phone to return to you." He took it from his jeans pocket and handed it to her. "Okay to grab a couple of chairs from the kitchen?" he asked his hostess.

She approved, and he and Harrison fetched the chairs to add to the circle.

Erika and Harrison sat down next to each other, which placed her between him and Mitchell. Harrison was seated next to James.

Erika tossed her cell phone into her tote bag and set the bag at her feet. "I want to thank you, James. I hear you saved my life today."

He waved it off. "From what I hear, it was a stupid plan all around." He directed a look of uninhibited disgust at Andrew, then turned back to Erika. "I'm glad you're okay, though," he said, his tone not altogether generous.

"May I offer anyone something more substantial to eat?" Isabel asked, the honeyed touch of her accent compensating for her son's caustic tone. She stood beside her chair across from her guests. The small walnut table between her and the chair presumably to be occupied by Andrew was laden with an assortment of crackers and cheese. "It would be no trouble, I assure you. The shepherd's pie is still warm."

"Thanks, but we've eaten," Harrison said. "Although if Erika...?" He glanced at her affectionately.

"Nothing for me, thank you." Harrison's housekeeper, Grace, had fixed them grilled cheese sandwiches and tea. Too tense for their upcoming surprise visit, Erika had only been able to down half a sandwich, and that, out of politeness.

"How about you, Lieutenant?" Isabel persisted.

"Come on, Mother, can we get on with it?" James said irritably. "This is not a fucking party!"

"James!" Isabel exclaimed, collapsing into her chair.

"I understand where he's coming from," Mitchell soothed. "Our objective is to discuss what took place today and to see where we go from here."

"No place, as I see it," James snapped. "After Andrew and Erika's screw-up, we're not going to be getting any follow-up ransom calls any time soon. You should have told me about the note, Mother. The Vittorio drawing is lost to us, probably forever—Andrew, will you stop hovering over us and sit down!"

"Yes, do, Andrew," Isabel prompted, cautiously glancing around, as if expecting a storm to erupt, but not knowing from where.

Andrew knifed another warning look at Erika and sat down.

"Erika screwed up?" Harrison belatedly fired at James. "Erika? After being dragged along with Andrew, here, only to get bashed in the face because—"

"Enough, Harrison, please," Erika reproved, touching his knee. "I'm fine. It's not worth getting excited about." To Mitchell, "You must have spoken to the on-scene officers," she gently nudged.

"Yeah, I sure did," he said, unknowingly co-opted. "Including Captain Brody, the officer who spoke to you in the hospital. Unfortunately, you didn't offer much in the way of information. He said you didn't remember what the person who attacked you looked like. That right?"

"Yes, I guess I blocked it out."

"Think hard, do you remember anything more now?"

She glanced sideways at Andrew. "I can't, no. I'm sorry." Andrew sat back in his chair.

She had her opening. Nothing thus far enacted or said would have prepared them. "I think maybe I'll have a cup of coffee, after all," she said, addressing Isabel. "I mean, if it's not too much trouble."

"Of course it isn't. Andrew will—"

"Thanks, Rosa," Erika inserted to Isabel, as matter-of-factly as her throbbing carotids would allow.

There it was, the flinch. Nothing more than the tiniest movement of Isabel's head, the arrhythmic intake of air. "Andrew, be a dear and brew us a pot of coffee, will you?" A fraction of a quaver more musical than the request warranted.

To detect the barest nuance of a reaction, Erika had directed her focus on her hostess as intensely as a raptor on its prey. But exclusive focus was needed only for an instant. She turned first to James to see fading from his features the slightly quizzical look that follows a slip of the tongue whose origin is of no importance. Then to Andrew: a portrait of repressed rage. "Don't bother, Andrew, skip the coffee," she said.

Andrew looked to his guardian for instructions. She fluttered her hand. "Never mind—unless Erika would like something else? A glass of wine?" Her focus skittered across the faces of her guests. "Anyone?"

"Mother, please!" James implored. "We're good. Everyone's good!"

Harrison touched Erika's arm, seeking her attention. "Rosa?" he half whispered as their eyes met.

She nodded. "I can explain." She glanced at her hostess.

Something had given way in the woman, she could see it in the uncharacteristic slope of her shoulders.

"Nonsense...fiction," the woman said, with attempted bravado. Andrew had reached out to her across the small table. She held out her hand without looking in his direction and he clutched at it, their fingers interlacing in knuckle-white tension; their dependence, one for the other, as tangible as their locked flesh.

"Stay cool," he said.

"What's going on?" James asked, glued to the tableau with an amalgam of fascination and distaste.

"Lies," his mother said weakly.

Lieutenant Mitchell clicked the top of his ballpoint pen; flipped to a clean page. "Erika?"

"I hardly know where to begin." James guffawed.

Erika smiled in sympathy. It did seem ludicrous, after bringing them to this pass, to come out with such an inanity. "Occam's razor," she said. "I guess that's how I can sum it up."

"'Occam's razor,'" James mimicked.

"It's a theory!" Harrison shot at him, glaring. "When you're trying to decide which of your hypotheses best fits the bill, choose the simplest one, the one with the fewest number of entities. Named after a Franciscan friar, if you want to know. Let her speak!"

"I don't want to hear a lecture, thank you," James balked.

Harrison jumped to his feet. "If that's what it takes, that's what you'll get!"

"Hey!" Mitchell barked, thrusting forward. "Everybody calm down." He waited for Harrison to take his seat, regain his composure. "I'd like to hear what Erika has to say without any interruptions. You can hold your questions until she's done. Is that clear?" Looking directly at his hostess: "But first, let me ask you, do you have any idea where this is going?"

"To slander," she said, barely audible.

Mitchell nodded. "I understand, but do you think you can hold your comments until we hear Erika out? Is that fair?"

"Will it matter if I object?"

Mitchell smiled, a silent offering before his unequivocal answer. "No, ma'am." To Erika: "Go ahead, then, you have the floor."

Erika tried not to feel like a gavel had just been struck. She folded her hands in her lap; unfolded them. "You see," she began, scanning the faces in the room in an attempt to be open and inclusive, "my idea—accusation, if you want to call it that —came to me as a kind of revelation, but in fact it was made up of a whole sequence of events and questions I"—she turned to Harrison—"we have been hashing over from the beginning."

She suddenly felt easier, less formal, addressing her monologue to Harrison. "You know how I told you I was sure Andrew was the one who'd attacked me in Schurz Park, warning me to keep my nose out of the Delaney investigation?"

Harrison nodded, and though he said nothing, Erika felt like they were engaged in conversation, his expression calming and receptive, neutralizing the grunts and gasps in the room elicited by her bombshell. "Well, it got me thinking, he might also have been the person who'd slipped the threatening note to me under my door, the note that was almost an exact replica of the note delivered to...Mrs. Fitch, Isabel Fitch. Remember, you ran after the guy, but he was too quick, so fit"—she smiled—"I mean, he had gotten a head start, after all. The important thing is, moments after I made the connection —Andrew, Schurz Park—I also discovered he was not just a delivery boy, he was involved up to his eyeballs in the scheming itself. That I discovered in the bathroom, right here, down the hall, when I tried to call you from his cell phone. I won't go into the mechanics of it, but then and there I realized it had been Andrew himself who just moments before had called Mrs. Fitch to give her instructions how to go about dropping off the ransom money, or at least the first installment.

"So, by the time I was fighting Andrew off in the back room of the Fitch Gallery, he was already in my thoughts as an active planner in the ransom scheme. He would have killed me, made it look like the nonexistent perp had done it, but

James came back, so he had to postpone the deed. Instead, he knocked me out. I lied to Captain Brody about this. I mean, I withheld the truth."

"You remembered? Your mind wasn't fuzzy, after all?" Mitchell uttered.

"I'm sorry, but I had to buy time, keep Andrew at bay until...well, now."

"What the hell is her motivation?" Andrew seethed. "All of a sudden coming out with a pack of lies!"

"Please be quiet," Mitchell politely warned.

"How come you get to butt into this crap story, not me?"

"Simple. I outrank you—Erika? You want to explain why you withheld your theory—whatever it is—about Mrs. Fitch?"

Erika put her hand to her cheek. The swelling had come down, but it still felt taut. "I needed to get a spontaneous reaction to my statement. Your ignorance was my only chance of that. Without it, either you or Harrison might have taken away the element of surprise with a word, an expression, however unintentional. Mrs. Fitch would have been prepared." She looked directly at her hostess. "Clearly, she was not."

Mitchell shook his head. "I don't get it. Why did you go along—cooperate with Andrew in the first place? Surely, you knew it would involve risk."

Harrison nodded vigorously. "Took the words right out of my mouth, Lieutenant."

Mitchell flashed a warning look.

"I went along," Erika answered, "one, because Andrew threatened he would take it out on Harrison and Sara if I didn't, and two, I wanted to get the story firsthand."

Mitchell tapped the nib of his pen on his pad. "Let's see if I follow your reasoning. Now that you've outed him, the threat is gone?"

She nodded. "You're forewarned, you'll know where to look if anything happens to me or any of my friends."

"Got it. Not saying I'm buying it," he added, with a placating glance at the rest of the group. "So. Where were you? Right. In the back room of the art gallery, allegedly getting punched in the face by Andrew."

A low sound issued from Harrison.

"Let me explain," she appealed, returning her focus to Harrison. "I was pinned to the desk, he had me pinned to the desk, and my skirt had risen up, and I remembered you tugging at Helen Gilmore's skirt to cover her knees. You remember? Such a kind act, one of those pictures that never goes out of the mind. That's when it happened, the two experiences —today's and the one in Southampton—came together, conjoined almost, Andrew becoming a party to Helen's assault, but not for his own ends—what would he have wanted with the contents of the safe deposit box?—but for Isabel Fitch's. In that same moment—without reasoning it through, it was only later I figured out what made the light bulb go off—Isabel Fitch and Rosa Ramirez became one and the same."

"Amazing how the mind works," Mitchell suggested, with more than a hint of cynicism.

"I know this must sound like it's coming from out of the blue," she said, addressing Mitchell, "but Harrison and I have been debating the pros and cons of any number of scenarios." Back to Harrison: "This is a hair's breath away from what we had already come up with. We've always believed, haven't we, that in all probability the three crimes—the original, in 1958, involving William Delaney himself, the second, involving Helen Gilmore, and the third, the theft of the drawing from this very room, were somehow related. But none of the people we discussed could quite fit the bill. "It's a stretch to think Bertram Morrison could have killed William Delaney. He retired from the art world immediately after the tragedy and without his imprimatur on any of the subsequent sales of stolen art, there's no credible motivation. Furthermore, his wife Tina's voluntary contribution of William Delaney's letters to him all but eliminates her from sinister motives of her own, both past and present.

"What about Rodney Smitts? Even if he, in our wildest imagination, had stolen the drawing, what would have been his motivation to seize the contents of the Delaney family's safe deposit box? And how could he have been related to the original crime? Through his grandfather? Uncle? I don't think so. I met his family.

"What about Aldo Fabbri? If he was so desperate to re-possess the only drawing sold from his Vittorio folder, why ever would he have choreographed its ransom? How about his father, Gian? Sure, like Morrison, he's the right age to have taken part in the original incident, the theft of William Delaney's storehouse of artworks and the cover-up murder, but why, again, would he have cause—or opportunity—to par-ticipate in the subsequent crimes? How would he even have known of the resurfacing safe deposit box containing the cru-cial 1957 inventory?"

She leaned toward Harrison, as if about to impart a secret. "What about Andrew? A reach, don't you think? Unre-lated to the original crime and not in his pay grade to come up with a Francis Bacon painting to spice up a threatening note. What about James Fitch Junior? Isn't his father connected, however directly or indirectly, to matters pertaining to the Delaney estate, past and present? Could he have dreamed up the ransom plot to deflect from his father's ancient mis-deeds?" She shook her head, staving off a possible outburst from the barely restrained art dealer. "No way. If James is a guilty party, he would never have so obligingly parted with a copy of the Vittorio bill of sale, which, you'll see, will turn out to be the choicest bit of incriminating evidence."

"Aha!" Mitchell broke in. "This, at least, I understand: the bill of sale transferring the Vittorio drawing from William Delaney to James Fitch in 1957. My department's handwriting expert compared William Delaney's signature on that docu-ment to the signature samples on letters written in the 1950s from Mr. Delaney to his friend Bertram Morrison. I discussed this with Harrison. I suppose he passed on the information."

"We never got to it," Erika said. "It's been a busy day."

James jumped to his feet. "Fuck this. I need a drink."

"Sit down, son," his mother said flatly. "There can't be much more to this."

Without a word of protest, James sat back down.

Remarkable, Erika thought, how order had been maintained throughout her long exposition. Was it owing to the authoritative presence of Mitchell, or to the same fascination that transfixes us to accident scenes, even our own? she wondered. "Thank you," she said, not knowing quite why, or to whom.

"Continue," Mitchell advised. "The bill of sale, the comparison of signatures," he prompted.

"About that," she said, responding more to Harrison's rapt look of encouragement than Mitchell's directive, "remember when we were going over William Delaney's letters to Morrison, how we discussed the possible scenarios of that sales transaction? We learned that the sale—any sale—of Delaney's art had to have been fraudulent, since Delaney himself would never have authorized it. He says himself in one of his letters that the only works he parted with were a couple done by Cuban artists that he donated to the National Museum of Havana. We knew therefore that his signature had been forged on the document, and we hashed over the names of possible suspects who came to mind. We also cast about for possible ways James Fitch Senior had been taken in by someone posing as William Delaney, or if he had in some way been complicit in the criminal transaction. We were caught up in an ever-growing heap of complexities." She took a breath. "Well," she said, including Mitchell in her focus, "I think we overlooked one scenario that would have simplified everything."

"Your Occam's razor," Mitchell suggested.

"Yes, Lieutenant. About your handwriting expert. I assume he did not find a match between the signature on Delaney's letters and the one appearing on the sale document."

Mitchell nodded. "There was no match. The result was definitive."

Erika looked directly at her hostess. "Was this the only comparative analysis your expert made, Lieutenant?" she asked quietly. This time, there was no reactive flinch. The woman who had been known for most of her life as Isabel Fitch had been prepared.

Her look was frozen in stoic resolve—or resignation.

"What other analysis are you talking about?" Mitchell asked, puzzled.

"My God, yes!" Harrison uttered almost beneath his breath. "Comparing the two signatures on the bill of sale itself," Erika said, in answer to Mitchell's question. "William Delaney's signature and that of James Fitch, the elder. I believe if your expert examines them, he'll conclude, also definitively, that these signatures were penned by one individual."

"And who might that individual be?" James asked, more curious than challenging.

"Your father, Jeff Davis," Erika said almost lightly, trying to avoid the delivery of a death knell. "He was the manager of William Delaney's sugar plantation in Guantanamo Province. In 1958 a band of rebels lay siege to the main building, making off with Delaney's art treasures—I should say the art treasures on display. Jeff Davis, along with the cook's assistant, Rosa Ramirez, were assumed to have perished in the fire that followed the attack. I believe they did not perish in the fire, that they in fact set the fire to cover their tracks, taking advantage of the general chaos of the day to further camouflage their actions.

"I believe in all likelihood they killed William Delaney before setting fire to the place, then took off with the balance of art works that were stowed somewhere on the premises." She gave a helpless shrug. "This idea is not something I grabbed out of a hat, James. Bertram Morrison, William Delaney's agent and close friend for many years, fervently believed that Delaney's murder and theft of the hidden cache of art was an inside job. Maybe if Delaney's widow hadn't shut herself off from the event so completely, or if the region hadn't been in a state of unrest, more effort would have been put into the investigation by the local authorities." To James's look of utter dismay, she said "I'm sorry," the apology hardly an adequate balm, she knew.

"I'm not sure I'm even close to believing this," Mitchell said.

"Compare the signatures, you'll be halfway there," Harrison said.

"Maybe." The officer looked from Erika to Harrison. "Either of you want to give me a blow by blow of how we got from there—the events of 1958—to here? The present?"

Their hostess heaved a sigh, opened her mouth to speak.

"Not a word!" Andrew cried. "Let her run off at the mouth!"

"Erika?" Mitchell asked, disregarding Andrew's outburst. "You want to fill me in?"

Erika deferred to Harrison with a soft-spoken "You." Hearing the story from his lips would be a kind of confirmation.

"I got it, you know, but only just now," Harrison said.

She smiled warmly. "I know."

Harrison sat forward and looked from one to the other. Professorial, Erika thought, feeling a tug of jealousy—untimely, foolish—toward his students.

"I don't suppose," Harrison began, "it would have been an insurmountable task for Jeff Davis and Rosa Ramirez to have purchased counterfeit documents of identification. Further, with all of Davis's military and commercial connections, it would not have been impossible to find an obliging agent to help transport the meticulously rolled up paintings and drawings out of the country." Harrison sat back. "At last," he said, "after their travails, the emergent Mr. James Fitch was able to draw up phony bills of sale, assigning them a date of execution prior to the actual date. Mission accomplished. Reality altered. The records would henceforth show that William Delaney, in the year prior to his death, had sold a substantial number of his art works to one James Fitch.

"With a starter collection of this magnitude, I imagine it would be a cinch to reinvent oneself as an art dealer. And that is just what James Fitch did, once he and his new wife, Isabel, took up residence in the States. I don't know the details of their peregrinations or how active a role Rosa a.k.a. Isabel played in the conception of the scheme—probably minor, she was so young and inexperienced"—he glanced at his hostess —"malleable, in love?" Addressing the group in general: "But that isn't important, not tonight, at least.

"What's important is the fact that Rosa has become, for all intents and purposes, an art connoisseur and a savvy business dealer—at least according to her son." He paused. "So what went wrong after all these years? Why did things fall apart?" To Erika: "At the gala, you spoke directly to Helen. You take it from here."

"How democratic," James commented, more forlorn than cynical.

Erika tried not to think about the torment James must be going through, a captive audience at his own history's demise. "Well, this is how I see it. James goes to the art gala at The Pierre. Later, in all innocence he tells his mother of conversations he'd been in on. This is how she learns that William Delaney's daughter, Helen Gilmore, has come into possession of the contents of her father's long unopened safe deposit box. Included in its contents, James notes in passing, is an inventory executed in the spring of 1957 itemizing the contents of William Delaney's art collection. His mother acts calm, but her alarms go off. What if the inventory postdates her husband's fraudulent bills of sale and lists those very artworks? If publicized—and it would appear that William Delaney's daughter, unlike his wife, is hardly averse to airing the past— it would invalidate those bills of sale! It would destroy everything! She has to retrieve the contents of that box. Also, who knows what else is in the box—photographs of Delaney and Davis? Employment contracts? Anyone's guess! All she knows is, without any hard evidence, any accusations concerning the fiction of their lives are mere theories, malicious rumor."

"What was the date on the Vittorio bill of sale again?" Harrison suddenly posed.

"January 8, 1957," Erika said, almost apologetically. "I looked at our copy a little while ago."

"Of course! I'd forgotten the month—or completely overlooked it!" Harrison's excitement was undiminished by his oversight. "So, Isabel—Rosa's—fears were confirmed right off the bat, when she checked the Vittorio bill of sale. William Delaney's updated inventory was dated in the spring of 1957, months after the bill of sale. That inventory would have listed all those supposedly sold works as remaining in his ownership. It would have proven the bill of sale was fraudulent."

"Exactly," Erika agreed. "What I think is, Jeff Davis thought it clever to have the bills of sale coincide with one of his boss's trips to New York. If anyone questioned the authenticity of his bogus transactions, at least the date would be a point in his favor. He made one small but costly mistake. He either forgot when in 1957 Delaney traveled to New York, or chose the wrong one of several trips made that year.

"I don't know if Helen Gilmore was meant to die; Andrew's assignment might have been limited to retrieval But after that tragic event, Rosa decided she needed a safety gap, something to counter potential suspicion. The ransom scheme, in which she was cast as the victim, was created as just such a diversion." Erika looked silently at those around her.

The stillness was laden with their responses on the cusp of expression. "Now, if we only had a way of matching the fingerprints of Jeff Davis and James Fitch Senior," she said, pre-empting them, "our proof would be incontrovertible."

Mitchell sat up. "Fingerprints!"

"Yes," she said.

Mitchell turned to Harrison. "Didn't you tell me Delaney recruited his manager from the Navy? Didn't you say the man was stationed at the Navy Base at Guantanamo Bay?"

"I think I mentioned it when we were talking about William Delaney's letters, vis-à-vis the signature matter."

"Well, then, as a Navy recruit, he would have had his fingerprints taken as a matter of course. My father was in the Navy. I saw his ID papers." To Erika: "I'll check to see if the records go as far back as the 1950s. I'm betting they do."

"Mother?" James cried, love and hate welding in the heat of his furor. "Why are you just sitting there?" The passion in his eyes was draining what was left in hers.

"No more, no more," she said, slipping her hand from Andrew's so she could hold herself around her middle. "No more," she said, rocking back and forth, as if she were cradling a dead child. "They understand nothing."

"It's not true, then?" James asked, his voice rising with bullying hope.

"Truth is not simple," she said slowly, each word a burden.

"This is my fucking life, and you're talking in circles?"

"Oh, my son, my son," she crooned.

"Am I your son?"

"Yes, of course you are our son."

Erika sat forward, seeking eye contact with her. Rosa's muted accent had become more noticeable, unmistakably Spanish, as if she was slipping into an earlier time. "You said we don't understand...Rosa. What don't we understand?"

"The human story." Rosa shook her head slowly. "My husband is past caring and no longer in need of my protection. Suddenly I am tired. Perhaps I, too, am past caring." She stopped rocking, folded her hands in her lap, then stared at them with a curious objectivity, as if seeing them for the first time. "Still, I want to speak our story. At last, to hear it."

Andrew slapped the table. "What are you doing? Keep

your mouth shut!"

She shook her head. "Be still, Andrew."

"They're putting ideas in your head, making you crazy!"

"You must know that is not true, Andy."

"I'll swear to it!"

"Do what you must, but shush now."

Smoldering, Andrew sat stone still, only his eyes giving him away. It was just a matter of time before he would erupt.

Momentum had to be regained at once. "You loved—love—your husband very much, don't you?" Erika asked, her words calculated to disarm. "Do you want to start there? Would that help us understand how all this..."

"Evolved?" James caustically supplied. He rolled his eyes.

"Heaven help us."

"Yes, I think it would," his mother said, targeting James with a beseeching look, to which he did not outwardly respond. She sighed resignedly and redirected her attention to Erika. "I love him—let me say his name now, for the first time in so many years—Jeff." And again: "Jeff." She tilted her head, as if listening for the name to be echoed yet again. "From the very first, there was fire between us, it could not be helped, there was nothing to be done. I was very young when William Delaney brought me into his home, and up to then I had never known tenderness or love, either toward me or within my own heart.

"Mr. Delaney was generous to me, but aloof. I never knew what was quite in his mind. Sometimes I would catch him staring at me, but when he realized I noticed, he would look away with a scowl. We did not speak much to each other, except about my chores in the kitchen, and sometimes about seeing to Mrs. Delaney, bringing tea and refreshments up to her room when she was feeling unwell or seeing to her hair—she liked when I brushed it, or put it up in braids. Kind, very kind, she was, but a little timid. She told me that she dreamed of moving back to the States, that she had always felt uneasy living away from home. She made me promise never to tell her husband that, and I never did.

"Only one time did Mr. Delaney frighten me. He was sitting at the desk in his office, and I was delivering the coffee and sandwich he had called down to the kitchen for. I was setting them out on his desk, when he suddenly ordered me out of the room. I was so startled, I spilled the coffee. I grabbed the towel from my belt and tried to catch the stream before it spilled into his lap. He grabbed my wrist and repeated the order, looking at me with such intense pain and loathing, it made me cry. I thought he would fire me then and there, and I did not know why. I thought he was a good man, but I did not understand this behavior."

"Naïve little thing, weren't you?" James muttered under his breath.

"It was different with Mr. Davis," Rosa continued, on her own course. "Another world, it seemed. When we were alone in the room, it was impossible for us not to touch, if only for an instant—his hand on my cheek, mine on his wrist. His love made me feel safe. I only needed to know he was somewhere near to feel no harm could possibly come to me." She gazed at Erika, or through her, a corner of her lips rising in a bemused smile. "I called him Mr. Davis then, I knew my place. But even then, before we pledged ourselves to each other, he was Jeff, and mine for life."

James moved restlessly in his chair. Andrew was motionless, unreadable.

Rosa's focus on Erika became more direct. "You cannot imagine what it was like the day of the attack," she said, looking her straight in the eye. "I was terrified. The three of us, Mr. Delaney, Jeff and I, hid in the basement storeroom listening to the frenzy overhead—the barking orders, the screams—any moment expecting to hear footsteps on the stairs. The men were ready with their rifles. I was unarmed. Jeff was my only protection. That was the way I saw it."

Mitchell cleared his throat, breaking the spill of words. "Did Mr. Davis turn his rifle on Mr. Delaney at some point?" he asked, flipping a page of his notebook.

Rosa's chin snapped up as if she'd been abruptly awakened. She eyed Mitchell suspiciously, at the same time pulling back in her seat. "I did not say that! Who are you to say it was not the rebels who shot Mr. Delaney?"

"If that was the case, they would have shot you all," Mitchell said blandly.

After a wretched beat, Rosa said, "Let me tell you, Lieutenant, Mr. Delaney had it in for me. Jeff told me so, and I had every reason to believe him. He told me that when the two of them saw the military trucks coming up the drive, Mr. Delaney said, 'This is Rosa's doing. I will see she pays for this!' Whoever killed Mr. Delaney saved my life!"

Rosa's cathartic narration was over, Mitchell had seen to that. Erika's heart was pounding. "Rosa," she said evenly, "didn't Mr. Delaney treat you kindly?"

"He did at first, yes," Rosa said, taken off guard. "He would ask how I was doing, how the cook was treating me, that sort of thing. But his behavior changed." She pressed her palms against her lap, fixing the thought in place.

"Yes," Erika answered agreeably, "and you were quite young, you didn't understand why Mr. Delaney's behavior changed toward you, why he became alternately distant and hostile. But I think that now you do understand. You may be unwilling to admit it, even to yourself, holding fast to your childish notions because they paint your husband in a more favorable light. It's easier to believe William Delaney's murder was an act of heroism rather than a seized opportunity, isn't it?"

Andrew uttered something unintelligible.

Erika paid him no mind. "Jeff Davis wasn't the only man who desired you, Rosa," she continued, unfazed. "William Delaney did, too, only he wasn't free to act on his feelings. He was a faithful husband tormented by what he considered his baser

305

instincts. His outbursts were expressions not of his anger toward you, but toward himself, his own weakness. He wouldn't have harmed you, and I think you know that."

"You have no grounds for what you say," Rosa protested, her hands fluttering off her lap like butterflies. "None at all."

"That's not true, Rosa," Erika said, steadfast. "Harrison and I have read letters written by William Delaney that do provide—grounds, as you say."

"I would like to see such letters."

"You can't. They don't belong to us."

Andrew jumped to his feet. "That's enough!" he shouted. "You're harassing her!"

"Quit your posturing," James said sharply, tossing Andrew a withering look.

"I don't know what the fuck that means," Andrew raged, "but you ought to be sticking up for your mother!"

"Stop it!" Rosa implored, clapping her hands to her ears. Just as suddenly, she threw them up. They hovered, then fell to her lap. "What am I doing? Stuck in the past, worrying about myself and my husband, who is"—she looked at Mitchell—"out of your reach... and mine." She shook her head with an almost sardonic satisfaction. "You cannot touch him. Take your notes. Write it down. It is all my doing. None of it Andrew's. I pulled the strings, he danced. I fashioned the threatening notes—to Erika, to myself—he delivered them. I said I needed to get the contents of the safe deposit box. I knew there must be papers that would incriminate my husband. I looked up the Delaney address, told Andrew where to go in Southampton. I told him to get the job done. Helen Gilmore walked in on him as he was collecting the items. The situation got out of control. I told him to get the job done!"

"I understand," Harrison said. "You feel remorse because you were responsible for Andrew's rehabilitation, and now you've set him back."

"Psychobabble!" Andrew yelled. "She gave me a life.

Without her I'd be dead!"

Rosa shook her head ruefully. "Oh, my faithful boy."

"Your faithful project," James amended.

"Rosa," Harrison said, with disarming sobriety. "Why did you send for Erika this morning?"

"I wanted her to see the note, to be a witness when I got the call giving me instructions on how to drop off the money." She looked at Erika. "But you saw through the ruse, so you had to be worked into it."

Erika held up her hand. "At first I thought you were as much of a dupe as I, that the ransom plot was Andrew's. It was only later I realized you were the mastermind."

"It was my fault the situation got out of hand," Rosa said. In a sudden burst of energy, she jumped to her feet and rushed to embrace Andrew.

"Enough of this bullshit!" James exploded, advancing on them. He pulled them apart. "Where's the stuff from the safe deposit box?" he seethed. "Let's see what we're dealing with!"

"I destroyed it," Rosa replied tremulously, holding on to James's arm to steady herself. She sighed. "No matter, no matter. The only thing that matters now is for me to protect Andrew."

"Right," James said wryly. "And allow me to go straight down the tubes." He suddenly swiped at the objects on the small table, sending crackers and cheese flying. "What did you and the little prick do with the Vittorio drawing? Nobody stole it, so you must have hidden it." His jaw jutting in his mother's face: "Or did you trash that too—you know, as incriminating evidence?"

"It's not ours, son."

He grabbed her shoulders, as if he meant to lift her off her feet. Mitchell stepped up to them, shoving them apart. "That's it!"

Unheeding, James kicked over Andrew's chair. "Where is the drawing?" he fumed, throwing Andrew a menacing glare. He closed in on him.

"Let's not fight, bro," Andrew placated, backing up against the writing desk, hands behind him, laying himself open to prove his point.

"Enough!" Mitchell bellowed. "I'm warning you!" James turned to confront Mitchell.

Erika saw Andrew's shoulders drop as he fumbled at the desk drawer. She took a wild guess at what he was after. "James —behind you!" she cried, leaping to her feet.

"What is it?" Harrison rasped, rising to her aid.

James swung around, but it was too late, Andrew had already whipped the gun in front of him. Stiff-armed, he swept it around the room. "Nobody move!"

"Come on!" James entreated, throwing up his hands in passive defense.

Reacting to the sudden move, Andrew smacked him in his ribs with the barrel of the gun, sending him sprawling.

Taking advantage of Andrew's distraction, Mitchell grabbed his pistol from under his sweatshirt, but was unprepared for Andrew's split-second response: continuing the arc of his swing at James, he took aim at Mitchell, just as the lieutenant was leveling his weapon.

Mitchell's gun dropped to the floor as the bullet struck his shoulder.

Keeping the muzzle of his gun directed at Mitchell, Andrew crouched to retrieve the fallen weapon, then jammed it under his belt.

"Andrew, please!" Rosa implored. "Think what you're doing, don't make it worse!"

"You've done enough, be quiet now," Andrew said. Calm almost. To James, stumbling to his feet: "Don't try anything. Stay put." He scanned the room, the muzzle of his gun following his shifting focus.

Mitchell splinted his injured arm to his side, holding it in place with his free hand. "She's right, Andrew, give it up. You can't expect to get away with—"

"Shut up and listen, all of you. I'm getting the hell out of here." Directing aim at Mitchell, Andrew moved toward Erika. Suddenly, his arm was around her neck, his forearm clamped against her throat, the muzzle of the gun rising toward her temple.

Harrison lunged at him, grabbing his wrist at a level with her shoulder and wrenching it from its trajectory. The gun went off, the bullet striking high up the far wall, as Andrew released Erika to fight off Harrison.

Harrison held fast to Andrew's wrist, keeping the gun aimed high. Erika tried to grab the gun, but Harrison warned her off as he swung round to face his opponent.

James staggered to his feet. Before Andrew could react, James was on him, prying the gun from his fingers, flinging it out of reach. As Andrew went for Mitchell's gun jammed under his belt, Harrison ferociously kicked his legs out from under him, landing him flat against the floor, Mitchell's weapon inaccessible, digging into his ribs.

Andrew, rising, tried to get at Harrison, reaching round to claw at his neck, drawing blood. Harrison jerked back his head and butted it against Andrew's, aborting the attack.

Mitchell's shoulder was bleeding profusely, staining through to his sweatshirt. Gritting his teeth, he bent to pick up Andrew's weapon. His injured arm hanging uselessly at his side, he gripped the gun in his left hand and pointed it at Andrew.

"Get Mitchell a tourniquet—a tie, a belt, anything!" Erika ordered Rosa, as she herself dropped to her knees to grab Andrew's ankles, aiding Harrison's and James's efforts to keep him immobilized. "Keep away, Erika!" Harrison shouted. "We've got this under control. Call for help, okay? Lieutenant, I thought you had back-up support!"

"I do—I paged them," Mitchell said.

As if to confirm his claim, a thunderous ramming issued from the front of the house, followed by the clamor of oncoming police officers, weapons drawn. An Emergency Medical

Team tagged close behind.

Within minutes, Andrew was in cuffs, Rosa was symbolically constrained by an officer's palm at the small of her back, and Mitchell was being prepped for transport to the nearest hospital.

Andrew was combative. "None of the crap in your notepad is worth a damn," he taunted Mitchell. "She wasn't read her Miranda Rights."

"That's okay," Mitchell retorted, as his gurney was being guided to the door. "Before she's officially interrogated, she will be. You, too."

The cut on Harrison's neck was bleeding, but there was no way he was budging from the scene. He allowed one of the medical personnel to swab and lather him with disinfectant and topical antibiotics, then stick an oversize Band-Aid on his wound. That was it. James's pain in his side was severe, but he too was not going anywhere, his thoughts obviously clinging to the only fact that did not spiral him into an alien universe. "Where's the damn drawing?" he railed at his mother as police officers were about to escort her and Andrew out to the waiting cars. "I don't care who it belongs to, it's been there all my life, maybe the only real thing in my life. I want to see it!" He pointed at the officer assigned to stay on site to wrap things up. "This man and I—"

"Sergeant Brooks," the young officer prompted.

"Sergeant Brooks and I, we're going to tear up the place looking for it!"

"Not without a search warrant," the sergeant demurred.

"I don't need a goddamn search warrant," James shot back, the veins in his forehead bulging.

"May I have a word with him?" Rosa petitioned the officer at her side. Receiving his nod of approval, she approached James. "Forgive me," she said softly, touching his arm tentatively, as if it were an object she'd just discovered. "The drawing is behind the Miro," she said, softer still. "I always thought of it as yours."

He nodded, put his hand on her shoulder, then quickly withdrew it and turned away, either too upset to see her led off, or summarily rejecting her, impossible to tell which.

After his mother and Andrew were taken away, James, without hesitation or explanation, headed directly to the bedroom area. A minute later he returned, bearing a large framed abstract painting in the unmistakable style of Joan Miro. He placed it facedown on the dining room table. A sheet of brown wrapping paper, held in place by the frame, covered the back of the canvas. "Would someone bring me a sharp knife, please?" he said, officious almost. "There's a rack on the kitchen countertop."

"I'll get it," Sergeant Brooks said, his tone leaving no room for contradiction. Returning with the knife, he reluctantly passed it to James, but not before his hand was firmly resting on his holster—where it stayed.

Erika and Harrison stood together at tableside, expectation passing between them like an electric current.

Delicately, James inserted the tip of the knife into the upper portion of the brown wrapping paper an inch below the edge of the frame. He held his breath and pierced the paper, then carefully drew the knife-edge sideways to form about a half-inch gash. He let out his breath and removed the knife, laying it on the far end of the tabletop, a safe distance from the parcel.

"Do it," Erika whispered.

He tucked his index finger into the gash, then slowly extended the tear until he was able to free the paper from the frame and draw it down, like a bedcover, to expose what lay below.

A hand-crafted poster-board folder Erika judged to be about thirty by thirty-six inches, lay flush up against the back of the Miro canvas. Cautiously, James opened it.

At first sight: recognition. Even before the details emerged—the distinctive cross-hatching, the confident stroke—she felt its core energy, the fusion of form and space, connecting with her own.

Harrison pressed closer to her side, widening the force field, her connection with him as authentic and indisputable as Michelangelo's drawing. It superseded her philosophical constructs, just as recognition of the authorship of the drawing superseded the prattling of art experts.

"The horse," he said quietly.

"Yes," she said, knowing he was referring to the Michelangelo drawing they'd seen at The British Museum, the one borrowed from The Ashmolean. It was depicted in the drawing before them, only with its forelegs in reverse position. "So clear," she said. "So much clearer than our photocopy." She tore herself from their immersion to keep from giving away their secret, although she hardly knew how, for so many years, the truth had escaped notice, that the pre- sumption of authorship had clouded sight. "This is a remarkable drawing," she said, with as much scholarly cool as she could muster. "It should be handled with extreme care." Addressing James, she asked, "Do you have a leather portfolio?"

"I know what to do," James said, not unkindly. He left the room to find a proper carrier.

Erika suddenly felt limp with exhaustion and relief. The day's events had taken a tremendous toll on her, but this was the first moment she was aware of it, or allowed herself to be. She put her hand to her forehead.

"Are you okay?" Harrison asked, slipping his arm around her. "This has been too much for you, and I'm at fault. I should have known better!"

"I'm fine," she exaggerated, "only I think I'd like to go." Already, despite her fatigue she felt her tendency to organize gearing up. With a little encouragement she could become tenacious about seeing that all aspects of the Delaney case—personal, legal, logical—had been considered. In regard to the nuances of criminal law, her input was especially uncalled for, but that wouldn't prevent her from putting in her unsolicited two cents.

Still, if she was going to get any sleep tonight, there was one thing she had to see to before she and Harrison left. "Sergeant, you think we could talk to you a minute in private?"

He acquiesced and the three of them withdrew to the steps just outside the front door.

Erika got right to the point. "The pen and ink we were just looking at is a very significant work of art. Would it be possible for you to take it into custody tonight and place it in a secure location?"

After a moment's deliberation: "I can do that, yes."

"Its ultimate destination will be The Metropolitan Museum of Art," Harrison said. "But in the meantime, we'd like to get approval from Delaney's next of kin, Natalie Gilmore, to release the drawing to an accredited expert for appraisal."

"I'm not familiar with the case," Brooks said. "If he's up to it, I'll ask Lieutenant Mitchell to reach this Ms. Gilmore, otherwise, someone will fill me in and I'll take care of it. Will Ms. Gilmore have the name of the expert?"

"We can suggest several names—Percy Clarke is one, although he's based in Oxford. If she'll allow us, we'll research the names."

"I'll make sure someone connects with you. Either of you reachable by cell phone the next couple of days?"

"Sure," Erika said. She eyed him closely. "We can count on you to keep the drawing safely under lock and key—oh, and in a cool, dry place and properly shielded, in contact with no other materials, nothing with ink or other contaminants? Now that I think of it, maybe The Metropolitan Museum will have the ideal storage area. You think you can arrange it with them?"

Brooks laughed. "Yes, I think I'm up to the task."

"Thank you!" She drew her arm through Harrison's. "You think we can go now? You need a break, too." She eyed the site of his wound.

"Definitely, we can go," Harrison agreed, "seeing as I was

about to drag you off with or without your permission."

"Is the cut on your neck painful?" Erika asked. "You want me to re-clean it or anything?"

"I'm fine. How do you feel?" Harrison asked warily, as he accompanied her to her bedroom. They'd been sipping de-caffeinated coffee and snacking on corn muffins for close to an hour, analyzing the evening's confrontation and marveling over the drawing they agreed would soon be reattributed to Michelangelo.

She smiled, causing a tug of pain in her cheek. "Relieved. Exhilarated." Arriving at bedside, "To be honest, a wreck." She slumped down onto the edge of the bed. As she reached down to remove her shoes, she was startled by the jangle of her phone, provoking another stab of pain. She grabbed the device from its cradle. "Hello!" she yelped too vigorously, over compensating for her fatigue.

"It's Natalie Gilmore. Erika? Are you okay? I just got a call from Sergeant Brooks!"

"I'm okay, Natalie. Thanks for your concern." She clicked on the speaker phone. "Harrison's taking good care of me," she added pointedly. "Sergeant Brooks must have told you about the drawing recovered tonight."

"Yes, and I'm thrilled," Natalie crooned. "And what do you think about Harrison's news?"

"News?" Erika asked, nonplussed.

"Stop!" Harrison declared. "She doesn't know. I want to tell her myself."

"You mean, you haven't?" Natalie asked in patent disbelief. Erika wondered when Harrison's apparent rapprochement with Natalie had taken place.

"What news?" she asked, after Natalie's call was hastily concluded.

Harrison smiled. "My mind was totally occupied. I can't believe I haven't told you."

"That makes three of us," Erika said, not sure if this was a good thing.

Harrison pulled the folding chair away from her desk table and planted himself in it. "I got a call from Javier Garcia," he said.

Erika was bewildered. "About the Cuban situation? Today? When was there time for a call?"

"This morning, after I left your office."

"You didn't tell me?"

"I got distracted. Your life was on the line."

"So was yours!"

"No. Only my reputation."

She smiled feebly. "You always know what to say, Harrison. Well, is your news good or bad?"

"Do I look dejected?"

"No, but you can be a hard read."

"That's not true, not for you."

"Quit stalling and tell me your good news."

Harrison sat forward, elbows on his knees. "My guy Garcia and Hector Martinez, the Cuban rep. They broke him."

"Luis Navarro, the black marketeer? They broke him?"

Harrison nodded. "Like a dry twig, they said. "First, there was nothing they could pin on me. Second"—flashing a wicked smile— "the office was bugged. My talk with Navarro concerning the five art works held by the Italian heir was captured on tape. Every word of it."

Erika squinted in disbelief. "Is it because I was hit in the head? Is that why I don't understand why you were put through all that hassle? Why you were placed under virtual house arrest?"

Harrison laughed. "No, your confusion is perfectly understandable. As was Garcia's, Martinez's and my own. You see, what none of us knew until the Minister of Art returned this morning from his trip abroad, is that he has been secretly bugging Luis Navarro's office for months. Suspicions of Navarro's criminal activities abounded, but he wanted positive proof before going public. Solid evidence would advance our perception of his sincerity; bolster his promise to seek justice, including restitution to any injured parties."

"A matter of diplomacy."

"Good will. Yes."

"Has the Italian been identified?" Erika asked eagerly, curiosity keeping exhaustion at bay. "Will Natalie be able to recover her grandfather's five works?"

"Yes. The statute of limitations may have elapsed, but the opportunity to drag a family name through the mud has not. The Italian will be paid a substantial sum for the stolen art and in return, his name will remain intact. Luis Navarro's fate under the justice system remains to be seen."

"I'm happy it's resolved well, really happy for you, Harrison," Erika said, pressing her fingers to her forehead.

"What's wrong?" Harrison asked, alarmed. "Nothing. Don't worry."

"I never should have let you exert yourself," he said gravely. "I've been negligent. Selfishly so." He combed his fingers through his hair. At a loss. "What can I do for you? You want an ice pack, would that help?"

"I'm okay. I'm just going to take off my shoes and keel over. You've been terrific, taking me home and all. You think you could let yourself out? That's rude, I can at least see you to the door!" She staggered to her feet.

"Sit!" He gently but firmly grasped her shoulders and urged her back down. "I'm not going anywhere. I'm staying here tonight."

"You're waiting to see if I slip into a coma so you can call 9-1-1?"

"That's not funny."

"But that's what you're worried about, isn't it?"

"I'm looking after you," he said, without denying her supposition. "This is non-negotiable."

She was too beat to object, and anyway, she wasn't sure she wanted to. She sat back down.

He studied her a moment. "I've been meaning to tell you something, but it never seemed to be the right moment.

This is probably the worst moment of all."

Her breath caught. "How mysterious."

"I don't mean to be."

"Still, you are."

"It's awkward, that's all. I'm going to be out of town for a while—I'm not at liberty to say why right now. We'll stay in touch by email, work on the Delaney project; we can do this long distance. And when, well, when I get back we'll talk."

She smiled gamely. "If you say so. Now, at least go sleep on the convertible couch. I promise to give a shout-out if I'm about to die."

He shook his head adamantly, like a stubborn schoolboy. "That would defeat the purpose." He folded his arms. Unmovable.

"You won't be able to sleep a wink in that chair. You'll be incredibly uncomfortable."

He took off his shoes and slung his feet onto the bed. "There. I'm perfectly comfortable."

She gave up. She slipped out of her jacket and tossed it onto the foot of the bed. "I'm too tired to argue." She kicked off her shoes and fell into a heap, her injured cheek hurting as it hit the pillow. She turned onto her other, non-habitual side. Facing away from him. "I'll never fall asleep with you sitting there like that," she said, already feeling herself drifting off.

"That's because the light's on." He reached over to turn it off. "There."

"This is absurd." She shoved over, leaving more room on her junior-size double bed. "Lie down here."

"I thought you'd never ask."

She heard him pushing back the chair. Felt the movement of his settling in beside her.

After a pause: "You're not supposed to strain yourself," he said. "So don't try anything funny."

"Not with a traveling man," she said sadly, too tired to feign transcendence.

CHAPTER 20

Erika fast-stepped up the Met's palatial staircase on the tips of her high heels like Cinderella hurrying to the ball. For weeks she'd been dodging social engagements, pouring her energy into work and becoming more and more remote, the dimming of her inner light closing down the colors of her shrinking world. Now, with the prospect of seeing Harrison—having their "talk"—her mood soared. Unreasonably, outrageously. She looked up toward the glorious Beaux-Arts façade. Suspended from the arches and loosely anchored by thin cords to the flanking pillars, the spotlighted colored banners heralded the museum's current exhibits: in tangerine, THE COURTLY ARTS; in cerise, BEIJING CLOISSONAIRE; in fuchsia, TITIAN REDISCOVERED; and gently billowing on the far right in lemon yellow, HOMECOMING: THE WILLIAM DELANEY COLLECTION.

The Great Hall continued the façade's Beaux-Arts theme. Taking it in at a glance, she was reminded of Escher's architectural lithograph, *Up and Down*, with its multiple arches, staircases, balconies drawn as one festive retinal warp. When she was little, the yawning complex space made her feel like Jonah in the belly of the whale—not scary, though, because she was holding her father's hand.

It was 7:00 PM and the museum had been closed to the public for an hour and a half. Two security guards were on duty, one to peer into purses and perform wand scans, the other to match IDs to a printed guest list and inform visitors how to get to the Petrie Café, where the group was convening.

After going through the drill, she headed off to the coat check area, where Brian Latham was handing over his trench coat to the attendant on the other side of the counter. He looked straight out of *GQ*—trim and confident in his tweedy sport suit and sweater vest. After she'd checked her coat, Brian looped his arm through hers. "Tell me," he said, leading her away, "did you add my bit about Michelangelo's pen and ink study for *Mourning Woman* to the catalogue in the works?"

"We did."

"Sotheby expert, Julien Stock, 1991. Discovered the study while leafing through a scrapbook during a routine inventory of Castle Howard. It's a work in progress, isn't it? Art history, I mean. One of the reasons I love it so."

"Yes," she said, thrown into self-reflection by the utterance of the word "love."

Climbing the granite staircase, Erika glanced up at the low balustrade forming the railing for the level above. She grasped the banister, remembering the dizzying fright when, as a child, walking close to the railing, and for a moment not clasping her father's hand, she imagined someone coming out of nowhere and hurling her over it. The capriciousness of the act, imagined so vividly in the moment, had instantly seared the thin line between life and death in her mind and belly.

Why was she recollecting childhood experiences with such accuracy and poignant connection with her father? As her hand slid along the cool banister, she wondered if it was because she was crossing some invisible line, saying goodbye to her long-practiced way of life, envisioning another.

A regiment of champagne-filled glasses was arranged on a table at the entrance to the Petrie Café. She plucked a glass from the front line. From the density of the crowd, she judged about half of the seventy or so guests had arrived. From a cursory glance, Harrison was not among them.

The plan, noted in the invitation, was to convene in the café for cocktails and then move on to the exhibit. Although entry into the galleries where the exhibit awaited them was not strictly forbidden, no one seemed to be venturing there on his own. It was as if there were an unspoken agreement to share the experience, as if it were a concert, the opening notes to resonate more deeply to a full house.

She wandered over to the food tables, where Amy Barlow was adding a trayful of hors d'oeuvres to the array.

"Mushrooms in fire roasted pepper sauce—*Quesadilla de Hongo*," Amy pronounced exuberantly, as if she were tasting the words themselves.

"Looks great," Erika said.

"Cuban-American fusion?" Brian inquired, holding up a prime rib tidbit before popping it into his mouth.

"Not fusion," Amy replied, eyes twinkling. "Contiguousness. Separate, but equal."

"Wonderfully diverse spread. I'm making the rounds."

"Our sponsor, Natalie Gilmore, told us the sky's the limit, so Matt and I just let the creative juices flow."

"As it were," Brian said.

"Exactly."

Erika polished off her champagne.

"Shall I get you another?" Brian asked, before resuming his tasting tour.

"No thanks," Erika replied, taking another look around for Harrison.

"Erika!"

She swung around.

"Sorry," the ever-observant Rodney Smitts amiably chided, catching her disappointment.

"Stop it. You with Natalie?"

"Strictly patron-protégé. She's been a marvelous influence on me; she literally inspires industry. Right now she's having a powwow with the museum director over the transfer of a painting from her grandfather's collection released into her possession only yesterday by one of the dot com organizations. She'll be along any minute." He glanced around. "Is that James Fitch putting on a brave front? I hear he's selling the family gallery, donating a bundle to the museum—atoning for the sins of his parents, poor guy. Speaking of which, how's the case going?"

"As for the murder of William Delaney in 1958," Erika said, "the statute of limitations probably doesn't apply, but it's a moot point, since Fitch Senior—Jeff Davis—is incapable of standing trial. Meanwhile, James's mother and Andrew will be standing trial separately for the murder of Helen Gilmore.

"I just learned that Andrew's cell phone was seized and his deleted phone logs were recovered. Taken with the records on the land line, evidence seems to be airtight that the fake ransom call was made by Andrew. He and Rosa are out on bail, and indictments have been handed down, but the lawyers are still wheeling and dealing. The trial dates have not yet been set."

"The gears of justice grind slowly—or something to that effect," Rodney commented.

"Yes. So, how go the gears of your career? Moving along?"

"Efficiently, thanks in large part to Natalie. She's quite a woman, you know. She deserves all the kudos she gets regarding this show, despite her modesty, which in no way is an affectation."

"Something like her mother, I think."

"Only more brazen—in a good way. She's made me more focused. I got myself back into the good graces of the Milgram Gallery. My show's been rescheduled." He looked toward the entrance, spotted Natalie, answered her wave with one of his own. "Catch you later, Erika." He planted a kiss on her cheek and hurried off, just as Sara Masden was approaching.

Pulling Erika aside, she asked, "Are you here with Wheatley? I haven't seen him." To Erika's slightly crestfallen head-shake: "So, another fashionably late arrival by our friend." Her eyes widened. "No matter, here's a more than adequate replacement advancing. Heads up." She blew Erika a kiss and gracefully withdrew out of Aldo Fabbri's trajectory.

"*Se bella ti ricordavo!*" Aldo greeted, swaggering near. He ogled Erika up and down, more alpha dog than she remembered, perhaps to cover up his embarrassment over his Michelangelo deception. "Beautiful," he said, translating the only word she'd understood. He gave her another once-over.

She was wearing a sheer gray chemise with a transparent lace border under a close-fit black suit jacket with a jaunty flare at the hem. The skirt hit just below her knees, hugging her body like a glove. Silver hoop earrings bobbed in and out of hiding with the movement of her shoulder-length hair. Sheer black stockings and black suede heels completed the picture, which was becoming more tawdry with every one of his salacious appraisals. Her gaze wandered in order to escape his. She spotted his father chatting with Greg Smith near the food tables. Since the favorable outcome of the Luis Navarro affair, Greg, along with Harrison, was back in Natalie's good graces and had, of late, been especially diligent in aiding her art recovery efforts. Erika's own feelings toward Greg had improved since her resentment over Harrison's solo trip to Havana had all but dissolved. She turned back to Aldo. "And how's your charming grandmother?" she asked, hitting on a neutral topic.

"*Ah, nonna—la vedo sempre mai soddisfatto,*" he replied, smiling broadly.

From the smile she knew it was good news. No way was she going to ask him to translate. She gave him a pleased-to-hear-it nod.

"You know, I've converted the short-term loan of my Michelangelo drawing to an extended one," Aldo said. "The document has already been drawn up and signed."

"That's wonderful," Erika replied with real pleasure. By agreeing not to publish Aldo's obfuscation of his Michelangelo reattribution, she'd persuaded him to lend the drawing to the

Met for the duration of the exhibition, along with his Vittorio da Luccas for contrast and historical context. Further egg-shell treading had led to his outright donation of two of the Vittorio drawings. The extension of the loan of his Michelangelo was a significant benefit to the viewing public.

"I hope the change will make the deadline for the catalogue," he declared.

"Barely—but yes. The museum moved so swiftly to make it all happen," she said, with a broad sweep of her hand. "This might be the first time one of their show's catalogues has lagged behind its opening."

In fact, the speed with which the exhibition had been mounted and publicized was unprecedented, owing to a confluence of factors of irresistible force.

In the spirit of boosting Cuban-American relations, the Cuban arts contingent had returned their dubiously acquired Delaney pieces to his estate, with the proviso that their magnanimity get full play in the media and that the show would be in full swing for the United Nations' trade conference slated for mid-December.

The National Museum in Havana wasn't the only party to forego the option to litigate. After the fingerprints dug from the Navy's files at Guantanamo Base proved without a doubt that Jeff Davis and James Fitch Senior were one and the same, most of the innocent purchasers who had bought "Fitch's" stolen works were willing to reaccession their pieces to the Delaney estate. The quid pro quos for not squabbling over the statute of limitations varied, from reimbursement of purchase price and decades of insurance premiums, to a percentage of the appraised value. One private collector had gifted his Gauguins outright and had added a sizable monetary donation to the Metropolitan in return for conspicuous acknowledgment in the museum's publications, including the special catalogue for the exhibition. Natalie had handled with kid gloves the acquisition of the five works held by the son of the Italian aristocrat. In this case the individual's guaranteed anonymity had been the only non-negotiable. There were several holdouts, digging in their heels and preparing for endless litigation, but at least fifty pieces were fully unencumbered and on view this day.

As for the show's centerpiece, the 1504 drawing credited to Vittorio da Lucca had lately been reattributed to Michelangelo by atypically amicable consensus. The drawing, now officially recognized as the master's study for *The Battle of Cascina*, had been relinquished by Rosa without objection. Rosa was bent on doing everything in her power to score clemency points with the judicial agencies dealing with her case.

As a final impetus, Natalie's father, in an attempt to avoid bad press and coincidentally to mend relations with his daughter, had agreed not to contest his estranged wife's most recent will. Natalie proceeded quickly, before he had a chance to renege. She had put up the funds for the event's publicity and a percentage of negotiation payoffs, to light a fire under the Metropolitan's directorial staff.

The sound of a utensil being tinkled against glass alerted the guests to an imminent announcement. The curator host was about to speak.

"Welcome!" the collegiate young man casually said. "We'll be moving on to the show now. I'll be there to answer any questions, although everything is pretty much spelled out on the introductory poster and on the text alongside each work. I can also pawn you off to those among us better informed than I am with details in their own special spheres regarding the Delaney project, like Greg Smith, Percy Clarke, Erika Shawn—and Harrison Wheatley, who I hope will be joining us shortly. Our honored guest, Cuba's Minister of Arts, would like to say a few words on site of the exhibit itself." He gestured toward the great expanse just beyond the café. "You're of course free to explore our Petrie Sculpture Court, where we've got a security guard"—mugging a comic's hopeless shrug—"working overtime, I should remind you. However, if you want to explore further, my assistant or I will be more than happy to escort you. I've spoken too long. Onward."

The group flowed north, through the sculpture court, to the galleries where the "Homecoming" exhibit awaited them.

"Are you overwhelmed?" Brian asked Erika, coming up alongside her. "Playing such a big part in its coming to pass, you must be."

"More like taken by surprise," Erika marveled. "I saw it being set up, but this is a different experience altogether." They were facing the partition wall marking the entry to the exhibition, which allowed a partial view of the rooms beyond. From her vantage point, she could see the two Monet paintings Greg Smith had helped Natalie recover after obtaining detailed descriptions of them from their original owners, the Winstons, the collectors Delaney had mentioned in several of his letters to Bertram Morrison, and on an adjacent wall, the brilliant Marcel Duchamp oil, returned to the Delaney estate by The Pushkin Museum in exchange for one of The Met's Tchelitchews. She could sense the presence of the other works on display, united under one roof as a family long separated, and felt a rush of pride at having played a part in its reunion.

On the partition wall itself, a brief history of the William Delaney collection and its peregrinations was mounted behind plexiglass, and Michelangelo's pen and ink study for *The Battle of Cascina* hung beside it, in quiet glory, stealing the show. Its history was posted below. It traced the drawing's established provenance, from Vittorio da Lucca to the Fabbri family to the Corelli Gallery to William Delaney. The provenancial passage from Michelangelo to Vittorio was left unresolved, to be answered by future study, or maybe not ever. Had it been conceived as a presentation drawing for a patron? A Medici perhaps? Or Piero Soderini, statesman of the Florentine Republic who in 1504 commissioned Michelangelo to paint the Cascina freso for the Council Room? Had Michelangelo decided it was not up to snuff and scrapped it? Had Vittorio saved it from extinction? Had Michelangelo given it to him, his lover in fact or fancy, as suggested by the line of poetry on the back of another of his drawings found in Vittorio's folder? "At your feet, I lament and weep." The line tantalized, would compel historians to search further.

"Did you write these descriptions?" Brian asked, closing in on the text to improve his focus.

"With Harrison," Erika said, as a group of attendees brushed past her into the first gallery.

The group at large had already begun forming a loose circle around the Met curator and Cuba's Minster of Arts. Erika and Brian joined them, skirting to the far end of the room where the crowd was sparser.

The minister delivered a short speech expressing his happiness in having played a major role in the recovery of William Delaney's lost treasures, and his privilege in working with Natalie Delaney. He said he knew this would not compensate for the tragic loss of her grandfather, and more recently, her mother, or for the many years the art did not grace their homes. There was no mention of William Delaney's confiscated property in Cuba, but then, no one in his family, from his wife on down, had ever applied for its return or reparations, and this was, after all, an occasion to mend relations between countries, not reopen old wounds.

The speech was greeted with a spray of applause, after which the minister's personal press photographer made the rounds with him, taking digital photos of him with featured guests, Erika included. The photographer was getting ready to take a shot of the minister standing between two of the Gauguin paintings returned to the Delaney estate by the National Museum in Havana. Erika was facing one of the Gauguin oils, one part of her mind stuck like a broken needle on the accompanying text, another caught on where is he? where is he?

"Professor Wheatley, about time!"

The greeting had come from the other end of the room, to the normal ear hardly distinguishable from the ambient buzz of conversation. To Erika's: loud and clear.

She turned; spotted him immediately. And knew. I love him.

A roomful of people separated them, and he hadn't seen her yet. The woman beside him, tall and lovely, pressed closer to him, slipping her arm around his waist as they talked to Percy Clarke. Harrison's focus twitched right then left, yet even so, his gaze paused on the woman, and he smiled affectionately.

"I can hardly hear you, sweetheart." The sentence, a dropped stitch, looped back into Erika's thoughts. Surely this was the woman Harrison had hastened from the Pierre to meet. The two must have reconnected in the lull of Erika's own relationship with him, during his weeks of preoccupation. Her heart sank, but not hopelessly. She loved and knew without thinking she could be loyal, unlike her father, and tougher than her mother.

She would fight for him, and if she lost she would recover. She strode confidently toward the couple, hardly knowing what she would say. But what was happening? The woman was approaching her and equally as determined! She was not prepared for a cat fight; words were her weapons, not claws. Think, think. Wait, the woman was smiling, her arms opening, and there came Harrison, trailing behind, looking—smug?

"Erika, at last!" The woman threw her arms around her, then stepped away to regard her seriously. "I've been hearing so much about you."

"What? I—"

"She's usually more articulate," Harrison submitted.

"Well, I mean, how did you—?" Erika began.

"How did she know who you were? I just pointed you out to her. Erika, meet my sister Nell, Nell Coleman. Nell, meet Erika Shawn."

Erika stuttered a laugh. "Sorry, you took me by surprise."

Nell touched her brother's arm. "I'm going to do the tour," she said quietly. "I think you two may have some catching up to do." To Erika: "I've been monopolizing my brother's time long enough."

She marched off without a backward glance.

"I thought she was the woman who called you at the Pierre," Erika said, coming right out with it.

"She was," Harrison said. "Come, let's walk through the sculpture court. We can talk more freely. It's still early, people won't go off exploring for a while."

"Do you want to see the exhibit first?"

"It'll wait. This can't—we can't." He put his arm around her shoulders. "I wanted to tell you at the very beginning—it would have been a big comfort to me—but I gave my word I wouldn't speak of it."

She nodded, too bewildered to speak herself. For now, knowing the weight of his embracing arm was enough.

"It's a wonderful space, isn't it?" he said, as they entered the court, modeled after a classical French garden and adorned by French and Italian statues. Except for the security guard at one end of the large expanse, they were alone.

Spotlights were set all along the room's high cornice, each trained on a single marble or bronze statue. The light haloing each figure cast the surrounding space in a soft glow tapering to a delicate shadow. Against the night sky, the glass-paneled ceiling was a kaleidoscope of reflections. "So different when the sun streams in on a bright day," Erika said. "Through the wall of glass—the south wall—too. It does feel like you're outdoors then, don't you think? This is my first time at night. It's kind of magical."

"It is now," he said, drawing closer.

She slipped her arm around his waist, entwining them more completely.

They ambled, not aimlessly, but with no definite end.

With a sudden hitch in his step, Harrison brought Erika to a stop before a bronze figure of a seated woman, knees bent, head resting on folded arms: *Maillol's Night*. "My sister lost her husband two years ago," he said. "Ridiculous word, 'lost.' He was killed in a car accident three blocks away from home. Nelly blamed herself."

"Oh how horrible—but she must know it wasn't her fault."

"He was on his way to the florist to pick up an arrangement for the dining room table. They were having friends over for dinner. He teased her about her perfectionism, but he went anyway."

Erika pressed against him. "Harrison..."

"Yeah, I know. And her daughter only made it worse. She blamed Nell, too, didn't leave her alone about it. You have no idea what guilt my sister suffered. Alexa was fourteen at the time, and very close to her dad. Fourteen is a rebellious age to begin with, and my niece took her anger to the limit, hanging out with a tough crowd, experimenting with drugs, then getting serious about it—doing drugs. Counseling didn't help, and of course Nell was a mess, too. That night, at The Pierre, I got a call from her. She was desperate, she hadn't seen Alexa in over twenty-four hours and asked for my help."

"You found her," Erika said firmly, as if her resolve could make it true.

He smiled. "I love you. Yes, we did. She was at a friend of a friend's, shooting up. But the story improves. As a last resort—it should have been our first—we brought Alexa to my parents' ranch in South Dakota. She went through monitored detox there, and her new therapist seems to be a good match. Alexa is lending a hand at the ranch, making herself useful, and the empathy she has for the special needs kids my parents work with is rewarded with trust, a kind of therapy in itself. I've been spending quite a bit of time at the ranch, trying to be supportive, another person to talk to. She's off drugs, we hope for good."

"She forgives her mother," Erika said with the same declarative hope.

"She misses her. It's a good sign. The important thing, Nell has begun to forgive herself. You can see how spirited she is. It's been a long time coming. I'm sure Alexa's turn-around has played a big part in the process. And finally, Nell's lifted the stigma of it from her life."

"And from yours."

"From mine, too, yes. She allowed me to share her story with you." He paused. "She knows how I feel about you."

"Oh?"

"She told me I should be more proactive with you. Really, that was the word she used. Like you were a cholesterol problem."

Erika laughed. "What did you tell her?"

"I told her I wanted you to feel comfortable with me, that I was going to go slow, take your lead."

"You said that to me a while back, I remember."

"I was going to call you before today."

"Me too."

"I thought maybe it was better face to face."

"I thought the same thing."

They walked on in silence, gazing idly at the row of marble portrait busts displayed along the east wall, in a corridor separated from the main area by several broad archways.

"So, how come you two arrived so late?" she asked, after a bit, as they wandered back into the central area.

He kissed the top of her head. "Nell was coming back from a visit to South Dakota. My driver Bill and I went to pick her up at the airport. The plane was delayed."

"Bill's back with you."

"Yes."

"I'm glad. He's a nice guy."

Harrison suddenly stopped short; faced her squarely. They were standing in front of a Rodin statue. "You've changed," he said, almost cautiously.

She stroked his arm. "I don't know how to explain it. It's like I've been in a plane, breathing in the same recycled air, my own hot air, I guess you could say, and now I'm free, and the air is great out here, and I'm still flying."

"Not scared?"

"Not very."

They turned to face the statue. It was *Eternal Spring*, Rodin's gracefully erotic conception of two lovers fused in a kiss.

"Rodin was inspired by Michelangelo," Harrison said. "I mean, in his break from classicism, he sculpted—"

"Real people, not ideals."

"'Real' being a relative term. They're marble, after all. Can't feel this"—he stroked her cheek— "or this"—he kissed it. "You know, Rodin was rejected by the Ecole des Beaux-Arts sculpture program."

"I didn't know." Her cheek was tingling.

"Three times," he said.

"Wow."

"Like me."

"What?"

"You rejected me three times. Or did I lose count?"

"I didn't recognize talent when I saw it. I should have known better."

"Damn right, you should've. Eternal spring, is this what you want?"

"Yes."

"With a guarantee?"

"Well..."

"Screw it. Be with me, what can you lose?"

"You."

"So we're even."

A couple had drifted in from the Delaney exhibit and were talking in hushed tones as they circled Rodin's monumental bronze, *The Burghers of Calais*. Their absorption made Erika's awareness of her own shared intimacy all the more distinct. She ran her palm over Harrison's face, felt the reassuring stubble of his beard.

In mirrored unison they turned to face each other.

He caressed her face, casually almost, and an image came to her, so clear it seemed to have come from outside herself, of Rodin's hand brushing the marble's cool surface, over the curve of the hip, this singular movement, like Harrison's, gone in the instant of recognition, yet suspended forever in time. Hungering—even hoping—for a lifetime of such moments suddenly seemed incredibly greedy.

"What?" he said to her silence.

"Nothing. I'm happy." She gestured toward the grand south wall, constructed entirely of glass, floor to ceiling. "Let's look out." They crossed the floor, walking past the couple who were still reviewing The Burghers from every angle and whispering conspiratorially, as if they were planning a heist.

They stood side by side, barely a foot away from the glass. "It's so different," Erika said.

He squeezed her shoulder. "Who would guess we're actually facing Seventy-ninth Street, which runs through Central Park?"

"Yes, and that right outside there's a big swath of greenery marking its entrance?"

The court's artificial light was causing the entire sweep of interior space to be reflected in the glass with startling clarity, virtually projecting it beyond the confines of the museum itself. Bisecting the reflected image, a string of cars, headlights gleaming, moved east to west, appearing to defy gravity, the street beneath them obliterated by the room's dominant reflection. Erika gazed at the montage captured by the light. She felt Harrison's shoulder against her own. His nearness, like the room's illumination, altered her perception of reality—or reality itself: two worlds intersecting, one suspended in the other, who knew which? The image of Michelangelo's David suddenly flooded her heart. All that was human was rendered in that marble figure, just as all of time was poised in this incandescent moment.

He skated his fingertips across her lips, then kissed her deeply.

Coming out of it, giddy almost, "You won't feel like that in fifty years," she said, parodying her old self.

"Wanna bet?" he said.

She shook her head. "Wouldn't have my heart in it."

"I love you," he said.

"I love you, too," she said, as much to state her own feelings as to hear his repeated, to etch them in stone—as if she could.

END NOTES

A Vassar dorm-mate of mine happened to mention, almost as an aside in a friendly exchange of personal histories at the start of our freshman year, that her father had once owned a sugar plantation in Cuba, but that it had been confiscated by Castro's rebels.

Years later, I was talking to my brother, Jonathan, an art historian and Professor at the University of Cincinnati, about my wanting to write a mystery with an art theme. He replied, without pause, "How about Michelangelo's Battle of Cascina —finding a lost study, a fragment of a cartoon, maybe?" As he gave me a little lecture on the subject, my Vassar mate's passing reference to her father's experience in Cuba serendipitously came to mind, dovetailing Jonny's suggestion. I had a story.

Aside from Jonny's—Jonathan B. Riess's—encyclopedic knowledge of art history, the sources I most relied on were: *The Complete Poems of Michelangelo*, translated by John Frederick Nims; *Michelangelo's Drawings/Closer to the Master* by Hugo Chapman; *Michelangelo: A biography* by George Bull; *Michelangelo: A Film* presented by Neil MacGregor, Director of the British Museum.

It should be noted that it is an historical fact that Michelangelo Buonarroti and Leonardo da Vinci were commissioned to execute murals described in the novel. Dozens of the artists' sketches depicting specific areas of their planned works exist. It is also a fact that there is much speculation regarding the murals' final conceptions, since no completed cartoons are in evidence. Whatever work Leonardo did on the Gran Consiglio wall itself was destroyed during Vasari's renovations of the Palazzo Vecchio in 1560. In all likelihood Michelangelo did no work on the wall itself. Aristotile da Sangallo's copy (c.1542) of the central section of the Battle of Cascina cartoon does exist. However, the unearthing of a Michelangelo presentation sketch, although plausible, is fictional, as are the characters in the story.

It goes without saying that I am grateful to Jonny, but there are others to whom I owe many thanks: My dear friend, poet Kay Kidde, who read the first draft and whose insights were invaluable. Editor Danelle McCafferty, whose sense of form and substance is impeccable. Marcia Rosen, whose savvy and generous humor guided me through the maze of production. Level Best Books, with whom it was so enjoyable working with. My dear husband, Bob, whose support on arid days was life-saving; on finger-flying days: icing on the cake.

ABOUT THE AUTHOR

Claudia Riess, a Vassar graduate, is a novelist and author/illustrator of children's books. She has worked in the editorial departments of *The New Yorker* and Holt, Rinehart and Winston, and has edited several art history monographs. Her first novel, RECLINING NUDE, was published by Stein and Day. Oliver Sacks, neurologist and author of *Awakenings*, commenting on Reclining Nude, wrote: "...exquisite and delicate...a most courageous book, full of daring, a daring only possible to a passionate and pure heart."

Claudia lives in New York City and the Hamptons.

For more information visit
claudiariessbooks.com

9 781947 915107